SON OF NO MAN SERIES

NORTHLANDER

BOOK 3

SON OF NO MAN SERIES

NORTHLANDER

BOOK 3

D. LAMBERT

Northlander
Son of No Man Series Book 3
Copyright © 2022-2024 D. Lambert. All rights reserved.

4 Horsemen
Publications, Inc.

Published By: 4 Horsemen Publications, Inc.

4 Horsemen Publications, Inc.
PO Box 417
Sylva, NC 28779
4horsemenpublications.com
info@4horsemenpublications.com

Cover and Typesetting by Valerie Willis
Editor Amanda Miller

Library of Congress Control Number: 2022933468

Paperback ISBN: 978-1-64450-490-1
Hardcover ISBN: 978-1-64450-504-5
Audio ISBN: 978-1-64450-488-8
E-Book ISBN: 978-1-64450-489-5

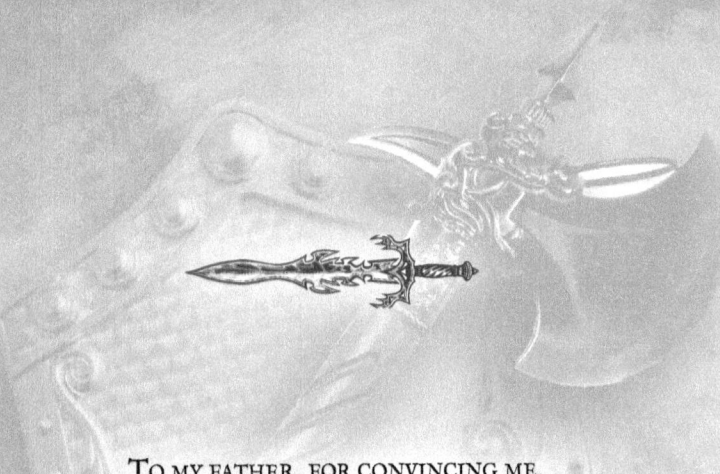

To my father, for convincing me
I could do anything I set my mind to.

Table of Contents

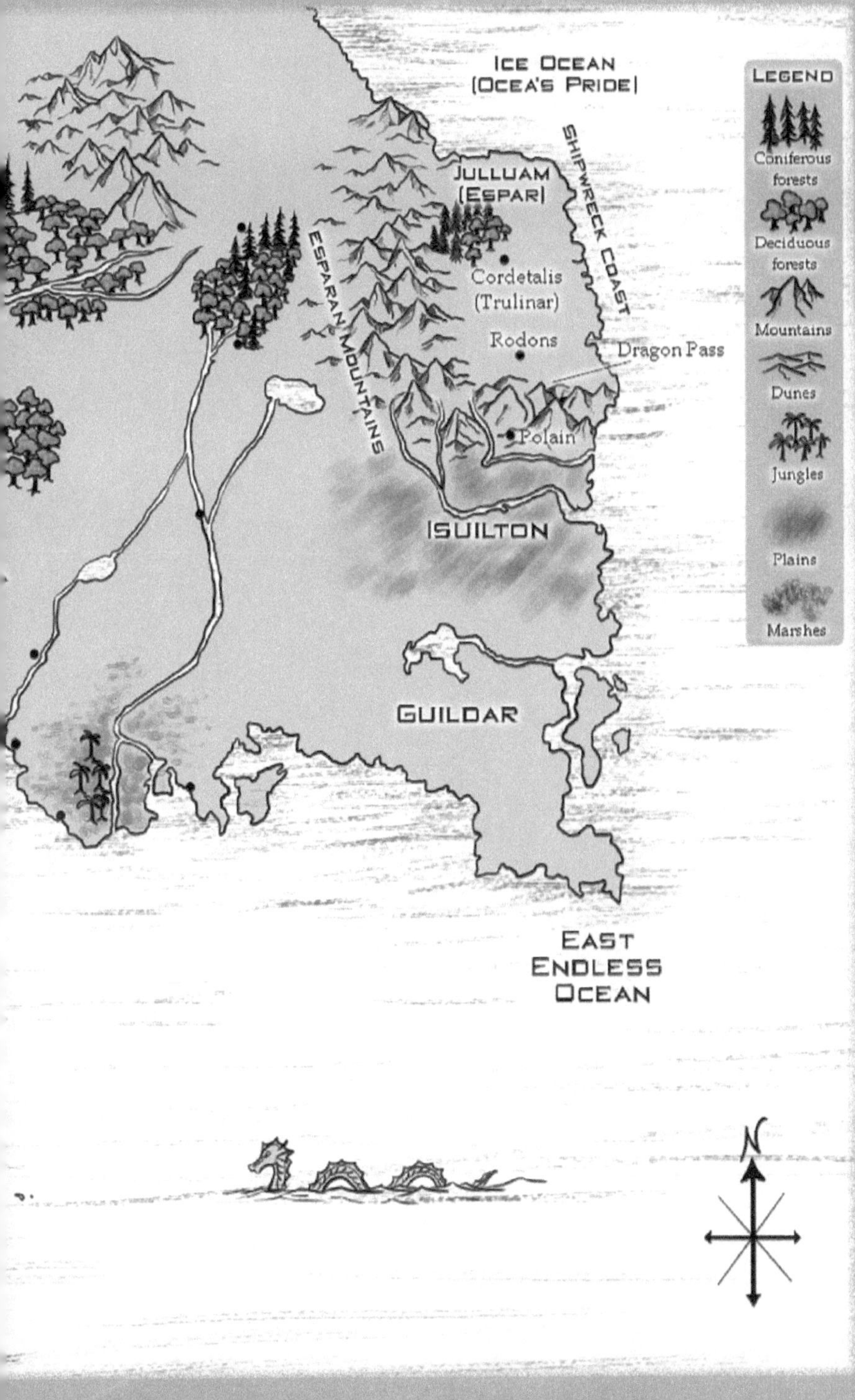

ICE OCEAN
(OCEA'S PRIDE)

JULLUAM
(ESPAR)

Cordetalis
(Trulinar)

Rodons

Dragon Pass

Polain

ISUILTON

GUILDAR

EAST
ENDLESS
OCEAN

ESPARAN MOUNTAINS

SHIPWRECK COAST

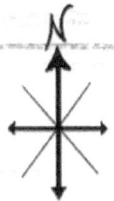

LEGEND

Coniferous
forests

Deciduous
forests

Mountains

Dunes

Jungles

Plains

Marshes

N

"ALWAYS FIGHT FOR SOMETHING
BIGGER THAN YOURSELF."

-DARKNIM DOOMDRAGON
OF THE EIDENLANDSA

Prologue

In the early dusk of the bog, Crawthran crept out from the den. Laorn followed him into the gloom of the thick marsh near their newest home, her shoulders slumped under the weight of the furs she wore. Mud covered her legs and feet, protection from leeches and the cold. It cracked as she moved, revealing her deeply tanned skin.

He ran a hand over her wide belly in approval. She was a strong female. With luck, the child she carried would be a boy.

The hounds quickly assembled, their bright eyes locked on the two humans, ready for action. With a guttural bark, Crawthran sounded the hunt, and the pack dispersed to follow him in his search. Beast, the eldest of the eight dogs, picked up the scent. He arrived at Laorn's side like a ghost and indicated the way with a look. As one, the pack turned to the north to hunt the intruders.

This was where the First Clan territory began. The chief had declared no one should pass through the Black Marsh, and Crawthran was more than pleased to enforce that law.

The pack found the humans in a clearing on the border of the marsh. Beast brought the pack in downwind. After scouting the region, they split again. Laorn took Beast and his pups to the west, and Crawthran took the remaining hounds in from the south.

The enemy had a dog with them, and it was this unfortunate creature that called the alarm.

NORTHLANDER

Crawthran threw the first knife, taking one of the invaders in the back, straight to the heart. The others moved away, into Laorn's charge. Venom, her sharp teeth flashing like diamonds in the gloomy light of the moon, caught the second man's throat before he could draw his weapon. Her brethren were not far behind her; they intercepted the remaining human. They knew the danger of a blade and circled the last man cautiously to keep him pinned until Laorn could slip between them. Laorn's double-handed, bladed fury forced the enemy back into Crawthran's reach.

There was no reason to prolong it. Crawthran slit the man's throat and let him fall.

Several groups had entered the pack's territory over the last few nights, but this was the last of them. Laorn showed her own sharpened canines as she approached the tethered horses where Beast was giving the final shake to the doomed watchdog. The three horses screamed as they fell to Laorn's blade. The hounds moved in to feast, for once not called off by their pack leader.

He was satisfied the last of the enemy was dead. None would pass through the Black Marsh. His chief had commanded it.

After gorging themselves, the hounds wearily dragged themselves back to the den for sleep that would last most of the next day. With the hounds gone, Crawthran and Laorn were left to dump the remains of the intruders into a deep reach of the swamp. Crawthran left the rest of the horses for the scavengers then found a clean pool where he and Laorn could wash themselves of the blood, taking turns picking off the ticks and leeches before they made good their bite. Done, Laorn covered him with mud once more, hiding his scent and protecting him. She let the contact linger, her eyes telling Crawthran of a different kind of hunger. Even as heavily pregnant as she was, slaying excited her. Now that the last of the killing was done, she came to him.

Crawthran lead Laorn, stark naked with her tattered furs slung over her scarred shoulders, back to the den but was interrupted by the sense of magic passing by.

He snarled, alerting his mate. It was not the first time they had felt the presence of the caster in the swamp, but as the power was only ever passing, he had been unable to locate or slay the flyer. He searched the undergrowth, sniffing the air and reaching out his senses, desperate for

any hint of the whereabouts of the enemy. He wanted to slay the flyer; it was his duty as a knife dancer.

But in a few moments, the magic was gone, and they were alone once more.

He growled as they carried on, his lust lost with the knowledge that a caster still patrolled the Black Marsh. But they had completed their task and defended the marsh. It was time to return to the Outlands.

He had to leave the caster behind.

Chapter 1

Atop the lake cliffs, the spectators lined the waggons and supply trunks. The crowd of observers, mostly Tohmas' trained protectors, seemed to get bigger every morning in the restricted space atop the hill. Since setting up the camp over the lake, it had been a long cycle of exchanging skirmishes with Northlanders, and the trapped men and women were glad for anything that would distract them. The occasional battle was interspersed with waiting, which favored the Northlanders and their access to outside resources. With the summer mooncycles ending, autumn loomed, threatening cooling weather and scarcer supplies.

Carsh, Tohmas' prime protector, sparred Rydan-style with his young tagalong, Sabian. Although Esparan, Sabian had taken to Carsh's weapons and style smoothly. While he was no match for the Rydan Knife Dancer, Sabian was getting better steadily, Tohmas had to admit.

It was a miracle Carsh allowed the eighteen year old Esparan to shadow him in the first place. It took great skill and strength to win over a Rydan's prejudice.

Tohmas sat apart on a barrel, leaning against an entrenched shop waggon, wishing he could be in Sabian's place and exercise his bored muscles. Instead, all he could do was flip a Lourite coin over his fingers, working the dexterity of his scarred left hand. But he was a Prince of Espar, even if his heart remained Rydan, and he had other duties this

day. He would have to take Carsh aside later for a proper match if he was to get a good challenge.

After, Tohmas reminded himself.

Once the spar was in full swing, Tohmas lowered his feet. "Protector Sanba, with me," he called.

The protector fell into step beside him, his tabard catching the wind. It had become stained by mud and blood, making it a mottled brown instead of green.

Tohmas moved away from the crowd to a place overlooking the cliff and the lake. Sanba joined him as Carsh kept the attention of the crowd off Tohmas by adding a flipping knife to his display. Sabian copied him, impressing the onlookers.

The other protectors followed Tohmas at a distance respectfully. Over the last year, Tohmas had come to know the protectors well, and they knew him equally well. So long as he stayed close, they were happy.

Sanba stood at his side, his blue eyes—an uncommonly bright shade like Tohmas'—scanning the lake then the cliffs. His stare lingered on the traps they had set along the sharp cliffs below to deter Northlander approach from the water. His posture tense, Sanba was ready to act should danger appear.

His steady resolve was one of the reasons Tohmas had picked him.

The wind picked up in the dawn and favored Tohmas with a gust down the slopes. The crash of the water against the cliff and the soft chirps of irate swallows kept his words from being overhead outside of immediate company. Farther to the right, a group of soldiers worked the nearby winch and drew water for the camp.

"You went to the Outlands once before, Protector," Tohmas prompted. "You delivered a greeting to the south border of Polthian."

"Yeh," Sanba replied, his word as curt as his nod. There being no other Rydans in the camp, he must have picked up the Rydan slang and accent from Carsh.

Tohmas smiled, vindicated in his choice of protectors to approach with his request. "I need you to do it again."

The older man narrowed his eyes, drawing his large eyebrows low enough to unite them over the bridge of his nose. He peered south across the lake to where another river began. The river there was treacherous and unpassable by boats. Still, it led toward the Outlands.

"Bit of a distance from here," the protector mused. "Three quarter-cycles? Maybe a full mooncycle to get there. Then I'd have to get back. Course you seem to be settling in, so maybe you'll still be here."

Tohmas followed the protector's gaze over the water and let his mind drift down the river to Solta's capital. From there, it was four princedoms to cross, including a rocky hillscape and a marsh. Most of it was forested. The fastest route would require navigation off the meandering roads.

"I can have you there tomorrow."

Sanba turned to him, a crooked smile cracking his dour expression. "Master Kitable, eh? I suppose that's why you princes spend so much damn money keeping wizards around."

"He can get you down there, but he can't get you back. If the Rydans catch any scent of magic, they'll kill you outright. So, no magic items, no enchantments, and no spells."

The protector nodded. "Take a message? Then come back?"

Tohmas envisioned the distant plains of the Outlands, picturing the tall grasses in enough detail to feel them swishing across his calves. He could practically taste the moist earth as the rain peppered down on his stalking position and hear the wren warbling a warning. In his mind's eye, the land was still within his reach.

But the lands of his upbringing were not for him. He was needed here, as was Carsh. He had to send another. It was best they never know how much he longed for it.

"A message, yes. Pay close attention because mistakes get you killed," Tohmas warned.

It did not seem to faze the protector. "When do I start?"

"Now," Tohmas replied, looking past the man. Lance Carraway, lacking his usual Gaidolon blue tabard, met his stare. "You need to be gone within the candle. It's going to get noisy later."

The protector frowned. "I'm going to miss out, eh?"

A cry went up from the crowd. At the cliff's edge, Sabian had launched himself at Carsh and stumbled. Thankfully, Carsh caught Sabian's belt and held him, his feet still on land but his body out beyond the edge of the cliff.

A hush fell over the crowd. Lance nodded to Tohmas. Without looking back, the high guardsman vanished back among the waggons.

Carsh heaved Sabian back and tossed the boy onto the stones atop the cliffs. For a long moment, Sabian stared back the way he had fallen, no doubt reliving the long look down the rocks to the cold waters far below. All anger was gone from his expression, replace by white-faced fear.

The Rydan sheathed one knife, stood over his Follower, and extended a hand to help him up.

The lesson was complete.

Tohmas heeded it as well: do not attack in anger. He could not rush in against DoomDragon. He was outnumbered and, for now, cornered. Fall was fast approaching. It was not the time to be rash and end up dangling off the cliff.

"Pack a bag. There will be a lot of walking," he told Sanba.

It was a terrible plan.

Lance felt like a rabbit being chased by a mountain cat as he darted between assailants. On one side, a broad Northlander swung his ax at Lance's head. On the other side, a soldier in a green tabard stabbed with his sword. Lance ducked the ax then slid sideways to dodge the sword. Using the slope of the hill, he skidded down the exposed granite to distance himself from both weapons.

At the bottom of his slide, Lance stumbled into a man with a streaked red-grey beard. He was Esparan, shorter than the Northlanders by a head, and a more reasonable width. He wore a thickly stuffed padded shirt and straps of leather over his shins and forearms, but he was not in Tohmas' green, Sol's red, Rairn's white, or the blue of the loaned Gaidolon soldiers.

A Northlander ally, Lance reasoned.

Lance skittered back, bringing his sword up between them and wishing he had a shield. Attacking risked the man recognizing Lance later, should he survive. Even if Lance killed the man, the confrontation could be spotted and damn Lance's mission.

But the mission would also be damned if Lance ended up dead.

Wait ... sword? Lanced checked again. Most of the villagers and farmers who had joined DoomDragon's invasion of the north had no

such weapons nor the training for them. This man had an Esparan blade and shield and was positioned to use them effectively. The sword looked well-used but also well-made. This was not a hastily forged blade of scrap iron.

Seeing uncertainty in the eyes of his opponent, Lance let his sword's tip lower.

"I'm with you," he lied. "Barlabian."

The red-bearded man brought his head slowly out from behind the shield. "You one of Rairn's?"

Lance nodded. "Got a little ahead of myself." He gestured up the hill. "The others are coming. Our prince is with us."

The stranger made a face. Someone else who didn't like the Prince of Barlaby?

"You're not in white," the man grumbled.

"I—" The stranger attacked before Lance could finish, crossing the distance between them in a single stride. He had dropped back behind the shield and lunged with his sword at Lance's unprotected left side.

Lance dropped below the man's line of sight, spun, and rolled his back across the shield, leading with his sword as he cleared the shield's edge. The tip of his sword cut over the man's shoulder, through the padded armor, and into his chest.

Lance kept turning, using his momentum to reef his blade free. The enemy stumbled forward and to the side, wrenched by the stab. He may have cried out, but Lance could not hear anything through the pounding of his heart in his ears.

He struck again, through the back, between the ribs, and into the heart.

Satisfied the enemy would not rise, Lance checked the area. The crowd of people was shifting. At times, there were mostly Galanth's green tabards clamoring over the stones, but then a wave of furs and leather would surge in and the Northlanders or their allies would take the region. No one appeared to have taken any note of Lance and his opponent.

The rendezvous was still a dozen paces farther down the slope, rightly so if there were still green tabards about. Lance pulled the shield from his now-dead enemy and took off once more.

"Nicely done!"

Lance started, brought his sword to bear, and would have struck if he had not spotted the many tattoos on the speaker's arms. Wadley had taken up an enemy's helm, hiding his face, but the myriad of tattoos was distinctive as he came up on Lance's right.

Lance had no time to reply as a Galanth soldier stumbled into their path. His hand was bleeding and missing a few fingers, and he had no weapon. Peering up with wide eyes, the fighter froze before them.

They were meant to be passing as DoomDragon supporters; an unarmed Galanth soldier was an easy target.

Lance glanced at Wadley.

With a shrug, Wadley hefted his sword and shouted. Woken from his panic, the Galanth fighter ran, sliding along the stones and trampled moss. Wadley and Lance gave chase, waving their weapons at the sky and shouting wildly. Deliberately, Lance fell to his right and knocked Wadley down the slope. He had intended for them both to slide and interrupt the pursuit of the helpless Galanth man, but the rocks broke under their combined weight and the stumble turned into a fall. With all his weight suddenly crashing into Wadley, it was all he could do to keep the sword from accidentally stabbing his friend. A tangled mess of limbs and weapons, they finally came to a stop a dozen paces down the hill.

They lay still for a moment, figuring themselves out. Lance's arm felt uncommonly heavy, and he realized he had landed on the shield, which had protected him from falling onto Wadley's mace. But Wadley's other shoulder lay across the shield as well, weighing him down.

He had to unhook the shield from his arm to come to his feet.

"That," Wadley said as he brushed himself off, "was embarrassing."

"Come on," Lance replied. He could worry about appearances later. They had more distance to cover.

They made it to the target outcropping and ducked behind the uneven edge of crumbling stone. The closest people were Northlanders and their Esparan allies, without a single green tabard to be seen.

One by one, the other guardsmen arrived, slipping in when they could be certain there were no watching eyes. Usually, picking out the blue and white of Gaidol was easy among the browns and furs of the Northlanders, but his guardsmen were not wearing any of their colors. He relied on recognizing their faces now.

Thinking about faces that could be recognized, his hand went to his upper lip. Would any enemy recognize him? He had shaved his moustache off that morning. His face still felt chilled.

As Lance counted the arrivals, Wadley and Shinat dug up the hidden store of white tabards and handed them out.

Lance let out a breath at seeing them. He could not think of any other Prince of Espar who would have dared attempt such a deception. But Prince Rairn had betrayed them. He deserved all he got. And, as Tohmas was fond of saying, *War is about death. The shorter the war, the better.*

Whatever means necessary, Lance thought as his Gaidolon guardsmen, each a loyal friend, donned the white tabards.

A horn sounded from the Galanth forces. Lance tried to envision the exchange, how one set of forces would advance while another retreated to give their soldiers a chance to recover. The signals were tight and frequent; many adjustments were being made.

"Rairn made his move," Shinat said, handing Lance a tabard. The tall, mustached man then went to the edge of the outcropping and peered around. He would alert them when Rairn's men reached this point in their retreat.

Lance and his ten chosen guardsmen were behind enemy forces now. With his forces, he could attack, cleave a dozen or more assailants, and give Galanth the upper hand in the current skirmish. He considered it. It was the easier route.

But they had a plan well beyond this engagement. Rairn would, according to Prince Tohmas, change loyalties. The Prince of Barlaby inadvertently gave Lance and his guardsmen a route into the Northlander's camp.

Lance slipped the stained tabard over his head and tied it down. It stank of dirt and sweat, but at least his lacked the green discoloration of vomit or entrails.

"This better work," he grumbled.

Wadley was at his side again. A chunk of moss had caught in the ridge of his helm and stuck up like a chopped plume. "It's been fun so far!"

Lance glared up at the guardsman. "You do enjoy a good scrap."

"Both sides trying to get us! Twice as many opponents as usual!" The man's bare tattooed arms were spattered with blood. Wadley preferred using a simple mace when not on his horse, and the effect was messy.

"Optimist," Lance groused.

"Time." Shinat's voice, a deep bass, cut through the banter, and the guardsmen tensed. Lance released his grip on his sword to wipe his hand. His bracelet of river pearls weighed on his wrist.

The afternoon was fading, and the warmth went with it. His fingers were chilling, making the hilt harder to hold. His heart was still pounding.

The guardsmen looked to him.

"Let's go," Lance said, brushing off his white tabard. He squared his shoulders. "Split up. See you on the other side."

"And have fun!" Wadley added as they dispersed.

Lance scowled at Wadley, knowing it would have no effect on the cheery man. His lip twitched.

Wadley laughed. "You're the one who said it. I'm an optimist!"

"Just keep up," Lance said, stepping out from the outcropping and into the flood of strangers heading back into the Northlander camp at the bottom of the hill.

This is a terrible plan.

The days in the far north were long, and the weather was good, but Tril did not pay attention to either. Although he spent his time helping the hunters set traps for the elk and skinning the kills, his nights were lonely. Since her illness, his wife, Nara, never traveled with him. The other wives helped him, but they did not have much time to visit or talk. It was for the best, he knew, for it gave him the chance to focus on his Aspect.

Forgoing sleep, Tril spent every moment by the fires, mentally seeking his Aspect across the empty plains. With each Scry, his disappointment was renewed. No animal spirit came to him, not like his wolf had. By the eighth day of the hunt, he feared none would.

A war waged in the south. His people needed him back in his seat on the Circle of the Raven, but that required he find an Aspect to

replace the one that had been stolen from him. He did not know if it was even possible for a Northlander to gain two Aspects in one lifetime, but he had to try.

He sat outside on the cold ground, keeping his eyes on the far-reaching skies above him, and searched.

As the seat of Divination in the Circle, Tril knew, with terrifying detail and accuracy, what would happen if he failed to find a new Aspect. When his *visaln*, his gift of magic, was active, his mind filled with visions. Some weak and unlikely, others strong and certain. Without conscious thought, he followed important ones back and forth, seeking causative events. He knew what the future would likely hold.

It terrified him.

Tril knew that, should the Circle not be complete to hold the ice pool, Master Terant would try to attack Master Kitable of Galanth by seeking Kitable out directly in battle. While the Galanth wizard often died in these visions, Terant would be exhausted by the effort. Most of the visions after included Terant's death on the battlefield.

That was not a worthwhile exchange. He needed to keep Master Terant alive; he was too valuable to DoomDragon.

One vision showed that Elder Ela, Tril's mentor and leader of the Circle, could keep Terant from taking the risk if Tril told her what he had seen. She would convince the wizard to wait until the next spring, but Ela's aging heart was close to failing. Tril suspected she was aware of her own illness, even though he had not, and would never, speak to her of it.

She would not make it to spring. If she died before Tril returned, the Circle of the Raven would never be complete, weakening DoomDragon's chances against the Esparans.

Since being declared an elder, Tril had known he was to replace Ela as the Voice of the Raven when she died. All the elders had agreed, but now that it seemed imminent, he sought another path. He loved Ela as a mother. He did not want to lose her, not ever.

He chased visions, seeking a solution. He sought absolutes in the cloud of possibilities, and it came always down to the same thing—Tril had to find an Aspect. If he failed, the Northlanders and their allies lost the war.

As he searched the tundra again for an animal spirit that would accept him, the visions continued to flow through him. The hunters would find elk the next day; if they killed any was uncertain. One vision showed a hunter being trampled and killed, but a different one predicted a cleanly killed bull.

One of the young girls was practicing with her sling. If she kept at it, she would take down a grouse in the dawn. But if she gave up early, she would miss the throw and toss her sling into the shrubs in frustration. The visions slipped ahead, following her down a path as a skilled tailor instead of a proud hunter.

In a moment of insight he seldom had and could never control, Tril saw Kyo, his brother's wife, coming to see him. The vision was strong.

After the evening food had been eaten and then stored against foxes and crows, Tril felt the predicted touch of the woman's hands on his shoulders. He had been mentally wandering the plains once more in search, but none of the elk called to him.

Dropping a Scry felt like closing his eyes, spinning in circles, and finding a different village. Tril kept his eyes shut to reduce the effect.

"Greetings, wife of my brother," he said without looking.

"Greetings, brother of my husband," Kyo replied. By her voice, she was smiling. Was that because he had identified her without looking or because of the irony of the title?

In the years before his Aspect, Kyo had agreed to marry Tril, not Bak. Tril's wedding hunt, meant to enforce the necessity of a continual hunt for the sustenance of his family, had been interrupted by the wolf. The failure of the hunt had cursed the union, and the elders had decided the gods opposed the joining of Kyo and Tril. Instead, after a year of uncertainty, Kyo married Bak.

Tril's sight returned to his own eyes. He opened them and found Kyo kneeling in front of him. The dimming cooking fire gave her a halo and cast a long shadow over Tril's fur-covered lap. In the dusk, the sky above shone cyan.

"Your family may have need of you," Tril warned. "Two sons are hard to keep track of for a man, particularly Bak."

Kyo smiled and tossed her head until her long blond hair flipped. Here, in the deep summer, he did not need his parka, and she did not need her hood. It seemed odd to see her hair down.

"Bak sleeps, and the boys as well. Did you not know that, Circle Elder?"

Heeding the tease, Tril smiled as he sat back on his heels. "I did not look."

Her smile faded, and she swallowed hard. "I wanted to speak to you about them, Elder Tril. .I am worried about Kohd."

Tril tensed. Kohd, now six, was Kyo's most recent addition to the family. The boy had misfortune surrounding his birth because of the illness he had caused in Nara, Tril's wife, and Tril was forever grateful that Bak and Kyo had been willing to take in the unlucky child. As a Circle elder, Tril was not present enough to care for Kohd. He had needed the surrogate family, and Bak, named Kohd's Eldafather at the time of the boy's birth, had stepped up.

"He was out here earlier today," Tril said, smiling through his nervousness. The boy looked more like Nara with every year, but he sounded like Tril when he spoke. "Declared that I was one-hundred and sixty."

The boy's adopted mother laughed. "Did you correct him?"

"To a child, one-hundred and sixty is the same as fifty-three. Neither, they think, will ever reach them." This time, when she looked toward the tent where her men slept, she had a sparkle to her eyes that offset Tril's fears.

"Kohd is showing talent. Maybe not with guessing ages," she amended when she saw Tril tilt his head skeptically, "but he always knows where his brother is, even if he has been gone for a halfcycle."

"The ties between families are strong."

"Yesterday, I dropped a garment coming back from washing, and he knew exactly where to find it."

"He could have seen you drop it. Or been out playing and seen it."

What father did not want his son to succeed? But Tril had to remain rational. The *visaln* was not inherited. As an elder, Tril dealt in truth.

Kyo's sparkling eyes would not be dissuaded. "Tril, it is more than that, I swear. You think me a pompous eagle and yet—"

"I am not saying you are wrong," he interrupted, looking beyond, to the tent where his family rested. Visions showed Kohd sleeping under his Eldafather's arm within the shelter. "Every Northlander, no matter their heritage or their tribe, has gifts, Kyo. You can nurture the gift—make it a game to him to find things—but even you cannot control if

the gift reaches the level of Aspecting." With a reminiscent smile and a small shake of his head, Tril added, "But perhaps one day he will be out hunting with his brother, and a beast will walk right into the camp, put its head on his lap, and reach out to his mind. Then your son will feel complete beyond anything he had ever imagined, and we—"

Tril was interrupted by a furry head being laid on his knee.

Kyo leapt to her feet with a shout. Tril only heard her faintly, lost in the black stare of the wolf. The portion of his mind that had been painfully empty was suddenly filled once more.

"You sneaky demon," he cursed in Esparan. "I just had to stop looking."

The familiar memories of an animal drifted into his mind and were welcomed. His vision changed to match that of the wolf, fading the colors of the sunset together. He heard Kyo running to her tent and rousing her husband. He even heard the soft flap of the tent door, although it was more than twenty paces away, open to let the family out.

Kohd was the fastest of the three, stopping short abruptly when he spotted the animal. Their eyes locked as the wolf, contently nestled in the back of Tril's mind, let her physical form go. When Tril could only see through his own eyes, he knew the soul was gone from the body at his feet.

Tril rose, and all the onlookers took a large step back, except for Kohd. The boy, dressed only in fur pants, rushed forward to pet the wolf's thick, stone-colored pelt.

In a corner of Tril's mind, the wolf nuzzled in next to him. Filled with renewed strength, Tril stood tall. She would never again run in the tundra, but she was content. She had found her true pairing, and the people around her had become her pack. Her thoughts, so closely tied to Tril's, were joyful.

"She had to come down from the north," Tril told his son. "Thankfully, she is not too late."

The visions answered. Now they could take down the Esparan wizard and grant DoomDragon victory.

The Circle of the Raven was complete. Kitable would meet his match.

Dropped by the spell just south of the Black Marsh, Sanba emerged disoriented and nauseated. He choked back his lurching stomach. With only basic supplies, he had no desire to waste his dinner nor soil his clothing. Further, Kitable had dropped him into an ideal campsite location, one that would be spoiled should he bring up the contents of his stomach into it.

At least I left the horse behind. Can horses vomit? Sanba took several deep breaths of air rich with petrichor and focused. He needed a camp. A nearby brook, which Kitable had already told him about, was downwind among the tall grasses. The breeze in the open plain kept the insects at bay as he set up the *Greet Po*—a spear bearing a cloth mark with a bloody handprint—Prince Tohmas had given him. He had brought a tent, usually shared between two protectors, and was excited to have the space to himself.

With all the extra room, it was a luxurious, but quiet, night.

Morning dawned too quickly, and soon the tent was hot and uncomfortable in the stilled air of dawn. Sanba rose.

A Rydan stood beside the post Sanba had erected, just as Tohmas had predicted.

Having become accustomed to Carsh, Sanba was not surprised by the man's crouching stance nor that he carried a dozen flint-chipped knives on him. The man had skin as dark as oak bark, and it looked as thick. His hair was cut raggedly short, and he was more muscled than Carsh despite being the same imposing height. Unlike Carsh's mischievous smirk, something about the man's feral stare made Sanba tense. He felt like he was faced by a mountain cat and had to prove himself inedible.

Remembering what the prince said, Sanba made a fist with his right hand and pressed the clenched hand into his left.

The stranger cocked his head, his ice-blue stare so pale as to be almost white. The stare flicked to the *Greet Po* then back to Sanba. The cloth attached to the spear hung flat in the still air of the dawn.

A growling noise, like gravel tipping down a slope, made Sanba look sharply behind him. In the bushes nearest the brook, two huge, black hounds had taken up post. One bared white fangs at him, blood-stained lips curled up widely. The beasts were nothing but muscle, sleek, black fur, and teeth.

He squared his shoulders and faced the stranger again. He was a Protector of Galanth and had been for twenty years. His prince had sent him on a mission, and he would be damned if he failed because some demon-cursed dogs gave him the willies. He had a message to deliver.

"I have a message for Chief Tamv from Prince Tohmas."

Sanba did not expect the Rydan to understand anything he said, but he was pleasantly surprised when the stranger echoed in a soft whisper, "Tamv. Tohmas."

"Yes," Sanba said, feeling like he was coaching a child through a new word. "Chief Tamv. From Prince Tohmas."

The man growled like the hound, and primal fear shot up Sanba's spine. For a moment, he thought the man in front of him was planning on eating him.

Show no fear, Tohmas had told him. To them, strength is everything.

Stepping up forcibly, Sanba advanced on the Rydan. He placed his hand on the hilt of his sword, ready to make good a threat. "Take me to Chief Tamv!"

The Rydan did not balk. Behind Sanba, both hounds growled in unison, the sound loud enough to make Sanba's stomach twist. He fought to overrule his instincts, which were insisting he run like a spooked rabbit from here to Wayburn. Instead, the protector held himself straight and stared at the Rydan in front of him, making a show of ignoring the hounds despite the weakness in his legs.

The Rydan examined Sanba with mild curiosity. Pursing his lips, the Rydan considered Sanba's weapon.

With a whistle, the hounds were called to heel. The Rydan gestured for Sanba to follow him away from the marsh, leading the way into the plains.

Sanba gathered his sack but was forced to leave the tent behind in his haste as the Rydan did not appear to be willing to wait for him.

Out of the grasses came another three hounds Sanba had not noticed, and the protector felt his legs shake under him.

He had probably come very close to being devoured. Without a doubt, it was the most terrifying thing he had, in all his twenty years of putting his life at risk for the sake of another, experienced.

Reminding himself that he trusted the prince who had sent him here, Sanba followed the Rydan further into the Outlands.

Chapter 2

F or nearly a mooncycle, Lance and his guardsmen pretended to be Barlabians allied with DoomDragon's Northlanders. For the most part, all DoomDragon's Esparans avoided the Northlanders, and Lance's men did the same. It was easy to disappear in the masses.

In the early evening, the guardsmen met up at a dice tournament. The games gave them a crowd to hide in while talking.

They arranged themselves without requiring discussion; Lance stayed near the center of his guardsmen, and a barrier of sentries camouflaged themselves with the crowd, creating a buffer against outsiders. Those within the group bustled about under the guise of bets, while in truth passing on reports and information about their findings in the enemy's camp.

"Something's up, without a doubt," Wadley reported on his turn. "My ... group, fyrd, whatever it's called, was just warned to be ready to move quickly, probably come morning. There was something about the Northlander Hunters going first and clearing the way, but then we follow."

"Without a doubt?" Lance echoed. He had known Wadley for too many years to buy into everything the man said. If there was any chance there might be fighting, Wadley would be there, watching in anticipation.

But their mission among the Northlanders was not to kill things; it was to gather what information they could. Wadley knew that as well as any of the guardsmen.

Lance checked their surroundings once more, but the crowd around the dice was still loud and no one was paying undue attention to them. He was being overly cautious, he knew. Everyone within earshot was his ally.

"It's gotta be soon. These idiots don't have long memories, and they bore quickly," Wadley said, and Lance nodded, trying to smile at the insult. Too many days of silence had put him on edge. Tohmas had ordered him to wait until the signal, but when would it come? During another skirmish? The two armies could sit staring at each other for another mooncycle without moving.

Lance rubbed his bare upper lip, missing his moustache.

"Well? What—" Wadley began.

"We wait," Lance said, the words all too predictable. He had said the same thing to many of the guardsmen tonight and would say it to the rest as well. "He knows what he's doing," he said, unwilling to specifically name Tohmas when there was even a small chance of being overheard. "We wait. No one does anything until we get..."

The sight of white robes made him pause.

The long robes, trailing feathers, were instantly recognizable. Although the celebrant's face was covered by a grey scarf, Lance had no doubt he had seen Celebrant Calanor passing by the campfire on the far side.

"I need to check that out," he told Wadley as the celebrant disappeared behind the tents. "Tell the others to stay in pairs and make sure their partners are out when things go to hell. I'll—"

"You don't have someone watching for you," Wadley warned, his tattooed arms folded across his chest. "Everyone else got paired up but you—"

Squeezing out from the crowd, looking for the celebrant, Lance replied, "Face it; you'd all miss me if I didn't come back."

He didn't wait for a reply but rushed after the celebrant, worried he had lost him. If Calanor was living in the camp, Lance wanted to know where and under what circumstances. There had been no visible escort. Was he a prisoner? A guest? How much had the celebrant of Totho been

involved in the fires that destroyed three of the four Temple Waggons within Tohmas' camp a mooncycle go? And how had a man once sworn to Galanth ended up living among its enemy?

In his bright white, Calanor wasn't hard to follow through the tents. Everyone moved aside, the Northlanders doing so with a subtle bowing of their heads. The Esparans occasionally nodded to acknowledge the celebrant but with less reverence.

At length, Calanor entered a hide tent. There were no markings and no sign of a Temple waggon. Since the tent was made of skins, not cloth, Lance presumed it belonged to a Northlander, but he could not see any way to identify the owner.

His task at an end now that the celebrant had gone where he could not follow, Lance turned to leave.

He jumped back; his path was blocked by two enormous Northlanders in elk skins. By the smell of the pelts, they were either fresh and improperly dried or old and never washed. His nose hairs curled at the stench.

"What you want, Esparan?" the warrior on the left demanded in halting, rough Esparan. The man's gloved hands, decorated with jointed bone plates over the knuckles, sat on his hips next to formidable axes. Like most Northlanders, the man had a beard that could be tucked into a belt, and the pale color of it made him look like a north bear.

"I..." Lance took a second step back so he could look the man in the eye without craning his neck. "I wanted to speak to the celebrant," he lied, "but I don't think he heard me call after him. It's no bother. I'll try again later."

The Northlanders exchanged long, suspicious looks, confusion on their faces. "Why?" the spokesman asked.

Feeling his excuses had been minimally understood, Lance decided to use as many words as possible. "Totho, the Gust, is the defender of secrets and the surreptitious, so naturally my business is not to be disclosed, at least not to any but the celebrant and servant of the guardian Spirit and Evening Star."

To Lance's satisfaction, he got two blank looks.

"We call him the Winter Star," another voice interrupted, and Lance spun around. Behind him, another set of Northlanders had exited the tent, somehow silent despite their bulk and weapons. At the center of

the new trio, an older man stood with his hands on his belt in readiness. He wore red and black dragon scale in place of elk pelts, and a huge, dragon-shaped ax hung over his shoulder.

Lance's heart skipped several beats and climbed its way up his neck. No other Northlander wore dragon scale, and the dragon ax was legendary among the Esparans in the camp. This was Darknim DoomDragon.

Lance and he had crossed paths before, but only at a distance. Lance prayed he looked different enough to avoid being recognized. Recognition meant death.

There was very little accent in the voice, and the sentence was spoken with confidence the other Northlanders lacked. Without a doubt, Darknim DoomDragon spoke enough Esparan to understand everything Lance said.

"So you sought Tothonar for a conference?" DoomDragon asked, no hint of suspicion or recognition visible. "I am willing to allow it, but you will first have to answer two questions."

With two Hunters behind him and three in front, Lance saw no alternative. Remembering that the Esparans in the camp, despite having very little direct contact with DoomDragon, generally feared the man, Lance respectfully straightened and lowered his head. In his mind, he imagined Prince Dorakon of Gaidol, Lance's patron, across from him.

"Of course, DoomDragon," he answered, his voice taking on an obsequious tone he had avoided using since leaving Gaidol. He had forgotten how much he hated it.

DoomDragon's beard was indeed tucked into his belt but was still long enough to permit a nod. "Where are you from?"

"Barlaby," Lance replied.

"You have a strange accent."

"My mother was Gaidolon, but I grew up in Chantsy, just outside of Field."

"So I have no doubt you know the village well enough to tell me where I would find the well," DoomDragon prompted.

Giving silent thanks to the many trivial missions Prince Dorakon had sent him on, Lance nodded. "South edge of the village, near the apple orchard."

"Next to the wall," DoomDragon agreed.

"There's no wall in Chantsy."

When DoomDragon met his stare, Lance looked away, hoping he appeared nervous enough to ease DoomDragon's suspicions.

How well does the invader remember the village he stormed? There was a chance Chantsy had built a wall since the last time Lance had visited.

The Northlander considered Lance for a long moment then nodded and gave a half smile. "Then for my second question: why is your brow pale?"

Lance paused. "I don't understand," he replied carefully.

"You see," DoomDragon said, advancing a step and pointing at the top of Lance's face, "Gaidolons wear a band of beads over their brow. The unfortunate downside is that you tan with a line."

Lance had no reply. He had hidden his moustache tan but not touched the rest of his face. His beads caused a line?

Demons...

"Dedan," DoomDragon finished, turning away dismissively.

Lance translated without thinking; "*dedan*" meant to arrest or hold in Rydan. He couldn't remember when he learned the word, or even if it had been Tanuka, Sori, or Carsh who had taught it to him, but he knew what it meant.

Certain of his death should he resist, Lance lifted his hands out and wide, showing he would not fight.

DoomDragon paused, glancing back at Lance. His thick white eyebrows lifted as two hands—the weighty grip of the Hunters who had first confronted him—landed on Lance's shoulders.

"You understood me."

Lance would have shrugged, but he doubted his ability to lift his shoulders under the heavy hands holding him. "I've been around enough to learn a bit," he said, smiling weakly, "and I know when I'm outmatched."

For a moment, the bushy eyebrows furled together. DoomDragon stared at Lance, the cold blue of his eyes making Lance shiver.

"You are Gaidolon and a spy," the Northlander said softly, a statement, not an accusation. His voice contained mild amusement.

In a blink, Lance saw his mental image of Dorakon be replaced with Tohmas. Lance smiled at the thought. "And you are Darknim DoomDragon, leader of the Eidenlandsa. You know, I expected you

to be younger—one of those full of ambition kids—yet this makes far more sense. An army needs a good leader, and very few hotheads are good leaders." Lance let himself slouch. "But I suppose I'm used to stories about heroes fighting monsters not armies. No measly hero I know could control an army."

DoomDragon cracked another smile, showing yellowed teeth. "I was going to have you killed, but now I wonder what else you may have an opinion on. How well did you—"

Before the sentence was finished, a man rounded the corner at a brisk pace then skidded to a halt when he saw the group of Northlanders with Lance at their center.

Lance sighed in exasperation. The gods were clearly in a foul mood.

Prince Rairn took one look at the gathering and paled. "High Guardsman!" he exclaimed.

"I even shaved, damn it," Lance said dryly.

DoomDragon chuckled, and Prince Rairn took a step back as if expecting Lance to somehow strike him. "What are you doing here? How did—"

"I have you to thank, Rairn," Lance happily informed the flustered prince. "When you swapped over, I tagged along, and in all the confusion, no one noticed. I thought you'd have known the men who served you better than that, but then I've been overestimating you for some time."

"You dare—"

The prince stalked forward, the insult sufficient to recover him from his shock. Lance couldn't help himself; he laughed. The thought of Prince Rairn getting through five Hunters was absurd.

Prince Rairn's arrival in DoomDragon's camp had been met with trepidation from the start. Darknim DoomDragon, as far as Lance could tell, had officially met with Prince Rairn once, and that was all. Despite the lukewarm welcome, Prince Rairn established his tent at the center of his new camp, his standard flown high as if to taunt Tohmas and the others still trapped on the hill. DoomDragon seemed to permit the arrogant gesture through disinterest, as if Prince Rairn was of too little importance.

Lance was curious how the prince would fare against the Northlander commander face to face.

Sure enough, DoomDragon, growling low, stepped into the prince's path. Prince Rairn came to an immediate halt.

"Our meeting is to be delayed," DoomDragon declared. Prince Rairn opened his mouth to object but closed it swiftly when DoomDragon touched a knife on his belt. It was a trick Lance had seen Tohmas use; the easiest way to silence the Prince of Barlaby was to threaten him. Near the end of their alliance, Tohmas had but to lift his hand toward his knife for Rairn to fall silent.

Surprisingly, Lance recognized the knife on DoomDragon's belt. Tohmas had left it as a gift at the crossing of MudCrow River.

"Of course, DoomDragon," Prince Rairn replied, his strained voice evidence of his irritation. "When would you have me return?"

Lance smirked to see the prince humbled. Everywhere the Prince of Barlaby went, he seemed to find himself under someone else's authority. For a man who had once controlled an entire princedom, it must be chaffing by now.

"When I call," DoomDragon dismissed. Prince Rairn's jaw clenched, but he left without saying anything. Once the prince was gone, the Northlander looked back at Lance. "High Guardsman, is it?"

"High Guardsman Lance Carraway of Varidee," Lance fully introduced himself with as much flourish as he could considering his company.

"You are close to Prince Tohmas then?"

"Define 'close.' I can't say I know his favorite color or anything. That said, I suspect it's red."

Again, the Northlander grinned through his thick beard. "You and I need to talk. Come along, High Guardsman Carraway. We have much to discuss."

Lance had no choice; the Hunters behind him stripped him of weapons and headed into the tent. He went along.

Keeping his hands at his side, Lance broke the thread that held Valia's chain of pearls around his wrist and flicked them to his right, hoping no one saw them drop into the broken tufts of grass by the tent pole.

By the second day of walking, Protector Varth Sanba recognized that the Rydan leading him had a partner. She was slight but muscled. Hauntingly beautiful, like a tragic ghost seen only by moonlight, she appeared when Sanba was feigning sleep and spent scarce time at the Rydan's side. Like Sanba's guide, who Sanba had taken to calling "Beastman," she moved with a hunter's deadly grace. Unlike Beastman, she had a downcast, angry feel. She reminded him of a beaten dog as she came to her master's side, eager to please but anticipating pain.

Sanba slept little and awoke instantly when he heard movement. In the pre-dawn light, Beastman regularly slunk away, leaving Sanba briefly unattended. He returned bearing meat without fail, yet Sanba never saw him light a cooking fire or gather food. Sanba was not even certain the Rydan skinned the animals he ate, but he often saw the man picking at his teeth with a bone shard. Unsurprisingly, Beastman's teeth were sharp like a wolf's.

On the third day, Beastman, without a word, made his hounds wait in the grasslands as they approached a gathering of homes. On the outskirts of the settlement, a sentry atop a boulder called out a harsh challenge. Working with Carsh had allowed Sanba to pick up some Rydan, but he did not recognize the word.

Sanba's guide walked on without replying. Sanba kept up, keeping his position three strides behind Beastman. He held himself tall in false confidence, shoulders tense.

The sentry, a spry youth, dropped to the ground and into a crouch. His spear, lowered for a quick thrust, led his way into their path. He reached a point a dozen paces ahead of Beastman, then froze. Knowing Prince Tohmas had warned against showing fear, Sanba was surprised by how the sentry scrambled away. The youth averted his gaze and cleared a path for Beastman, making a flicking motion with his hand—a sign to ward off something?— as the man passed.

The sentry's expression changed to profound confusion as Sanba passed.

Beastman led the way into the heart of the shelters, every Rydan scuttling out of his way. Even children, usually oblivious to displays of authority, fled like a monster was on their heels.

Sanba wanted to call the area a town, but the smattering of shelters, all made of stretched hide over bent boughs, was not substantial enough

to earn the word. He tried to take in all he could, wondering if he was the first Esparan allowed so close to the Rydans' homes. Everything looked temporary, as if ready to be plucked from the ground and thrown over a shoulder. The homes themselves were built as tunnels of short brush and grasses, long enough to lie down within. At least these Rydans were cooking their food and did not have the same bloodstains on their faces as Beastman did.

As he walked among the hovels, Sanba realized there would be little point to making the shelters taller. The homes had no windows to let in light. The insides were filled with deep darkness, and Rydans did not have candles or lanterns. Sanba was shocked when two children and a woman crawled out from one shelter. He kept glancing back, trying to figure out how they had all fit in the tiny space.

Near the heart of the village, as best Sanba could gauge it, a single structure loomed. Unlike the tiny shelters, the sun-bleached, wooden building was tall enough for a man to stand comfortably within without touching the stretched hide roof. A mountain cat pelt hung over the door, decorated in beads and stained red. A host of warriors, some of the biggest Sanba had ever seen, huddled in the shade of the building while a small herd of untethered horses grazed just beyond it.

Since the building was the only tall structure in the entire village, it must be the chief's home, a *shella*.

Out from the *shella* stepped a huge Rydan. He bore a certain similarity to Carsh with his ropey, muscled form and had similar green-tinged eyes. His hair was ghostly white, although he still had a full head of it despite his creeping age. Sanba, at forty-eight, guessed himself to be about the same age as the Rydan but then felt inadequate at the comparison. The Rydan squaring himself up in the doorway of the *shella* could live another twenty years and not fade at all, Sanba was certain.

The Rydan placed his hands on his hips, and Sanba's eyes were drawn to the weapons hanging there——short, bone-handled, hooked blades. The man's grass bracelets were stained chief's red and matched the pelt over the door. Sanba, familiar with Carsh's bracelets, knew Rydans wore beads among the grasses, but the chief's bracelets were nearly all beads and little grass. He was wondering about the significance when the tilt of light reflected the white. Those were not beads at all, he realized. Those were human knucklebones.

Are all Rydan bracelets filled with bones?

Beastman paused, and Sanba did the same. Once the chief fixed his stare on Sanba, Beastman moved on. Without a word to any, the feral man slunk back into the plains to rejoin his hounds, his duty done.

Sanba lifted his hands to make the usual Rydan salute—hand to palm—but caught himself before finishing the gesture. Tohmas had said to do the other salute—right fist to left shoulder—to the chief.

He quickly corrected himself, pressing his clenched hand against his left collarbone.

The rising tension lessened around him, but the narrowed eyes of the chief made it clear the error had been noted.

Sanba held his position stubbornly, waiting for permission to speak to the Rydan chief.

With deliberate care, the chief lifted his hand from his blades, a sign of acceptance. He stared down at Sanba and demanded, "State your business."

The Esparan words were sloppy but decipherable. Knowing the Rydans were accustomed to little by way of chatter, Sanba replied, "I carry a message from Prince Tohmas."

A humming surrounded him, a sound he often heard the prime protector make when he was thinking

"Speak."

The hum intensified. Sanba did not turn his eyes from the chief, concerned that hesitation would offend the chief.

Sanba cleared his throat. "Prince Tohmas says 'Ready.'"

"Goh," the chief said, smiling. Sanba preferred the man's scowl; the smile felt like a rabid dog snarling. When the chief stepped down from the *shella*, Sanba involuntarily moved back a pace.

"Burlotak!" the chief barked, and one of the warriors came forward, falling into a half-kneeling position in front of his chief. Although one knee was close to the ground, it did not quite touch, letting the man be ready to leap up. *"Cawl 'em alh. 'Af col way. 'Af Brinkhan."*

Sanba held his breath, his heartrate skipping like a spooked horse. Although the chief clearly had not expected it, Sanba had understood the instructions.

The chief was ordering his men to enter the *Brinkhan*, the Rydan name for the Black Marsh. The First Clan occupied the territory

immediately south of Galanth, and only the Black Marsh separated them. If the Rydans were entering the Black Marsh, they would be in position to threaten the Princedom of Galanth.

Sanba's mouth went dry.

He had to return to Prince Tohmas immediately and warn him. He could be in Wayburn within five days if he pushed it. At the least, he could warn the fyrd there of the threat. From Wayburn, he should be able to contact the prince; Master Kitable kept an eye on the city and could relay a message. He didn't know what the prince or Master Kitable could do, but they could not let their home be threatened by Rydans.

Sanba had to get to Wayburn.

Trying to keep his fear buried, Sanba waited until the chief had dismissed his messenger, Burlotak, and turned to him.

"Have you a reply I can carry to the prince?" Sanba asked, forcing his voice to be even.

The chief abruptly moved. Before Sanba could close his hand on his sword's hilt, a hooked blade was at his throat. The blade was chipped shale with an edge so thin it was translucent in the sunlight. Sanba had no doubt it was sharp enough to sever his head with little effort.

A Rydan approached from behind him and neatly removed Sanba's bag then sword belt. All his belongings were placed atop the step into the *shella*.

"You will not go back," the chief said, his voice a hiss. The pressure of the keen edge against Sanba's skin drew blood, but not deeply. Sanba tried to avoid swallowing, not wanting to move even that much with the blade so near.

He stared up at the venomous green eyes and willed himself not to blink. He had been born the son of a hunter and learned his father's trade. In the woods, he had come across mountain cats several times. Then too, he had stared down the predator, knowing that to show fear was to be identified as prey and eaten. He would not be intimidated. He was a protector of Galanth.

But as he studied the man before him, he realized his assumptions about this man being a hunter like Carsh were mistaken. This man was not killing for food and need; he stood over Sanba as a master to a slave. His desire was not to survive but to control. He wanted servitude. And a challenge among the Rydans could not be left unanswered.

CHAPTER 2

Sanba turned his stare aside. He did not look down, thinking that would show subservience, but let his gaze shift to one side.

Not mountain cats, Sanba decided. Rydans were wolves, much like Beastman. He had been challenged by the chief of the pack, and if he wanted to survive among them, he had to yield.

Their prisoner now disarmed and deferring, the chief lowered his blade, his smile whimsical.

"You know your place," he said. Turning his back dismissively, the chief returned to his *shella*, pausing only to gather Sanba's belongings.

His hands were wrenched behind him, and thick ropes tightened over his wrists. A rope collar and tether followed. He was led away.

By morning, the first of the outlying Rydan warriors began trickling into the Chief's camp. Plans to travel north solidified, and despite his best efforts, there was nothing Sanba could do about it.

Chapter 3

Trying not to shiver, Lance sat naked, his legs curled against his chest. He had tried other positions, but only bent with his knees up kept his core from freezing. He still had to alternate to a position on his knees when his backend numbed from the cold. They still had almost a cycle of autumn left, and yet the ground felt frozen under him. In the north, winter would come early.

As far as he could tell, he had been left overnight. The tent must have had some enchantment on it for him not to have frozen to death. As morning dawned, the tent seemed to keep the cold from getting out instead of allowing the warmth in. Even by noon, Lance kept his legs drawn up, shivering. By evening, he had no energy left with which to shiver.

He would not survive another night.

Hearing someone arrive, Lance opened his eyes and peered over his knees. DoomDragon had returned. Behind him, a dozen Hunters milled about. Among them, hidden in the back, the white-robed celebrant passed by briefly but flitted away like a dry leaf on the autumn wind. Lance wondered if Calanor would drift back but thought it unlikely. What would the celebrant want with a high guardsman?

DoomDragon dropped a pile of furs beside Lance then knelt and untied Lance's hands.

"A more uncivilized man would just cut the rope," Lance commented as his hands were allowed to fall to his sides. He resisted the

urge to rub his sore wrists, certain it would make the watching Hunters laugh. With his nudity, he didn't want to give them anything else to find humorous.

"Waste of rope," DoomDragon replied in Esparan as he released Lance's feet. As DoomDragon stood, he lifted the pile of furs. It fell into a long robe.

Lance stared up at the Northlander leader. He had to clear his throat before speaking. "Please tell me you don't expect me to wear that." He rose to his feet unsteadily, his joints complaining loudly at the freedom of movement. There was no hope of being modest; he had been stripped of everything. Trying to cover himself would be futile.

"Tonight," DoomDragon replied as he dropped the furs into Lance's arms, "you are my dinner guest. You must be dressed."

Lance examined the furs, keeping one eye on DoomDragon as the Northlander moved away. The dragon ax on his back was within Lance's reach. He could lunge for it.

The presence of the nearby Hunters made Lance dismiss the idea as suicidal.

He reconsidered. Suicidal could be good. It might be better than his current alternative.

But I'm sure I can find a better way to get myself killed given enough time.

Lance pulled the robe over his shoulders. Escaping would be easier if he did not have to focus on not turning blue.

A Hunter tossed him a huge belt embossed with shells and rocks.

Grudgingly, Lance tied it around his waist. "Not like I'll be running anywhere," he grumbled, lifting his arms in experimentation. The weight of the furs forced him to drop his arms back to his sides quickly. "Clever."

The Hunters next carried in a short table and set two places. Unlike the formal dinners of Esparan princes, DoomDragon offered only a slab of slate as a plate and a cloth as napkin. He set the cup—a tusk wound with braided hair—deliberately at the top of Lance's place and filled it from a jug.

A Hunter dropped a chair in front of Lance before shuffling away. DoomDragon gestured to it with a welcoming smile.

Dumfounded, Lance sat, his robe weighing him down into his seat. He tucked his feet up under him, hiding them in the warm fur. Soon, feeling returned to them.

Having missed all meals that day, Lance felt his hunger acutely. Still, he was in the company of enemies and dared not lose control of himself. Keeping his voice light, he said, "I love last meals. They always taste so sweet, even if you're only eating beets and bark."

DoomDragon lowered himself into the chair opposite Lance, his expression one of amusement. "And how many last meals have you had?"

Lance shrugged but he doubted DoomDragon had seen through the thick robes. "This will be my fourth. Are those parsnips?"

The Northlander passed Lance the bowl of steaming vegetables, and Lance decided it counted as permission to begin. He placed two parsnips on his slate, twisted them so they broke open, and while he waited for them to cool, picked a rib from the meat platter.

DoomDragon made a plate for himself as he asked, "So you do not think I am poisoning you?"

"Why would you? You can kill me anyway you please. I figure this is you trying to trick me into talking about Tohmas and the camp on the hill. You named the game. I'll play."

He took a mouthful of beef to prove his point. It had been flavored with a bittersweet spice Lance did not recognize.

DoomDragon sipped at his cup and leaned back in his seat. "You don't have to die."

Lance laughed. "No? Oh well. The meal is lovely nonetheless." He paused to pick at a parsnip. When DoomDragon didn't immediately reply, he added, "Here's where you tell me what I have to do for you so that you spare my life."

"Tell me what Tohmas offered you, and I'll match it," DoomDragon surprised him by replying.

Lance cocked his head. "Now that's a backward way to approach it. Not what I expected." He tapped his fingers against the slate to shake the grease off them before choosing a piece of bread. "Still, I fear you've failed because you asked the question."

"You continue to intrigue me, High Guardsman. Will you explain?"

Lance ran the words over in his mind and found none that would help the Northlander. They were safe. "Tohmas didn't promise me

anything. There's only one thing I want, and he can't give it to me. Neither can you."

"But he never offered?"

Lance shook his head. The confusion on DoomDragon's face made Lance smile. "I joined him because I didn't like where I was, and whatever happened, he was going somewhere new. That's all most of us need."

"A distraction?"

"Hope," Lance corrected. "Hope that our lives will not be meaningless. Tohmas keeps that alive too. We're outnumbered again, aren't we? But no one on that hill cares. You've taken higher losses than we have, and if we can keep that up, we'll be the last ones standing."

"You still think you're going to defeat us?"

Lance chewed slowly as he considered his reply. Would it sound cocky? More importantly, would it be true or just what I want to believe?

"Do you think you're going to push us off that hill? Who's going to run out of tricks first?" Lance asked.

DoomDragon stabbed a piece of meat with the jeweled knife Lance recognized. "That, I do not know. I do not know my enemy well enough."

"Which is why I'm here. You're looking for an enemy."

The Northlander cocked his head. He chewed thoughtfully, swallowed, and replied, "A backward way to approach it indeed. Explain?"

Lance chuckled to hear his words turned around. Feeling generous, he said, "The way I see it, you didn't have an enemy before Tohmas. You raided villages for survival. Prince Sol was never your enemy, else you would have defeated him long ago. Now you've moved beyond petty squabbles, and you're looking for a cause. For that, you need an evil to defeat. You think you've found one in Tohmas. You're clinging to it; you have to. Heroes have to have villains. And you're a hero, at least to yourself. Probably to your people too. So, you want to know everything about him to convince yourself that he's worth fighting."

"You seem to think you understand people. And you claim he is worth fighting *for*."

Lance tried to shrug again and failed under the weight of the robe. "I cannot explain your obsession. If there's another reason, by all means, correct me."

"Why bother?" DoomDragon asked, another smile under his white whiskers as he wiped aside a clinging bit of meat. "I will not convince you otherwise."

"So now you think *you* understand people. You know, you're cleverer than I expected. Everyone thought you were a brute with axes wanting to split skulls. Everyone except..."

"Except Tohmas," DoomDragon finished.

"See?" Lance popped the last of a parsnip into his mouth. "You're obsessed. I could have said anyone."

"But you were going to say Tohmas."

Lance saw no need to contradict him. "Tohmas sees the best in people, even his enemies. Everyone else underestimated you. Probably why they're dead."

"He saw the best in you as well, High Guardsman?"

Lance considered his cup again. The meat was dry, and he had been given nothing else to drink. Although poison did not concern him, too much drink might doom him. He could not lose sight of the dangers. This friendly tactic was already disorienting enough without adding wine.

North wines were renowned for being weak, he justified.

Lance sipped at the wine and wrinkled his nose. At least the poor quality of the wine might keep from drinking it to excess

He cleared his throat and replaced the cup. "Prince Tohmas expects the best in people until proven wrong, then he is an unforgiving bastard. The combination works brilliantly; people fear to disappoint him. Kind of the way I'm not going to disappoint him, no matter what you say or do."

"Not even if I said I would release you into his camp, so long as you agree to help me?" DoomDragon asked.

"Would you really believe me if I agreed?"

DoomDragon laughed aloud, the scales of his dragon skin armor flexing as he moved. "No. You stand in Tohmas' camp, and yet you wore the beads of your homeland. Loyalty to you is sacred. You will not be coerced."

"So, we are done then?" Lance asked, wiping his fingers on the bread. "Should I hurry to finish?"

DoomDragon pushed his chair back, leaving his plate of food half eaten. "I am finished, with one exception. Tell me, High Guardsman, why you understood the word *dedan*."

Lance thought of drawing out his reply but recognized he would only be delaying the inevitable. As nice as the meal was, Lance had spent the last day metaphorically staring at the executioner's ax. He was already tired of it.

"It's Rydan with a Trulin accent, if such a thing existed. You slur your words in a similar way at least. Your consonants are harsher, but the general laziness of the language is like Rydan," he said.

DoomDragon stared at Lance as if looking for the lies to reveal themselves. Lance chose another chunk of meat while he waited for a response.

"And you understand Rydan?" the Northlander asked in a softer voice.

Is it so unbelievable that I understand another language? Lance had found the similarities to Northlander unexpected, but DoomDragon's curiosity was focused on Lance's proficiency with the foreign language.

"I'm not great at it," Lance confessed. "If Carsh starts ranting, I lose him, but he usually sticks to single words, or single syllables for that matter."

"Carsh?"

Lance smiled, his mouth full. Quickly swallowing it all, he pushed away from the table. "I think I'm finished too. You want your robe back?"

"Naw. Since you have finished your meal, I will depart and invite Seria to take over."

Lance's throat went dry as a petite woman stepped into the room. She was Esparan and small. Lance could only think of one reason for her to be accepted among the burly Northlanders.

"Demons," he choked out and stood, the weight of the robes pressing on him. He thought to step back but decided it wouldn't be effective enough to warrant the effort. The bottoms of his feet burned on the cold ground.

Lance had heard of DoomDragon's casters but had not thought them Esparan.

The woman paused beside DoomDragon. A tiny smile sat on her lips as if someone had told a pleasant but not overtly funny joke. Her eyes stayed on Lance.

"Anything in particular you would like to know, DoomDragon?"

The Northlander turned away as if not wanting to watch. "The supplies across the lake. I want to know where they are coming from, and when and how they're getting them up the cliffs. I also want to know everything about the defenses. Those are partial walls. There must be openings. Anything about internal politics too. Tohmas has plenty of enemies. Other than that, he's yours."

The tiny smile took on a sinister feel. Lance flinched. The stones on his belt clunked against his hips through his robe.

"And what state would you like him in when I am finished?" Her voice was flat, but her eyes were filled with enthusiasm.

"Gutted and filleted or roasted whole?" Lance asked pessimistically.

DoomDragon did not look back but did not immediately join the Hunters awaiting him. Lance didn't know what to make of the hesitation. What was there to decide? Did he still think Lance would be useful?

The Northlander gave a long sigh then replied, "Alive."

Recognizing the broad range of states that would qualify as "alive," Lance winced. He did not find his voice again in time to comment before DoomDragon disappeared, a flap of hide falling behind him. Lance was left with the little Esparan woman and her magic.

She stepped around the table, and her eyes flashed. "This is not going to be gentle."

Swallowing hard, Lance forced himself to smile. "I can honestly say that is the first time a woman has said that to me and meant it with such sincerity."

Her smile left, replaced by a scowl. She raised a hand, and a force wrapped around his hands, pinching his skin and slamming him to the ground. Something cold stabbed into his forehead.

Lance's vision went black.

Chapter 3

It was morning, Celebrant Sedgan had a headache, and he was out of wine. There had only been enough wine in the jug for two cups, and he had drunk both of them. Now he had to decide if he should get an acolyte to fetch more or if he was able to do it himself.

Standing in the room at the back of the Temple Waggon of Inac, Sedgan felt awful, which had become common. He was not hungover— he had drunk a single cup of wine the night before—but he felt like it. He forlornly picked up the jug, wishing for Loni. She was a pleasant distraction, especially on mornings when he felt like a waggon had run into his skull and then been set on fire.

But Loni was not there and had not slept with him in several days. There was no question Sedgan could have others, but he disliked taking lovers into his personal quarters. Loni was a Celebrant of Inac. No other compared anyway.

Sedgan stared into the jug, distracted by a film of red-stained powder.

There should not have been sediment in this vintage.

He ran his finger along the inside of the container and came up with a layer of fine crystals. It smelled and tasted like the wine, but the aftertaste was bitter.

Well, he thought, his head throbbing, I know how to find out what this is. And they will have something for my head.

He wiped up the residue with a rag and placed it in his belt pouch. Assigning his eldest acolyte, Tamort, to the afternoon prayers, Sedgan left for Fixer City. With the forces of Espar encamped over the winter, the gathering of tradespeople and shops had established a permanent location, making it easy to find the Match and Mixer shop.

He must have been the apothecaries' first customer of the day, for the daughter was outside opening the side of the vardo when he approached. The counterspace dropped down to chest height, leaving her a small space to stand behind it without being in the curtained-off living area within the waggon.

"Welcome to Match and Mixer," Shimmer Weaver cheerily greeted him. Her hair, a brilliant shade of red held back by a gold and black headband, flowed over her arms as she leaned onto the counter. In place of her dancing clothes, she wore a loose-fitting blouse that fell off her shoulders. Four necklaces dangled from her neck, each one a different style of charm.

Sedgan's throat was painfully dry despite the earlier two cups of wine. His voice croaked as he said, "I need another identification."

Shimmer leaned back into the vardo and shouted, "Papa! Celebrant Sedgan for you! Open the side door!"

She ushered him around the vardo and into the company of the yawning apothecary. Sedgan did not think he had awoken the man, for he was fully dressed in his ostentatious, patchwork garments. But as Dust let Sedgan in, he was clearing sleep from his eyes.

"Have a seat," Dust invited, taking a seat at the low table between bookcases in the vardo. Sedgan folded himself onto the nearest cushion. The girl followed him in, closing the door behind them, then disappeared behind the purple curtain to the front sale area. The many hanging herbs and dried goods waved in her wake, releasing a spicy scent.

"What can I do for you?" Dust asked.

Sedgan laid the rag on the table. "I want to know what this is."

Dust felt the crystals between fingertips then smelled them. "Soaked in a good Forsinth wine."

Sedgan would have nodded, but for the pain of his head.

"There may be more than one thing in there. There's definitely a crystallized substance, but I think I feel a powder. If you want a full breakdown, it'll cost the same as last time."

Sedgan placed the silver shard on the table. He considered asking about something for his head, but the smell of the waggon seemed to have lessened the ache for now.

Loni can probably get me a few pain pills from the cutters later.

Dust picked up the coin piece and, without his hand going anywhere near a pocket, made it vanish. He collected the rag and scraped the powder onto the table surface.

"Shim!" he called while his fingers worked the substance into a pile. "Where's Markin's Lists?"

"Second shelf, fifth book from the left, Papa," came the muffled reply from behind the curtain.

The apothecary went to the bookcase that encompassed almost the entire wall and found the book exactly where his daughter predicted. As before, Dust gestured and chanted random-sounding words. His eyes closed, he brought the invisible spell to a climax, and the mountain of powder divided itself into two piles and a small puddle.

The puddle rapidly soaked into the table and stained it as red as the apothecary's hair.

"Waste of good wine," Dust pined.

The first pile was a fine powder. A sniff and a taste made the apothecary's eyebrows furl, but he remained silent. If the man was thinking, Sedgan did not want to interrupt.

Dust checked the bigger pile. He remained pensive until he gingerly tasted the crystals.

Sedgan had seen the girl spit the willar's weed out the last time they identified something for him, but the speed with which the man spat surprised him.

Dust shot to his feet. "Where did you get this?" The apothecary's hands seemed to be moving without requiring guidance. He selected a variety of dried leaves and roots and threw them into a dish.

"What is it?" Sedgan countered. "I'm paying you to answer my questions, not ask me questions."

"I... I need to run a quick check." Dust massaged together the mix from the dish and popped it into his mouth. He chewed loudly as he crouched at the table, staying on the balls of his feet. "I will need your hand."

Ire rose in Sedgan. "Why? What does my hand have to do with any of this? You know what it is, don't you? Why are you hiding the answer?"

"I need a second living creature to help channel the energies," Dust replied, his voice milder with each word. "I will be handling the powers, so you need not worry. It is safe. Shimmer is busy, but if you want to wait a few candles, I may be able to find another who would be willing. Or I can try on my own, but then I would have to insist on charging more for the increased—"

To stop Dust's rambling, Sedgan put his hand on the apothecary's outstretched palm.

Dust's fingers gently wrapped around his wrist. "Perfect. Thank you." Seeking a new page in the same book, the apothecary spoke again in the strange language. There was no gesturing this time.

A tingle, like brushing a cactus, swept across Sedgan, ending at his fingertips. He had never felt magic, although he had used trinkets before. It was not painful yet left Sedgan feeling profoundly uneasy.

Suspicion filled him.

The apothecary opened his eyes, took a deep breath, and swallowed hard.

"You owe me answers, apothecary," Sedgan snapped. "Enough of this nonsense! What was in the wine?"

Dust Weaver stood slowly. He looked to be distancing himself. "The fine powder is fennal extract. It calms the mind. Unfortunately, it also dulls one's reasoning. It, as Prince Tohmas once put it, makes people as dense as a log."

Sedgan felt himself flush. He had drunk it only that morning.

"The dose here is mild, so the dulling would hardly be noticeable," the apothecary carried on.

Through clenched teeth, Sedgan asked, "And the other?"

Dust cleared his throat. "The other is commonly called frozen freedom. It is an extract from a south-growing weed. In high enough doses, it can be fatal."

"Poison?"

"It does not linger in the body, so it has to be delivered in high doses to kill. Smaller doses provide an addictive euphoria. How long have you been taking it?"

"Taking it?" Sedgan leaped to his feet. "What makes you think I am taking anything?"

"Your sunken eyes, the tremor to your hands, the way you sit slouched when you used to sit straight," Dust replied calmly. "You have pain in your eyes, which makes me think your head probably feels like it has been trampled by every horse in HillTop. I remember how withdrawal feels."

"My hand!" Sedgan snapped despite the accurate description of his aching skull. "You did not need it for any spell! You cast something on me! How dare you!"

"Celebrant Sedgan, the demon-cursed stuff gives the worst downswings. You must realize you are on one now. Calm down, please."

The apothecary's voice was soft, but his words failed to sooth. Sedgan reached for his blade as he considered the easiest way to get around the table. He had been betrayed. The man had lied to him. The Bitch Goddess required vengeance for the slight. They were merely traveling entertainers. Who would miss them?

CHAPTER 3

The arrival of Shimmer Weaver and her colorful dress disrupted Sedgan's thoughts. Heat replaced anger.

Shimmer was a shapely young woman. The way her blouse drifted off both shoulders under her thin vest, while still leaving her middle bare three fingers below her navel, told him she liked being looked at. The gold hoops from her ears reminded him of Loni, as did her bright red hair.

Shimmer shot a glare at her father, who rubbed the back of his neck and shied away. "Papa, I am aghast." She raised an eyebrow at Sedgan. "Has he offended you, Celebrant?"

"He cast a spell on me without my permission! Of course, I am offended," Sedgan snapped.

Shimmer scowled at her father, profound affront on her otherwise fair face. "You cannot treat a celebrant like that, Father!"

Shimmer's smile was soft as she approached Sedgan with graceful steps that reminded him again of Loni. He had seen Shimmer Weaver dance. She was as good, if not better, than Loni.

Sedgan let the young woman slip up beside him. The scent of flowers made his breath come easier as she ran a hand up his arm to his shoulder.

"Anything we can do to make this right, Celebrant, please, let me know. We cannot have a celebrant slighted in our shop."

Her pale hand slid up to his shoulder, and the contact lingered. Sedgan fixed his stare on the obviously uncomfortable father across from him.

"The Lady of Lust has a few suggestions," Sedgan said.

Shimmer's arms drifted down around his shoulders in a loose embrace. When next she spoke, it was a whisper in his ear.

"*Entouran.*" She dropped her arms and jumped away.

Sedgan tried to turn but bumped into something. He tried to lift his hands, but they were pinned at his sides by an unseen force.

"You harlot!" he shouted.

Ignoring him, Shimmer went to fan the flames of a small brazier where she hung a teapot. When she spoke, it was factual. "What you got, Papa?"

"Combination of fennal and freedom, Shim," Dust replied. While he spoke, he collected dried herbs from hanging bunches and powders from jars.

"Fennal and frozen freedom? That's like getting the prime protector drunk and poking him with a stick! Who came up with that?"

Her father shrugged.

"How dare you hold me!" Sedgan shrieked. "I will have your heads for this. The soldiers—"

"The vardo is surrounded by a permanent one-way Wind Barrier," Shimmer said from beside the brazier. "That means no one can hear you. Shut up."

Sedgan paused. I'm a captive?

The apothecary filled the silence. "Up for a Sweep?" he asked Shimmer.

"A what?" Sedgan shouted. He lashed out against his invisible cage, but nothing changed. As if tied, he stood rigid.

The daughter made a face. "Against freedom or fennal?" Her father handed her the mix, and she dropped it into the teapot. After a quick stir, she filled a cup and placed it on the table.

"Both."

"Don't you dare touch me with more magic!" Sedgan felt like he was trying to contact Totho by shouting down a well. His words were getting nowhere near the two other occupants of the vardo.

"A double Sweep is beyond me, Papa."

"I'll take one. You take the other."

"No more spells! No more! I will not allow it!" Sedgan yelled.

They ignored him and, after a few deep breaths, stood on either side of him. Once their words changed to something other than Esparan, he knew it was useless.

It felt like a slow, creeping illness. He could tell Shimmer started with his head, swept down his right arm, did each leg in turn, and finished by dragging her magic through his left arm. He did not feel the movements of her father nearly as acutely as he felt hers.

His headache returned with a vengeance. His every muscle shook. Sedgan slumped against the invisible walls that held him stationary, suddenly too weak to stand. A prick to his finger made him flinch, but he

was only distantly aware of the blood trickling out of his fingertip. He squeezed his eyes shut in pain. His anger flared as nausea struck.

"You vile wretches," he muttered.

The vardo was slow to come into focus as Sedgan opened his eyes. Dust was tying a bandage on Sedgan's hand. If he was close enough to touch him...

Both apothecaries stepped back as if to admire their work, and Sedgan threw up his arms to find his cage gone. With his teeth gritted against the pain and his stomach spinning, Sedgan reached for his knife.

"The only thing that is going to help you right now," Shimmer said, pointing, "is that cup of tea. Drink it, Celebrant, or I will shove your demon-kissing ass out of the vardo. I may aim for the lake."

Sedgan wanted to scream but could hardly draw breath. She could do it without laying a hand on him if she had to.

His eyes found the cup when Shimmer pushed it in his direction.

"No more," Sedgan begged. His head chose that moment to throb. He lost the power in his legs and fell to his knees with a cry. Neither of the Weavers moved to help him. With her face dark and her arms crossed, Shimmer stared at him. Dust looked away, his lips drawn tight.

Sedgan clutched his knife, but his hands shook too much. He had to let the blade go to take the cup.

The moments between swallowing the sour tea and having it ease his ache dragged by like candles. Slowly, from the back of his skull, the headache lessened. Within another few flickers, the room came into focus. For the first time since arriving, Sedgan noticed the clutter under the table and the three musical instruments on the wall. When he moved his head, the room did not tilt or fade. He felt though he had opened his eyes for the first time in days.

Dust slowly returned to a seat at the table. "We should be alright now, Shim. You can go."

Shimmer did not move. "I'm not leaving. I let him through the defenses. I trusted him. I'll not trust him again."

To Sedgan's surprise, Shimmer's words wounded him. With his outrage, he had not expected to feel guilt, but now he saw his actions in a new light. He had considered killing them, with no regard for trials, justice, or even morality. Part of him could justify it—they had used

magic on him without permission—but without his rage to push him on, he wanted to know why they had done so.

The apothecary did not argue with his daughter. Despite Dust's obvious fatigue, which certainly had nothing to do with the early morning, his stare was firm.

"Where did you get the drugs?" he asked Sedgan.

Sedgan took another ragged breath. For the moment, he wanted answers as much as Dust did. "Bottom of a wine jug."

Dust made a face. "I'll need more than that."

"It's true. I found it at the bottom of my wine jug." Calmer now than he had been in mooncycles, Sedgan sat straight and placed his hands on the table. Smears of blood crusted both of his index fingers. He turned his hands palms-up to examine the wounds.

"We bled both substances out of you," Dust explained. "It will heal quickly."

"I asked you not to cast any more spells," Sedgan said, folding his hands against the pitted table before him.

"Asked?" Shimmer repeated, but her father shook his head, and she did not press the point.

Dust gave Sedgan an apologetic smile. "We had to get the drugs out of your system. Frozen freedom makes for a nasty confrontation. We did what we did to give you a chance." Dust drew a long breath. "How long have you been drinking out of that jug?"

A chill shot up Sedgan's spine. "Years. It's from the temple in Wayburn. Why? Do you think this has been going on for longer than today?" If he had been drugged for days or cycles, how would he know? Now that his mind was clearing, he doubted much of his memory.

"The shaking, the headaches, and the rage all point toward long-term use," Dust replied.

"I have only had headaches for the last mooncycle," Sedgan corrected.

"In the morning?"

Sedgan nodded, but his brain throbbed at the movement, stopping him short.

"Then your use must have been not much more than a mooncycle and a half. Who filled that jug?"

"I did," Sedgan objected.

"Where did the wine come from?"

CHAPTER 3

"A vintner in Wayburn. I doubt—"

"No, it had to be added more recently."

"Rule One, Papa," warned Shimmer's soft alto.

Dust shook his head with a smile. "Right you are, my dear. I apologize."

"Rule—" Sedgan wondered.

Dust interrupted one last time. "Celebrant, do what you will with the information I have provided. You can take your chances with the withdrawal, or we can mix you a pill that will get you through the worst of it. The other choice is to keep taking it every morning to stop the headache and live with being reliant on the drug."

When Dust sat back, Sedgan felt cheated. He did not like any of the options.

Although he was certain they were trying to con him, Sedgan's now-clear head dragged him through a review of the last mooncycle. Sedgan closed his eyes in grimace. Some of his memory was vague beyond recognition, but he recalled moments of strange behavior. He felt he was merely an observer to his own actions. Some of the actions horrified him.

The final memory was something Dust had said.

"You have experienced this," Sedgan realized aloud.

"Small doses of freedom are often used by musicians and artists for inspiration. I sold the stuff and worked with many people who regularly used it," Dust confessed.

"But if you remember headaches, you must have taken it for some time at least."

"Well, I think we can safely say the fennal is out of your system," Dust said with a laugh. "Very true, Celebrant. I got rid of it when Shimmer was born. I didn't need it once I had my little girl."

His "little girl" continued to stab Sedgan across the vardo with her stare.

"So, what do you recommend?" Sedgan finally asked.

Dust flashed his daughter a victorious grin. "We will make a series of pills for you to take. It will include a dose of freedom, among other things, but a reducing dose in each pill. The rest of the pill will help you cope with the withdrawal signs. It will be expensive."

"I have very little reason to trust you," Sedgan pointed out.

Dust shrugged and rose from his seat in search of ingredients once more. "You know it was for your own good. And besides, you will trust us because you know who was drugging you."

I do know, Sedgan realized, although he was loathed to admit it.

Loni had started sharing his bed a mooncycle and a half before. He could even understand why she had done it.

The memory of the burning waggons flashed into his mind. Burning the Temple waggons had been her idea. The thought of his hands barring the waggon doors to keep the acolytes and celebrants inside made him nauseous. He was not sure if he had been entirely himself at the time.

"Fine," Sedgan said. "Get me your pills, but I swear, after these, I will not purchase anything further from you."

Soon the father and daughter team produced a sequence of pills, which they strung together on a string. With another frown, Sedgan handed over a silver disc.

"Oh, I am sure Inac can spare it," Shimmer grumbled.

"Inac is not who I am worried about right now," Sedgan replied. "How long will your tea keep me sane?"

Dust opened the door for him. "Another candle, probably less. As soon as your head hurts, take the first pill. After that, swallow one each morning. Since you have forsworn any further assistance, I hope it will be sufficient."

"As do I," Sedgan agreed bitterly. Under the accusatory glare of the apothecary's daughter, he made his exit.

"Good luck, Celebrant," was the last thing he heard from the apothecary.

He took advantage of the calm the tea provided to plan. By the time he got to his Temple waggon, he had to swallow a pill.

He went in search of Loni.

Sedgan found Loni's fire in Fixer City and was greeted by several of the girls. He tried to return their affections. They, unlike their mistress, were not guilty.

Loni's green eyes narrowed upon his arrival to her campfire circle, but she still smiled. It felt hollow, like a worn actress who had given up on trying.

"You look unwell," she said.

"I have had a vision," he said in a loud whisper.

CHAPTER 3

The crowd of girls gasped and, in respectful awe, backed away. *Loni has trained them well,* Sedgan mused.

Loni's eyes sparked dangerously, and her smile gained sincerity.

She was a fanatic. He had known that all along yet forgotten it of late. He had to play this carefully.

"I do not understand my vision. I hoped you would help." The deference to her, as he had hoped, soothed her.

"Tell me your vision. We shall see what interpretation the goddess gives."

He sat on a log by the fire, for his muscles were still suffering from the lack of drugs. Loni perched across from him like a vulture.

He had practiced the words on his walk over, the lie so clear in his mind he could see it. "I saw a great mountain made of fire. Rivers of molten stone flowed down the sides. Men stood around the fires with weapons raised—swords and hammers. It was a city of some kind, for there were houses and children. Yet the fire flowed right beside their homes, and they did not fear it. A man stood atop a great golden anvil."

"The Princedom of Lour! StonePeak," Loni declared. "The great capital of the mountain princedom of Prince Loritat. His mark is a grey anvil on a golden field. They are the greatest weaponsmiths in Espar."

"Of course! StonePeak is also situated in a dormant volcano, is it not? I had forgotten!" Sedgan said with false enthusiasm.

"What interest does the goddess have in Lour?"

Seeing she needed more prodding, Sedgan continued. "The man standing atop the anvil held a great sword of green and silver unlike any I have ever seen. It glowed like fire."

Loni leaped up. "Green and silver! The Champion's colors are green and silver! This sword must be for Prince Tohmas!"

Sedgan kept his head lowered to hide his smile. "But how would a sword be found in Lour when we are so far north?" he asked, filling his voice with confusion.

"Someone must go and fetch it," she decided.

It's a great comfort to have my wits back. Would I have believed this nonsense so easily?

"But I cannot go!" he exclaimed in exasperation. "By my oath to the Prince of Galanth, I am bound to his presence. If only..."

The pause pulled hard on Sedgan's nerves. For a moment, like the flash of metal under a lamp, Loni's eyes narrowed. His stomach knotted sharply. If she suspected he was lying, she would turn on him. She did not shy from murder, and he could not match the desperate power that Loni channeled when enraged. She would smile at his face and happily put a knife between his shoulder blades if the whim struck her.

Before he could draw his next breath, the moment had passed. Her sultry smile returned. "I will go! I will fetch this blade for my prince. This is the Goddess' will!"

Sedgan did his best to look aghast. "But how will you leave HillTop? It is dangerous!"

Loni stood slowly, an actress perfect in her timing. She composed herself regally, her words theatrically dramatic. "I will find a way."

For the sake of the audience, Sedgan bowed his head in reverence. "I am the messenger," he agreed in mock surrender, "and you are the vessel. You are right, Celebrant, but you must hurry. There is only one blade that will do for him, and Lour is a long way to travel. Winter approaches."

She seized his hands and brought him to his feet. It was all he could do to hold his ground when she placed a kiss on his lips. He struggled to show no disgust.

"I will leave for Lour at once and return with a blade worthy of the Champion of Inac or never return at all," she promised. In her madness, she could not see his lies. She would walk to Lour, mooncycles away, to retrieve the weapon he had invented.

He could not have asked for more.

Chapter 4

One cycle after the last raid that had placed Lance and his men among the Northlanders, Tohmas heard a horn in the dusk. It was not his horn, but it sounded from inside his defenses.

In the next instant, the Northlanders charged up the hill. They had been ready for the signal, he recognized, but had been going about evening business to fool watching eyes.

They had succeeded.

People had a tendency of rushing to him when things went wrong; he was rapidly surrounded. Far criers used their horns to call the all-up-and-out, and a horn carried a message to the Guardians of Boro and Rest to get their men to the west, where the greatest assault approached. The rest of the horns ordered the soldiers to group in readiness behind the front lines by a hundred paces. Tohmas wanted the fighters to have room to organize, but that meant relying on those on defense to hold temporarily.

Another horn warned the attack was occurring from both sides. The Fyrd of Arrow answered by claiming they had it reasonably under control. They would be pressed but did not expect to break.

Unable to spare men from the west, Tohmas took them at their word. That his largest fyrd was occupied annoyed him, but he would have to make do.

He was grateful when Master Kitable arrived at his side.

"Any chance you can slow them slightly, Kit? West slope. We're getting butchered." The defenses standing between his men and the charging Northlanders were not doing their duty at all. While they still forced the enemy to weave between walls, no one seemed to be cutting them down as they advanced.

DoomDragon must have cleared the Galanth soldiers there, although Tohmas did not know how or when.

The wizard frowned. "I am not as well prepared for dueling as I would like, but I can probably convince some of those fools this was a bad idea."

Tohmas snatched the glass orb from his pocket and tossed it to the wizard. "You said it would help against wizards," he reminded Kitable when the wizard held the orb at arm's length.

"Had you shattered it..." Kitable said, his voice dripping with disapproval, but Tohmas waved him off.

"Nice catch then. Geddit!"

Kitable paused for only a moment more. Need won out.

Prince Sol arrived the moment Kitable left, Prime Protector Severin behind him.

"I need your fyrds on the west side of the hill," Tohmas told Sol. "Provide a reserve for those caught on the front line then for Boro and Rest once they get in position."

"What about the rest of you?" Sol asked, but he tossed his token to a runner. The runner headed out to pass on the order to the Guardians of Solta.

"We are going to move some things. Just make sure your men do not follow those Northlanders back down the hill."

Sol balked. "Down the hill? What makes you think they are going to be going *down*? They look intent on coming *up*!"

Lifting his own horn, Tohmas called for Lance, certain the high guardsman and his men could help shift the tides in Galanth's favor.

Meanwhile, Kitable made himself known closer to the defenses. Carsh shivered visibly at Tohmas' side.

Magic blocked the sun, potent and terrifying.

The Hunters advanced in the late afternoon. Magic was not required; the Hunters had dressed themselves in torn grasses and slunk like snakes through the broken grasses. Using what little they had learned from the high guardsman, they approached the west defenses. One by one, the spiked walls erected in a staggered formation were conquered. The hill camp lay in silence, unaware.

There, they waited. When the sun touched the horizon, the horns sounded. DoomDragon's warriors leaped eagerly from their evening fires and charged the hill camp.

Watching from a place farther back, Darknim glanced at the celebrant who stood stoically beside him.

"Will you give us the blessing of the Gust?" he asked.

Tothonar's stare stayed on the hill as he whispered, "Wind cares not for conflict like this." The celebrant then turned his pale grey eyes, so like those of the god, to DoomDragon. "I will pray for the spirits that come of this. May you all find a place among the stars for your bravery."

"It is not bravery. It is survival."

"We—" Seria prompted from Darknim's other side.

"We are going," he interrupted. He shot her a coy look. "I hope your fighters get you where you need to go, wizard. I am tired of going back and forth with magic."

She straightened at the challenge. "We were only delayed because your Circle was broken, DoomDragon. Now that Elder Tril has returned, we can attack from a distance." Her grin was vindictive. "When Kitable shows himself, we will kill him." Her promise came with venom in her eyes. For a moment, he almost feared her vehemence.

Despite all her failures, she never seemed to lose faith that she was, if not perfect, nearly perfect.

"Then go. Everything is ready."

As she sauntered away, Darknim pulled his ax and readied his remaining Hunters for their charge. He made sure they were all ready to meet with a caster, just in case.

He still did not believe her.

"Who is she?"

Lance's answer was the same as it had been the other hundred times. "No one."

Although the voice was familiar by now, Lance could not see, or identify, the speaker. He existed in deep darkness, surrounded on all sides yet profoundly alone.

He didn't trust the voice, but he could no longer remember why.

"You think about her. She's pretty. A little young for you, High Guardsman. Who is she?"

In Lance's memory, Valia danced around an apple tree, shaking the trunk to make the blossoms fall. It was a memory from years before— she was barely showing signs of womanhood—but his chest tightened upon seeing her.

"No one," Lance insisted, and Valia's image faded. His head hurt for a moment. The voice spoke again, distracting him from his pain.

"So much attention on her. How can she be no one?" The voice lightened. "I think she's sweet. You two belong together. I'll help you win her over. Who is she?"

Now dressed in her riding skirt, Valia skipped onto her horse. She was laughing as she glanced over her shoulder, goading her guardsmen on. Of the six of them, only Lance was fast enough to be mounted when she spurred her horse out of the stable. Only Lance kept up.

For a flicker, he almost answered. She was Valia Lodaton, the most beautiful free spirit in all of Gaidol. She was the missing part of his heart, the dream he never wanted to wake from. She was...

Although he did know who asked or why, Lance was certain they meant her harm. He would not let anyone hurt Valia.

"No one," he repeated. "No one at all. A pretty face, nothing more."

The speaker abruptly sounded close at hand, disappointment in their voice. "Stubborn man. Let me help you. Who is she?"

Lance threw his arm out to strike, surprised when his arm felt weighed down. In the darkness around him, he had no visible target. He hit nothing. His arm fell back heavily. "No one!"

"Stubborn man," the voice repeated, now farther away. The voice faded into the distance. "Why defend someone so insignificant? Useless. And if you're useless..."

A cold hand closed over Lance's throat, digging into the grooves on either side of his windpipe. He threw his hands up to throw off his assailant but struck nothing. The momentum of his strike tossed him backward onto the ground where he lay, the cold slowly creeping through his back. He felt pinned as if by shackles.

In his mind, Valia was still riding through the fields, seeking a way to lose her determined escorts. Her flashing eyes made him smile through the pain of his throbbing skull.

The clamp on his throat released.

"Useless," the voice muttered. "Stubborn and useless."

The cold seeped through him. The darkness pressed around him, wrapping him up like a blanket freshly pulled from a mountain river. His muscles tensed until it was hard to breathe, but the frustrated tears he expected refused to fall, instead lingering as a burn in his eyes. He shivered.

"He dead?"

"Don't know. Poke him again."

The silence lingered. Like a vaguely remembered dream, Lance could not make sense of the words he heard above him.

"Maybe he's dead."

"Still breathing though."

"I'm not leaving if he's not dead."

"Kinda looks dead."

His mind slowly sorted through the words, gradually waking. He knew the speaker. He trusted them.

"Carthy," Lance croaked.

"Well, he can hear," Carthy's voice said from the darkness above him. "You going to open your eyes too?"

It took effort, but Lance commanded his eyes to open and they slowly obeyed.

He first became aware of light, although it was dim, bleeding through a crack in the dried hides above him. He was indeed on his back, a weight sitting on his chest and holding his arms on his lap. The fur of the robe tickled his nose.

Four faces loomed over him, all of them indistinctly backlit.

"About time. Told you he wasn't dead," another voice, Wadley's, said. "Can you walk?"

Every muscle felt filled with sand when Lance tried to sit up. His head ached like someone had smashed it against a cliff face. He fell back.

Valia's smiling face flashed before his eyes in the darkness.

He remembered the questions, many of them aimed at Tohmas' position on the hill. He was in DoomDragon's camp. He had been interrogated through magic.

The Esparan caster. How long was she in my head? And how deep?

He had to get up. They had one chance to escape.

"Guess not," Carthy grumbled. "Well, we can't very well carry his demon-kissing ass up the—"

"I can walk," Lance interrupted. "Undo my hands, you louts."

Two faces pulled away, and Lance heard shuffling. Finally, someone grabbed his hands and cut the ties from them. The leather had dried into his wrists, and his guardsmen had to peel the thong from his skin.

Once his hands were free, Lance found the buckle of the belt and released it. Instead of standing, he rolled to one side, leaving the robe that had smothered him behind. The frigid air prickled at his skin, but he was able to rise.

"You can't walk around showing your white ass to the enemy, Lance!" Wadley objected. "All the Northlanders will get their hopes up!"

"Might blind them," another guardsman added. "We could all strip. At least then he'd blend in."

"Still not subtle enough," someone else warned. "And no one wants to see Carthy's spindly legs."

Lance hardly heard them, his fingers tracing the lines along his wrists and finding them sticky with blood. The robe lay like a dead bear at his feet.

Dead, or was it sleeping?

His head throbbed again.

"Where we at?" he asked. He wanted to kick the robe, but unnecessary movement might aggravate his aching head.

"Us? I'm standing to your left, Shinat's across—" Wadley's voice was crisp.

"We're in DoomDragon's tent, at the heart of DoomDragon's camp," Carthy replied. "And we need to be somewhere else. We had to take out two Hunters to get in. We're pushing our luck with every flicker spent standing here."

"The signal?"

"None yet," Carthy answered. "But DoomDragon sent his warriors toto HillTop. That's why we had the shot at grabbing you."

"If DoomDragon attacks Tohmas, he'll call us back, right?" Wadley asked. "Now's the best chance we have."

"What day is it?"

Silence answered. At length, Shinat's voice, deep as a well, asked, "How hard'd they mess your head up?"

Lance turned to Shinat, and his brain tried to break out of his skull. He winced, bringing a hand to his temples, but it didn't help. He remembered more questions—something about the cliffs behind the hill. Tunnels? Defenses?

Weaknesses?

"That bad, eh?"

"It's the seventh of the sixth, and it's the fourth candle of the evening." Of the lots of them, only Carthy seemed able focus on the task at hand.

They all understand, Lance corrected himself. Their casual queries and distractions were designed to make a mockery of their foes and the situation. They were surrounded by enemies. They could panic, or they could jest.

"Dusk," Lance realized. "He's waiting for the sun to sink behind the west ridge. It'll blind Tohmas."

He glanced at his bare feet and shivered. The cold wind cut to his bone.

"You can't run around like—"

"I'll wear the robe," Lance decided. "Don't have a choice. We go in by the east. If DoomDragon's main forces are west, then we have a good chance of getting through on the east." A draft wrapped around his ankles. "The east will be quiet, so less chance of the wrong side killing me."

Someone snorted in disgust.

"Try to kill you, you mean. No north-raised pansy with caribou fat for brains is going to..."

Another guardsman retrieved the robe, pausing as he lifted it clear of the frozen ground.

"Demons! This thing weighs as much as a horse!" Between two guardsmen, they hefted the robe. Once the belt had fallen clear, they presented the fur to Lance.

He took it and threw it over his shoulder without the belt. The weight forced him to slouch, but at least he didn't feel like he was dragging a waggon by his waist.

"You sure?" Carthy asked.

"No choice," Lance answered, pulling the robe closed in front of him. The draft around his feet made his toes hurt, but he would not freeze. "They took everything."

"Not everything." Wadley placed a string of pearls in Lance's palm. "It's how we knew where you were. No one else has such a useless piece of junk."

Against the chill of the darkening evening, the pearls were warm. The moment he closed his fingers over them, Lance's chest let go of a pang he had not even been aware of.

He remembered more questions, and Valia's light laughter echoed in his ears. Reminded about Valia, and the promise he had yet to fulfill, Lance forced himself to stand tall. "Let's go."

Shimmer beat her father out of the vardo by what felt like ages. Although she did not know what the horns of the Galanth forces meant, she recognized the sounds of fighting. Around her, the people of Fixer City cautiously peeked out from their shelters. They had all quickly retreated into their homes.

Dust hooked up the horses. If they had to move, they were going to be ready. It did not seem to matter that they had nowhere to go.

She stood, not helping, until he finally caught her stare and, with a roll of his eyes, said, "Be careful."

Shimmer rushed from Fixer City. Part of her wanted to see Kitable in action and another part wanted to help him. A third part warned that he would not need any help from her, so the first part answered, and she added a skip to her run.

She ducked, unseen, into the main camp. Following the sounds of battle, she found a place on the hill from which she could see the lines

of Esparan actively holding the Northlanders back. While she searched the area for any sign of the master wizard, magic reared behind her.

Only a hundred paces to her left, she spotted Kitable taking long strides between tents. With a breathless curse at having neglected it, Shimmer activated Spell Sight and marveled as magic twirled around him at a dizzying pace. A few slingshot stones warned that the Northlanders had recognized him as a threat, but they bounced, with a burst of energy, off a Missile Deflector. Ignoring the brief annoyances, Kitable's spell reached completion, and the largest illusion Shimmer had ever seen took form.

Kitable extended his arms from side to side. The outline of the wizard went black as night, then stretched in all directions. The emblem of a silver and green tree, embroidered on the wizard's shirt before the spell, was the only color remaining in the new form, the crest glowing in the black. He enlarged so much that Shimmer had to step back to fully appreciate what he had done.

Wings of black stretched out from one edge of HillTop to the other as a long, serpentine neck reached over the fighting. The terrified cries of the Northlanders reached her ears. Tohmas' men, recognizing the emblem on the dragon's chest, nervously cheered.

When the illusionary dragon's head reared back and blew a brilliant spray of fire into the battle, the enemy's cries changed from alarm to pain and panic.

To Shimmer's altered vision, the whole thing trembled yellow. Nothing about the dragon or its fire was real; Kitable had created an elaborate, moving illusion.

Seeing auras tied to the "fire" that the dragon generated made Shimmer's jaw drop. A thought spell was bound to the illusionary flames. It was weak, but when it touched the Northlanders, it gave them terror. Even the toughest of them fled.

Behind the dragon, Galanth's fyrds reorganized. Soon enough, the dragon shrank back into the wizard. The path was clear for the soldiers of Espar. They rushed in, pushing the Northlanders back.

Shimmer ran toward Kitable. She was not certain what she would say, if anything, when she met him face to face, but she wanted to be in Kitable's shadow this day.

Kitable was alone when she again spotted him surveying the battle from a rise beyond the tents. Northlanders were pushing in several directions below him—Shimmer could spot at least three groups—but Esparan squads held off, needing no magical assistance.

She was wondered what his next magical miracle would be.

Powers flashed from down the hill; a force spell pushed a dozen men aside, and a group in red and black, with a woman at their head, rushed into HillTop. Horns below blared warnings to the remaining fyrd. They moved to cover the gap.

It was not fast enough.

As Kitable turned, an aura of orange and yellow formed a circle above him, unnoticed. The edges of the circle flashed purple in linking, and a waterfall of magic poured through, engulfing Kitable completely. Like a rainbow-hued cloudburst, auras of every domain and flashes of every element blinded Shimmer. The most prominent, to her confusion, was the smooth aura of alteration. Purple showed up the brightest—binding magic.

Alteration of bindings made no sense to her.

The woman smiled viciously and advanced toward the torrent unobstructed.

Seeing the multitude of spells bound to the woman, Shimmer hesitated despite her desire to help Kitable. Her father would never forgive her for breaking one of their most fundamental rules. And the woman was powerful enough to make any interference ill-advised.

A gust of wind-like purple burst from Kitable's location. While the spell washed over all the invaders without doing any damage, the spell surrounding Kitable and the circle above him vanished. It came short of Shimmer's position but passed over the woman. She froze as if expecting more, but nothing came of it.

Kitable lay on the ground, no longer buried in a magical avalanche, but not moving. Magic still hovered around him randomly, less than half of what had been there prior to the spell. He lay prone, not so much as lifting his head.

The woman headed toward Kitable, leaving her spells behind. The flash of purple made sudden sense; although the spells themselves were unharmed, the bindings had been broken. The stranger walked right out of her defenses, including a brilliantly green Molded Shield spell.

Kitable vulnerable, Shimmer's resolve strengthened. She could not let them hurt Kitable. But she certainly could not stop them, not realistically. Shimmer had no spell strong enough.

She changed tactics. Her family avoided confrontation. There were many other elegant solutions.

Shimmer dropped a Concealment spell over Kitable, and he disappeared. In the next heartbeat, she realized her success meant she had targeted him without difficulty, a sobering prospect. He had no defenses left. And if *she* could bind him, so could the enemy.

The strange woman cursed in Esparan when Kitable vanished from sight. Shimmer would have expected the woman to see the presence of magic, but Spell Sight was a bound spell. And like her Molded Shield, the woman had left it behind. She could not see the simple spell Shimmer had used for now.

Shimmer froze in her position, crouched by a collapsed tent, hoping she looked enough like a cowering innocent to be ignored.

To her disappointment, the woman and her warriors headed up to where Kitable had "disappeared." Shimmer bit her lip. Kitable was hidden, but he had not moved. If they stepped on him, they would recognize the ruse. All the woman had to do was cast Spell Sight, and the ploy would fail.

But the fighters stopped and stooped to collect something from the ground. They presented it to the woman. The caster cursed and, like a child, stomped her foot before casting a Sending that went in three directions.

Shimmer cast the fastest Eavesdropping spell of her life and managed to target the last of the Sendings before they escaped her reach. In Esparan, she heard, *He was hit and definitely weakened, but he still used his Relocation spell! To Wayburn!*

The caster and the soldiers with her shoved their way back to the north at a run.

Once Shimmer was certain they were gone, she crawled up the hill to find her fallen wizard.

Using a Reveal spell, Shimmer looked through her own illusion. Kitable's only injury seemed to be a badly cut hand where he had, apparently, smashed something. The pieces were strewn about and had likely

been what the soldier presented to the other caster. How that meant a Relocation spell, Shimmer did not know.

A group of Galanth men rushed past, narrowly missing Shimmer as she knelt beside the hidden master wizard.

If she dropped the Concealment spell, he might be targeted and killed, but if they remained where they were, someone was going to trip on them.

Shimmer hefted his limp body over her shoulder.

Halfway to Match and Mixer, Shimmer started snickering. Her father had been wondering when she would bring a man home. Unconscious and slung over her back was probably not what he had in mind.

After leaving DoomDragon's tent, the Gaidolons made their way to the east slope. As much as Lance expected, and hoped, for the recall to come from Tohmas in today's fray, he had already decided he would have to return whether the call came or not.

Lance tried to stay out of sight when possible then walked like he knew what he was doing when hiding was impossible. If he appeared confident, no one would have the gall to question him. He certainly felt important in his long, heavy robe. He prayed no one noticed his bare feet.

They made it to the east approach, and Lance went back to hiding behind tents and waggons. When a horn sounded, the Northlander forces and their Esparan allies charged the hill.

As Lance predicted, the main forces charged the west slope, leaving only enough soldiers in the east to keep those manning HillTop's defenses from supporting the west. The winding north slope, banked by steep drops and gravel slopes, was left open.

DoomDragon probably knew about the traps Tohmas' men had set there. They might even know that the only defenses Tohmas had in the west were the barricades—wooden spiked walls mounted in an alternating pattern that made attackers weave between them. Unmanning the barricades would allow a steady flow of enemies into the thinner populated western side of the camp.

Lance turned his sights to the eastern side of the hill where Esparans loyal to DoomDragon were making their run. They outnumbered Lance's guardsman by four easily, but the numbers did not worry him. Brigands often outnumbered the guardsmen sent to break them in Gaidol. These attackers were the same—undisciplined, sparsely organized, and unprepared.

The guardsmen came together in a wedge formation with Lance at their center. Usually, the position was reserved for the man best able to adapt and assist the others around him. It should have been Shinat's place, but Lance did not protest, lacking the strength to wield a weapon. He would be a liability in any other position.

Catching the enemy from behind, the wedge ruthlessly cut its way up the slope. Carthy, at the head, waved a green cloth as Shinat blew a horn to identify them as part of the Fyrd of Arrow as they reached the Galanth defenses.

The run was torture. The cold mud stabbed into Lance's soles like a field of thorns. The strain of the interrogation manifested as physical exhaustion, and Lance struggled to reach the top of the hill. With each step, he forced his weary legs to lift by threatening them with amputation should they fail him. Around him, his guardsmen slowed their run, taking the opportunity to prove their skills against the mob, but Lance was not fooled. They were only slowing for him.

Thankfully, none of the warriors below were armed with bows. He just had to run and keep running. So long as the Galanth fyrd manning the defenses did not shoot him, Lance would soon be safe.

An age later, he reached the top of the hill, and the guardsmen wove their way into HillTop unopposed. Someone recognized them. Voices called encouragement. At long last, they were through the defenses, and the formation came to a halt.

Lance's legs trembled under him. The robe was too much. As embarrassing as it was, he could no longer stand under its weight, and he dared not be thought a Northlander while he stood among the defenses.

"It's our fyrd," one of his guardsmen whispered down at him. Someone else pressed a sword into his hand.

"Demon piss," Lance cursed quietly. Had another fyrd been on the defenses, he could have found a place to collapse and let the on-duty guardian repel the invaders. But these were *his* people. Guardsman

Dolvan was leading for now, but he recognized Lance. Lance raised his head, and Dolvan lifted an eyebrow at him.

If I don't take command, what will they think? That I'm defeated? Will they fear their enemy more?

Lance forced himself to stand, raising his sword.

"You've got the defenses arranged, Guardsman Dolvan. Tell me where you need me!"

Someone cheered, but Lance was too tired to notice who.

"I want fresh guardsmen digging in here," Dolvan promptly answered. The location was the back of a choke point between barricades. "Eyes forward! Archers, platforms! Let fly. Keep 'em high, and leave those closest to the barricades to us!"

Above them, arrows arched into the advancing enemies. Those leading the chase reached the barricades. Before Lance could worry again about his feet, he was called forward to relieve those clashing at the barricades.

He dropped the robe, counting on the threat of death and the fury of battle to keep him temporarily warm.

Stark naked, armed with a sword, and holding Valia's pearls in his left hand behind a shield, Lance joined his guardsmen.

He smashed into the invaders furiously, but soon ran out of opponents. The attackers retreated from him. More than one made a warding sign then chose an approach against a different defender.

He stationed himself at the center of the defenses and watched the enemy try to go around him, to their disadvantage.

As the battle quieted, a guardsman gave Lance a green tabard, but it didn't cover him enough to protect his modesty. The attackers continued to avoid him until there were none who would try the hill.

Dolvan announced victory for the east front with the horns.

A horn from the west warned the success in the east was the only kind being celebrated. The Fyrd of Rest needed assistance. Soon enough, Prince Sol also called for help.

The guardsmen gathered around Lance.

"You want command back?" Dolvan asked, then skeptically examined his commander. "You want some pants?"

Lance shook his head. "Those who were in DoomDragon's camp stay with me; we'll hold. Take the rest of the fyrd to the west."

"You'll hold?" Dolvan asked, but the rest of the imminent argument didn't follow. One look at Lance's sparsely covered body, spattered and bruised, was enough to convince the guardsman to obey. The majority of Fyrd of Arrow announced their intention to assist and marched out.

Lance assessed the state and numbers of those remaining. His count came up one short.

Seeing his confusion, Carthy said, "Shinat's dead. Straight through the neck. Saw it but couldn't stop it."

The mood collapsed under the weight of the admission, and the guardsmen collectively froze in homage.

Lance let the silence continue only two breaths. "Start collecting bodies," he ordered. "I want those Northlanders thinking the entire fyrd is right behind us."

Lance took a place on the defenses, still wearing only the tabard.

The east went quiet. No attacker took so much as a step up his slope again, unwilling to face the naked man.

Lance followed the battle horns to the west. With the support from the Fyrd of Arrow, Tohmas' soldiers drove DoomDragon's forces out of HillTop. Someone called a pursuit but was overruled.

As night darkened, the horn calls reassembled the fyrds at their posts. There was no victory announcement. Instead, a runner arrived with the Fyrd of Arrow as it returned to its post. The missive to Lance was short:

Welcome back. Report when able.

Lance called together his guardsmen, not daring to approach the prince himself. But who to send? He didn't trust himself, not until Kitable checked him over, but the others were also potential risks. They had come to get him. Had DoomDragon been expecting it? He'd certainly made it easy enough, or had that been luck?

Lance tried to think like DoomDragon. Who would he pick to become a walking trap? Someone obvious like burly Carthy? Or someone nondescript like Norin? And would he expect Lance to suspect the ploy? Would he try to avoid the obvious?

A bluff or a double bluff?

When he had needed to focus on defending the hill, Lance's head had stopped complaining. Now, his headache returned with a vengeance.

In his agony, his vision briefly blanked, only to return a moment later, spotted with white lights.

It was useless.

He decided on two guardsmen, increased his odds of getting at least one right, and sent them to Tohmas to report. Afraid of what might be lurking at the back of his mind, Lance selected a place on the outskirts of HillTop nearest the lake. With the help of the closest Galanth guardian, he found shelters and finally procured normal clothing and shoes. He refused the sword that was offered and insisted all guardsmen give up their weapons as well.

Lance retrieved the bear-skin robe. He dragged it to the cliff and, with finality, dropped it into the icy water below.

"Down the hill? What makes you think they are going to be going *down*? They look intent on coming *up*!"

Ignoring Sol's question, Tohmas reached for his horn.

After collecting strangers from every walk of life under his banner, Tohmas had combined the forces of three princedoms. Initially, he had been unsure if he would ever be able to rely on them. Now, with Kitable applying himself and the soldiers working together, he did not doubt.

They would push the Northlanders back.

The first half of the answer to Sol's question was the illusionary dragon, which spooked even sturdy Northlanders into retreat. The second followed the moment the dragon faded away; the army answered the assault.

Given full freedom, the archers launched their volleys. The arrows had been used sparingly before—they were in limited supply and too valuable to waste on long, ineffective shots—but now they drove the attackers back.

Tohmas called his men back to the second line of defenses behind a row of emptied tents. Several fyrds announced their intentions to use the "backbite" retreat, which had one part of the fyrd retreat faster than the others, drawing the Northlanders into a hall of Galanth fighters. The maneuver was completed when the surrounding parts of the line cut the

over-enthusiastic Northlanders off from their allies. They left a trail of enemy bodies along their retreat.

Once the fyrds confirmed they had reached their retreat marker, the archers fired again. The Esparans among the enemy hid behind their shields, but the Northlanders, standing on the level crest of the hill directly in sights of the archers, were sharply cut down.

"Hold!" Tohmas ordered, and a far crier echoed the command on the horn. "Boro, back ten paces. Rest, forward two!" The horns relayed the commands, and the soldiers followed the instructions with precision.

The line of men he created was neatly angled, aiming toward the lake cliffs.

He allowed the enemy to crash into his lines, and his soldiers held. Once they were tangled, Tohmas mounted Honest Justice and drew his sword. Somewhere near the north slope, magic light flashed. Tohmas ignored it, trusting Kitable would contain the wizardry.

His protectors followed him to the lake cliffs and along the edge. Once ahead of the main lines, Tohmas led the charge.

They ran down the lines, forcing the enemy north. Those unable to leap clear met the trampling hooves of a hundred war horses. Some launched themselves against their opponent to get clear, but the angle of the line made their advance a risk; their opponent's neighbor could strike at their flank or back. While it forced many of the Galanth men to attack over their left shoulders, it was a maneuver they had practiced repeatedly. The Northlanders did not have that advantage, and their left sides were weak, bearing no shield.

A few scattered Northlanders pulled back to the defenses, while others retreated north. There, they were forced into the north hill's descent, which alternated cliffs with pits. Once they started down that road, Tohmas no longer worried they would return.

Behind his charge, his soldiers retook the second line of barricades, then the third one. Tohmas was surprised they massed so quickly until he recognized that the numbers had been bolstered by the Fyrd of Arrow. The fyrd fought with new energy that the Northlanders struggled to match.

Tohmas had to heed his own command not to pursue as the last of the enemy was pushed from HillTop. Fyrds assigned themselves

to replenish the defenses, and the wounded were gathered in the Healing waggons.

He took a moment to survey the damage from atop Honest Justice before dismounting and making his way back to the vantage point. *Fortunately*, Tohmas thought as he rubbed his shoulder, *Darak will be able to deal with the other wounded*. Now that the wound had healed, his shoulder did not ache, although it was still more fatigued than he expected.

He was halfway back to his standard, where his guardians would seek him, when a runner handed him a token and reported that a spear with a horn slung over it had appeared in camp.

"*Greed po*," Carsh guessed. Tohmas had to see it to believe it.

He found a circle of soldiers around the spear that had been stabbed into the ground inside the defenses. A feathered braid of hair rope attached a carved horn to the spear shaft.

"Anyone seen Master Kitable?" Tohmas asked.

In answer to the shaking heads, he turned to Carsh. The prime protector crouched and drew a second blade as he slunk forward like a cat stalking a bird. After two circles around the spear, he stood and, with a frown, put away one blade.

It was not magic.

At a nod from Tohmas, the Rydan picked up the horn. He turned it over in his hands as he trotted to Tohmas' side.

It was a horn made from an animal tusk Tohmas did not recognize. A pattern of gold and silver, undulating like fire, decorated both ends. The center of the horn bore the proud silhouette of a rearing dragon.

There was no real word for "gift" in Rydan. The closest approximation was *gef*, an item given in battle to acknowledge a fight well fought but lost. Tohmas had twice now left a *gef* for DoomDragon.

But Tohmas had never received a *gef* himself and was not sure what to do with it. He turned the horn over a dozen times in his hands. Then, with a small shake of his head and a smile that felt out of place, he took it with him.

Half of a fyrd had been lost when the Hunters took the defenses, the damage amplified by their presence in HillTop. Hundreds were wounded to the point of being unable to return to service. Overall, a quarter of his forces had been lost in the brutal exchange.

CHAPTER 4

Victory belonged to DoomDragon. The *gef* had been appropriately given.

Chapter 5

Dusk lingered long enough to see the end of the fighting. DoomDragon's warriors were pushed back to their camp but not before exacting a heavy toll. The chill wind rose.

The darkness was meaningless to both camps, Calanor was certain. Neither side had the energy to repeat what had been done in the sunset. It was no coincidence that peace came when Inac's chariot was gone from the sky.

Calanor regarded the game pieces set on the table between him and Darknim DoomDragon. As he considered his next move on the board, the wind blustered outside the whale-skin tent. Totho's fury had picked up, collecting the souls of the dead. Once the spirits were all gathered into the stars—when the wind died down—Calanor would go out to pray for those who had been lost that day.

He moved a soldier playing piece toward the Northlander's lead figure. Darknim sat forward to examine the move.

DoomDragon had taken a few blows in the day's fighting. The elders, with what Calanor had identified as a combination of a celebrant and a healing mother, had mended him well. A bandage over his right forearm was the only reminder of the injuries.

They had not discussed the battle; his host was either honoring Calanor's insistence that Totho wanted nothing to do with the killing or was trying to save Calanor grief. There was little doubt Calanor knew some of the people DoomDragon had cut down.

As Darknim considered his options, voices came from behind one of the tent partitions.

"What happened?" demanded an unfamiliar voice. "Everything was perfect! How could he have Relocated?"

Darknim lifted one thick, white eyebrow but made his move on the game board instead of getting up. The words were not directed to either Darknim or Calanor.

Sure enough, a woman's voice answered. "I saw the crystal remains! He used his pendant. Kitable must have gone to Wayburn!" This voice, Calanor knew. She had searched him the first day he awoke in Darknim's camp and had taken his magical trinkets. Her name was Seria, and she was an Esparan wizard who had lived in the Princedom of Tanble. As Seria pointedly avoided Calanor, he still did not know why she was following a Northlander into battle.

"He is missing," said a third voice, and Calanor cocked his head. It sounded surprisingly familiar, but he could not place it.

Darknim leaned back, having used his wizard piece to steal land from Calanor's side of the board. "The children are bickering." He placed his hand on his bog-iron pendant as he looked at the divider separating them from the squabbling Esparans.

"Missing?" came the first man's voice. "How? He was *not* in Wayburn, nor had he been anywhere near it! Besides, if he was hit by that spell, there would be no remains!"

"Why not?" Seria asked.

"Master Terant struck Tohmas' wizard today with a spell he has been boasting about for years. Apparently, they are unsure of the outcome," Darknim softly explained to Calanor then glanced at the board. "Your move, Tothonar. If they are bothering you, I will send them away."

Calanor shook his head and made his move. The voice he almost recognized—the second male voice—teased the edges of his memory.

Master Terant's voice was sharp. "My Full Reversal was designed to send him over the edge. If it worked—"

"What edge?" Seria interrupted. "You never explained!"

"Fool!" Terant shot back. "What happens to a wizard who takes too much magic?"

"Spell Burn," was the matter-of-fact reply from the unidentified man

"No!" Terant cried, infuriated. "Not what happens if you try to *hold* too much magic, you idiot! What happens if you *grab* too much?"

Dropping his pendant to hang on his chest once more, Darknim yawned and sent a mounted soldier to block Calanor's piece. Calanor answered by cornering the wizard with his trickster. DoomDragon's eyes narrowed as he pursed his lips in thought.

Terant's voice was pained, but it softened. "Let me simplify. If you request more than you can pull, instead of *it* coming to *you*, *you* go to *it*."

"Ansa's ghost," Seria said.

"Or the tale of the hermit of StonePeak," the second male voice agreed.

"Or any other case of a wizard simply disappearing during a difficult spell," Terant added. "By returning his spells to him, I bypassed all his defenses. Yes, any magic that lingers would be Spell Burn, but he should have been thrown from the world with this much influx. But the glass shards—"

"And the One-way Dispel," Seria interrupted.

"—and the One-way Dispel," Terant allowed, "indicates it may not have worked perfectly."

"He is still missing," the second man said. "No one has seen him, not even the prince. I've been unable to locate him."

"He may yet turn up. Keep an eye on the Healing waggons. He has hidden there before," Seria said.

"He wasn't there, but I'll look again," the unidentified voice promised.

When Darknim reached for his playing piece, he glanced under Calanor's hood. Without a doubt, he saw Calanor's frown.

"He is a spy," DoomDragon confirmed as he gave up on saving his wizard and moved a mounted fighter to attack Calanor's. "I imagine Tohmas has a few around my camp, too. The wizards all think you are just that, Tothonar."

Calanor lifted his head and met the stare of the strongest man in the Northlands. "I obey the Wind and no other."

Darknim flicked his eyes to the tent partition, and Calanor took Darknim's lack of concern to be faith in Totho. He moved his own wizard to the far side of the board to threaten the Northlander's leader piece. In the Esparan game, it was the prince, but here, it was a large warrior.

"And what about Carraway?" Terant asked, his voice now calm. "We set a trap and yet—"

"It's ... difficult, but I'll get him. We should be able to use him yet." Having heard that tone from Seria before, Calanor imagined she was pouting.

"We cannot afford to lose this opportunity," Terant warned.

Calanor had heard Darknim and Seria discussing Carraway earlier. While the attack on the hill had been in their favor in terms of simple numbers, Darknim always worked multiple angles. Kitable's defeat and Carraway's return to HillTop had been part of his plan.

A long pause answered. Seria had no reply.

"Carraway has kept himself apart for now," the spy said.

"He suspects something," Terant replied, his voice grating.

"It doesn't matter what he suspects," Seria insisted. "I designed the anchor to move, so it's not even on him."

In an apologetic tone, the spy explained, "He keeps his entire group segregated."

"But Kitable can't help," Seria said dismissively. "It is only a matter of time before the spell's in position."

A pause lingered. Calanor felt its weight.

Darknim sighed as he examined the board. "I had better see what they want. Besides, I cannot salvage this particular bout. I yield, Tothonar. Your match."

The leader of the Northlanders knocked over his leader piece to signal surrender and rose from his seat. "Another match after I have dealt with these children?"

Calanor nodded. Over the last six matches, they had each won three. They had to break the tie or neither of them would sleep.

The wind was still howling outside. Totho had many souls to collect.

When Kitable opened his eyes, he was ecstatic to see a ceiling and not the dark, vacant space of nothingness he had lingered in during his unconsciousness.

A dream? He'd last dreamed at thirteen years of age, when he had been new to magic. He never remembered dreams now, but this event was a significant exception.

He remembered falling in darkness but not landing. There, in the black that could not be penetrated, a twirling array of magic auras had lit the distance. Unable to slow or stop himself, he had been dragged toward the light, a smooth surface slipping under his feet.

Then pain from his right hand had cut in, strangely dulled. In that instant, his movement had stopped, dropping him onto the black surface that did not reflect the light of the distant magic. He remembered looking down and taking a painful, fire-touched step back. He had been on the edge of the black surface. A bare step in front of him had been a drop.

The drop remained a concept, not a sight, and he did not know how he had recognized it. There remained no doubt in his mind that he had been standing on the brink of the solid surface, looking down into a void that separated him from the lights.

Nothing changed for an age after that. He had been stuck in the blackness, no landmarks except the chasm he had barely avoided falling into. He had been trapped, lost in a place of such complete nothingness. It made him shiver to recall it now.

In the real world, where there was light enough for him to recognize a waggon's ceiling, he let out a sigh of relief. Every muscle ached, making his sigh tremble.

Lying on his back, Kitable reviewed the spells he had cast during the Northlander attack. An illusion. That could not be the cause. There had been a woman, an Esparan, but he did not remember seeing her cast. Certainly, a spell had hit him, but even that did not explain why he ached.

He recognized the pain as Spell Burn as his head cleared.

Magic channeled through the mind but not used up in a spell caused Spell Burn, scorching flesh from the inside out. Due to his lack of formal training, Kitable had spent the better part of his childhood in a constant state of severe Spell Burn, but none of his previous experiences had come close to what he felt now.

As he considered trying to move, familiar faces appeared over him. The first face was covered in white and black fur and had a long pink

tongue hanging out of its mouth. Oddly, the dog's breath was minty, so he did not mind the lick to the forehead as much as usual.

Cutter Darak's bearded face followed, his beard tangled and untrimmed. "You comfortable?" asked the gruff cutter.

"No."

"Oh, good. I was going to pull out some blankets. Anything to keep you from coming back so often."

Kitable knew he would probably appreciate the sense of humor later, but all he could do at the moment was wince.

"They all think you were a soldier hit by powerful magic in the fighting," Cutter Darak explained in a hushed voice. "Care to tell me what happened so I can fix it?"

Wanting to be rid of the view of the waggon ceiling and the grinning face of the cutter, Kitable lifted his hands to push himself up. The dog had gone to lie beside him, as she did for every patient Darak spent more than a flicker visiting.

The pain was expected, but Kitable's right hand was heavy. He brought it into his sight. It had been bandaged.

"Ah, yes, that," the cutter said. "Usually, when I spend a candle picking glass out of someone's hand, it's because they threw themselves at a temple window. Don't laugh; it's happened. But since there are no glass makers in all of HillTop, and the shards were in your palm, I presumed you crushed something. Any idea what it was?"

Kitable let his wrapped hand drop and lifted his left hand to search for his crystal pendant. Rather than the pendant, he found only skin.

"Your things are over there," Darak said.

Kitable did not check where the cutter pointed but stared at his left hand. His skin was red. Every bit of skin was bright, poppy red.

"That," the cutter added helpfully, "is the reason you are currently not wearing anything. I had to make up the story about the spell because of that too. I fear the only alternative I could dream up would have you streaking through camp in the bright sunlight for days, and surely, someone would have noticed that. How you got so badly sunburned, I do not know."

"Spell Burn," Kitable muttered, lowering his hand. He was, he could now tell, indeed wearing only a blanket. The trouble was the burn was

not on the skin at all. Despite a long history of experiencing Spell Burn, Kitable had never even read about a version harsh enough to be visible.

Despite the ache, he turned his head in search of his belongings. Among the pile laid beyond his reach was his crystal pendant.

It would not have made sense anyway. Breaking that would land me in Wayburn.

The cutter cleared his throat. "If you tell me what Spell Burn is, I may be able to help."

Kitable closed his eyes, thinking back to before the blackness and the void. As he did, he answered. "If you ran around the HillTop as fast as you could, cutter, why would you ultimately have to stop?"

"My legs would be sore, I presume."

"Run hard enough, and they will burn."

"True enough."

"Now, imagine that burning feeling in every muscle in your body, down to the soles of your feet."

"That's how you feel?"

The orb, Kitable finally realized. Tohmas had given it to him before the fighting started. How Kitable crushed it, he did not recall, but at least he knew why his hand was sliced up. Unfortunately, that did not explain how he had gone from the battlefield to lying in a Healing waggon.

Kitable opened his eyes to find the cutter sitting pensively on his heels, stroking his beard.

"Are you still warm?" Darak asked when he saw Kitable was again attentive.

"Yes. How did I get here?"

"A girl from Fixer City brought you in. Do you ever go over to Fixer City after dark?"

Kitable nodded. "A few times, watching for trouble."

"She dances after dark. She and her father—"

"Weavers," Kitable grumbled. "Speaking of trouble."

Cutter Darak nodded enthusiastically. "The pair of them brought you in and gave me a list of things they had given you. Hearing what you say about this Spell Burn, their treatments now make much more sense."

Kitable cursed under his breath and ran his good hand over his face. "I need to check my belongings."

Lance waited at first, expecting Kitable, but instead of the master wizard, Prince Tohmas sent a replacement.

Lance smiled to see the colorfully-clad young woman duck into his small tent. Despite the deepening chill, which had dropped snow overnight as if to erase the evidence of the Northlander assault, Shimmer Weaver's blouse only reached the bottom of her ribs. She had donned a cloak, but it hung open in the chill.

Sori, seated behind Lance, growled like a she-wolf. Lance batted the Rydan's hands, which were on his shoulders, and she heeded the chastisement by falling silent.

"Wine?" Lance offered. "I have a wineskin somewhere around here."

The dancer shook her head, but her smile was warm as she knelt in front of him, one eye on Sori. Both women sat as if ready to leap to their feet.

"Sori, get out," Lance commanded.

Sori snorted then crawled to the exit. She shot a glance back to make sure Lance knew she was annoyed at being dismissed.

"And don't give me that look!" Lance called after her.

With a final wrinkling of her nose, Sori joined Tanuka outside.

Shimmer smiled again. "Trouble with the miss ... ah, missus?"

Lance shrugged. "They found me again. Every time I move, they find me."

"But you're not—"

"No!" Lance accidentally shouted the word. He quickly reined himself in. "As far as I can tell, they have nowhere else to go. I was nice to them once, that's all." Lance frowned at Shimmer. "If people think I need two Rydans for company, I wonder what they'll say when they hear I hosted you, Miss Weaver."

Shimmer chuckled. "Right now, no rumor compares to you, naked, fighting Northlanders." She fished in her sack as she spoke and produced a stone medallion. "I thought you'd like to see this."

From the smooth black stone, a white etching of a naked man with a sword looked back at Lance. The inscription underneath read "The Naked Sword."

"Just one of many pieces now for sale in honor of your shameless fighting style."

"They move fast," Lance replied, returning the necklace and trying to hide his embarrassment.

"You've got a song too. Something about 'rather being naked than dressed in their skin.'" She flipped her hair back and threw her arms up like a bard at the climax of a tale. "'Kill 'em wearing nothing but a grin!'" she sang.

Lance put his face in his hands.

"'The Naked Sword' is a very popular song right now. It's also at the heart of at least two poems. I think there might even be a play on its way."

"It wasn't deliberate," Lance muttered into his hands. "I didn't have—"

"Don't try to justify it, High Guardsman. No offense, but no one out there cares. They have a story to tell. It's better than hearing another rendition of 'Talking to Dragons' or 'From the wastelands, I come wasted.'" She settled and sat back on her heels, folding her skirts over her knees. "Don't worry. It'll pass."

He lifted his head again, certain his face flushed. She flashed him a wide smile. "You will be known as 'The Naked Sword' for a while though." Her smile grew in seeing his discomfort. "But that's not why I was sent to visit. I hear you've had trouble with casters."

"Messed with my head. I managed to stave off some, but I don't know if the bitch is still in there."

Shimmer raised an eyebrow. "You refused?" Her eyes narrowed pensively. "High Guardsman, I—"

"Lance," he corrected. "'High Guardsman' never sounds right."

There was brief frown on her face, as if she debated another topic before dismissing it. "Lance," she tried again, "if the caster was at all competent, you had no choice. Don't be ashamed of it. The interrogator was probably reading your thoughts. As soon as you think the answer, they see it. It's not your fault."

"I didn't answer everything. After a point, I stopped having to reply, so I didn't. I..." Lance's chest tightened. "You don't look like you believe me."

Shimmer's expression was apologetic. "Thought magic is nasty. Regular people can't defend against it."

"I didn't tell her everything. She asked me about my home, and I just didn't have to answer that question. After that, she never got another reply from me."

Shimmer stared at him, a small frown on her fair face. At length, she sighed. "I suppose it doesn't matter. What was or wasn't said isn't my business; talk to your prince about it. I'm supposed to make sure you're not still enchanted."

"You still don't believe me."

She shrugged. "People can't control their thoughts. Wizards get better at it with practice, but they know what they're up against. Unless you had something... or maybe..."

For a long moment, Shimmer sat with her eyes distant, biting her lip and fiddling with a lock of hair. Lance tried not to watch the fidgeting; the lock was dangling down her front and her blouse was low over her breasts.

A chill, like a draft under the tent wall, crept up his feet as he waited for her to focus. His fist tightened at the drifting cold, and his pearl bracelet dug into his raw wrist.

The cold dissipated. Valia laughed in the distance.

Leaping into a crouch, Shimmer exclaimed, "Oh, that is amazing!"

Lance started to his feet, his hand reaching for his sword. He groped at air; he had surrendered his blade. It took him a moment more to realize she was excited, not upset. Shimmer peered at him with undisguised interest.

"You're using a Focus! How? I realize it's probably something you care a lot about, but what is it? What—"

"No one," he answered in reflex.

She leaned back, her eyes bright. "Ah, understood. Not my business anyway." She retook her kneeling position, and he mirrored her nervously. "But very interesting, High ... I mean Lance. You've achieved something many wizards never do. You're right. You resisted. You shouldn't have been able to, but you did."

Lance unclenched his hand as he settled into his seat. "Does that mean she's out of my head?"

Shimmer sat up straighter. "No promises on that," she said, brought back to the task at hand. "Having a Focus can dispel magic, in theory, but bound spells might dodge that." She straightened proudly. "Most

casters would use Spell Sight to see if you have spells on you, but any wizard worth a copper leg would protect a spell like that from Spell Sight. I'm going to use a Reflection." Shimmer rummaged in her bag once more and pulled out a chain of beads and a tassel.

"You do this much?" Lance asked.

"Most work I get as a caster is to investigate suspected enchantments. People like to think spells are involved a lot. It's usually an excuse to avoid responsibility, but yes, I do this a lot."

"And what do you need me to do?" Lance asked, his hands spread. She glanced at his open hands briefly, her eyes on the crusted cuts along his wrists. Her stare lingered on the pearls around his right wrist. He had the impression she saw far more than just a chain of pearls.

Her smile was less confident. "Just sit still. Try not to block me, please. Basically, I'm going to cast a spell on you which will detect any lingering auras and use Divination to follow them back to their original spells. Complicated spells linger longer, so it can detect those back several days."

"But little spells only for a short time? Less of a chance to catch them?" Lance guessed.

"You ever think of training to be a caster? If you can set up a Focus completely untrained..."

His brother had been a caster, and Lance had seen those powers misused. He had no interest in magic.

Placing his hands on his knees and breathing deeply, Lance said, "Just tell me if I'm free."

The chill came again, crawling over his feet and up his legs, but he resisted the urge to tighten his fist. With the cold piercing through him, he shivered, but he did not otherwise move.

When Shimmer cleared her throat, Lance opened his eyes, not aware that he had closed them. Her smile had less energy when she looked at him.

"Quite a few spells on you," she confirmed. "But they've all fallen off. One was a binding spell though, tied to trigger when you were touched."

"Touched?"

"It was to transfer the spell to another person. The caster must have expected you'd get checked. The spell moved."

"Who has it then?" Lance asked.

Shimmer shrugged heavily and stood, her movement slow. Sweat on her brow glistened in the light through the door. "I don't know. Call together your guardsmen, and I'll check them. If it's one of them, we'll keep him isolated. I can probably come up with something to break the spell."

Lance rose to his feet and lifted the tent flap for her, fearing she would walk right into it in her daze.

"Probably?" he echoed as Shimmer ducked through. He tried not to think about the rumors that would circulate once it became known Shimmer Weaver had come into his tent and emerged, exhausted, shortly afterward.

"I'm not Master Kitable," she warned. "I can't even cast an Eight-layered Dispel. I can target a given element, so long as I can identify it, but if it's complicated or trapped or..." She put her hand to her forehead. "Don't make me think too much, please. Just get the men together and I'll do them all." She paused and furled her brow. "Please don't quote me on that."

"Let them bleed over the winter."

Darknim grimaced but was uncertain if the prince on the throne saw it. DoomDragon was pacing and had his back to his patron when he replied. "And do what? Stare at them? You wanted them to come north. We have Galanth and Solta in position. If you want the others, we need to bait them."

Prince Marfaie chuckled low, the sound echoing in the large hall. "Is the young upstart irritating you, Darknim?"

Darknim stopped pacing, his hackles up. "He has inflicted more damage than we expected. It will be worse if he survives until spring."

"But the others are still not showing interest. We need—"

"If I kill their nephew and capture their brother, do you think they will be apathetic?" Darknim snapped.

He had watched too many bodies burn over the summer. Sol had been easy to predict, but as the fighting continued, Tohmas matched Darknim blow for blow. Even if DoomDragon brought the full force of

his army against the camp, he did not think he could push the defenders off. He had other plans. And they included revenge.

There was silence from the throne.

"A bold plan," the prince eventually said. "Can you do it?"

"Sol is ours to take whenever we choose."

"You missed him once already."

Darknim snorted. "A product of bad luck," he said, dismissing his patron's doubt. This time, he would ensure Carsh and his tagalong Esparan were not nearby. "I will take the attack to Tohmas' door. That will keep his prime protector out of the way. My Hunters need only to get through Kitable's defenses, and Terant or Seria can do that. Or at least, they claim they can."

"You do not sound like you believe them."

"Seria is a spoiled child who does not understand the consequences of what she does. When she fails, she blames others. She never learns."

"She wields more power than—"

"Then have her command your army!"

The long silence that followed made Darknim smile. The longer it lasted, the more profoundly he had offended his patron, the more satisfied he was.

Even if the man on the throne gave the commands, it was Darknim's people who died on the front lines. Darknim was eager to remind him of that.

"Power is not the same thing as skill," Darknim said. "You asked me to command, I presume, because you thought I was skilled enough to bring the sons of Zayban to you. Yet you do not heed my advice. You have held me back. Now, I present you with the opportunity, and you refuse. Have I done something to make you doubt me?"

The silence lingered once more. For a moment, Darknim thought he felt the pendant around his neck twitch. The hanging sword and circle had been given to him by Marfaie over a decade before and acted as a continuous reminder of their agreement and the reasons behind it. The weight seemed heavy for a moment, but the sensation was gone as soon as he noticed it.

"Prince Habal is already dead. To win this war, his son must join him in death. They are weakened. Let me send my Hunters," Darknim insisted.

"Very well," the Prince of Tanble agreed. "Kill Tohmas if you wish, but capture Sol. We need him to bait his brothers."

"Thank you, my Prince," Darknim replied, turning without waiting for a dismissal. He knew the Esparan protocols but saw no need to acknowledge them. He was Northlander. He had taken the Esparan vow of loyalty, but it never mentioned acting like a fool.

"One last thing, Darknim," Prince Marfaie called, stopping him. "Master Terant tells me you are holding a Galanth prisoner."

"I killed the only prisoner we took, and that was mooncycles ago in BellRoost. The other, a spy, escaped," DoomDragon corrected. "We need no prisoners." Expecting a converted man to fight his friends was folly. Darknim barely tolerated the Barlabians; Prince Rairn held a place of contempt to Darknim and would never be trusted.

"He says you hold a Celebrant of Totho in your own house, the Celebrant of Totho for Prince Tohmas himself."

"Tothonar came to us, my Prince," Darknim confessed. "But he is not a prisoner. He is a celebrant."

"Celebrant or not, he is a threat. I do not like taking chances. Be rid of him."

Even knowing Esparans did not follow the same religious teachings as Northlanders, the statement surprised Darknim. "He is a *celebrant*!" he objected.

"He is Galanth," the Esparan prince answered. "Unless you can show me he has been of use—"

"I will not harm a celebrant!"

"Enough blathering!" snapped his patron, standing. The tattoos on Marfaie's face twisted as he grimaced. "You will do as you are told, little dragon. If you cannot do it yourself, get one of the Esparans to do it for you."

The pendant went cold against his chest. Faint twinkling lights, like reflected sunrays over ice, shimmered in Darknim's vision.

Remembering his oath, Darknim stood for long moments with his head bowed and his teeth clenched. To harm a celebrant was to attack the god. If he laid a hand on Tothonar, he would lose the favor of the god. Winter had arrived fully in the north with the turn of the cycle. It was a bad time to be offending the Winter Star.

But disobeying the Prince of Tanble would cost him everything he had gained over the last ten years.

"I can use him," Darknim said, the words making him cringe.

"Then make use of him. But if you cannot give me a good reason to keep him, little dragon, I will have him slain."

The words, "As you command, my Prince," stuck in Darknim's throat as he said them.

Chapter 6

All of Kitable's belongings were accounted for. He thought about casting Reflection spells on the items to see if any of his enchantments had been tampered with, but he did not have the strength. The Weavers had had plenty of chances to hurt him, especially recently. He had to assume, for the moment, that it was safe.

Cutter Darak surprised Kitable with his insight when he had the other cutters and their assisting acolytes dump Kitable into a large barrel of cold water. After the brief dunk, the fire in Kitable's bones was extinguished, and he was left feeling like a runner after the race of his life. While they no longer burned, his muscles were still stiff. After drying off, he was able to make his way slowly to his vardo. He used a traveling coat, the hood up, to conceal his reddened skin.

Kitable spent the next few candles in his vardo, casting one-handed. It was tricky, but he knew how to manage.

Once he had cast sufficient defenses, he finished with an illusion over his skin. Ready, Kitable ventured out in search of answers.

Tohmas was pleased to see him, but nothing the prince said clarified what had happened. He advised Tohmas, gave one of Lance's guardsmen sleeping pills, then turned his attention to finding what had driven him into the darkness.

He had no choice; he sought out the Weavers.

He found Shimmer Weaver sitting on a log beside a large, patchwork tent. When she spotted him, she perked up. He was still wearing

the traveling cloak, his face covered, but the way her eyes sparkled said she recognized him.

"You are up!"

"Surprised?"

She lowered her bright eyes. "Never." She fiddled with one of the many layers of her dress, as if running her fingers over the cloth would remove its many wrinkles. For a performer, she was remarkably bashful. "Did you take a look at Guardsman Nivant yet? I saw the spell but—"

"It was trapped. You were right not to attempt a dispel," Kitable confirmed.

"But you broke it?" she asked, her shy glance raised. "How did you get around the—"

"Sleeping dust."

She squinted at him, her shyness dismissed as she considered his reply. "But why would extract of Julian's moustache flower break..."

He waved her question aside, unwilling to discuss the nuances of magic bindings on the sleeping individual. Wizards had written books on the topic. If she had not read them, he did not feel inclined to provide an abridged version.

"I want to know what happened yesterday," he said instead.

"I thought you may be able to tell me."

"What did you see, Weaver?"

"Shimmer," she corrected.

He drew a slow breath, reining in his irritation. Yelling at her was unlikely to help.

"What did you see, Miss Weaver?" he compromised.

The small victory brought another smile, more reserved than the first, to her face.

"I saw your dragon," Shimmer said. "Beautiful illusion, Master Kitable. I cannot figure out how you bound thought magic to the illusionary fire so seamlessly. I saw it actually flowing with the flames as if—"

The dragon had done exactly as he had intended—slow the attackers until Tohmas' men could retaliate. It was not worth discussing.

"After the dragon," Kitable interrupted. If he let her continue, she might ask for an explanation for that spell as well.

Shimmer's head dropped like a chastised child, and her alto voice softened. "After the dragon, there was a woman who broke through the

soldiers. Then there was a scrying circle above you, and the spell struck through that."

He remembered the woman caster, although he had not seen her face. The scrying circle was new.

"What spell?"

Shimmer shrugged her bare shoulders. She must have been wearing a spell for warmth, for it was too chilly to have that much skin exposed comfortably.

"I don't know," she said.

"Any chance you had Spell Sight active?" Kitable asked, and she nodded enthusiastically. "Describe it."

"Primarily alteration of binding magic, but a little of every element. I couldn't see a pattern until there was this burst of destructive binding magic—a One-way Dispel—but I couldn't figure out why someone would alter binding only to destroy it unless—"

"The dispel was my doing," he interrupted, regretting his words immediately. He made a point of not telling people things, especially when those people were casters.

"From the middle of that? You were completely covered! How did you do it?" She was hopping in excitement, her bashfulness again forgotten.

Kitable saw no need to explain how smashing the orb had done it for him. "What happened next?"

Biting her lip and keeping her gaze level with his, she continued. "The woman was hit by your One-way Dispel. She paused when she realized she left her spells behind, so I dropped a Concealment on you, then one on myself to keep her from—"

"Wait," Kitable stopped her. "You had a third person Concealment spell hovering? Why would you—"

A new voice interrupted from inside the colorful tent beside them. "Shim, send in the next lot!" Dust called.

Kitable closed his mouth. Shimmer had told him she and her father often had to move without warning. Having hiding spells would be prudent.

"One moment, please," she said. Without waiting for his reply, Shimmer leaped atop the log. In a voice more appropriate for a woman

who spent her spare time performing around a campfire, she addressed the crowd Kitable had not noticed was gathering.

"Step up! Step up! See the ice woman of the Eidenlandsa with your own eyes! One copper leg to get in! Catch her before she melts! Have your coins ready!"

A queue formed at her log, and Kitable stepped away to give them room. He was still within earshot when the line started moving, one at a time, in exchange for a copper leg bit.

One man winked at Shimmer as he reached her. "I got a different leg for you, sweetheart. How much that cost?"

To his surprise, Kitable was incensed by the man's presumptuous comment, but he quickly corrected himself. Shimmer Weaver was, by all accounts, a dancer. She was probably as bad as any of Celebrant Loni's lot. If it had not been for the celebrant being untouchable, he expected Shimmer and Celebrant Loni would have shared a fire.

Unlike Kitable, the red-haired dancer did not bristle at the remark. Instead, Shimmer fell into one hip and tossed her head. "That which the gods fear, the poor have, and the rich need, of course."

The man's plump brow creased heavily, drawing his eyebrows over his eyes entirely

She kissed him on the forehead like a grandmother would. "When you figure it out, ask me again politely."

A shove from the rest of the crowd moved the man into the patchwork tent. Her deft hands snatched the copper leg coin as he passed.

It was a riddle. She had asked the man for "nothing."

Once she decided there were enough people in the tent, Shimmer told the rest they would have to wait for the next wave then turned back to Kitable.

Her confidence stayed with her. She met his gaze with her bright eyes.

"You dropped a Concealment spell," he prompted.

"The woman and her soldiers came up, picked up a piece of glass, they spoke, she sent three Sendings, then ran off. She didn't have her Spell Sight because of your One-way Dispel, so they didn't see you. When they left, I took you to Match and Mixer, and we treated your Spell Burn before turning you over to Healing Mother Gracie's waggon.

I didn't think you, of all people, would suffer from Spell Burn, but if you were casting a One-way Dispel in the middle of..."

He let her prattle on and turned his attention to what he had learned. Unlike what Shimmer believed, he had not been casting. The One-Way Dispel had been from the shattered orb. *So where had the Spell Burn come from? An outside source?* It was unheard of, but as he started considering what she had said about the alteration of binding magic, he began to see how it could be done.

They had targeted his spells, dominated the bindings, and through alteration, reversed them. They had, at a fundamental level, un-cast his spells, releasing the magic back along the bindings.

The orb had destroyed the binding magic. Without bindings to target, the reversing spell had nothing to target and petered out. *But why? What were they trying to accomplish? What happens if every spell I wear is undone?*

He could not imagine a worse Spell Burn but...

He remembered the void he had narrowly avoided and how his rapid approach to the swirl of lights had stopped at the throb in his hand. If he presumed that pain was him crushing the orb, his sudden stop was also likely due to the dispel. He had halted because he had ended the attacking spell early.

Would I have gone over the edge into nothing?

He shuddered at the memory.

When he next focused, Shimmer was staring at him inquisitively.

"You going to tell me what hit you?" she asked.

"No. It's nothing you have to worry about." She's safer than I am. The more spells, the worse the Spell Burn and closer the drop comes. She's got too few for it to be a threat.

"Do you want to know what she said in her Sendings?"

Kitable cocked his head in surprise. "You also had an Eavesdropping spell ready, did you?"

The sarcasm, surprisingly, made her smile. She played with a curl of her ruby hair as she answered. "I did a full cast! Usually, I have trouble with Eavesdropping since I use it so seldom, but sometimes the words just flow right and—"

"What did she say?" he interrupted.

"Three branches of the same Sending. Two went into the lower army, and the third to the northeast. She said..." She cleared her throat. "...that you had been hurt but still managed to cast your Relocation. She said they should go to Wayburn."

His bad hand involuntarily went to his crystal pendant. Someone knew. Despite every defense he had cast against Scrys, they had somehow determined that the crystal around his neck could get him back to Wayburn.

"I take it that means much more to you than it did to me," Shimmer speculated. "The last time I checked, you don't use material in Relocation. What was the glass—"

"Shim, send in the next lot!" came a perfect echo of the first call.

Her lips pressed in objection at the interruption, but she jumped onto her log once more. Her shouts formed another queue, and she collected another handful of copper coin fragments in exchange for entrance into the tent. This time, her claims caught Kitable's attention.

"What's in that tent?" Kitable asked once Shimmer was again on the ground beside him.

She giggled. "I told you that the woman left her spells behind, right? Well, once I told my papa, he went and got her Molded Shield."

Kitable's knew his eyes widened, giving away the significance of her nonchalant confession. He corrected himself a moment later. "It must be exhausted by now."

She grinned wider. "Papa knows an opportunity when he sees one. He punched a hole in it, filled it with water, then cast Freeze. Now, we have the only full-size ice statue of a woman in all HillTop!" Her smile became mischievous as she added, "Only a copper leg to see it, Master Kitable."

He looked at the patchwork tent, seemingly made from scraps and broken tents. Poles splinted together made it tall enough to enter without stooping. A duplicate of his opponent could be useful thing. There were a hundred possibilities, but he was rapidly dismissing them. There would be a way, he was certain, of defining the caster from the statue. He was not quite sure how yet, as the most obvious methods had large flaws, but he would find one.

"I imagine it will cost me far more than that, since I want a private viewing." Her face lit up. "Take your bill to Prince Tohmas. Keep that statue undamaged. I will contact you when I want to see it."

When he turned, her face was no less bright, but she was pouting. "You know I would never dare ask Prince Tohmas for payment!" she objected, and Kitable shrugged his sore shoulders.

It took Master Kitable two days to request an audience with the frozen statue, but the Weavers immediately accommodated him. It was a shame to lose the crowd-pleasing feature, but if he could bring down an enemy wizard and free them from the hill, Shimmer considered it worthwhile.

She had left him alone, but as the night drew in, Shimmer decided to visit. She had saved him then successfully answered all his questions. He knew her name. Better still, treating his spell-burned skin from his forehead to the soles of his feet had shown her that, without doubt, he was nothing but a man under all his robes, trinkets, and arrogance.

An unexpectedly attractive man in her eyes.

He was unattainable, but she did not let her certain failure deter her.

The warm air over the campfires, combined with the lingering chill, made it difficult to decide if what fell from the sky should be called snow or sleet. The silence of the night fell likewise wet and cold. The weather soaked her, flattening the curls of her hair and making her dress look like a poorly stored bedsheet instead of dancing clothes. Nevertheless, she entered the blue-lit tent confidently.

The ice statue stood at the center of the tent with a ring of rope around it. Dust's casting would last for days still, but it was focused enough to keep the statue cold without chilling the tent more. With the enchantments on the tent, the cold was kept out, the temperature more like late spring than early winter.

The traveling cloak she had pulled from the back of the Match and Mixer was already damp, but it was better than her current soaked clothing. She needed to change.

Master Kitable sat beside one of the tent walls with his legs folded and his back straight. A small globe of blue light glowed steadily behind his head to light the area. His half-closed eyes opened upon her arrival.

A glance was all he needed. Master Kitable resumed his straight position and let his eyes close again.

"I thought I said I wanted to be alone," he said without looking at her.

"True enough." Shimmer wrung the melted snow-water out of her hair then dropped her bag by the door. "But there's a ribbon on the handle to Match and Mixer, so I cannot go there, and it is sleeting."

"There are at least a dozen young men out there who would love to share their tent with you tonight," the master wizard grumbled. "Why not visit them?"

"There are thousands of young women who would love to share a tent with you any night," she replied. "Why not visit them?"

Although he had an expression of horror on his face, Kitable's open mouth did not actually form any words. His fully alert stare, she was pleased to note, was now on her exclusively. Shimmer enjoyed the attention.

She pulled off her vest and hung it on a tent post, very aware of his stare. A moment later, he looked away.

"Magic is about seeing the world with different eyes. You need to stop seeing with just your head," Shimmer said.

Normally, she would have taken off her skirt's outer layers, but she did not really want to see him become as red as Spell Burn. She wrapped herself in the traveling cloak. It was cold, but it would warm.

"So," Shimmer said, as she made her way to his side, "any luck?"

"If you are going to stay, at least have the decency to be quiet, Weaver."

"Shimmer," she corrected, but Kitable glared at her. It took her only a breath to decide he was not going to reply. "I take it you wanted to spend time with the statue to see if you can define the woman from it then bind her. Clearly, it's not working."

Since he was ignoring her, Shimmer went on. "It was made from a Molded Shield, so you could cast a Molded Shield on it to reproduce the original then target the person who wears a shield like that. Most wizards who know that spell use it regularly. You could catch her with it at some point."

"There are several problems with that suggestion," Kitable said, but his disapproval backfired; she now knew he was listening.

He could have chased her out. Since he didn't, Shimmer assumed he was not that bothered by her presence. Maybe he appreciated having someone to talk to.

She reconsidered her solution. "Molded Shield sits a distance from the skin. You would have to rewrite the spell to eliminate that distance if you wanted to use the statue to match the original. That's not hard. Even I could do that."

His silence told her the answer was incomplete.

"The spell targets the skin," she thought aloud, her eyes on the frozen statue. *That's why our ice woman is so popular; she's naked.* The buffer zone between the skin and the shield meant the statue was a little larger in all dimensions, but the men certainly had not seemed to care. "Her being in different clothes would not affect it, and there is no way there could be another identical shield anywhere. Even if she had an identical sister, they..." She had found the second problem, she realized.

"But something could have changed. If she got a cut or, demons, a pimple, the shield would change slightly. Huh." Shimmer slumped her chin onto her knees, curling herself up in the warming cloak. The shield had probably changed in some miniscule way. Magic took everything literally; it would have to be perfect.

She sat in contemplation for long moments before Kitable surprised her by asking, "Are you going to stay here all night?"

When she lifted her head, he was looking at her. Her heart fluttered. "Yep. I like solving problems."

He turned his stare back to the statue without replying.

They sat, side by side, as the sleet pounded down on the tent, Shimmer grinning all the while.

Long after the traveling cloak had warmed around her, Shimmer felt the thickening of an already-present spell. When she looked at him, Kitable had opened his eyes. Half of a smile crept onto his unshaven face, his stare fixed on an invisible spot somewhere between the statue and the roof of the tent.

"Got you," he muttered, coming to his feet.

She followed him. The spell he cast was a simple Scry using a pre-established anchor, requiring no complicated targeting sequences. He had only to put his hand out and grasp the thread of binding magic he had established.

She dared not cast Spell Sight. She had learned very young that interrupting even the most basic spell was dangerous. Further, casting within a dozen paces of Kitable when he was concentrating was likely to trigger a reflexive counter. Instead, Shimmer stood, biting her lip and listening attentively.

Like her father, Shimmer had learned to close her eyes during Scrys to avoid upsetting clients, but Kitable stared up, his vision distinctively elsewhere. It was unsettling to see him look through it all.

He seemed to forget about her as he mumbled, "Solid defenses, and a cover against thought too..." Shimmer held her breath, straining as his voice dropped until it was incomprehensible. The last thing she made out before he casted was, "Two and two and four then."

His eyes refocused partially, and it made Shimmer's skin crawl. Her father was either scrying or fully present, but Kitable seemed capable of holding the Scry with half an eye. His right hand moved reasonably well, although it was obvious to Shimmer that it was stiffer than his left. The cuts had, thankfully, not been deep.

Shimmer listened to his next spell, which defined a Two-way Dispel targeting binding and fire. It was complicated by the need to use a binding without the dispel destroying it. By the end of the code, her head hurt, but she thought she understood.

But Kitable was not finished. Using hovering spells, he sent three other spells down the binding after the Two-way Dispel. Through it all, one hand held onto the anchor he had made.

The third spell was by far the largest. Shimmer wished she had Spell Sight active when she felt it build then vanish along the thread Kitable held. Her jaw hung open.

He spoke one final trigger word as he released his hold on the thread. The result of the spells appeared just out of arm's reach in front of him.

The blonde woman, wearing a semi-transparent nightgown, jumped to her feet. Her pale eyes were wide as she stumbled on the uneven ground. She collided with whatever containment spell Kitable had chosen.

"What have you done?" the woman exclaimed. She examined Kitable, and Shimmer saw realization rise as the woman's blood drained from her face. "Demon-piss."

Shimmer laughed in delight. What a fascinating combination of spells! He had summoned her!

"Make yourself useful, Miss Weaver," Kitable said. He pulled a leather token from a belt pouch and gave it to her. "Fetch the prince."

Shimmer was torn. She wanted to stay and see what he did with the prisoner, but she equally knew he was trying to get rid of her. Still, Prince Tohmas needed to know what was going on. Kitable's request was valid.

Snatching up her sack, she left the tent at a run.

Funny, she mused as she ran. He speaks as if there is only one prince in HillTop.

Chapter 7

When Tohmas entered the Weavers' tent, he thought Kitable had somehow frozen his prisoner. Movement beyond the ice statue of a woman showed him his error; a live captive was present beyond the statue. Kitable stood beside the tent wall with his eyes on the small Esparan woman.

"I thought you had given up on catching one of their casters," Tohmas said.

Shimmer snuck in behind him and put her bag by the door. Tohmas let her come. Kitable seemed to have enlisted the young woman's help, and there was a chance he would need the Weaver again. The girl had the right to see her own handiwork.

"I had to develop a new descriptor," Kitable said, shrugging as if the effort had been minimal. "I'm a little surprised it worked on the third try."

Tohmas took that to mean Kitable was used to considerably more failure.

Carsh entered behind Tohmas, his attention fully focused on the far end of the tent.

"*Da flya*," Carsh confirmed. By the woman's cringe, Tohmas assumed his brother had flashed her a smile. "Bridge," he said, identifying her as the caster he had leaped on outside of BellRoost. Teeth bared, Carsh creeped forward like a wildcat ready to pounce. His hands bore long

knives like claws, ready to strike. A stride from the woman, he froze, waiting for permission to kill the caster.

Wanting to see what Kitable could get out of the woman, Tohmas did not acknowledge Carsh's request.

The woman stared down the Rydan. "You vile—" was all she said before Kitable interrupted.

"Another word, and I will Vox you," the wizard threatened, his voice poisonous.

"I'm surprised you haven't yet," she snapped.

"The only Vox I have at hand comes with a Black Agony and a Permanency component."

"You are despica—"

"Finish that, and I will shove that Vox down your throat," Kitable replied tersely.

The prisoner's mouth shut, and she leaned back against the invisible spell that surrounded her. Tohmas assumed she had been contained, although he could not see it.

That's a trick to remember, Tohmas thought. By leaning against it, she would know the instant the spell ended.

Tohmas waited a moment longer. Once he was certain she was not going to say anything further, Tohmas waved Kitable over, and the wizard, keeping an eye on his captive, joined him by the entrance. Kitable called back, "Carsh, if she casts, put a knife between her ribs."

Although Carsh grinned wider, the spitefulness of his wizard made Tohmas pause. Kitable did not make threats lightly; he would follow through without hesitation. This caster was a threat.

"So what are the odds of her knowing something that would help us?" Tohmas asked softly enough not to have the woman hear them. "Is she the Northlander version of you or a Weaver?"

"Probably more like me," Kitable replied. "She's the one High Guardsman Carraway dealt with, and it sounds like she's the one Carsh attacked on the crossing into BellRoost too. She definitely deals with DoomDragon directly."

"What are the odds of her telling us what we want to know?"

Kitable frowned. "Slim. Wizards are notoriously immune to torture."

He had to stop himself from chuckling for fear of offending Kitable. "Can you explain that?" Wizards were generally physically unimposing.

Clarin was the perfect example, but even Kitable was a head shorter than Tohmas and a quarter the weight. Either magic had a way of stripping fat from bones or wizards made a point of not eating. It was not exactly the impression he would have expected from someone who was "immune" to torture.

"With very few exceptions, pretty much every spell comes with a mild burn, my Prince," Kitable explained without taking his eyes off the prisoner. "Since we typically cast dozens in succession when preparing hovering spells, wizards spend their lives in pain. Combined with the amount of time we spend completely detached from our bodies, physical torture is generally useless."

"There's a difference between old pain and new pain," Tohmas answered. "But you're the expert. You wouldn't have gone to the trouble of capturing her if she's going to be useless. What are the odds of us finding out what we want?"

"Pretty good, although I'll make no promises on the depth of information."

"How do you recommend doing it?"

For the first time, Kitable pulled his stare from the glaring woman and met Tohmas' eyes. "I can disguise a Thought Scan, a mind-reading spell. There are ways of going deeper, but they are highly invasive and can damage the information retrieved."

"Out of curiosity, on which ground are you refusing to do one?" He had the impression that was exactly what the wizard was doing.

"If I practiced them more, I would never damage the extracted thoughts," Kitable replied. Tohmas nodded in acceptance. Kitable continued without pause. "There are a few issues with the Thought Scan as it stands. Firstly, I will have to cast a defense on you to conceal it. If she knows I have cast it, she will defend against it."

"She can cast? I thought..."

Kitable shook his head. "I won't let her cast, but the Thought Scan only reads surface thoughts, which are under conscious control. If she suspects I have cast it, I'll get poetry or some other deliberate distraction. If she's developed a Focus, I'll get nowhere."

"Like Lance," Tohmas said.

"A Focus is a bit like sleep; it disrupts magic, although it's inconsistent. Very few wizards have ever managed to create one. Don't ask me why. No one understands it."

Tohmas shrugged, and Kitable continued. "If I target her, she will easily guess the spell, so I am going to use an area scan. That means I will be able to see everyone's thoughts. I will likely read a few surface thoughts off you all at first."

"Do people normally think in words or pictures, Kit?" Tohmas asked.

The wizard cocked his head curiously. "Usually words with image flashes, but everyone is different."

"Then we have no problem. I agree, and so does Carsh."

"Lastly, if she does not think about the things we want..."

"...you will not see the thoughts we want," Tohmas finished. "But," he continued when the wizard again opened his mouth, "if we are obvious about it, she counters and you get poetry."

"Basically."

Tohmas raised his voice. "Then put up a defense, so I can find out for myself."

Soon Kitable was whispering his strange words, and Carsh's smile dropped, recognizing there would be no killing just yet. He did not otherwise adjust his poised position.

At a nod from Kitable, Tohmas stepped forward.

The woman's attire was something he would only have expected to see under intimate circumstances with a wealthy Esparan woman. It was a delicate garment woven with pearls, and he could not guess where she had gotten it. Beyond the transparent piece of cloth, she was adorned with a few rings and a very short necklace. Her size was the first thing that had warned him she was not Northlander, and her thin face and long, straight hair, which flowed like spun gold down to her buttocks, further confirmed it. She seemed more like a sprite than a person.

But she squared her shoulders, crossed her pale arms across her chest with finality, and declared, "I will not tell you anything."

"So Kitable tells me," Tohmas replied, taking on the part Kitable needed him to play. "If I decide that's true, then the only decision I have to make is whether to slit your throat or gut you." Kitable needed her unfocussed.

Her eyes went wide, and the sharp reply she had almost spoken was halted. Her jaw fell open.

He was surprised. The girl had been living with Northlanders. She should have been accustomed to some degree of brutishness.

Must be living isolated from the Northlanders. Or perhaps she didn't expect it from an Esparan.

"So I need to decide if you know anything useful, and how likely I am to get it from you. It's already late, so I'm not going to waste time. Start with your name."

He got an angry stare.

"What would you have me call you? The prisoner? The woman caster?" Still, he got nothing, so he shrugged. "I cannot say that is promising."

It was possible, he supposed, that Kitable now knew the answers to every question he had asked. *Have to go over it with him later.*

For now, he wanted the questions flowing. "What I want to know about, little caster, is DoomDragon. I want to know the man. I want to know where he came from and why. I want to know how it is he has convinced you, an Esparan, to stand against your own people. I want—"

"I follow power," she said, shifting her position. She still leaned against the invisible wall, but her crossed arms lowered.

Tohmas laughed. "Is that what you told him? Was he flattered?"

She clenched her teeth and said nothing.

"I don't believe that," Tohmas said. "If you followed power, you would have joined Kitable the moment you showed up here, which I assume he would have mentioned." Kitable made a face, giving Tohmas his reply. "You have been out-done. Kitable defeated you. We are more powerful than DoomDragon."

"He will defeat you!"

Tohmas cocked his head. "Are we still talking about DoomDragon? Your Northlander is, believe it or not, slowly losing this war. I've killed a greater portion of his people than he has mine. If you follow power, you should be following me."

It was sounded silly, but it fit the image he was cultivating for his enemy.

When he got no answer, he continued. "So you say he's powerful. What else? What has he planned for me? Would he even tell you if he

had plans? What part did you play in his army? Leader or follower? Servant or master?"

She looked away, and he knew he had reached the end.

"Well, little caster, I don't think you are going to be any help and that—"

"I would have a few words with her before anything drastic, my Prince," Kitable interrupted.

Tohmas nodded. He was unsure what, if anything, they had gotten from the exchange, but if Kitable thought he could get more, it was worth a try.

"As you like. When you're done, let Carsh know. He may have a few thoughts on a wizard's immunity to torture."

Tohmas saw her fear despite her efforts to conceal it. He could not blame her. *Kitable said they could resist torture. He didn't say they enjoyed it.*

He had other things to be doing.

"Have fun, Kit," he said. Carsh sent the woman another grin before following Tohmas out. The last thing Tohmas saw was the woman shrinking back as Kitable stepped up.

He was a little offended that she found the wizard more intimidating.

When the Thought Scan spell went up, Kitable desperately avoided reading Carsh's mind. Firstly, he was uncertain how sensitive the Rydan would be to the intrusion, and secondly, he did not want to know what was going on in the man's mind.

The result was a slightly closer look at Tohmas' mind than he had intended, but since he did not understand the few words he overheard and could make no sense of the flashing image of a field with a spear, he did not feel he had intruded. Images of himself casting beside an ice statue reminded him that the apothecary's daughter was present, but all he heard were speculations on how he had cast the spell that summoned the prisoner into the Force Cage.

The prisoner's thoughts were, as he had expected, well controlled. Even if she had not seen him casting, she was expecting him to be looking for information.

Drither, drather, still a bit farther. Passed the bridge and through the gate, I'll meet my love. I shan't be late....

It was not poetry. Instead, she was singing in her head.

But Tohmas disrupted the woman's thoughts. The words "slit your throat" triggered a memory of an Esparan man being stabbed by a spear. Kitable heard a few words in a gravelly voice that, combined with her emotions, made him shiver.

He assigned a portion of his mind to keep out the other thoughts in the room. The rest of his mind focused on listening to, but not feeling, the woman's thoughts. There was a slightly larger chance of missing a thought by distancing himself, but if he felt her emotions too closely, he would mirror her reactions and reveal his spell.

She thought her name—Seria—when Tohmas asked, though she did not speak it aloud. He did not recognize it.

When Tohmas mentioned DoomDragon, Seria's thoughts showed the Northlander in detail. The man had an old face with a long, beaded beard and a fur-lined hood that made him look like he was part bear. Deep grey eyes and a large nose completed the weathered face of the man Tohmas was seeking.

Drither, Drather... The song stabilized Seria's thoughts.

Questions on DoomDragon's origin yielded nothing but more song, but the reference to her "people" broke through. For a moment, Seria's thoughts were completely on Tohmas, and Kitable saw his prince from her point of view.

She did not hate the Prince of Galanth. She feared him slightly but thought him stupid and so was confident she would resist this interrogation. She had lived a lifetime with brutes belittling her and expected it of everyone she met.

"I follow power," she said, meaning to taunt Tohmas.

A flash of a memory came with the thought, but Kitable did not fully catch it. It was a man, of that he was certain, dressed in wizard robes covered with trinkets. Kitable could gain nothing further from the vision of an older face he did not recognize.

"So, you say he is powerful. What else? What has he planned for me? Would he even tell you if he had plans? What part did you play in his army? Leader or follower? Servant or master?"

The word "master" brought Seria's thoughts back to the man in robes. He was casting something.

Like movement in the corner of his eye, another memory snuck in. A waterfall of magic auras cascaded down over a memory of Kitable as Seria looked on smugly.

But if he saw Seria in the image, protected by Esparan warriors amidst a melee, it could not be Seria's memory.

Recognizing the source, Kitable remembered that Shimmer Weaver was still present. The apothecary's daughter had, with a stray thought, confirmed what Kitable had assumed; Seria had been the woman on the field that day. That was worth investigating. Would Seria know more about the spell that had nearly thrown him out of the world and left him Spell Burned? Through her, could he find the secret to reversing spells?

Passed the bridge and through the gate. I'll meet my love...

They had not gleaned much more by the time Tohmas gave up. The only additional information he gathered was that Seria's job was to kill Kitable. She expected to have help during their next confrontation.

What kind of help? Kitable wondered.

Once the prince and his prime protector left, Kitable felt Seria's fear intensify. Her overconfidence facing Tohmas had calmed her, but she now mentally sang louder in fear.

When he stepped toward the trapped woman, Shimmer Weaver shadowed him gingerly.

Kitable paused, turning his glare on her. "Why are you still here?"

Shimmer shrugged. "Because there's still a ribbon on the handle of Match and Mixer and it is still sleeting."

"What kind of code is that? What does that even mean, a ribbon?" Kitable demanded.

To his surprise, she blushed. "It means my Papa is entertaining tonight, and I am expected to not intrude."

He regretted the question immediately, but before he could command the end to the conversation, his wandering awareness caught a thought from Seria.

Lying disrobed on a bed of pelts, he saw a man of medium build that could be neither DoomDragon's great bulk nor the master's thin figure. He could not see the face, but Seria's memory came with strong lust.

If she had a lover, he wanted to use it against her.

"Does he do that often?" Kitable asked Shimmer instead of chastising her, hoping to get more from Seria.

Although she raised an eyebrow in bemusement, the apothecary's daughter replied, "Whenever he finds reason to. He is popular with many but chooses few."

I shan't be late, was all Kitable heard from Seria.

"Unexpected for a man of his age. How does he find so many willing?"

"Despite what you may think," the Weaver insisted, "my Papa actually loves everyone he takes to Match and Mixer, and I assure you, they are each the better for it. He may not stay long, but that does not..."

Kitable found himself sharing the memory of a kiss, but there was no image to go with the sensation. *Had she closed her eyes?* The person was taller than she was, and she sensed magic surrounding him. Her lover was a wizard.

DoomDragon had three wizards working for him: Seria, her master, and her lover?

The memory was interrupted by the image of a Northlander stabbing Kitable's chest with a bone-handled knife. Kitable flinched.

He turned his eyes to the prisoner. "Boring," he said aloud.

The song resumed in her head as Seria smiled wickedly. "I thought you would like it." They had interrupted Shimmer, but the dancer slunk out of the conversation inconspicuously.

"That thought wasn't realistic. You will have to do better than that."

"I am sure I can come up with something. I will make you earn every moment you spend in my mind, demon."

Shrugging, Kitable found a place beside the wall and lowered himself to the ground. Shimmer sat out of arm's reach to his left, but he did not acknowledge her. He did not want Seria to see him bicker with a girl.

"I would not expect any differently," he said. "So tell me about the spell you used against me, Seria. And tell me about your master, that man you fear and respect and have lived with for so long. You were an apprentice, I presume, or you still are. Does he even know about the lover? Would he mind, I wonder?"

He kept his questions flowing for nearly a candle, accepting whatever snippets of thoughts that escaped her singing. Her opposition meant tolerating several more images of his own death under an array of circumstances. She had, if nothing else, a good imagination.

He learned that DoomDragon spoke Esparan, fought from the front like Tohmas did, argued often with casters, and did not like Seria. He learned that Seria's master lived farther north and had designed the spell that nearly killed Kitable. The scrying circle during that altercation had come from another source, one Kitable was in the process of investigating when he was interrupted.

One of his tethered spells ended. None were due to end.

Confused, Kitable sorted through his remaining spells and located the missing one.

"A ward in the prince's tent has been broken," he realized aloud, forgetting entirely about the audience of casters.

He fired off his Vox spell as Seria opened her mouth to comment. The Black Agony tied to the attempted use of speech instantly caused the woman to keel over in pain.

"Maybe someone went for a visit," the Weaver muttered, half asleep beside him.

"People *trigger* wards." He wove together a Scry. "Only wizards *break* them."

He could not target Tohmas; the man was not sufficiently unique. Carsh, on the other hand, would be simple. It was possible the Rydan would object later, but Kitable did not care. He had to know what was going on in the prince's tent.

Through the Scry, Kitable viewed Tohmas' tent, looking down at the table and chairs that Tohmas complained about every time they stopped. Carsh, his target, was leaning back in a chair, his feet on the table. On the edge of the vision, Tohmas knelt barefoot beside his altar.

The Rydan sat up straight and drew a blade, but Kitable assumed that was because he had detected the Scry. Unfortunately, the prime protector turned toward Kitable's Scry, which put his back to the entrance.

Behind Carsh, a darkly painted figure slunk through the entrance. The only color Kitable saw was the silver glint of a throwing ax in each hand.

Kitable threw a blind anchor into the vision, targeted it, and activated his Relocation spell all in a single breath. By the time he felt the magic pulling his body down the tether, the assassin had thrown the ax.

Kitable was too late.

From his place kneeling by the altar, Tohmas was aware of Carsh's movement. Opening one eye, he watched the Rydan tense and turn, implying magic. Since Tohmas had been expecting something from Kitable, he was unconcerned. He was only surprised it had taken the wizard so long to get bored with his captive.

But in turning his head, Tohmas spotted movement by the tent entrance.

He snatched his sword from the altar, turning on his knees and drawing his knife in readiness. Carsh was faster. Although the Rydan initially had his back to Tohmas and the entrance, he jumped off his chair, leaped over the table, and set himself between the intruder and Tohmas in a blink.

Carsh intercepted the enemy's thrown ax, snatching it from the air on its path toward Tohmas. With the same speed, Carsh returned the throw, the ax taking the intruder in the neck and felling him.

Carsh spun when Kitable appeared behind the chair Carsh had toppled. To Tohmas' shock, he threw a knife sluggishly at Kitable. The knife skipped off the table and into a nearby trunk without coming anywhere near its target.

Tohmas' heart sank. Carsh had missed.

Tohmas ran to his brother. He led the movement with a throw of his own, putting a second blade in the downed intruder by the entrance, but the assassin did not move; the first blade had killed him. By the time he reached his brother's side, Kitable had finished casting, presumably defenses should there be other attackers.

Carsh staggered, pitching against the table.

The Rydan lifted his right hand, glaring at the thin line of blood drawn across his palm by the assassin's ax. The word made Tohmas shudder: "Snake'd."

Poisoned.

Tohmas lowered the Rydan to the ground and clamped a hand over his brother's upper arm to slow the blood. With his free hand, he tore free Carsh's vest and turned it into a tourniquet.

There, he faltered. He had no access to Rydan treatments. No soaked bandages or river leeches. He could bleed the wound, but he could do nothing more.

"Runnah!" he called to summon the protectors. It took an agonizingly long moment for two protectors to arrive. Tohmas did not know where the closer two had gone. "Get me Darak! Now!"

"Weaver," Kitable said as if speaking to someone standing beside him, "we have a poisoning in the prince's tent. Get your father here immediately."

Tohmas spared the wizard a glance, but he doubted Kitable could help. Healing was the duty of celebrants, not wizards.

To his surprise, Kitable knelt over Carsh and began casting.

Most spells Tohmas had heard the wizard cast were measured in words, but the spell Kitable cast over Carsh felt like it took pages. When it was finished, the wound's bleeding stopped.

Wanting as much of the poison out as possible, Tohmas reached for his knife, ready to cut the poisoned wound open.

Kitable's voice was strained. "I have stopped everything. Wait for the healers. I will hold him until then."

Tohmas sat back on his heels in silence, the tension in his gut moving into his chest.

There was no choice. He had to wait.

And while he waited, Carsh was dying.

"Brudda," he said to the Rydan, not caring if Kitable heard it. "Dohn die."

There was no reply this time.

Chapter 8

Shimmer was rushed through the entrance of Prince Tohmas' tent by protectors. She skipped over a body in the entrance, certain that the knife in the man's throat was deadly and dismissing him as irretrievable. Two more steps in, Shimmer paused, realizing that the man had been Northlander. She almost turned around, but the sight of Prime Protector Carsh motionless on the floor at Prince Tohmas' feet brought her attention forward. Master Kitable, who knelt beside Carsh, wore a frozen expression of deep, concentrated concern.

Her father, surprised by her sudden halt, ran into Shimmer from behind. Dust cursed as he disentangled himself. When he stepped out from behind her, he straightened, ready for business.

Someone had managed to poison the prime protector. Her stomach tried to leave through her ankles when she realized she was the one meant to save the Rydan defender. The consequences of failure would be particularly unpleasant.

"Oh, demon piss..." she muttered.

"Shim!" Dust snapped. "Cast Healing Hands. I'll take identification."

She started out of her contemplation to obey. To have any hope, they had to act quickly.

"How was he poisoned?" Dust demanded as Shimmer rattled off the incantation for the Healing Hands spell. Dropping her bag beside Carsh's hip, she knelt beside Kitable.

"A scratch. His right hand, across the palm," Prince Tohmas replied.

Sure enough, a quick glance found blood on the ground beside the prime protector's hand. The bleeding had stopped already.

Her spell complete, Shimmer reached out to touch the prime protector and anchor it. As her hand advanced, she felt the presence of powerful magic. Not daring to pause for fear of losing her spell, she pressed her fingers to Carsh's chest. Her skin tingled as she passed through another spell, but that magic did not prevent hers from taking hold.

Once her spell was anchored, Shimmer assessed the multitude of new auras now visible to her. Each part of him—heart, lungs, gut, mind, and muscle—showed as healthy or diseased. She expected to see warning red auras but instead found a new color——the grey of death.

His heart and lungs were not moving, and the magic colored them grey to show they had failed. The Prime Protector of Galanth lay without heartbeat before her.

She glanced to her right, seeking Kitable. Shimmer certainly did not want to be the one to tell the prince that the attack had been successful and there was nothing they could do.

Seeing Kitable's tightly calm expression, Shimmer reconsidered. Kitable was maintaining an open spell. *Why would he waste such effort on a corpse?*

Shimmer examined the rest of the magic around Carsh.

"Holy flame! You have a Time Distortion on him!" she cried.

"I will not be able to hold it much longer, Weaver," Kitable said softly.

"That you're speaking while holding it is a bloody miracle. Hold as long as you can," she said, turning her attention to Carsh. "Papa! I've got time to set up a Comparison if you're sure it's poison."

"I'm sure, Shim," her father called from the far side of the table where he had placed a throwing ax. He had dumped *Markin's List* on the table. "I'll know what in a moment." He launched into a Decomposition. The complicated spell built around her father slowly.

Shimmer shoved herself to her feet and searched the tent, wondering who she could use for the Comparison. She could not use herself; females and males differed too much for the spell to be useful. Kitable would be good, but she would have to get through his defenses, and that risked interrupting the spell that was buying Carsh time. Dust was also unacceptable; she had no way of knowing what he had been doing recently, and she dared not interrupt him either. A cutter had arrived,

but Shimmer did not know the man well enough to judge his appropriateness as a target for her spell. The protectors dealing with the body?

Prince Tohmas stood by the table, looking like he would pace if he could do it without appearing anxious. She felt his smothered fear in his tightly controlled actions.

Best choice.

"Have you been drinking?" she asked the prince. He nodded. "Has he?" she next asked, pointing to Carsh, and Prince Tohmas nodded with more certainty. "Good enough. Hold this."

Without hesitation, the Prince of Galanth accepted the black globe Shimmer handed him. She activated the orb and allowed it to take a reading from the prince. Once it had become crimson, indicating the reading was complete, Shimmer took it back. In passing, she noticed that the two men were going to have matching scars; Prince Tohmas had a scar across his left palm, but it was old and healed.

Shimmer activated the second part of the spell by touching the orb to Carsh's forehead. Blinking quickly to adjust her vision, Shimmer tried to interpret another set of auras the spell revealed.

Overlaid on the Healing Hands spell showing Carsh's stopped vitals, Shimmer now saw flecks of light. Each color of light represented something that was present in Carsh but not in Prince Tohmas. There were a dozen different colors.

Only three of the light flecks were clustered around the wound. They were the likely poisons, but all three were already diffused around the body.

"Dark root, Shim!" Dust called.

"There are three things here, Papa. Dark root may be one, but it's not the only one."

"Dark root takes vannac as a counter," a new voice offered. Glancing up, she saw the cutter had taken a place across from her, his sack of tools next to her bag.

"I have some," she told the cutter, pointing to her bag. "If you know it, grab it."

The cutter flipped open the flap of her bag.

The Time Distortion dropped, and Kitable, seated beside Shimmer, fell back onto his heels, breathless.

Dark root was known for stressing the heart, and sure enough, the Rydan's heart immediately started pounding, going from grey to the alarming red aura of danger. That alone would kill him if they were not fast enough in administering the vannac to calm Carsh's pulse.

Shimmer grabbed the cutter's wrist as he moved to put the vannac leaves under Carsh's tongue. "Something's wrong."

The yellow of what she assumed was dark root lined the heart and lungs. While his heart raced, the Rydan's breathing was not harried. The aura around his lungs showed the breathing was of normal depth and substance. "His breathing is slow, Papa. With dark root in here, he should be panting."

Green sparkles, one of the colors around the wound, flashed among the yellow in the lungs.

"Two components?" the cutter guessed.

"Demons!" Dust cursed. "There's bellanon in here!"

While dark root sped up the heart and breathing, bellanon acted to slow the breathing. Giving vannac to calm the heart could very well stop the breathing all together.

The cutter swore as well. "Clever bastard. What slows the heart without touching the breath?"

"There's still that third compound," Shimmer pointed out. "Any counter could be hindered by that." There was a brief silence when no one could argue with her. "Papa, we need a Sweep."

Her father must have run across the tent; he landed on his knees across from Shimmer instantly. The cutter managed to pull the bags out of his way by a slim margin.

"Sweep?" asked Kitable wearily from her right.

"It's a spell Shimmer and I developed," Dust informed the most powerful wizard in the world flatly. "And we do not have time to teach it. I can handle one, Shim. Can you—"

"I'll do the other two." In preparation, she turned to the cutter and, for the first time, met his stare.

He was younger than Dust but older than Kitable and had a thoughtful expression that sparkled with child-like curiosity. There was little chance he understood what they were suggesting, but he did not seem worried. Then again, she had never known a cutter to panic. Either

they were going to save Carsh, or they were going to fail. According to cutters, that was in the hands of their god.

"When we're finished, we should have all the poison in the vein here." She indicated the vein behind Carsh's knee. "You will need to bleed them out."

The man smiled from behind his beard. "You are asking a cutter to cut, dear girl. I can handle that."

As if to prove his point, he drew a curved knife and laid out a selection of suture, needles, and bandages. He rolled up Carsh's right pant leg to expose the skin, revealing dozens of old scars.

Shimmer turned her still-enchanted vision to the body. "Demons ... Double Sweep."

Her father gingerly laid a hand on her hand in comfort and encouragement. With a wink, he then activated a binding between them to share the Comparison spell. Since he could now see the lights indicating the poisons, she pointed him to the green and assigned herself the blue and yellow.

Shimmer cast the Sweep spell as quickly as she could, careful to get every syllable correct. Once she was finished, she cast a second.

Bit by bit, she passed the spells through the Rydan's body like a fisherman trolling a river. It took all her concentration to tease the different sparks out of their places in the body and move them to the blood. She started with the heart to get the dark root clear as soon as possible but had only cleared the chest before her energy sagged. The blue flecks, whatever it was, continually slipped through her first net and seemed to dodge the second net entirely. She tried leading with the other net, but it dragged. The effort of alternating nets along every limb, then chasing the blue sparks back out of the tissues, left her trembling.

Soon enough, she felt as if she had been the one poisoned by dark root; her heart pounded, and her breathing became rough. The chill of sweat prickled her brow, but she dared not spare a thought on wiping it away.

She held on, determined to force the poisons out. She could rest once it was done. If she failed, the Prime Protector of Galanth would die.

With her concentration on the spell, Shimmer only distantly felt a gentle touch across the back of her neck. A hand wrapped around her outstretched arm, and the supportive pressure of a body leaned against

her back. She did not know who was holding her until she felt the influx of power.

Warm energy flowed from her neck and down her arm. Her fatigue faded. Her clearer mind found maneuvering the two nets easier, and she brought them closer together to stop the blue flecks from escaping. The extra strength was maintained until she had gathered the poisons at their destination.

Shimmer dared not speak in fear of losing the nets, but her father had been watching and told the cutter to go ahead. She watched the sparkles of light flow from the wound with the blood, and the moment the last fleck had flowed onto the floor, the support was gone.

Her muscles failed, and she fell. While her vision went black, Shimmer felt gentle hands propping her up.

As the cutter stitched the wound he had created on Carsh's leg, Dust scrambled to Shimmer's side. Enervated, Shimmer collapsed backward into the arms of Master Kitable. *Sadly, she's not conscious enough to appreciate the close contact with her hero,* Dust thought.

The master wizard, hardly any more conscious, propped Shimmer up for Dust to put a pill in her mouth. Dust then offered one to the wizard.

"What is it?" Kitable asked.

"Rejuv pill. Mimics a Rejuvenation spell, only without the resulting coma. It provides a non-magic boost for enervation recovery."

Master Kitable shook his head and slowly got to his feet. Shimmer was already waking thanks to the Rejuv pill and lifted herself into a sitting position. Although her eyes were still glazed and her posture weak, she was conscious, and that was more than Dust expected after her exertion.

The raised eyebrow from Master Kitable implied he was also impressed.

Dust offered the pill for a second time.

"I do not need it," Kitable insisted.

"Take it anyway. Use it when next you find yourself enervated. I assure you, you will be glad you did."

Despite his scowl, Master Kitable accepted the pill. Likely, the master wizard would swallow it once they were gone. Dust had worked on his Rejuv pills for decades and knew of nothing better for enervation, but he also knew Kitable's pride would stop him from buying any in the future, since that would admit he had tried the first one.

"Is there anything further the prime protector requires?" Kitable asked, business once more.

The cutter and his dog had moved in to check Carsh, but Dust already knew what they would find. The heart rate would remain fast and thready for a while, but the breathing would be normal. His muscles would be sore from the lack of air, but that would pass. Carsh would remain unconscious for a candle or two yet.

The biggest concern was how long the dark root had lingered in the heart. Since they had used a spell instead of vannac, Dust did not know how bad the damage might be. He also did not know the effects a Time Distortion spell might have on the progress of the poison. Certainly, no one had ever treated the poison with a Time Distortion before. As far as Dust knew, the spell had never been applied on an area so large, let alone on a person!

"I should be able to figure out that third component now, which will help us decide how to treat him," Dust said.

The cutter gestured to his dog, who was nudging him. "Stitches here thinks it's Fanont's dust. If it is, the choice of not treating the bellanon was very wise. I think he owes your... ah..."

"Daughter," Dust said.

"...your daughter his life." Patting and pushing away the hound's head, trying to stop her from poking him further, the cutter added, "But I would appreciate you checking too. Regardless, he will need something to help his heart. How long—"

"He will be fine," Prince Tohmas interrupted. "The Rydans are a hardy bunch."

"Probably as impossible to keep down as you are," the cutter said dryly. "Does this mean he will not take medicine?"

Prince Tohmas smiled sadly. "Not unless you want to shove them down his throat."

Dust laughed at the suggestion. The mental image of one of them—or all of them, for that matter—trying to hold Prime Protector Carsh down was ridiculous.

The cutter let out an uneasy sigh. "Correct me if I'm wrong," he said to Dust, "but dark root weakens the heart to the point of exhaustion."

"Even people who get vannac immediately tend to live, at most, fifteen years after exposure. It's one of the nastier poisons out there," Dust agreed.

Prince Tohmas' face blanked, as close to fear as Dust expected to see in a man who refused to show his emotions.

"We got the message about a quartercandle ago," Shimmer said weakly, pushing her hair out of her face and rising to join them. "But he was stopped by the spell between then and when you went for the vannac. His exposure could be anything between a quartercandle and the length of our spell. I swept it out first, but..."

The three of them exchanged uneasy looks as they did their calculations.

"Then he has up to ten years," the cutter hesitantly offered.

"That's assuming the Time Distortion froze it. If he was exposed for the full quartercandle, I would be surprised if he saw spring," Dust finished. With their diagnosis made, they turned to the prince.

Prince Tohmas' expression was a wall. Dust expected anger, but nothing followed. Prince Tohmas stood like a statue, his jaw locked. Just as Dust turned his head to check with the cutter, wondering who would speak if the prince did not, Prince Tohmas said, "No one is to tell him."

Shimmer's jaw dropped. "A man deserves to know that he is going to die."

Prince Tohmas shook his head, a hard look in his eyes. "If you tell him his heart may give out in the next two mooncycles, I promise you he will be dead before two cycles pass."

"But he could live ten more years!" the cutter objected.

"He wants to die fighting. If you threaten to take that from him, he will seek it. You are not to tell him."

It was not the prince's rank that made Dust nod in acceptance. The prince and his prime protector were close friends, as close as brothers. These were the wishes of the Rydan's family. And what he said made

sense more than Dust wanted to admit. Even Master Kitable, seated at the table, nodded.

"You cannot make him take the pills for the same reason," Shimmer whispered, tears in her eyes. "You would have to tell him." Without support, he was unlikely to make it even ten years.

Through inaction, they were shortening his life.

"Apply what treatments you can now, Darak," the prince commanded the cutter. "Then none of you ever mention anything again, to anyone."

They did not argue, but the silence weighed heavily over the room.

After doing everything they could, Dust led Shimmer out of the tent. The sleet had shifted to snow, the flakes large and lazy. Against the ground, the snow melted to slush. She paused beyond the entrance to pull on her traveling cloak, covering her head.

Joined by the cutter, the three healers stood outside the tent in silent unhappiness. At length, the cutter turned to Shimmer with a sad smile.

"Very impressive work for a young lady," he commended. She was too tired to blush but did offer him a small smile. "Acolyte training?"

Shimmer shook her head. "Just my Papa's teachings."

The cutter turned his smile to Dust. "Well, if either of you ever need a cutter, ask for Darak and Stitches in Healing Mother Gracie's waggon." For the last, his gaze was on Shimmer alone. "I would be glad to help however I can."

She ignored him, hefted her bag, and made her way back to Match and Mixer. Once out of sight, Shimmer accepted Dust's arm for the walk home.

Carsh woke only a few moments after the crowd left. Kitable had lingered the longest, as if to make sure the rest of the casters were in fact gone, then excused himself to return to the prisoner. He made no mention of his visible enervation.

Although there was little doubt that Carsh was still groggy, he rose at once. For the first time since they had left the Outlands, Tohmas spoke to him in fluent Rydan.

He told his brother that he had been snake'd by *tri-wa* venom but the cutter and healers had gotten it out of him. He would feel a bit off for the next while.

"*I sah nah die*," he finished with smiling chastisement.

Carsh rolled his eyes. "*Esparans be preddy*," he said, meaning they might look good but were generally useless. "Protector! Hah! *Tunnabot*?" There would be revenge for the attack. He wanted to know when.

"Better clean up first," Tohmas replied, switching back to Esparan.

Tohmas let Carsh wash the blood off himself then called for the protectors. They reported finding the missing defenders behind a wood stack. Both were dead.

Before he had time for the news to sink in, two of his protectors escorted a Soltan soldier into the tent.

"Prince Sol is gone," Protector Derry informed Tohmas. The protectors nodded to the man with them, the man's green rank rope paired with the black and red tabard identifying him as a Protector of Solta. "His protectors are asking for you."

"Gone? Voluntarily or involuntarily?" Tohmas asked the Soltan protector.

"Something blocks our access to his tent, and no one answers our calls," the Soltan protector replied.

Tohmas let out a slow breath, fetched his footwear, and sent for Kitable once more. Then, Carsh following him, Tohmas followed the Soltan protector to Prince Sol's tent.

Kitable joined them along the walk. In a quiet voice, the tired wizard informed Tohmas that the prisoner was gone.

"Gone, meaning what, exactly?" Tohmas wearily asked. His attention was on Carsh, who was taking long, careful steps instead of prancing as he normally would have. The limp from his stitched wound was subtle but not the only thing slowing him down.

"Meaning someone waited until Shimmer Weaver was gone then broke down my Force Cage and Relocated away with her. She may have been able to do it herself," he confessed. "But I cannot imagine how she managed to cast through a Vox, let alone while under a Black Agony. There are other wizards working for DoomDragon, my Prince. One of the others could have done it while the other broke the wards on your tent."

NORTHLANDER

Tohmas' step slowed. "You warded my tent?"

"Carsh agreed to it a mooncycle ago, so I didn't think you would object."

With a shrug, and a silent moment of amazement that Carsh would ever agree to the use of magic, Tohmas continued his walk. "Well, one of the others also attacked Sol, apparently. We have need of your skills again, Master Kitable."

If he had been expecting a reprimand for having lost the wizard prisoner, Kitable was not going to get one.

When they arrived at the Soltan tent, they were met by a crowd of fighters with green ranks ropes and red tabards. They parted to form a path to the entrance, but Tohmas stopped among them first.

"I need an explanation," he demanded. No one moved, each man among them standing at attention. Addressing them, he checked with each blank expression in turn. "I'm going to make a few assumptions, and I need someone to stop me when I get it wrong. First, I am assuming Master Clarin was with Prince Sol in that tent." Nodding heads answered. "Second, Master Clarin is reputably a decent wizard, but he is no fighter. So you have someone, or several someones, who act as prime protectors in his stead." There was no nodding this time, but no one corrected him. "I want to talk to them, now."

At length, all eyes turned to a pair of protectors. Tohmas' next question was directed to them. "You cannot get in?"

The taller of the two nodded. "Prince Sol always speaks to the protectors last thing."

"His prime protector knows nothing about being a protector, so he managed you directly? You went for your meeting and could not get in?"

"We tried shouting, pounding on it, cutting through the fabric, but we were hoping..." The way the man's stare went to Kitable finished the sentence.

"Well?" Tohmas asked.

Glittering eyes looked back at him. He did not know when Kitable had cast Spell Sight, but there was no mistaking the effect it had on his eyes.

Kitable wore a profound grimace as he reported, "At least six levels of walls. Complicated too. They're layered and connected. Breaking one will trigger another. It's essentially rigged."

"Why?"

"To make it dramatic or maybe so that if I mess up, it kills everyone inside it and several people outside. Wouldn't that be good for morale?"

Tohmas smirked at the teasing, if tired, tone in the wizard's voice.

"Solutions?" Tohmas pressed

The wizard sighed. "I'm sorely tempted to ask for divine assistance," he admitted.

Carsh shook his head. "*Naw goh.*"

"Unavailable?" Tohmas interpreted.

The Rydan shrugged. Loni and her magic-nullifying presence, Tohmas took it to mean, was temporarily absent.

"It will take a while for me to unravel it," the wizard warned. "If I miss a single thread, I could destroy—"

"Actually, I was thinking that maybe we should be paying attention to Pari right now since Inac is unavailable," Tohmas interrupted.

Kitable cocked his head but followed Tohmas to the tent wall. He kicked a stone, looking for loose soil.

Kitable smiled. "Digging, I can do. Stand back."

Carsh went through the tunnel Kitable made under Prince Sol's tent wall first. The ground beyond the tunnel had no magic, although the walls still tingled his senses. Once he was certain the space was safe, he called his brother forward.

Magic was making him tense, but he did not know why his chest ached or why his left hand struggled to hold his knife. He knew why his leg hurt; Tohmas had explained that. The rest did not make sense.

He ignored it all. Flyers were around. Someone had already tried to kill Tohmas. Although Carsh would have expected to be excited by the prospect of more fighting, he felt unusually tired. Nevertheless, he was ready when his brother climbed out of the pit, Kitable on his heels.

Carsh searched. Nothing looked out of place, although one area buzzed with magic beyond the spells on the walls.

Carsh narrowed the affected area down to a spot one stride wide beside Prince Sol's empty cot. The magic was potent enough to give him gooseflesh as he circled it.

"Alteration, illusion, creation..." Kitable said as he approached. "Again, there are a half-dozen spells here. The biggest one is ... Concealment?" The wizard raised an eyebrow. "Something is contained here and hidden from view."

Carsh carefully poked at the magic area with his knife. His knife hit something solid. The thing moved.

Kitable jumped back, somehow aware of the movement. "Someone is in there."

"Sol or Clarin?"

"I can guess, or I can hit the area with an Eight-layered Dispel. None of those spells are explosive or third-person targets or—"

"If it's safe, do it," Tohmas said.

Carsh made a point of standing well back.

With a word from Kitable, all the magic in the region by the cot vanished.

Master Clarin pitched forward. As pale as unstained cotton, he had a fever-like sweat covering him. Every muscle, from his face to his trembling hands, was flaccid and looked sunken over his bones. Kitable always looked like he lost a stone of weight when he was enervated; Carsh assumed the same condition now affected Clarin.

"Sol..." Clarin grunted then collapsed, unconscious, into the dirt.

Carsh confirmed the man was still breathing, but that was all he could bring himself to do in aid of a caster.

Kitable remained staring down at Clarin, his expression one of uncharacteristic concern as Tohmas called forward the Soltan protectors. They cautiously emerged from the hole under the wall, did their own search of the area, then retrieved their prime protector. Their movements were cautious, like a Follower honoring his Leader. He did not understand their deference until one muttered, "Gods protect us now..."

Although Carsh had never liked Clarin, the Master Wizard had been Solta's sole defense against the enemy's casters. They had relied on him, and he had failed them. They were frightened, left without shields against the unknown enemy.

Even Carsh had to acknowledge they were all worse off having Clarin out of service.

Carsh's chest renewed its ache. He resisted lifting a hand to it. For a moment, it was harder to draw breath.

CHAPTER 8

Kitable broke his silence with a choked voice. "They wanted me to kill him. Had I attacked the outer wards, I would have triggered—"

"You didn't fall for it," Tohmas interrupted. He paused, but the wizard remained silent. "Can you tell if they got Sol?"

Kitable shook his head. "I can't know for sure, but it seems likely. While a caster was here, the other was saving our prisoner. Now that they have Seria back, that makes three casters with DoomDragon. One of them is very powerful."

"Bested Clarin," Tohmas agreed.

"Bested me that day on the hill," Kitable cautioned. "I was lucky to survive. Their scrys are impossible to detect, and they have proven they can break my defenses. I do not like it."

Kitable sank into a chair. His posture was slouching more than usual. "We can only hope Clarin hurt the caster enough to give us a little reprieve. I cannot defeat three alone. I need Clarin up, and soon." He looked as pale as Clarin.

Tohmas nodded but did not speak. It was a dark day for the Esparan forces.

They left Kitable in the tent, where he promised to carefully disable the enchantments.

Tohmas and Carsh walked in silence, the pain in Carsh's chest and the continual weakness in his limbs slowing him. It was not until they reached the command tent that Carsh recognized Tohmas had walked in contemplative silence. He was plotting something.

Good. Carsh enjoyed revenge.

Chapter 9

Kitable tried to make it back to his vardo from Prince Sol's tent but dismantling the elaborate enchantments had sapped him entirely. He had to take a break against a waggon, only a hundred paces away from Sol's tent.

Gritting his teeth, he pulled the Rejuv pill from his pocket. Dust Weaver had said it would help enervation recovery. Shimmer had become conscious rapidly after her collapse.

I need that energy tonight. Although a Rejuvenation spell could also suffice, it stole energy later, forcing the wizard to sleep for a fixed set of time in compensation. He could not afford to be so limited.

He turned the black bean-shaped pill in his hand. It looked like the same thing the apothecary had given his daughter, but that could have been a trick. *Why give me something for free if not to gain an advantage?*

Kitable swallowed the bitter pill. He could not be weak.

After a dozen heartbeats, strength returned to his limbs, and his foggy mind cleared. Now, when he walked slowly it was not because of fatigue but to give himself time to think. He still felt worn, but not on the verge of collapse. He was begrudgingly impressed that herbs could do so much. His energy grew, his legs becoming sure in their stride.

Three casters, he repeated to himself. He was facing three enemy casters.

The first was the slight Esparan woman from Tanble. Seria's skill was not overwhelming. She would match Clarin's strength approximately, which put her below Kitable, but not by as much as he liked.

The second wizard was Seria's master. Since he had trained her and Seria feared him, the master was likely her better. Further, he'd been responsible for the spell that had nearly thrown Kitable out of the world. That made him powerful and creative, a dangerous combination. He must have defeated Clarin and captured Prince Sol. He was the only one Kitable thought had sufficient power.

That meant the third caster had disarmed the wards in Tohmas' tent and freed Seria, requiring him to be able to disable wards and dispel a Vox. Either he had Relocated to the location, or he was a skilled scryer if he had performed the feats from a distance.

Kitable was certain they were lovers—or had been. For all he knew, the lover may not have been in DoomDragon's camp at all. None of Seria's memories of her lover had included Northlanders.

The third wizard remained a mystery. If it had not been for Shimmer Weaver's mutterings, Kitable would not know about him at all.

Kitable reached his vardo and paused. The third wizard was a middle-aged Esparan caster of middle magic prowess who was possibly living outside DoomDragon's camp.

"Demons," he grumbled.

He suddenly wished he had not swallowed the apothecary's pill, no matter how tired he had become. Now he had to pray Dust Weaver was more honest than Kitable suspected, and Kitable had little faith in gods.

He turned back without setting foot in his vardo. His destination became Fixer City.

Dust Weaver was more powerful than he let on—and not just with herbs. At odds with his bumbling persona, he had developed the Sweep spell, a formidable divination. Further, the man had not been accounted for earlier. In fact, his daughter had been sitting next to Kitable. *Keeping an eye on me?*

He had let Shimmer listen in as he trapped Seria. He never shared spells, and he certainly had no patience for other wizards listening to his casting. Why allow her into the tent at all? He had not needed her aid. She had been a distraction at a time when he should have been focused on his enemy.

Her, the distraction? Kitable mused. Her father, a deception?

Bile rose in his throat. *I called for their help! I brought them to Tohmas to save Carsh.* Kitable had forgotten his usual prudence and trusted them. Would they have truly helped, had Darak and Kitable not been present to keep them honest?

If he had been deceived, whether by her distracting flirtations or by Dust's pill, he had damned everyone in HillTop.

He had to know where their loyalties lay, and he had to know now. If they had betrayed him and endangered the camp, they would die.

By the time he reached the Match and Mixer shop, doubt had snuck into Kitable's mind. He felt good. The effects of the Rejuv pill seemed to be lingering. *Would they not have sought to poison me, given the opportunity?*

He had to know.

The door was warded and locked but not much of an obstacle. He wanted them off their guard. No delays. No escape. No chance to summon aid.

Kitable's Eight-layered Dispel hit the door, followed instantly by an Incursion spell. Both the locks and wards fell clear as Kitable pushed opened the door.

Shimmer rolled out of her hammock and landed crouched on the floor in half-awake confusion. Her thin underclothes fell tight around her, her unbound hair creating a halo of red.

Her father lifted his head over the edge of his hammock, large bags under his eyes illuminated in the limited light through the window.

"What happened? What's wrong?" Shimmer asked.

The moment Dust moved to stand, Kitable threw a Force Cage around him. With an undefended target, it was easy to encircle the apothecary tightly and pin his hands at his side. The daughter gave a surprised cry and seemed to consider casting, but with reluctance, she stopped herself.

For the best.. Had she opposed him, he would have targeted her next.

Kitable's voice sounded somehow less like him "I have three wizards working against me, only two of which I have faces to. I may be wrong..."

"You *are* wrong," the apothecary objected from within his cage.

"...but I have to be certain."

Shimmer's face was red to match her hair. "You cannot believe either of us—"

"You were keeping an eye on me, Weaver," Kitable said, glaring at the scantily-clad woman. "And your father was nowhere to be seen when the ward was disrupted. When you spoke of your father, the prisoner thought of her lover! Then the moment I left, she escaped. Suspicious to say the least!"

Shimmer pressed her lips, her eyes flitting from her held father to Kitable. He read her expression as both furious and calculating. She was going to defend her father. Only enervation held her back.

Unlike his daughter, Dust remained calm. His voice was smooth. "I am no ally to DoomDragon, Master Kitable."

"Then provide an alibi for tonight. If, under a Lie Light, she can attest to your—"

"No." Dust shook his head within the confines of the spell. "I cannot, for his sake."

"Then I will take a Geas," Kitable declared. "I need to make sure Carsh's poisoning remains a secret regardless."

Silence followed. The spell itself would be complicated to cast, but he was, thanks to the Rejuv pill, capable of doing it twice tonight if he needed to.

Shimmer's face blanched. Dust fell into an uneasy silence.

"A Geas requires a willing target," Shimmer said, her voice tense. "Neither of us are willing."

"A thought creation, and you will be. You can accept, or I will force it upon you."

Dust gritted his teeth, nodding thoughtfully. He opened his mouth to speak, but Shimmer interrupted.

"No," she said tensely. Her steady stare met Kitable's. With each word, she seethed. "If you want to track us from a distance, develop a definition of us. If you want to bind us, break down our defenses. If you want to question our loyalties, cast a Lie Light or a Contingency. I will not permit a Geas on either of us."

She was no match for him at the best of times, and she was enervated worse than he was. Kitable could force it. Her determination was not a true barrier.

NORTHLANDER

But as he considered what spells to activate, she spoke again in a soft voice that made him hesitate.

"Please think about what you are suggesting, Master Kitable. You would never accept the same on yourself."

"My loyalty is not in question."

The bemused voice of the apothecary replied from the hammock, "Nor is mine as far as I am concerned!"

Shimmer pressed on. "You are suggesting binding us. No defenses. No protection. You would be able to see our thoughts, even alter them. You could kill us without even having to get up from your seat! There must be an alternative. Please. A Lie Light—"

"Your vardo is likely warded," he refused. He had considered the idea and dismissed it during his walk.

"Not against—"

"That cannot be proven."

"Use a Contingency then. It was your demon-cursed invention anyway."

Her idea had merit. It would easier to cast and only short-term. He would know instantly if the man was a traitor and avoid an unnecessary strain on his already-stretched reserves.

Although he hesitated because it was Shimmer's suggestion, her dogged stance convinced him. She was going to fight him if he tried to Geas either of them. In her state, it would kill her. That, for a reason he did not understand, suddenly seemed like a terrible waste.

"Fine," Kitable grumbled. "But I will not cast in your home."

He attached a binding to the Force Cage and pulled it out the door behind him, dragging Dust out with his hammock. Shimmer followed. Once clear of the vardo, he hit the apothecary with an Eight-layered Dispel, releasing him from the Force Cage and destroying all remaining hovering spells. The apothecary stood up and untangled himself from the hammock, making no attempt to run.

Kitable cast the Contingency with Shimmer listening, wanting her to hear it. Even when he set the consequence of a lie to be a Four-way Destructive spell that would certainly kill her father, she did not move.

The spell locked onto Dust, and he flinched. Feeling no warning was required, Kitable demanded, "Whom do you serve?"

"I have no loyalty to DoomDragon," Dust replied, and the lack of his immediate death confirmed he spoke truthfully.

"Are you loyal to Prince Tohmas?"

The apothecary smiled sadly. "I have no loyalty to Prince Tohmas, Master Kitable. I am not sworn to him like you are. I like the man, but my loyalty is to myself and to my daughter."

"Did you disrupt the wards around Prince Tohmas?"

"I did not disrupt any wards placed to protect Prince Tohmas Galanth."

The knot in Kitable's stomach began to release. "Did you help the caster Seria?"

"If I have met a woman called Seria before, I do not remember, Master Kitable. Maybe under another name?"

"Have you slept with her?"

"Possibly," Dust admitted. Nearby, Shimmer rolled her eyes, but a smile came to her lips. "If you don't know another name, can you give me a description?"

After Kitable described the woman, Dust shook his head. "Don't think I've ever had a lover that short. I prefer someone with reach."

Having found nothing else, Kitable let the spell drop and turned to the daughter.

He had been wrong. Dust was innocent. Whoever the third caster was, it was not the Weavers.

When he faced Shimmer, she pushed herself up and met his stare squarely, belying how enervated she still was.

"Satisfied?" she asked in an almost playful voice.

"No."

She sighed, but she was smiling. "But you never will be, will you? You survive by being the first one to attack, and that means jumping to conclusions as fast as you can." Shimmer's voice was soft, not accusatory, but Kitable felt momentarily shamed. "Not all wizards try to kill each other."

He wanted to hate her. It was simpler when other casters were his enemy and he killed them before they killed him. *Where do Shimmer Weaver and her father fit in this if not as enemies?*

"You are the one following Master Clarin," he countered, but the comment made her laugh.

The sound brought a smile to his face despite himself. He quickly removed the evidence of amusement.

"So, we are a little paranoid ourselves. We have something in common. Why is it no wizard can trust another?"

Clarin did, Kitable realized. Clarin had always trusted Kitable, even leaning on him during times of vulnerability. He had let the Weavers stay in BellRoost without suspicion. Somehow, Clarin alone had been immune to the animosity that grew between wizards.

Perhaps there is merit in that. Tonight, at least, he had found an ally. They had helped save Carsh. Kitable's trust in them had not been entirely misplaced.

"Go about your business, Weaver. I will be watching you."

To his back, she replied, "I hope you like what you see."

She could not have seen his smile as he walked away. This time, he let it remain.

One prince captured. Both prime protectors injured but not dead. The Galanth wizard enervated.

Darknim sorted the tokens on the table. The northern approach to the camp—apparently the Esparans were calling the camp HillTop—was protected by pits and traps, and the eastern slope was too narrow for significant forces. The south cliffs were no longer an insurmountable problem, since the Galanth wizards were enervated. His warriors could attack from the south and west, and Tohmas would have nowhere to go but through his own traps. Darknim could probably get some Northlanders directly Relocated into the HillTop too, so long as Master Terant was not too worn.

It was a poor substitute for simply assassinating Prince Tohmas as Darknim had planned, but it would do under the circumstances.

Darknim felt his pendant grow heavy as he sat at his table. When he brought a hand to the symbol, his fingers warmed to the touch of magic. A cloudy purple aura encircled the pendant hanging around his neck.

He knew little about magic but guessed the pendant was working like the chest the Circle of the Raven had once used to track Tohmas' army. Master Terant had assured him the item was protected from any

besides his allies, so the binding must have been the master wizard or Prince Marfaie himself.

Darknim waited, expecting a message from Marfaie. Instead, the magic continued to rise. He recognized the colors as they flashed—a Relocation spell.

Someone was coming to visit without even the courtesy of announcing themselves. As far as he was aware, none of the casters knew Darknim could see magic auras. This intruder was intending on taking Darknim by surprise.

Darknim waited for the person to appear opposite him at the table. Before the wizard could move, DoomDragon snapped his ax out, stopping it only a finger's breadth from Master Terant's neck.

The master wizard flinched. Shields may have prevented the ax strike from landing, but the reflex satisfied Darknim.

"Rather rude," Terant said with a sneer, gingerly pushing the ax away with a finger.

"Next time, use the door," Darknim replied, allowing his blade to be directed away. He placed the ax on the table within easy reach. Since their disagreement about Tothonar, Darknim had no humor for the arrogant caster.

"In a bad mood, are we, DoomDragon?" Terant asked, a sickening smile on his thin face. His usually well-kept appearance was ruffled, but Darknim knew that smile well; Terant was delivering news he expected to annoy Darknim. *Why else would you come in person if not to witness my reaction?*

Darknim glanced at the entrance and spotted a white aura surrounding both the door and the walls of the tent. Sounds would not escape now, keeping their conflict private from the Hunters.

"Get to the point. I have work to do." Darknim took his seat.

"Actually, you don't," Terant replied, leaning over the table and picking up a token to admire. In doing so, he disrupted the careful piles. "Prince Marfaie commands you wait."

"Why?" he snapped, on his feet once more and looming over Terant from across the table. Unfortunately, Master Terant was not easy to intimidate.

"We ensured Sol's brothers heard of his predicament. Prince Barnon has left Rabarch, heading north with his soldiers," Terant said sweetly.

"Better then that I kill Tohmas now lest he be strengthened by new allies," Darknim objected.

"But if Tohmas dies, Barnon has no rally point. He may not come. And our spies say Dragal is also considering joining despite his own failing health."

"We have Sol as bait. They would come for him even if their nephew lies dead."

Looking smug, the master wizard tsked. "Oh, Darknim, little dragon, don't you see that they are only now joining because they think they have a chance? Tohmas has given them the impression they can win. For now, we need him. Once the other sons of Zayban have arrived, demand a ransom for Sol."

Darknim clenched his teeth, wanting to tell the wizard to fly up a dragon's backside, but he censored himself. He had been fighting for this since Barrow's Hills, slowly getting revenge for the many lives lost. He had been told to win this war. That meant striking now.

But he was forbidden from doing so.

"Tohmas will not be fooled by a ransom offer," Darknim pointed out.

"He doesn't have to be. His refusal will alienate him from his uncles, especially if we ensure Prince Barnon and Prince Dragal knows Tohmas' rejection condemns their brother. We tried it your way, and it failed. Now, we do it our way."

Darknim glared at Terant, hating how much pleasure the wizard took in delivering the frustrating news. "I could take him down now," he said through clenched teeth.

Terant waved him off dismissively. "So could I. Kitable has been forced to ask for aid. He leaves Tohmas under Clarin's protection now."

"When Clarin watches, Carsh is always on hand," DoomDragon corrected. He had seen that opportunity but could not bring himself to rely on it. He had seen Carsh fight. Even when he watched them now through the Circle, Carsh kept a skeptical eye on Clarin at all times. There was no trust there to be exploited.

For once, Terant lost his smile. "Clarin can kill both Tohmas and his prime protector upon request," he snapped. "You have not been fooled by the ruse he plays against the Galanth, have you? That Rydan is no match for a wizard like Clarin."

It was hard enough to have his prize lost, but to know that Master Terant was taking it for himself irked Darknim more. He wanted to shout at Prince Tohmas for being so easily misled. The man deserved better than to die by treachery.

"Is that pride I hear?" Darknim asked spitefully. "You do not usually show such devotion to any of your students."

Terant's glare narrowed on Darknim, his jaw clenched to cut off more tempting retorts. Instead, the master wizard said, "You are commanded to wait for Prince Barnon to join the fight. Then, demand ransom. And if Prince Dragal decides to follow into the north, we wait for him. Are we understood, little dragon?"

Darknim nodded once. His pendant seemed to pull him down as he retook his seat.

"Then I will leave you to your waiting. Good day, Darknim."

Magic flashed through the air, leaving Darknim seeing spots of light as Terant vanished. The purple light and the weight faded from the pendant.

Darknim recounted the stone tokens representing the dead and laid them out. He sorted the remaining tokens into new stacks, focusing on defense, not offense.

He was set for a winter siege—he had no worries about supplies or weather while the Circle aided him—but boredom would threaten his ranks. Still, the orders were clear. The sons of Zayban would come.

For the first time in ten years, Prince Marfaie's vengeance was making progress, and yet Darknim was disappointed. He could not decide who—Marfaie or Tohmas—was disappointing him more.

If he failed to recognize the danger in his own ranks, Prince Tohmas deserved his undignified death at the hands of a traitor.

Chapter 10

Without wind, the thick clouds choked the sky, granite-grey by day and pitch black by night. In the mooncycles after Sol's capture, it snowed. Tohmas' men kept warm by clearing the snow from the defenses and stacking the snow around the tents. The extra layers insulated them surprisingly well against the cold.

Prince Barnon of Rabarch and his soldiers arrived early in the winter, rushing DoomDragon's fighters from the west. They pushed through and joined HillTop with minimal losses. Tohmas was not deceived; DoomDragon had allowed the youngest son of Zayban to join him. While it bolstered their forces by a few thousand, it put extra strain on his resources for a longer siege and, most importantly, divided command on the hill once more.

Time passed as slow as honey in the cold. Skirmishes up or down the hill interrupted frequently enough to keep both sides vigilant. They also helped break up the monotony of their trapped position.

By the end of the Eighth Mooncycle, winter lightened. In the south, it would have started to thaw before the Ninth cycle, but here, where the grey sky lightened only around midday and sunset followed only a few candles later, the snow and ice lingered.

Supplies ran low. DoomDragon's Northlanders had set a new camp atop the frozen lake, cutting off travel via river for supply for escape. Kitable and Clarin warned against bringing anything in magically; lowering the wards could have disastrous effects. And moving any

significant amount of supplies would sap the wizard performing the feat, possibly opening them for attack. Only the deaths from the raids and disease made the supplies stretch.

At the first indication of thaw, Tohmas met with Barnon in his tent. The horn, a *gef* from DoomDragon, hung across one of the chairs at the table. Every time he called his soldiers together, they took turns avoiding the chair.

Tohmas took the seat, the press of the string against his back reminding him of the shrewdness of his enemy.

As soon as Barnon arrived, Tohmas remembered why he had resented Sol so much during the earlier part of the campaign.

He did not sit but paced like an agitated schoolboy denied allowance. "You should have told me they offered ransom for Sol!" he snapped immediately. His prime protector slunk back to the tent wall, giving his prince space.

Offered? I would have said "demanded." And how did DoomDragon get that information to Barnon? Another spy for Carsh to kill? Carsh had not been complaining about any effects from the poison, although Tohmas still worried. He would probably enjoy the assignment.

Bored with the conversation already, Tohmas remained seated and removed his mitts to free his hands. "And what would you have done if I had?"

"Sol is my brother and your uncle. We could have paid that barbarian off!" Barnon paced the length of the tent then pivoted back sharply. His thick felt coat fell open as he spun. He was sweating. *Did he run? Or is it just the agitation?*

Tohmas folded his mitts on the table calmly. "And then he would have taken the money and supplies and left us with nothing, Prince Barnon. Do you not think it's strange that he waited until *now* to make the demand? If we are careful, we have enough supplies to make it through. If we are careless, we do not. Hungry soldiers do not fight."

"But Sol would be safe," the youngest son of Zayban protested.

"No," Tohmas corrected. "They would not return him for a handful of horses and our supplies."

"We could try," Clarin argued lightly, and Tohmas glared at the Prime Protector of Solta. He had almost forgotten the wizard was standing against the wall. Kitable had insisted on having one of them present

at all times, although the majority of the time the Master Wizard of Galanth took care of it himself. Whenever he couldn't, Clarin attended. He usually stayed silent. Tohmas preferred that.

Since the loss of Sol, Clarin had never been without Spell Sight, giving him a constant flicking, color-filled gaze. Tohmas could not remember what color the wizard's eyes were naturally. With his magic, he required no additional clothing despite the cold, although his sandals were now solid shoes.

"It will not work," Tohmas answered.

"We will not know until we try," Clarin pushed.

"It will not work, and that is final. Mind your place, Prime Protector Severin."

The wizard opened his mouth to speak—Sol's protection was indeed his place—but Carsh inched forward. Clarin flinched back. His mouth closed.

Tohmas turned his attention to the other prince. Prince Barnon might have been the youngest of Tohmas' uncles, but he was still more than a decade Tohmas' elder. Barnon had been a teenager when he inherited Rabarch from his father. Defending the land had fallen to Zayban's allies. In the years since, Barnon had fought no real wars.

I have more experience than the whole family now, Tohmas mused.

Tohmas took a slow breath to calm his voice. He spoke evenly despite his irritation. "Even if I believed DoomDragon would honor those ransom conditions, which I do not, I will not have my warriors starving for the sake of one person."

"He is the Prince of Solta," Barnon objected.

Tohmas sneered. "He is just one man."

"He is your uncle!"

"He is just one man," Tohmas repeated.

Silence filled the tent.

Barnon let out an exasperated sigh and sat beside Tohmas at the table, frowning like a chastised child.

Behind Barnon, Carsh glared down at the prince, and Tohmas shared his pessimism. *Are Barnon's soldiers worth the headache?*

He hoped so. Nothing else seemed to be working. Inac had turned her gaze from them. Celebrant Loni was missing. Sedgan claimed she had gone on a quest before the first snowfall and would return when the

Goddess willed. Totho was shunning them, and no one spoke of Ocea or Pari. In the eyes of the gods, Tohmas was vulnerable.

"Sol spoke highly of you," Barnon interrupted Tohmas' thoughts. "Whenever we talked through Clarin, he commended you. He told me that you were making progress against DoomDragon and that you were making your father so proud. I came up here because of what he said."

Deference was not what Tohmas had expected. Barnon did not have Sol's confidence at all.

Tohmas smiled, and he hoped it looked comforting. "Then trust me. We cannot bargain with DoomDragon. We are not ready to deal the blow we need. We must wait."

"Wait?" the Prince of Rabarch echoed. "What are we waiting for?"

"You will see."

Protector Sanba would have delivered his message to Chief Tamv by now. The reinforcements were late, perhaps bogged down by bad weather and hostile terrain, but they had to be coming. And Tohmas had made arrangements with the Weavers. Everything was ready. They would deal the final blow to DoomDragon when the Rydans arrived.

Barnon nodded, suddenly content. His acceptance gained depth and confidence. Like a celebrant before an altar, Barnon's expression was one of faith.

It was a disquieting realization.

Shimmer walked among prostitutes, thieves, and thugs in the night. She kept her head high and her stride confident. A dozen spells hovered around her, and hundreds more awaited in her memory. No mugger or pickpocket dared cross her path.

Despite the snow and the dangerous company found in Fixer City at night, she walked. Walking helped her think, and she needed to think.

Fixer City, kept stationary through the changing seasons, had settled into a sort of village. Packed roads wove between the waggons. Snowbanks buried the wheels, making the waggons permanent snow sculptures in the fresh moonlight. Tonight, the half-moon finally broke through the stormy skies, its light brightened by the reflections off the ice and snow.

HillTop had formed in the late summer, and it had weathered the autumn with poise. Winter was a different matter. Rumors said Prince Tohmas had run out of tricks and was waiting for winter's end, but Shimmer knew differently; Prince Tohmas had commissioned the order in her bag.

It still left her uneasy. She had used new herbs she had never dared to touch before to make the order.

Her father had not only known how to use them; he had been able to source them quickly. It worried her.

Comfortingly, Shimmer carried a vial of the antidote. She was uncertain if they intended to use it.

As she walked, she wondered what Prince Tohmas was going to do with poisoned knives and whether it would change anything for her and her father. Winter had pinned them. After Prince Barnon's arrival, the Northlanders had even claimed the frozen lake. Tohmas' forces were surrounded.

Not much had happened for too long. The cold seemed likely to linger through the Ninth Mooncycle and into the new year.

Shimmer was reconsidering her reasons for staying when she walked into an area of potent magic. Shimmer froze in anticipation, but nothing followed. Curious, she activated Spell Sight. To her surprise, she saw no auras.

Instead of searching with her sight, Shimmer concentrated on feeling for the magic. One hand extended, she followed the increasing power to her right for a dozen steps.

Light appeared, a multitude of magic auras glowing before her. The brightness of the combinations made her step back in amazement, and in that moment, they vanished.

It's a wall, she realized. Kitable had put up a shield against Spell Sight to hide his defenses.

The master wizard had been in semi-hiding since the night Prince Sol vanished, moving his vardo often. Although she spied on him often enough to know he was alive and well, their paths had not otherwise crossed. Perhaps it was time to change that.

She stepped forward again to admire the auras then walked around the otherwise nondescript vardo. At the front, the carthorses were blanketed and tethered. Kitable's deaf waggon driver, Colt, sat at a fire at the

base of the vardo's steps. His fire, unlike others that burned dung and scraps, was a clean yellow with no visible fuel.

Of course, Master Kitable would not need firewood.

As Shimmer watched, a spell appeared above the vardo. At first, she thought it a Sending but reconsidered when it continued to develop. It had to be a full Scry.

It broke free of the vardo and shot off to the north.

Her curiosity flared to the strength of a bonfire. She knew that spell. She could follow him.

When she stepped into the campfire circle, the waggon driver's half-smile welcomed her. He extended the enchanted stone that allowed him to hear her, recognizing her.

With one hand on the stone, she asked, "May I share your fire for a short while?"

"You are welcome," Colt replied. He shyly pocketed his stone and returned to his cooking.

Thanking him, Shimmer settled in front of the fire on a stone she assumed usually accommodated Kitable.

The Scry required a full casting, leaving her far behind Kitable by the time she pulled her consciousness from her body. She could still follow him. Instead of disguising the thread binding his wandering mind to his body, Master Kitable had defended it with a dozen spells. The anchor glowed like a row of firebugs because of her Spell Sight.

Knowing she would never be able to defend her own anchor sufficiently, Shimmer made it as thin as possible. Next to Kitable's brilliant thread, she thought it effective camouflage.

Following Kitable's thread, Shimmer sent her consciousness north. It took about a quartercandle to leave the fields of the Princedom of Solta. She had no concept of distance except that she recognized when she passed over BellRoost. The next landmark was the deserted ruins of a town she did not know. Snow covered the shambled shells of the houses and empty streets. A fountain buried in snow reminded her of Gaidol, making her believe the ruins were Esparan, not Northlander. Despite its abandonment, the city looked peaceful under the snow.

Since Kitable's spell was nowhere in sight, she moved on and did not linger over any of the other broken cities passing below her in her travels. No life stirred among the rubble.

At the third city along the road markers they seemed to be following, Shimmer's Scry slipped her hold. A full candle had passed, and she had seen no sign of Kitable. She could no longer concentrate well enough to maintain the Scry. It was time to go back. She would not catch up with him today.

Instead of retracing her steps, Shimmer braced herself and let the spell drop. Her mind reeling, she was suddenly back in HillTop, the waggon driver looking up at her from where he was oiling the harnesses, having finished eating. It did not surprise her that Kitable's coachman would be able to sense magic, so she merely smiled at him and pushed to her feet.

"Thank you, Colt," she said, bowing to him. She winked and blew him a kiss to be sure he understood her meaning.

Shimmer was rapidly on her way again, her steps lighter. Although she had not even caught a glimpse of her wizard, her heart felt brightened. The abandoned cities had reminded her why the forces of Galanth were in Solta. Knowing that Kitable was still working against their enemy made the winter feel less cold.

Tohmas would have a good reason for his purchased poison.

As Darknim had predicted, the ransom was rejected. Tohmas refused it without telling Barnon, but Darknim made sure the Prince of Rabarch found out that Prince Sol had been damned by his nephew. To Darknim's irritation, it seemed to have little effect; Prince Barnon remained loyal to his nephew. Tohmas defended his actions well.

Just when Darknim thought his chance would come, Master Terant delivered more bad news; Prince Dragal had decided to come north. Darknim was to keep Tohmas pinned, harassing him when it seemed likely to be in his favor, but was forbidden from doing anything else.

Prince Dragal traveled with only a few hundred men, Darknim heard. *Like a man coming to die.* The imminent arrival of another son of Zayban pleased Prince Marfaie immensely. At last, they had progress.

Darknim was to wait for all the princes. Then, and only then, could he destroy the entire family.

Terant's visit was followed immediately by a call from the Circle of the Raven. He left his whale-skin tent immediately.

As he approached the Earth Lodge, he pulled his ax from his shoulders, knowing the handle of the ax would otherwise gouge the low roof of the corridor when he ducked within.

But before he could enter, Seria, breathless from a run, called to him. "A quick matter of business," she said, stopping before him. She looked as pleased as Terant had.

"Your master already told me," Darknim groused.

"New information, DoomDragon. Prince Marfaie asked I speak to you directly."

"He knows how to find me. Why send it through you?" *Why send it through either of you? Am I too much of a nuisance to speak directly to?*

"I suspect he wishes to be certain you obey him, DoomDragon." Her voice was light, teasing.

"And when have I given him cause to doubt me?" His thoughts were treacherous, but he could not stop them. The constant constraints and disrespect wore on his patience. *Have my ten years of service to Prince Marfaie earned me no respect or trust?*

"He says that you've failed to justify the continual presence of your guest. He commands the Galanth celebrant be slain."

Darknim froze, his grip tight on the handle of his ax. He wanted to object, but it would only serve to justify the prince's failing faith in him. Further, if he was going to refuse, he would do so to Marfaie, not to the prince's messenger.

"If you are unwilling to do it, I am to do it for you," Seria said when he paused. Delighted, she sounded like she might enjoy the task.

Darknim cut off a growl and replied, "I will do it. Tothonar is my guest."

He could not look at her. He headed down the dark tunnel into the Circle's chamber while Seria stormed away.

Elder Ela's golden eyes lifted from among her feathers when Darknim ducked into the cavernous room. He stood there for a long while, silent. Despite his many dealings with the Circle of the Raven, he never knew where to start. All too often, Elder Ela knew his purpose better than he did himself.

The pool was shaped like a rabbit in full run this time. The cold within the cavern was the same as outside, although the air was without piercing wind. They had built the Earth Lodge into a permanent structure, held by stacked stones and mud, not snow and ice. It reminded Darknim of meeting the Circle for the first time in his village when they had given him the ax. The lodges had been smaller, temporary things since. It felt good to have a strong building to shelter the Circle as they waited for permission to take the hill camp.

"You requested me," he said, eyeing the purple light connecting the Circle together. "But I can see you are Linking. Shall I come back another time?"

"You wish to speak to us and so are welcome," Ela said.

"You asked me here before I even knew I had cause to request a meeting. How..."

Darknim's gaze paused on the youngest Elder. Tril had returned to his place as the seat of divination with fortitude, his beard having gained more white in the last mooncycle.

"We knew you would need advice," Elder Tril said.

"You used to speak of possibilities, Elder Tril. Now you speak with certainty. I did not know that was possible for the Circle of the Raven."

The smile beneath Elder Tril's beard showed long canines, but it was Elder Ela who spoke. "You have a harpoon in your side, dragon. Shall we tell you who pulls you where you do not wish to go?"

He shook his head. "To what end, Elder? I know his face well."

The Circle members nodded when Elder Ela did, all at the same speed. "We see that you do. We feared you would be blaming your pain on the wrong side of the borders, DoomDragon, but the white of your hair is well earned. You are not so easily misled."

Her words brought him no comfort. DoomDragon was beginning to suspect his enemy was not the people cornered on the hill but was where his ax was committed.

Yet here, in the Circle's presence, his treacherous words were safe to speak aloud. They would know them anyway.

Darknim released his frustration. "Our people die for Prince Marfaie's cause, and still, he doubts me. I am weary. I need to be free of this barbed alliance. Help me find the way."

When a thought went out, a pulse of purple light flashed along the Linking. The Circle elders fixed their semi-bestial stares on him.

"You are divided within," Elder Cark said in her high, singing voice. "Warriors will not follow a divided soul."

"I stand facing the wind," Darknim agreed. "My word and my actions point me one way, but the gods now whisper disapproval. The Goddess Inac stands with my enemy."

"She is but one of four," Cark replied.

"I do not know what Water or Earth wish of me, for they hide their faces, but I had thought the Winter Star with us until today."

There was surprise in Ela's voice when she finished the thought, having seen Darknim's mind. "He commands the death of the Wind."

The Circle stirred uneasily. Darknim shared their fear. A slight against Totho's celebrant was a slight against the god. *How can we expect to survive the winter if we offend the God of Wind?*

"And so you seek our council," Elder Tril said, his smile victorious.

"The arrival of Tothonar was a good omen. He is an emissary from the Winter Star, I am certain, but now I am commanded to slay him. I have delayed in obeying for as long as I can."

"The Winter Star will curse you should you harm one of his messengers," Ela confirmed.

"No victory will ever find you should you allow the Wind to die by your hand, DoomDragon. I see no other future but that, should Tothonar die." The declaration was made with such conviction, Darknim stared at Elder Tril once more. Divinations had never been so absolute.

Darknim shook his head to clear it. "I will not argue with anything you have told me, for you echo my own heart, but tell me what I might do! This is an ice crevice. I am trapped."

In the silence, the wind howled outside the cavern as if in mourning. It was painfully fitting.

He could not kill the Wind Celebrant. His belief in the gods discouraged it, but his friendship with Tothonar completely forbid it. And yet, he must obey Prince Marfaie.

"There is a way," Elder Tril said cautiously. "It must be done carefully, but it would silence Tothonar. He would no longer be a threat, and his life would be safe."

Darknim cocked his head in surprise. "How? Even if I cut his tongue, wizards can take a man's thoughts."

"Not if his faith is strong enough," Tril explained, his expression confused as if every word was occurring to him as an individual thought and he did not yet know how they went together. "There is a way," he repeated.

Does he know he already said that? Darknim wondered. It did not matter. If there was a way, Darknim would take it. "This war makes less sense as the days pass. A family that murders each other would not be expected to chase after a lost member. Why would my patron have expected the princes to come for Sol? Why was he correct?"

"Is it their cruelty or the compassion of the sons of Zayban we have misjudged?" Tril asked.

"Tothonar will give me that answer," Darknim decided. It was Tothonar's only hope. "Tell me what I must do."

Tril's eyes focused, and his expression was suddenly sad. "It is not pleasant, but it will save his life."

"So be it," Darknim answered.

Behind him, the wind sang across the entrance.

Chapter II

Seria hated the cold. She wore every piece of clothing she owned, yet the wind over the lake still gave her gooseflesh. There had been warmer days of late, enough that she had been hoping for spring. But the season remained frigid, keeping the lake frozen.

DoomDragon had commanded her to check the lake camp to get her out of the way, she was certain, and that made the cold worse. He was a terrible liar, perhaps because he seldom practiced the art. For the last mooncycle, Seria reminded the Northlander commander daily to kill Tothonar. He had procrastinated and dithered, claiming other duties stole his attention. He directed raids against Prince Tohmas, reassigned Hunter scouts to watch for Prince Dragal Galanth's arrival, and visited the Circle of the Raven often. But Seria kept reminding him, and finally, that morning, he announced his intention to slay the Galanth Celebrant. The decision put him in a sour mood. Knowing he was still reluctant, Seria placed a Scry to track his progress as he took the celebrant away.

As she walked along the frozen edge of camp on the lake, her feet crunching over thick ice, Seria's magic kept one eye on DoomDragon and Tothonar. She expected a trick. Why else would he take Tothonar to the far edge of the cliffs facing Tohmas' camp? She looked forward to catching the Northlander.

Through her Scry, Seria heard DoomDragon tell Tothonar of his orders. The celebrant sighed, and that was all. He could have tried to flee,

even if he had no hope of escaping, but the Galanth Celebrant accepted DoomDragon's decision emotionlessly.

"The most important thing is that you be silenced," DoomDragon said. "Would you rather die or accept silence?"

"'I am a whisper and a spirit,'" the celebrant replied cryptically.

DoomDragon nodded as if he understood.

Seria watched out of a sense of duty. She expected an execution under the dragon-wing ax, but instead, what she saw turned her stomach.

DoomDragon cut Tothonar's hands at the wrist, but the celebrant made not a sound. The Northlander finished by taking the man's tongue, and still the celebrant was placid. Done, DoomDragon turned his back on the huddled form and walked away, leaving the man alive but maimed.

In the snow, it was going to be terrible death. It seemed uncharacteristically cruel for DoomDragon.

Seria paused and focused on the Scry. Tothonar was still breathing, at least for now. There was not as much blood from his severed wrists as she would have expected. She checked but saw no magic. *Do I have to finish this?* The celebrant would die slowly. Should she watch the entire time, to be sure? She was already bored.

Feeling the hairs on her neck stand up, Seria pulled her thoughts from the Scry briefly. A man stood in the middle of a row of pickets, staring at her from across the defenses.

She had reached the farthest south point of the camp where cut trees formed barricades at the edge of the lake. Behind her, the tents sagged with melted snow, and the daily cooking fires had been extinguished. The lone man struck her as odd. Where were the other Northlanders?

Covered in mismatched, unidentifiable pelts, the stranger tilted his hooded head as if sniffing the wind then lifted his gaze to hers. Fixing his stare, he slunk toward her like a stalking mountain cat.

Her blood became ice in her veins, and the feeling had nothing to do with the wind.

He must have thought her one of Tohmas' allies, so she called, "I stand with DoomDragon. Identify yourself!"

Although she did not see his hands move, a dagger deflected off a defense in front of her face. A second knife, then a third, followed in rapid succession. None succeeded in getting through.

Seria dropped her Scry. Tothonar would die with or without her intervention. Her attention was required here.

Calmly, Seria lifted her hand and activated a Dilapidating Dart spell. The Dart would knock even DoomDragon back several steps; the stranger would be knocked flat.

To her amazement, the intruder ducked the Dart and continued his approach.

Seria followed his movement with her extended hand. He had, she presumed, heard her speak while pointing and ducked instinctually. The Dart had no visible component. He could not have seen the spell.

"Vile demon," she spat. "You cannot surpass my defenses."

He was still advancing cautiously, but none of her words made him flinch. Certain he was unprepared for her next spell, she kept her voice even as if she was beginning a new sentence. "*Vahsin,*" she said, activating another Dilapidating Dart.

He threw himself into the snow and rolled clear of the spell.

For the first time, Seria's pulse accelerated.

He had deliberately dodged. How had he known the spell?

Another knife bounced off her defenses as he sprang up from the snow, a knife in each hand. She was suddenly reminded of another encounter with a lithe, muscled man.

He was not Prime Protector Carsh, but he was much like him.

Rydan.

She had been unable to use a Molded Shield since Kitable used it to track her, and her other defenses were not as comprehensive. She was not ready for a fight like this.

With a lunge, he closed the distance, snarling with sharpened teeth.

Seria activated her Relocation spell, grabbed the anchor in her tent, and vanished. A blink later, she had left the cold winds of the lake camp behind and was safely in her tent in the main camp.

She threw open the flap. She had to warn DoomDragon of the danger before the new arrival took them by surprise.

But DoomDragon had not yet returned from executing the celebrant.

"My turn to keep watch," Kitable told Clarin. He took up a place inside Prince Tohmas' tent, clearing the exit for the Soltan wizard to leave.

Clarin cocked his head wearily. Thick bags hung under his eyes. "You sure? You keep taking the longest shifts. Don't you sleep?"

Since Sol's abduction, Kitable could not justify leaving Tohmas undefended. He felt better when he took the late afternoon and night shifts, putting him beside Tohmas whenever Carsh wasn't on duty. Clarin also had the help of the full contingent of protectors during the day should he require it..

It had been a long winter. The days were short, the nights long, and both were freezing. Between keeping Tohmas safe and maintaining defenses over HillTop, Kitable wore thin.

But he saw no alternative.

"I'm sure. Go rest. Eyes are on us outside, remember." Wards kept them safe within the tent, but Kitable had sensed the Scrys on him outside. The reminder of the three wizards against them and their inexplicable inactivity worried him.

Tohmas continued his conversation with Prince Barnon, not acknowledging Clarin's departure. Carsh momentarily sheathed a blade, slipping it away for the briefest instant before returning it to his grip. He never felt safe enough to have only one blade in hand now. Tohmas' gaze flicked to Carsh, acknowledging the signal that Clarin was no longer close enough for Carsh to sense.

Holding up a hand to interrupt Prince Barnon briefly, Tohmas glanced at Kitable. "Anything new?" he asked, now able to discuss sensitive matters without Clarin overhearing. Had he waited because of Kitable's preference for privacy regarding magical affairs, or did he also not completely trust Clarin?

Nearly a mooncycle earlier, Kitable had snuck past the defenses of the Northlanders and scryed without their interference. What he had seen had amazed him; instead of burned out, ravaged Esparan villages and cities, there were thriving cities in the north. He had been trying to repeat the feat to better understand where these cities were and why the Northlanders had not raided them, but he had thus far failed. Despite being confident the burnt-out hollows of abandoned homes and streets in every northern city he scryed on were illusions, he could not see

through it. He did not even know how he had circumvented the illusions the one time he had.

Kitable shook his head. Nothing new. No success.

The prince went back to his conversation with Barnon.

While keeping one ear on them, Kitable mentally worked his counter for the Scry outside. If he could take it down, perhaps the same technique could be used on the illusions he kept running into.

In the middle of a question from Barnon, Tohmas and Carsh sat up sharply. Kitable snapped to attention but sensed no powers in the area. Barnon, oblivious, answered his own question and carried on the conversation alone.

"Carsh," Tohmas interrupted, his eyes on the entrance. "Did you hear...?"

The Rydan nodded. "Howl."

Kitable had heard a dog's howl as well, but he had not paid it any mind. There were many dogs in HillTop.

Barnon paused, his mouth open.

With hesitation Kitable was unaccustomed to seeing, Tohmas stood slowly and called, "Runnah!" A protector popped into the tent like a spring-loaded toy. "I need a live goat. I don't care how, but I need it now."

"A what?" Prince Barnon asked, but Tohmas did not seem to hear him. The protector, with a mildly baffled expression, left at a run.

Tohmas headed for the exit, passing Kitable. "Runnah!" came the next command, and another protector rushed in, stumbling back when he nearly ran headlong into Tohmas, who did not break stride as he left the tent. The protector caught the token thrown over Tohmas' shoulder. "I want every man in HillTop up and at arms, now. Have a runner sent to each guardian. I need them all at a full halt. Get me the Far Criers too. Geddit!"

Kitable followed him out, the baffled Prince Barnon joining him.

Tohmas changed to a light jog, his protectors falling into his wake.

Running behind the prince gave Kitable a chance to watch Carsh, and he was surprised to see the Rydan nigh-on skipping. While some could have made the movements seem joyous, in Carsh they signified readiness and, more importantly, recognition of danger.

Tohmas stopped above a central cleared region in HillTop usually used for drills. He turned to Barnon. "Give the same orders to your men.

Get them ready but have them stand at a full and unconditional halt. No one is to move unless I say so."

Barnon opened his mouth as if to question the order but then stopped, perhaps sensing Tohmas' urgency. "Do you want them assembled anywhere in particular?" he asked instead.

"Here," Tohmas replied. "Criers!" he shouted at the messengers who had followed with the protectors. "Once the soldiers are assembled, call a complete halt. Repeat it a dozen times if you have to, but no one is to move!"

As the men scurried around the tents, Kitable suddenly had the stare of his prince focused on him.

"You'd better drop your spells."

"Drop my what?" Kitable snapped, unable to rein himself in. "You cannot—"

"Kit, this will all fall apart if you are seen as a wizard right now," Tohmas replied with tension in his voice that snagged Kitable's attention.

By the time Kitable could form an answer, Tohmas had already taken the halter of a goat and moved away. Kitable had no idea where the protectors had found the creature, it being so late in the season. The owners would have not let it go for cheap.

"I hope you know what you're doing," Kitable grumbled. He still had magic items. But if he was seen by the scryers without spells...

With great pangs, Kitable identified every spell he had bound to himself and dismissed them. A feeling of unreserved fear crept in. He felt naked.

While Kitable pulled his castings apart, Prince Tohmas tied the goat to a log at the center of the open area. The soldiers assembled around him in layers. Their ranks filtered between waggons and tents on all sides, extending well beyond the drill grounds. They left a small place at the center clear for the prince and his goat.

The Far Criers sounded the full halt, and Kitable was pleased to see the soldiers straighten into a firm stance. Kitable glanced up, wondering if the enemy was watching. He felt like a bullseye was painted on his forehead.

Carsh following with a shifting, anxious skip, Tohmas stepped back from the goat and shouted, "Listen carefully! *No one* is to move. I don't

care what happens! I will personally gut anyone who steps or speaks out of turn!"

Tohmas returned to his place beside Kitable, leaving the goat a dozen paces ahead of them.

There was a long silence.

Tohmas and Carsh stood firmly among the soldiers but separated by a wall of protectors.

Kitable watched the goat, his mind tangled. *A holy rite? A sacrifice? What demonic magic is this?*

In heed of Tohmas' threat, the soldiers seemed unwilling to blink, let alone move. The goat's pawing at the ground was the only movement.

A towering figure stepped into the gap between the tents and the soldiers at halt. The pelt-covered man did not walk; he stalked. With each step he took coming up between two fyrds, his eyes were on the goat, mercifully paying no attention to the astonished gazes of the soldiers he passed.

A Rydan, Kitable recognized. He appeared more feral than most, but there was no doubt he was one of the Outlands' people.

The goat pulled against its halter when the stranger finally reached it, but it could not escape. The man circled the animal twice in inspection. Then, without a cry, the goat died. Kitable had not even seen the knife, yet the animal's throat was expertly cut when it fell.

The nearest Esparans flinched, but not one of them stepped back or spoke. Their stolidity became even more impressive when the intruder tilted his head back and howled like a wolf.

A shiver ran through Kitable's core at the inhuman call, but the army held their perfect halt, as did the princes and prime protectors overseeing them. Barnon flinched, but glancing at Tohmas reaffirmed his confidence, and he steadied.

More movement down the column caught Kitable's attention; a row of hounds, each as tall as a man's waist and covered in thick, dark fur, rushed toward the intruder. Behind the beasts, trotting calmly, came a woman.

With the furs covering her, it was only her pregnant belly that revealed her gender. Although slower than the hounds, once the woman was at the carcass, her snarl and kick sent the nearest hound cowering, and she had her turn at the meat.

The man in furs cut free a cursory piece of raw goat flesh and chewed it slowly as he wandered around the clearing, inspecting the soldiers. The thought of eating raw meat made Kitable's stomach roll, but he, like the forces of Espar, held his ground.

Halfway between the carcass and the prince, the intruder halted and narrowed his pale eyes directly on Kitable. The hunter fell back into an aggressive crouch. A knife was visible in his hand.

The shiver he had felt at the howl shot through Kitable again.

"*Naw Flya!*" Carsh suddenly shouted from his place on the other side of Tohmas. Kitable jumped at the harsh sounds. "*Naw Flya. 'Ee be bane o' Flya. And stand wid.*"

The intruder's stare shifted to Carsh, considering the words.

Kitable took the opportunity to lean over to Tohmas and ask, "What's going on? Do I need defenses?" The way the stranger looked at him was predatory. Kitable did not intend to be eaten.

Tohmas whispered back. "Don't cast; he'll kill you. Believe it or not, Carsh is defending you."

Kitable could not reply. Although they had not been at each other's throats recently, he had not expected the Rydan prime protector to ever warm up to him or his magic.

"*Wisavi*," Carsh added. "'*Ands wisavi.*"

"What's '*wisavi*?'" Kitable asked.

Tohmas cracked a small smile. "A wise man who advises a leader. It is a very prestigious post. I hope you like it, Wisavi Kitable."

"Is a wisavi allowed to use magic?"

Tohmas' smile vanished. "No more than any other Rydan."

"Meaning 'no.'"

"Meaning a big, emphatic 'no,' Kit, but he may see you as my responsibility. I forgot about your items. He probably picked up on them. Better than active spells though."

The intruder's cold stare passed over Kitable once more, and Kitable straightened. If he was to be a *wisavi*, he had to look the part.

"*Wisavi*," the intruder whispered in a disused voice, as if seeing if the word fit. "*Wisavi.*"

Carsh stepped up with a prince's confidence and pulled up the sleeve of the coat they had only recently convinced him to wear. Cold

as it was, the scars on his forearm stood out purple. One particular scar, from Carsh's elbow to his wrist, was prominent.

"*Wisavi*," Carsh insisted.

The intruder took a step back. Nodding, he pressed his right fist against his left forearm in a low salute. "*Arm stand. And?*"

The frigid stare landed on Tohmas.

The prince rotated his left hand to show the scar that crossed his palm.

Images of a handprint in blood flashed in Kitable's mind. When Tohmas had, twice now, made a standard, he marked it with a bloody handprint with a line across the palm. It suddenly occurred to Kitable that he had been identifying himself by the scar.

The stranger's right hand now pressed a fist into his left palm, and he gave a toothy grin.

He recognized Tohmas by that mark.

"*Tey come*," the Rydan throatily declared. "*Seten wa.*"

The hunter returned to his dogs.

The moment the stare of the stranger left Tohmas, the prince let out a sigh and closed his left hand. He took several steadying breaths before calling for the guardians.

"Fyrds of Flystead, Barmore, and Lariton, form up facing the west hill. Boro, stand as a reserve there. Arrow, you're taking east reserve. The rest of you, form up on the east. Push when I say, then pull back at my call. It'll be short, so don't go deep."

As the fighters rushed off, Kitable found himself staring down at the two Rydans and their dogs. His chill would not be shaken.

But as Carsh followed Tohmas off, Kitable found his voice. "Thank you, Carsh."

The prime protector shrugged, and with another glance at the dogs and two humans gorging themselves on raw goat, said, "Family."

Barnon watched in silent admiration. Sol had been right. After conversing with a feral man, Tohmas organized his forces into a powerful assault smoothly. With one charge, the combined forces pushed the Northlanders out of the west and off the frozen lake to the south. It helped that the enemy's camp on the lake apparently had no one on

the defenses. Barnon guessed the Rydans had been responsible for that unexpected advantage.

The last time Barnon commanded armies, he had been defending his princedom after his father's death with help from old family friends, seasoned warriors who had sworn to preserve Zayban's legacy. Watching Tohmas now made Barnon realize how little he had understood about those battles.

From the south, Rydan horses pounded into the Northlander lines, and the Northlanders broke under their hooves. It had not snowed recently; the packed ground provided ideal footing. In a hundred heartbeats, the blockade at the base of the west-facing hill was uprooted by the combined efforts of the Esparans and Rydans.

It was spectacular. Having never seen Rydans in battle, Barnon was surprised by their speed. Their horses towered over anything but a Trulin warhorse, and they seemingly enjoyed trampling their enemy. There were no saddles or bridles, yet the horses and riders moved as one through the trampled snow, spears flying ahead of them. The tangled mess of people resolved over time, leaving bodies strewn in red snow as the rush moved on toward the Northlanders' camp.

Everyone stopped at the barriers of DoomDragon's main camp as Tohmas had commanded. A large force of Northlanders, the burly DoomDragon among them, manned the barricades. The Rydans had lined up for a charge, an attack Barnon considered folly, when a horn cut through the air. The warhorses were brought up short—a feat in of itself.

The Esparans returned to HillTop. The Rydans collected behind the stolen defenses of the lake camp, their enormous warhorses among them. The Northlanders did not follow.

The lake camp, once the greatest obstacle to renewing HillTop's supplies, was now in Rydan hands.

Barnon could not stop grinning. The west hills behind the rocks provided a safe path down. They were, for the first time since he had arrived in HillTop, not cornered.

The Rydans appeared to be unpacking; the lake camp now belonged to them. As Barnon watched shelters be claimed by Rydans, a group of six Rydans headed up the hill toward Barnon. *No, not me*, Barnon realized. Prince Tohmas was waiting for them.

Are they mercenaries? How had Tohmas procured their services? And at what cost?

Master Kitable made a face and quietly said, "I think I had better be elsewhere. Call me if you need me." By the time Tohmas nodded, Kitable had already rushed away, leaving Carsh, Tohmas, and Barnon alone at the top of the hill.

The man at the head of the group of Rydans was burlier than Carsh but of equal height. His fur coat parted, showing off his thickly muscled, scarred chest decorated with a tattoo of a grinning, fanged jaw. Like all Rydans, they wore clumps of grass tied around their wrists.

Protectors edged in around Tohmas, but the prince waved them off and stepped forward with only Carsh at his side. In response, the lead Rydan put aside his double-bladed walking stick weapon. He pressed his right fist first to his left forearm then into his left hand. Finally, with enthusiasm, he punched his fist against his left collarbone.

Without a word, Tohmas and Carsh copied the final gesture, and the man grinned to reveal fangs matching his chest tattoo.

The Rydan gestured behind him.

Barnon had been mistaken; five Rydans had come up. The sixth person was Esparan. Tanned hides covered him as the Rydans escorted him to stand before Tohmas. Beneath the hides, torn cloth fluttered in the cold wind. The long beard, reaching to the man's sternum, was unkempt. Squinting, Barnon made out the dusty green and silver rope hanging from the man's shoulder. His hands bound, he was coated with filth from hairline to boot. Although thin, his legs were ropey and strong. His unkempt hair did not wave in the gusty wind, so thickly was it matted.

"Welcome home, Protector Sanba," Tohmas said.

"*Sta*!" Carsh snapped, wheeling to face the protectors in anticipation. Barnon checked over his shoulder. Sure enough, the protectors were reaching for weapons, but they paused obediently, their eyes leaving Carsh to stare at Tohmas expectantly.

Barnon had heard that Tohmas was fiercely protective of his sworn people. There had to be repercussions for treating a protector poorly, even if the offender was an ally.

Tohmas met the lead Rydan's eyes, and something seemed to pass between them. Alone, the Prince of Galanth stepped toward the bound

protector. The muscles along the Rydan leader's arms tensed like mooring knots holding a wave-swept boat, but his weapon remained lowered.

With deliberation, the prince pulled his knife and cut the ties that held the protector. No one moved.

The prisoner freed, Tohmas returned to the protectors. He did not assist the freed man. Instead, the protector pulled his shoulders square, flicked his wrists to limber them, and followed.

Protector Sanba took up a place behind the prince, perfectly duplicating the steady presence of the other protectors despite his stark appearance.

"Carsh," Tohmas invited softly.

Prime Protector Carsh advanced, and the Rydan leader came up to face him. Together, the two Rydans crouched into the slush to sit on their heels. When they started speaking, Barnon stopped listening. He could hardly understand Prime Protector Carsh when the man was making an effort in Esparan. Having two Rydans speak their native tongue at their native speed was a lost cause.

"You all right, Sanba?" Tohmas asked without turning.

"Stiff," the protector replied in a matched tone. "Wouldn't mind something other than wildwater to drink. Beyond that, fine."

Tohmas smirked, but the expression was quickly erased. "Go rest up," Tohmas said. The protector bowed to Tohmas' back, and the mass of protectors quickly encompassed him like a thick mattress enveloping a weary child.

An Esparan runner was admitted as Sanba left. Tohmas tore his eyes from the conversing Rydans to accept a token.

"Guardian Rusk requests you immediately, my Prince."

When Tohmas moved, Carsh cocked his head in silent inquiry. Tohmas shook his head, telling him to stay behind. Knowing he would learn nothing from the Rydans, Barnon followed Tohmas and the half of the protectors that went with him.

"Tohmas!" Carsh called as the princes left. "Tamv be 'ere."

Tohmas nodded.

"Who is Tamv?" Barnon asked once they were on their way, following the runner through the mud. The air was warmer, the snow underfoot turning to slush.

Without looking at him, Tohmas replied, "Chief of the Outlands."

"Which clan?"

"All of them."

Barnon would have asked more, but Guardian Rusk had spotted the Prince of Galanth and rushed to meet him. The one-eyed man had forgone any bandage over his blinded eye, and the milky-white half-gaze gave Barnon chills. Although it had to be cycles old, the scar that had blinded him still had the blue-pink of freshly stitched tissue, complete with pinched points where the sutures had been.

"He kept askin' for you," Guardian Rusk said, pointing into the crowd. A lone Rydan stood among the Esparans. Both the Rydan and the Esparans held their blades in readiness, an uncertain tension between them. The Rydan appeared to be guarding a body robed in white that lay at his feet.

The Rydan was a boy about fifteen and had no tattoo on his chest. Seeing Tohmas, he grinned wide and punched his right hand into his left palm. He did not release his weapon—a long dagger—to do so.

It marked the second time Rydans had used the gesture to Tohmas. A salute?

The boy spoke, but Barnon could not decipher the rattling words. Tohmas gave a nod as acknowledgement then move up and crouched over the body in the snow. The Rydan skipped back to give Tohmas permission and room.

Since the fighting had been downhill, the body must have been carried up. Strangely, Barnon saw no blood in the snow nearest the white-cloaked form.

Tohmas flipped the body over. Whoever it was, Tohmas was startled enough by the face to step back.

"Get me a cutter!" Tohmas called.

Among the whispers of the onlookers was a name— Celebrant Calanor.

"The little whippersnapper wouldn't let us near the celebrant. Glad you talked sense into him," Guardian Rusk said in a sarcastic tone. He waved forward the cutter who had been waiting. The celebrant in the slush was breathing in short, shallow breaths. After a quick assessment, the cutter called over soldiers to carry the celebrant away, presumably to a Healing waggon.

"What happened?" Tohmas asked the Rydan.

The Rydan's eyebrows furled, and his eyes narrowed dangerously. His grass bracelets seemed to shiver in unease.

"*Port*!" Tohmas barked, and the boy immediately calmed. He replied in rambling Rydan which was, to Barnon, incomprehensible.

Tohmas seemed to fare better and wore an expression of satisfaction. "Protectors! You four," he selected from the first to answer the call, "are now in charge of making sure Calanor lives. Limit who sees him if you have to. Am I clear?" Each of the four nodded. "*Geddit.*" The four rushed after the celebrant.

The Rydan tilted his head and raised an eyebrow.

Tohmas smiled. "*Va goh. Ged.*"

The boy beamed and accepted the command with another punch to his left palm. He left at a run, heading for the lake.

"You speak Rydan with surprising ease, Prince Tohmas," Barnon commended as his nephew watched the boy go.

The Prince of Galanth shrugged dismissively. "All you need are two words, Prince Barnon. *Goh* means good. *Ged* means get or go away. Everything else is just yes or no, and for that, you nod or shake your head."

As much as he wanted to ask more, Barnon heard tension in Tohmas' voice and decided his queries were unwelcome.

"You knew he'd live!"

Terant's voice was accusatory, but DoomDragon only yawned. Seria was the spoiled child; Terant was the arrogant teenager. He was bored with them both.

Darknim had suggested it would be wiser to move away from the outside campfire for privacy, but Terant had launched into his verbal attack without heeding him. Now, all nearby Northlanders could hear Terant sputtering. Darknim normally protected the appearance of the Esparan allies, but if they were so determined to make themselves appear foolish, why should he stop them?

"Totho surely wanted him to live," Darknim replied. "I am glad I did not try too hard to disrupt Totho's plan."

Although he had placed tourniquets on the limbs before severing Tothonar's hands, the exposure and the blood loss should still have killed the celebrant. That he lived proved Elder Tril had been correct; the celebrant had accessed the powers of faith and staved off death. Now, he was silenced but alive. And no wizard would be able to steal his thoughts.

Darknim had been pleasantly surprised to learn Tothonar had been taken in by Prince Tohmas' forces. He was waiting to see if the Prince of Galanth had showed that mercy because of the potential advantage—Tothonar had stayed with the Northlanders—but that would come. When the Prince of Galanth discovered he could not get any information, not by word, writ, or magic, what would he do?

"You disobeyed—"

"I was told to be rid of him, Master Terant," Darknim replied, leaning back with a hot cup of tea in hand. "Now I am." He paused. "Would you like more time to curse, or are you ready to move onto more important things?"

Terant pulled himself up, making himself tall as if to intimidate Darknim. DoomDragon looked up at the shorter man from his seat on a stone, keeping his expression neutral.

"More important things?" Terant growled. "You mean the Rydans?"

"Yes, the Rydans you did not see coming," Darknim replied, smiling sweetly.

"They moved under—"

"I do not care how they got past you," Darknim interrupted. "They are here. Tohmas will use them. We have a day, two at most, before he attacks. I want to bring him down. That means doing it before Prince Dragal arrives."

"Dragal is only three days away!" Terant objected.

"We have only a day or two before Tohmas attacks," Darknim repeated. "I am not going to let Tohmas butcher my men so you can use him as a rally point. Dragal is close enough. We can catch him even if he turns back. Are we agreed?"

Terant clenched his jaw hard enough to be grinding his teeth flat, but he nodded.

"Good," Darknim said, rising to his feet. He refreshed his tea and began the walk back to his tent. "I'd best get to arranging his defeat. I

expect you to deal with Kitable, Master Terant. Tell Clarin to be ready to go in for the kill, but you deal with Kitable."

Terant still failed to get a word through his clenched jaw. The silence suited Darknim well.

As he made his way into the tent, Darknim was struck by a sudden feeling of loss.

He had a wizard within reaching distance of Prince Tohmas, able to make short work of the man. Terant would be on hand to deal with Kitable. Carsh was formidable, but his clansmen were not going to have the chance to prove themselves; Tohmas and Carsh would be dead before the battle started. Once command fell to Barnon, it would be simple.

It was disappointing. He had come to expect better of Prince Tohmas.

I had been hoping for better, Darknim thought as he sat as his table and examined the disrupted tokens. He had almost come to believe that a prince could be an honorable enemy. He thought they could have been good friends, if they had not been on opposite sides of a war.

Prince Tohmas had, after all, taken Tothonar in, saving the celebrant's life.

It was a shame he would die, but there was no other way.

Chapter 12

W hen night fell, a hush came with it. With Rydans on the lake, the Esparan army felt hopeful, but uncertainty mixed with their optimism. No one quite knew what to make of their unexpected allies.

The quiet of HillTop was striking compared to the ruckus of the Rydans.

Tohmas waited until dark before leaving. Timing the patrols, he chose a quiet moment to cut a slit through his tent wall. One of Carsh's many blades stitched the opening shut as they slunk away. It had been a long while since he had snuck away from the protectors; they did not seem to expect it. He left his green tabard and, most importantly, his black rank rope behind.

Carsh paused after a few steps and regarded the people assembled in front of the tent. As he had for the last two mooncycles, Sabian sat at a campfire beyond the tent.

After a moment of consideration, Carsh whistled softly.

Sabian glanced over. When Carsh gave the whistle for a second time, the boy stood, picked up a pot as if to dump cooking water, and headed toward the noise. The protectors watched him go but did not leave their posts.

Tohmas was surprised that Carsh wanted his Esparan Follower to come. With Carsh moving on ahead, Tohmas invited Sabian to leave the cooking pot behind and walk with him.

Once on the slope, Tohmas quietly said, "You've picked up Rydan habits, Sabian." The boy cocked his head but, true to Rydan form, did not reply. "You no longer ask questions," Tohmas pointed out.

"If you watch, you get the answer," the boy said softly, his breath fogging in the chill.

"Where are we going then?" Tohmas teased.

After a moment of thought, Sabian replied, "Carsh is looking for someone. He wants to find them before they find him." Sabian paused, considering his next words cautiously, as if worried about causing offense. "He is also nervous."

"He is hunting another knife dancer," Tohmas confirmed. "There are only two at the moment: Carsh and Crawthran. Most know Crawthran as the Pack Runner because of his dogs."

"Knife dancer," Sabian repeated. The comment did not come out as a question.

Sabian had no way of knowing what a knife dancer was—Carsh certainly would not have told him—so Tohmas explained. "Essentially, someone put a knife in his hand when he was six years old, and he has not been without one since. They always seek each other for practice. The fights can be deadly, so a knife dancer is either very good or dead at a young age. This ought not be so dangerous. Both Crawthran and Carsh are First Clan; they usually pull their blows. That said, few people have ever seen two knife dancers fight, even in practice like this."

Sabian cast a quick glance at Tohmas. "You have."

Tohmas smiled.

Without enemies between them, HillTop could access the Rydan forces on the lake down a rocky path. Most of Fixer City's tradespeople appeared to have mobilized, offering services in exchange for the Rydans' fresh meat and horsehair blankets. A line of excited woodcutters, able to reach the woods beyond the Rydan's camp, rushed up the hills, arms and sleds loaded. There would be many large fires tonight.

Tohmas and Sabian filtered through the crowds unrecognized.

A hundred paces from the rough trading post on the shores, where the lake was dunes of snow, Carsh appeared ahead of them. He had removed his heavier coat, but Tohmas had no idea where. Under the light of a half-full moon, Carsh's stance had changed. Before Tohmas could guess where the Pack Runner was, Carsh caught a blade.

Following the throw back, Tohmas spotted the fur-clad Pack Runner crouched near the edge of the lake. Crawthran had not changed in years. The Pack Runner was still lean and had thin, wispy facial hair. A few years Carsh's elder and a hand taller, he had the advantage of experience and reach.

With a visible target, Carsh rushed in to close the distance and deny the Pack Runner some of his advantage. In a flicker, they were entangled. The spar became short jabs and feints to prevent the Pack Runner from utilizing his long, arching strikes. The occasional thrown blade landed in the snow around them, making Tohmas keep his distance.

To Tohmas' relief, neither seemed to be landing hits. They could keep this up for...

Carsh's heart! Tohmas' stomach sank. It had been only two cycles since Carsh had been poisoned with dark root. Carsh knew no greater challenger than the Pack Runner. *Can his heart manage?*

Tohmas strained his ears. Despite the speed of their exchange, neither Rydan was breathing heavily. A knife dancer knew to keep calm and, for the sake of endurance, carefully control his breathing and the beating of his heart. Carsh was not stressed; he was focused.

Tohmas still thought he should send a prayer to Pari in the morning for the continued health of his brother's heart.

A soft step behind them made Sabian draw his blade, but Tohmas had already seen the woman joining them from behind a rise of ice.

"Laorn," Tohmas said.

Sabian tilted his head. "You know her."

"Knew her. I knew her before she became the Pack Runner's mate. Now, I don't know her at all." Tohmas rubbed his hands to warm them. He could not wear mitts when he might need his weapons.

Unlike Crawthran, who seemed as spry as when he was sixteen, Laorn had aged drastically. The darkly shrouded creature that slunk up behind him looked nothing like the attractive girl from the Outlands he had known. Laorn had been a proud girl on the verge of womanhood when the Pack Runner had come in search of a mate. Crawthran had been intrigued by her outright refusal, but with Chief Tamv's blessing, the Pack Runner had carried Laorn away kicking and cursing.

The girl should have been flattered, but instead she had been furious. Over the following years, the appearance of unwanted female infants on

the Chief's *shella* steps confirmed that the Pack Runner and his mate lived, but Tohmas had not seen Laorn again.

The Pack Runner needed a son, and by Laorn's swollen belly, Tohmas assumed he was working toward it.

Taking his cue from Tohmas, Sabian re-sheathed his long blade and faced the knife dancers. He kept one knife, a short stabbing blade, openly in hand and left his coat open to access his baldrics if needed.

Laorn, fur-clad and stiff, took a place on Tohmas' right. Like him, her eyes were on the sparring men. After a few moments, she glanced to the side. Pointing to Sabian with her stare, she snorted. "*Preddy Esparan. Naw be havin' place 'ere.*"

Sabian, Tohmas was pleased to see, met the woman's stare evenly.

"*Naw preddy. Strengt,*" he replied, and Tohmas concealed a smile. The boy had been picking up Rydan.

She sneered. To keep the peace, Tohmas interrupted. "*Fallo o' Carsh. Fallo o' Arm.*" Sabian was a Follower of Carsh, the Arm among the Rydans. She needed to know as much.

Laorn immediately cut off her reply.

When she went back to staring at the sparring pair, Tohmas winked at Sabian. Begrudgingly, she had accepted him. She would not forgive him for being Esparan, but she would no longer complain about his presence. To insult Sabian now was to insult Carsh.

Long after any two Esparans would have collapsed, the two Rydans finally knocked each other over. In the light of the moon, Tohmas spotted a blade at Carsh's throat as he lay in the snow. But the way Carsh's hand was tucked low between them threatened to disembowel the Pack Runner in return. The neck blow would be more instantly deadly; Crawthran had won.

Tohmas let out a single relieved breath. They had each pulled their final blows. It was easy for knife dancers to forget that vital detail; they were trained to make killing blows at every opportunity. Tohmas assumed Crawthran's loyalty to Chief Tamv was the reason he spared Carsh.

The match decided, both participants rose and made their way to the spectators, retrieving all the knives they could. Whoever found the knife kept it.

Relief flooded Tohmas. His brother was still taking deep, calm breaths as he and the Pack Runner joined Tohmas, Laorn, and Sabian.

When Tohmas met Crawthran's stare, a chill ran down his spine. Only two men in the world frightened Tohmas, and the Pack Runner was unquestionably the better fighter of the two. More than a decade before, Tohmas had been marked as someone to watch, and he did not want to disappoint the man who had marked him. Having Esparan blood made the need to prove himself all the stronger.

The Pack Runner flipped his blade over his knuckles and gave Tohmas a curt nod. Tohmas' turn had come.

Tohmas pulled the heavy woolen coat from his shoulders and—sword in his left hand, knife in his right—followed the Pack Runner to the trampled snow. He was going to be beaten, but he would make sure the Pack Runner at least worked for it.

Chapter 13

Sabian had considered the matches between Carsh and Tohmas the pinnacle of one-on-one combat. He reconsidered when he saw Carsh finally challenged then beaten. Carsh was spectacular, and yet the Pack Runner was better. It frightened Sabian deeper than he allowed to show.

It was then Tohmas' turn.

Tohmas' spar was not as fast-paced, but he held his own. The woman, who was now beside Sabian as Carsh watched from Sabian's left, raised an eyebrow.

"*Bedda*," she conceded.

"*Ahlway*," Carsh replied. He had retrieved his hide coat and donned it but left his tattooed chest open to the wind. His pants had been soaked by the melted snow and were beginning to frost.

They stood for a moment more before Carsh glanced at the woman and asked, "*Darcina be 'ere*?"

Laorn snorted. "Be 'ere, ya, bud ya be findin' herr?"

"*I be findin' herr*," Carsh confirmed with confidence.

As much as Sabian wanted to know who Darcina was and why Carsh was asking after her, he held his tongue.

Tohmas spent time in the snow when the Pack Runner tripped him, but the prince was quickly up and ready for the next attack. The match ended when a blade stopped only a hair from Tohmas' chest and only

because the Pack Runner chose to stop it. Although the Rydan was not even winded, Tohmas' steps dragged when he returned to the observers.

The Pack Runner followed Tohmas over then looked at Sabian.

His eyes glowed in the moonlight like the reflection of a hound's stare. Sabian almost took a step back, but he could not look weak in front of Carsh. Carsh called him a Follower. He had to earn that status.

"Esparan," the Pack Runner said with a snarl. "Bah."

Sabian dared not speak this time. The Pack Runner was, without a doubt, a killer that Tohmas and Carsh respected. If Sabian said something out of place now, he feared the repercussions would be deadly.

"'Ee be goh," Carsh informed the Pack Runner. "Fan Esparan, ee be graye."

The Rydan's pale eyes narrowed on him, and Sabian forced himself not to shiver.

"Esparan. *Arm eik*?"

Sabian translated the Rydan easily; Carsh was boasting that Sabian was a good fighter, great when compared to a typical Esparan. The reference to the "Arm," which Sabian had heard Tohmas use earlier, confused him. It was being used as a title. Calling him a "Follower of the Arm" surely meant Carsh was the "Arm," but what *that* meant was beyond him.

"*Arm eik*," Tohmas replied as he fastened his coat once more. His sword and knife fit over it snugly. "*Enn 'And eik, 'ee be goh*." To confuse matters further, Tohmas referred to the "Hand" with the same authority as the "Arm."

When the Pack Runner began circling him, Sabian thought of the goat. Was the Pack Runner assessing him as a fighter or as dinner? Eating victims seemed very much like something the beast-like man would do.

After a single circle, the Rydan faced Sabian and nodded. With a flip of a blade over his knuckle, the Pack Runner walked back to the patch of packed snow.

"You can refuse if you want," Tohmas said. "You are Esparan. You have an excuse."

Sabian's heart paused then stagger to catch up. *He's inviting me to spar?*

Excitement shot through him. He fought to keep his voice level as he told the prince, "You're Esparan too. You did not refuse." Beside him, the woman growled, but a gesture from Tohmas stopped her.

"Then go," Tohmas said with a shrug.

Sabian peeled off his coat, and the prince obligingly took it. It left Sabian in a cotton shirt but gave him full access to all his knives in readiness. His feet were chilled from the walk, but the waxed leather had kept out the moisture. Their grip would be questionable in the snow.

Sabian's steps were slow as he went to meet the Pack Runner. It seemed very possible that he was going to die. Both the Pack Runner and his mate clearly held Esparans in a different category than Rydans. *Is this a prank? If I die, will they find it funny?*

Without preamble or formality, the Pack Runner attacked straight and fast. Sabian deflected it easily. The second swing came around with the speed of a diving hawk. The Pack Runner's fist—the blade in it turned away—struck Sabian's ribs, knocking Sabian back a step. The softer snow gave him traction, letting him keep his feet and be ready when the man came at him again.

The first strike came again, straight and hard. Sabian deflected it farther, giving him a flicker more before the fist came around. While one knife warded off the punch, Sabian cut at the Pack Runner's hip with his left blade. Shifting his body to avoid Sabian's strike, the Pack Runner's punch went wide. He did not hit the knife Sabian had positioned, but he came close.

Although Sabian had watched the Pack Runner fight Carsh without any repetition, now the Rydan presented a sequence of blows that started anew when Sabian failed to counter one. As soon as he stopped the last attack, a new one was introduced. There were times he progressed through several at once but others when he was stuck at a given combination multiple times.

No killing blow was attempted. When Sabian staggered back too far, the beast-man waited for him to right himself and step back up. Then the game continued.

It exhausted Sabian. The Pack Runner showed no sign of slowing, but Sabian's muscles went from cold, to hot, to burning. Simple defenses that had been easily preformed earlier were soon failing. His mind slowed, then stopped, and he was left reacting solely by instinct. The knife cut into his skin shallowly as he faded.

He went blow by blow, counting on his muscle memory to guide him. Like during the heat of battle, Sabian did not think, he acted. He

progressed through the sequence, barely fast enough to stay ahead of the blades.

When another punch knocked Sabian back, the Pack Runner deviated sharply from his sequence by throwing a knife from the folds of his furs. It narrowly missed Sabian's knee, disappearing into the snow. Instinctually, Sabian returned the action, snatching a blade from his baldric and throwing it. He cursed the attack the moment the blade left his hand. Throwing a knife was a way of killing someone; it was not something he practiced on allies!

The Pack Runner caught the blade, holding it for a moment in its path to his sternum. With a flick of his wrist, he flipped the blade and held it by the handle.

Sabian swore as he staggered back another step. The shock broke the flow of his mind and muscles. Fatigue hit like a shield bash; Sabian's shaking legs nearly dropped him in the snow, but determination kept him upright. "I can't believe I did that."

The Pack Runner made a sound part word and part bark, a call that brought his mate to the fighting area.

Sabian grimaced. *Now*, he thought, *I'm dead*.

Carsh and Tohmas followed Laorn but stepped to one side. Sabian lacked the energy to even follow the movement of the Pack Runner when the Rydan circled him again. This time, Sabian was certain he was the goat.

After two circles, the ghostly eyes of the Pack Runner scrutinizing Sabian from every angle, the Rydan looked at Tohmas and said, "*S'plane.*"

"Explain?" Tohmas echoed. "What am I expl..." The answer dawned on him, and his face blanched. "You..." He glanced at Carsh, but the prime protector seemed just as shocked.

"*S'plane*," the Pack Runner repeated.

"He wants to test you, Sabian," the prince said. "You only get a warning because you're Esparan, so consider yourself lucky. You must have really done something right, boy."

"*Cowsmowt*," Carsh interrupted. Sabian's tired mind recognized the word as a mild insult, but he could not find the translation through his fatigue. The cold was setting in.

Tohmas smiled with a small sigh. "He is going to test you. The only advice I can give is, don't move. That's more than we ever got."

Tohmas nodded, indicating the explanations were over. The Pack Runner resumed circling, but it felt less like a vulture stalking his prey to Sabian. Prince Tohmas had said "we." He and Carsh had survived. *Maybe I'll live.* And not moving would be easy; he was too tired to move. He had been forced to lock his muscles to stop his trembling.

He focused on a campfire on the lake, watching the uneven light as shadows danced around it. In watching the motions of people in the distance, he became aware of a distant beat. For a moment, he thought the drums matched his heartbeat.

Pain lanced through his shoulder, and Sabian fell into the snow. He clamped his jaw shut, but a cry still escaped him. His knife fell from his grip, and he clutched at his left shoulder. Wet warmth warned him he was bleeding.

Uncontrolled tears fell. From his place kneeling in the snow, Sabian saw only Laorn's feet as she rushed after her mate. He knew she said something to the prince and prime protectors, but he hardly heard it and could not understand it.

After the two Rydans had left, Tohmas knelt in front of him. "Breathe, boy."

Sabian consciously released the breath he had been holding against the throbbing. His voice whined, but at least he stopped seeing sparks.

"Do you carry bandages?" Unable to speak, Sabian shook his head. "You should start," the prince advised as he opened a pouch and produced rolls and squares of cloth. "Now pay attention. You're going to have to learn how to do this yourself. Shoulder wounds are a demon to bandage."

"What ... by the hells ... just happened?" Sabian hoarsely asked between throbs from his shoulder.

"What an Esparan thing to say," Tohmas said, smiling. "You got tested, Sabian. I think you did well."

"Why?" Sabian choked out the word, his head tilting. He could not see the shadows of the fire anymore. His entire vision was Tohmas.

Tohmas pried Sabian's hand off the wound and replaced it with a bandage as he answered. Sabian let the hand fall into the snow, where it felt no chill.

"You impressed him, which is a remarkable achievement no matter where you come from. Carsh should be very proud."

CHAPTER 13

"Bah!" the prime protector dismissively called.

"But I lost." Paradoxically for the wet weather, his throat felt dry, and he was beginning to feel light-headed. He could not tell if it had been the workout or the injury; he did not even know how deep the wound went or how much blood he had lost. The multitude of smaller cuts from the spar were probably not helping.

"You learned as you went, Sabian. You adapted. He recognized in you what Carsh did: you have a good head for fighting. As hard as it is to understand, that wound is a compliment."

If I survive it, Sabian thought.

The bandage tied, Sabian leaned back into the snow and clutched at his shoulder. The extra pressure made it hurt less.

"We'll take you back up the hill. You should take it to a cutter but..."

With Carsh's help, Sabian rose to his feet. Tohmas draped his coat over his shoulders, the weight of the sheepskin enough to pinch against the bandage. Once he was vertical, Tohmas provided an arm to help him keep his balance.

"Do not tell anyone how you got that wound, Sabian," Tohmas said, his voice taking on a tone of command. "It's important that no one knows we were down here or that you met the Pack Runner, understand? Make up a story so you can get treated, but do not tell them what really happened."

Sabian checked with Carsh, and his Leader's frown confirmed Tohmas' command. Sabian had to obey, even if he did not understand.

Once they reached the top of the hill, the nearest Healing waggon was only a dozen paces away. They let him walk on his own. He heard them as they turned to go back down the hill.

"Naw be tellin' Tamv," Carsh said.

"Inac herself would have to come down to convince me to mention this to Tamv, Carsh," Tohmas answered. "No, we are not telling Tamv. Ever."

At Lance's fire, Tanuka remained distracted all evening, forcing Sori to take over her chores. Lance said nothing about it until night fell and Tanuka remained outside, staring off westward.

Drums thrummed in the distance.

Sori ostensibly went to her bedroll and curled up beside the fire, putting her back to the sound of the Rydans, but Tanuka stood, her face pained, outside the firelight. Figuring she would not sleep, Lance joined her.

From their place atop the cliff, the fires stretching over the Rydan's camp were like firebugs trapped in ice. The flickering shadows hinted that no Rydan slept yet, and the drums made Lance think no one else would tonight either.

Tanuka stood firmly, her arms crossed. He guessed her tight expression to be one of longing.

"You can go if you want. They're your people, aren't they? If you want to go home, go," Lance said.

Tanuka turned her head sharply away, pressing her lips. He thought, for the first time in his life, he might see a Rydan cry.

"Naw home," she replied.

"Wouldn't they take you in?"

Tanuka shook her head, her eyes glassy.

"She be Third Clan," Sori said from behind them, making Lance jump. He had not heard her leave her bedroll, but she had joined their sentry atop the rise. Her face was dispassionate as she examined the distant lights. "They be First Clan."

"So not friendly?" Lance guessed.

Sori snorted. She glanced at Tanuka, an expression of pity crossing her face then vanishing in almost the same blink. Her voice went back to being factual.

"*Yahnah*," Sori said, speaking as if her friend was not present. "Tanuka be lucky. She be havin' nice face. She be findin' husband enn dey take 'er in. She could be First Clan. Naw me. I naw be havin' nice face."

Lance sorted through the rough Esparan and recognized what Sori was doing. She could not compliment Tanuka or advise her without insulting her, but she could talk to Lance about it. Tanuka could seek marriage. An army of Rydans certainly had many bachelors.

Realization was slow. First, Tanuka lowered her crossed arms. Then her weight shifted forward. She had the opportunity to return to a predicable life, one where she did not have to struggle with a strange language or customs. It would be a relief for her.

"Go, Tanuka," Lance said. "Take care of yourself. Do not let anyone treat you poorly."

With haste, Tanuka pulled off all her knives except one, an acceptable number for a Rydan woman, and placed the extras onto a seat by the fire. She left at a jog, nearly skipping in joy.

Lance retrieved the knives and passed them to Sori. "You will not go?"

"I naw be wandin' fort husband," Sori answered, adding the knives to her collection. He could not imagine her giving up her extra blades.

"Fourth? You're barely what? Sixteen? How by the hells have you had three husbands already?"

Sori shrugged as if three husbands was a perfectly normal occurrence. "I naw be wandin' First Clan husband."

"What's the difference? First, Second, Third?"

Sori glared down at the distant fires, her fingers running along the handles of her knives as if seeking an excuse to draw one. "Second Clan attack First Clan. First Clan fight back. Third Clan attack First Clan because dey be weak. First Clan kill ahl."

"All?" Lance pressed.

Her eyes were hard when she met his stare. "All," she said, correcting her pronunciation. "I be Second Clan, last one. Tanuka be Third Clan. Tatim, Third Clan gawn."

The extinction of the Third Clan did not seem to bother Sori. With a sigh, she returned to her fire and crawled into the bedroll she and Tanuka had been sharing. Without each other, the night weather would have frozen them.

Lance felt he had no choice. "Come on, Sori. Share my tent. It's too cold for you to be sleeping alone."

As Tohmas approached the Rydan lake camp with Carsh at his side, a weight lifted from his shoulders. His fatigue from the spar with the Pack Runner dissipated.

At long last, he was home.

A shout went up when they were spotted. Flooded with excited welcomes, Tohmas and Carsh were surrounded by their Followers

and escorted into the new settlement. Tohmas' mind hiccupped as he swapped to speaking and thinking in Rydan. It seemed a strange sound after Esparan for so long.

"Tamv wants to see you as soon as you arrive," Dakn warned, making his salute hastily, his grin painfully large in relief. If Carsh or Tohmas had died in the foreign land, their Followers would have lost their rank among the Rydans instantly. Seeing them in the flesh seemed to assuage their unspoken concerns about the long absence.

"Point the way," Tohmas answered. The group adjusted their direction, obeying the chief immediately.

"Cold enough?" someone asked. "If you wanted snow, we could have sent you up into the mountains!"

"Bored yet? What do you do all day with Esparans anyway?" came another voice.

"I'm surprised there are any still standing!" someone else replied.

"Hey Carsh!" Dakn teased, "I just saw Darcina! She sends her warmest welcome and—"

The rest of the comment was cut off when the prime protector caught the Follower by his shoulder and tossed him off into a drift of snow. The presence of only one blade in Carsh's hand, which would be expected even if Carsh was completely alone, confirmed that the jest had been accepted as that.

"You couldn't handle her, Dakn. And you can't convince me you've been anywhere near her," Carsh told the fallen man.

"You could let me try," Dakn suggested, his voice muffled by snow.

Carsh snorted. "If I ever tire of you, I may. Then I will be rid of you entirely."

It is good to be back among friends.

No one dared obstruct the sons of Tamv and their Followers on their path to the central fire. A *shella*—a half hide, half wood building built at every stop a chief made—had been erected on the shore. A large bonfire blazed a dozen paces in front of it. Standing in the doorway in the chill, stood Tohmas' father.

Tamv had not changed. The *shella* entrance, built a pace above the ground, amplified his father's already significant height. Despite his age, the muscles on the chief were still strong and prominent. Since his hair had always been pale against sun-darkened and clean-shaven skin,

it was hard to say when it had changed from sun-bleached to white. He was dressed in bear fur, but his coat was open to expose his chest tattoo despite the cold. Hooked blades dangled on either side of his hide belt. His red-stained grass bracelets identified him as chief and overflowed with knucklebones.

As pleased as Tohmas was to see his father, he did not immediately present himself. For the moment, Tamv's attention was on someone else. Tohmas' eyes narrowed at the figure standing below the chief.

"Baont?" he grumbled. "I'm surprised he even came."

Baont had lived along the border of the Second Clan and assisted the First Clan's raids, a traitor to his own Second Clan heritage. In the years since the defeat of the Second Clan, Baont had gained rank under Tamv. Although he was cautious to support the Chief, he remained a quiet contester for the chief's position. Should his support ever hesitate, Tohmas expected to find the man's corpse.

"Chief insisted. Smart to keep him where we can see him," Krahr said. The grey-eyed man was one of Tohmas' first Followers and six years his senior. He boasted he was wiser due to his advanced years regularly.

Tohmas had to smile. Baont had many sons who, since their family Leader had come north, would be in the crowd. Rows between Tohmas' Followers and Baont's sons were common. They were also, he recalled, a lot of fun.

"Promises were made," Baont declared to the surrounding crowd. He faced Chief Tamv again, lifting his chin boldly. He had grown his thin beard out into a point, decorated by bone beads the color of blood. An imitation of chief's red?

How much as the absence of his sons weakened the chief that Baont dared be so bold to command him?

The reply was immediate. "Tohmas!" Tamv called.

Tohmas left his Followers at a run and presented himself to the chief, taking a position of readiness a step forward of Baont, showing himself to be of higher rank than the man. He pressed his right hand to his upper shoulder in acknowledgement of the chief. Instead of letting his leg touch the ground, he half-knelt and put his hands on the hilt of his weapons after the salute, showing he was ready to act. It was for the best; the terrain here was still mud and trampled snow, although the rock below revealed the shore. The fire was hot on Tohmas' back.

The chief spoke again to Baont. "Select your challenger."

Tohmas grinned back at Baont, daring him to take the chance himself. Had the chief grown weary enough of the influential Second Clan man?

"Ganer!" Baont shouted, and Tohmas' Followers snickered. Ganer was, unless Baont had been productive with his wife for the first time in many years, the youngest son. He would be hardly sixteen. Not a challenge at all.

The crowd around the fire cleared an area for them, and at a nod from Tamv, Tohmas stood. By the time he turned, he had both his sword and his knife out.

Upon his father's call, the boy stepped up and, like Tohmas had, took up a brief ready position before rising and drawing his own dual weapons. They were *hooknyes*—short, curved blades with bone and cloth handles. Carsh usually had one or two on him at any given moment. Since the chief had shown a preference for them, they had become popular weapons.

Between the two of them, Tohmas was the unusual one in his leather armor. Like most Rydans, Ganer wore hide breeches with fur against the cold and prominently displayed his grass bracelets. He had slightly longer hair than was normal, but it was tied back.

Tohmas walked with his weapons low and circled the cleared area, testing the footing. Although there were clumps of ice farther from the fire, the traction was overall good.

Ganer mimicked his movement by pacing the improvised arena. He moved fluidly, a typical Rydan style.

"What did you do to so annoy your father?" Tohmas asked him.

"You talk too much, Tohmas," the boy replied. "You always have." The insult was wasted; what any son of Baont thought of him was irrelevant.

"I already had to prove myself to the Pack Runner this evening," Tohmas taunted, using the time to assess his opponent. Ganer had been gangly when Tohmas had left the Outlands. He had filled out since.

The boy straightened, and the crowd hushed. No matter their loyalties, everyone feared the Pack Runner.

But Ganer kept his eyes on Tohmas. Once the challenge was issued, looking away could be a deadly mistake.

The duel struck Tohmas as odd. What was Baont playing at, bringing his youngest into a fight he would lose? And why would Tamv allow the duel at all?

"Better than he was," a quiet voice said behind Tohmas. Krahr had edged his way to the front of the crowd and given the warning as Tohmas passed. There was no chance to clarify what his Follower meant.

Ganer lunged his with his *hooknyes*, slicing in with both hands at once. The inexperienced would leave their core open, but Ganer kept his attack tight, giving Tohmas no means to retaliate.

He blocked instead, his sword crossing to the right and his knife to the left. With his immense strength, he pushed, uncrossing his arms, and slashed his weapons back at Ganer.

His bulk was his disadvantage. Ganer's knife caught on his forearm as he tossed the boy back.

As fast as Carsh, Ganer lunged in again, forcing Tohmas back a step to dodge.

Someone's been training. This would not be as easy as he had expected.

Ganer arched his *hooknyes* through the air as he advanced, making it hard to determine which strike would be real and which a feint. Frustrated, Tohmas attacked with sword and knife, but both were deflected by a spinning knife.

Refusing to give the boy a chance to repeat the assault, Tohmas attacked again, and then again. Each time, he was deflected, but Ganer had no chance to turn his blades against Tohmas either. One cut, shallow across Ganer's thigh, got through the spinning defenses. It matched the cut on Tohmas' forearm well.

"*D'aem'd* Esparan," Ganer spat.

The duel made sudden sense. *Esparan.* Ganer saw Tohmas as Esparan. His father, Baont, was among those who refused to acknowledge Tohmas' prowess or rank among the Rydans. No doubt Baont had leveraged Tohmas' blood against Tamv, taking advantage of Tohmas' absence to criticize Tamv's choice to take Tohmas as his eldest son. If Tohmas lost to a son of Baont, Tamv would be proven wrong for elevating Tohmas. Baont would have further reason to challenge the chief.

Well, Tohmas thought, if he believes me Esparan, then I will show him what an Esparan can do.

On the next attack, Tohmas swung low. Ganer blocked it, then swung to stab Tohmas' shoulder as Tohmas moved in. Ignoring the blow, Tohmas kept Ganer's knife pinned and sharply brought his knee into the flat of his sword, bending Ganer's wrist back. Ganer's wrist popped and cracked.

When Ganer staggered back, he dropped one *hooknye*, his wrist kinked unnaturally.

Tohmas passed a silent thanks to Protector Sanba for having shown him the trick. Without the armor, the attack to his shoulder would have ended the match, possibly even reaching the large vessel under his clavicle and killing him. But Tohmas was well accustomed to the weight and use of the armor now. He was pleased to use it to its full advantage. Ganer's strike had cut into the leather but had not reached Tohmas' skin.

Tohmas pressed the attack. Despite his broken wrist, the boy blocked two of Tohmas' attacks. But when the *hooknye* was occupied with blocking Tohmas' sword again, Tohmas stabbed his knife under, then through, his opponent's arm. Ganer dropped his second *hooknye*, the tendons to hold it severed.

The path open, Tohmas twisted his sword and slammed the hilt into Ganer's sternum. The enemy fell, sprawling into rocky slush.

Tohmas followed, placing a knee on the boy's shoulder to pin him down. The edge of his knife pressed against Ganer's throat.

There, Tohmas paused, looking at Tamv for instructions.

The chief sneered and shook his head.

For a moment as short as a flickering wick, uncertainty shot through Tohmas.

Lives were wasted this way. The boy did not deserve death as a demonstration. It was wrong.

But his response had to be instant. Obedience to the chief was all. This was Baont's fault, not Tohmas'. To remind Baont of his place, his son had to die.

Tohmas slit the boy's throat.

A knot twisted his stomach. Inac would never approve of such needless killing.

Baont began to object, but Tohmas stepped squarely into the Rydan's path before the man took more than a step toward Tamv, blood dripping from his knife.

CHAPTER 13

No weakness.

"Have you qualms with me, Baont?" he demanded.

Baont's mouth slammed shut. When Tohmas continued to meet Baont's stare, the man offered a belated salute to the Hand by pressing his fist into his palm. Other men were seeing to Ganer, but Tohmas paid them no mind.

"Sons, to me," Tamv called, halting the confrontation.

The call was as effective as Carsh's whistle. At a jog, Tohmas retook his place of readiness at the feet of his father, the fire at his back once more. Carsh arrived and mirrored the position on Tohmas' right.

"We have much to discuss. Come."

Without another look, for he had faith that his Followers were protecting his back, Tohmas followed his chief into the *shella*.

He had no desire to see the faces of Baont or his remaining sons anyway.

When a ward was disrupted, Kitable instantly Relocated to Prince Tohmas' tent. He was surprised to find it empty.

But with a bit of searching, he found a slit in the tent canvas held shut with a bone-handled blade, the type Carsh would carry. There was no sign of battle, and no lingering auras of magic involvement.

It had been a while, but Tohmas and Carsh were known for sneaking off alone.

Cursing, Kitable left by foot. Sure enough, the protectors outside the tent were still on duty, but the boy who shadowed Carsh was absent from his customary place at the campfire beyond Tohmas' tent.

If Sabian was gone, he was following Carsh. The prince and his prime protector must have snuck away, that was all. Of course Carsh would want to visit his people. And Tohmas and Carsh were nigh-on inseparable. Tohmas has shown he could handle the Rydans well enough. Kitable should have anticipated it.

Unpanicked, Kitable walked back to his vardo. Even if the prince was surrounded by strangers, they were officially allies, and he still had his best bodyguard with him.

Once in the safety of his vardo, he settled back into his position and began casting to confirm his suspicions. He had to be cautious. Although not all Rydans appeared to sense magic like Carsh or the Pack Runner, Kitable did not dare test his theory by casting a tracker onto Prince Tohmas when the prince might be surrounded by the magic-hating people. Instead, he located the prince with a spell then set an anchor high above him. After casting a visual amplification spell usually used at sea, he re-cast his Scry, found his anchor, and settled back to search.

With his Scry high in the air and the amplification spell providing enhancement of the image, he located a house-like structure. A fight was happening in front of the house, a man dressed in furs, grass, and bones overseeing it from the doorway. To Kitable's chagrin, one of the combatants was Tohmas. Carsh was watching on without concern.

Before Kitable could decide if he shoulder intervene, it was over. Tohmas disarmed the challenger and pinned him down. At a nod from the man in front of the house, Tohmas then killed the defeated Rydan.

It was done in such a careless, haphazard manner that Kitable almost dropped his Scry in shock. He had never seen anyone kill anything so emotionlessly, let alone another person. Even Carsh, with his enthusiasm for fighting, killed with passion, not disregard.

There was no retaliation from the Rydans, although Tohmas paused to speak to one man who seemed more irritated than the others. The Scry provided no sound, so Kitable did not know what was said. Still, no one stopped him from entering the house.

Carsh followed, but Kitable did not dare. He would have to send his Scry inside the building, and that would certainly allow Carsh to detect him. Instead, Kitable watched a celebration begin. He kept one eye on the door in hopes of seeing the prince again soon.

Chapter 14

No son of Tamv would be outdone by a son of Baont. Ganer had clearly been chosen to embarrass Tohmas with defeat, yet Tohmas' skill proved Tamv's supremacy. Carsh was pleased.

As the second son, Carsh followed Tohmas into the *shella*, but once within the walls, the sons simultaneously adopted a ready position, half knelt. Tamv was both their chief and their father. The salute to him was instinctual.

It was not as cold under his feet here. A dry reed mat hid the wooden platform the *shella* had been constructed upon. A ring of stones cordoned off a small fire pit stocked with hot stones, and the hides hanging on the walls kept the heat in.

"Rela," Tamv invited, and they rose. Now that they had been given permission, Carsh perched on one of the logs around the fire, warming himself and ready for questions. Tohmas remained standing, indicating he wished to speak.

Tamv acknowledged him.

"What was that about?" Tohmas asked. The formal challenge of the Hand's authority had been a surprise. There had been little doubt the sons of Tamv would be assessed upon their return, but only a fool would have thought them vulnerable. Carsh had not expected an actual fight, let alone a formal one.

"You talk too much, Tohmas," the chief said, tossing Carsh a water-skin of wildwater. "You always have."

Tohmas flinched as if he had been dealt a blow. Ganer's words had been meaningless, but hearing them from the chief was different, particularly when the chief then honored Carsh by offering him drink before Tohmas. The brothers had considered themselves equals for years, but Tohmas was still the elder. Tamv was offering Carsh the respect due to the elder.

Despite being chastised, Tohmas pressed, "I understand the need to prove myself after being away, but why Ganer? It was a waste. Why—?"

To Carsh's shock, Tohmas was behaving like an Esparan!

"Enough!" Tamv snapped.

Tohmas immediately knelt with his head down and his fist over his shoulder in salute. The command had effectively slapped Tohmas on the back of his head.

Tamv left Tohmas for a long moment. He accepted the waterskin back from Carsh and took a drink, waiting. When he was satisfied Tohmas had heeded the reminder, he said, "Rela, Tohmas."

He offered Tohmas a hand to rise, and Tohmas accepted it. Esparans would have apologized or tried to explain themselves, but Rydans needed no such words. Taking the Chief's forearm showed that he would do as Tamv wished now.

The moment Tohmas stood tall, the chief gave Tohmas the waterskin, and Tohmas drank obediently. Leaving the waterskin in Tohmas' keeping, Tamv took his place on the bone and pelt *traon*. Sitting on the pelt-covered seat put him above even Tohmas' impressive height.

"Tell me about the Esparans," he ordered.

"They obey," Tohmas said, perching like Carsh on one of the log seats by the fire and seeking another drink. When Tohmas handed the waterskin back to Carsh, Carsh smiled. He had been rationing his supply of wildwater. Tohmas knew how much he had been missing it.

"Some would follow," Carsh offered. He would not have suggested as much a few mooncycles ago, but he knew the Esparans better now. He had found strength among them. The chief needed to know that.

Tamv cocked his head. "Followers among the Esparans?" His frown deepened in disbelief.

Tohmas nodded. "Sabian."

"Lance," Carsh supplied.

"Kitable," Tohmas added, a touch cautiously.

"Maybe a dozen of the protectors," Carsh agreed, not remarking on Tohmas' suggestion of the caster. He knew he could trust Kitable, and the man was strong. He made a good Follower, particularly as a wisavi. "Good men all, and loyal."

"What of the princes?"

Tohmas shrugged. "I have dealt with more than half of them in passing but fought alongside only three. They obeyed."

"They obeyed? No longer?"

"One still obeys. Another has been captured but is apparently still alive for reasons I do not understand. The third *dearn'd*."

At this, Tamv looked surprised. "And he lives still?" To *dearn* was not merely to change sides in Rydan, it was an open abandonment of family, clan, and honor. Even the Esparan word "treason" did not express the same contempt as was due for a *dearn'd* man. Any who *dearn'd* was given a death sentence.

"His life is meaningless to me—he is leader of a fallen people—and I used his betrayal to smuggle my men into my enemy's ranks. When we defeat DoomDragon, he will die." The word Tohmas used for "fallen people" was the same Tamv had used for the Second Clan upon their defeat.

Tohmas won a satisfied nod from the chief. Into the pause, one of Tamv's Follower entered in, a basket of hot stones in hand. He swapped the stones in the pit to keep the warmth in.

"And?" the chief asked.

Carsh looked to his brother for the reply. Tohmas had mentioned that DoomDragon's assassination attempt had given him an idea, but he had not elaborated.

Tohmas stared up at the chief, visibly thinking. Once the Follower had left, Tohmas finally said, "I was awaiting a reason to attack him. He would be suspicious if I attacked without expecting to win. With the Rydans here, I have that reason. We can finish it."

"Explain," the chief said, his head cocked. He did not fidget or shift his weight, willing to listen.

Tohmas spread his hands over the fire, the blood on his wounded arm crusted already. The scar across his palm warmed to pink in the glow of the stones. "DoomDragon leads a divided army. He controls his Northlanders, a gathering of confused Esparans, and Prince Rairn's *dearn'd* men. The title of the DoomDragon holds the Northlanders together. His reputation holds the Esparans loyal. When we kill DoomDragon, the Northlander clans will divide and the Esparans will scatter. We clean up the pieces."

"What DoomDragon tried to do by killing you," Carsh agreed. Killing Tohmas would have broken the alliance between Solta and Galanth just as surely.

"Only he missed, and I do not intend to miss." Tohmas looked up from his hands, awaiting the chief's response.

Tamv's bracelets rattled, and both sons listened. The bracelets held knucklebones from dozens of wise allies of Tamv's. They were due respect.

"What support do you need?" Tamv asked.

Carsh grinned, and even Tohmas released the tension in his shoulders. He had redeemed himself.

"I request the full force for a single strike tomorrow. We can do everything else."

With a slow nod, the chief agreed. Tohmas began to smile.

But two words took the grin from Tohmas' face.

"And then?"

Tohmas again chose his words carefully. As the first son of the chief, his duty was to expand the power and territory of his chief. *Is the timing right?* It was happening so quickly.

"Espar stands divided. We can take it all," Tohmas declared.

The chief smiled, which made Carsh's heart skip, and for a moment, an ache flashed through his chest. It faded in an instant, leaving his arm numb. As Tamv had his head turned to pick up a bag from beside the *traon*, Tohmas cocked his head at Carsh. His flinch had been noticed.

Carsh gave no answer. He required nothing.

Tohmas drew no attention to the lapse.

They brought their attention to Tamv as the chief pulled out a bag of stones. Once, Tohmas and Carsh memorized the Esparan princedoms and politics with the same stones.

Tamv stepped down to the planning circle stained into the mat and crouched there, dumping the bag out. Tohmas and Carsh joined him.

Fourteen stones, each painted with a symbol on a colored background, looked up at them.

Tamv waited.

Tohmas picked up the green stone with the grey tree and turned it over in his hand. "Galanth trusts me. I am their prince in every way. That is ours already." He placed the stone outside the circle with one hand while the other hand picked up another. This one was red and black—Solta.

"Sol, if he survives, is in my debt again. If he dies, we choose another until one of his sons is old enough. A child will need support to take command. We maintain control." He placed the stone beside Galanth's. "The rest of the sons of Zayban," Tohmas continued as he picked up three stones at once, "consider me family. If I show them what we can do, they will obey." Tohmas dropped the white and red stone then briefly examined the brown and grey one. "Forsinth has no choice," he said, dropping it into the pile. "Even if his bonds with Galanth are weakening, he cannot act alone." It was not Rydan to tolerate weak leaders, but Tohmas knew his Esparans well. It was temporary. Carsh approved.

Tohmas glanced up to judge the chief's expression. Tamv sat immobile, listening and allowing Tohmas to continue.

Carsh's brother then turned over the third stone in his hand, the blue and yellow representation of Clandac and the last of Zayban's territories. "Dragal may be a problem, but the man is ill. I will give him a chance to die well. He will do the rest for us. Two men have claimed his daughters. The one we support will rule. We have Clandac."

The blue and yellow stone landed in the pile. Carsh handed Tohmas the next three stones: red with a raven for Meloch, black with a sword for Tanble, and white on white for Barlaby. This part Carsh knew well.

"The north is ours when DoomDragon is taken," Tohmas explained to Tamv. "What has been lost can be given to any we choose. Barlaby will lose its prince before I am through. I will appoint another."

Tamv gave no reply, implying acceptance, but Carsh was at a loss. The remaining princedoms were not well known to him. If Tohmas thought them weak enough to be conquered, he had a plan. Carsh was keen to hear it.

Not disappointing him, Tohmas picked out the yellow stone with the grey anvil without hesitation. "Lour will follow the highest bid. If we are buying the most metal, they will obey. Despite their strength of arms, they will not act against us."

"Polthian," he went on next with the blue and red stone in hand, "is unhappy with me, but Prince Polthian is in no position to act. He has a close fighter companion, a high guardsman." Tohmas met Carsh's stare meaningfully. Carsh had met with High Guardsman Ranth while Tohmas spoke to Prince Polthian.

Carsh smiled in understanding, the single blade in his hand spinning faster in his excitement. "As much as he respects wisdom in Leaders, High Guardsman Ranth will take action if he believes Polthian is not acting rightly," Carsh said. "He believes Prince Polthian to be prone to overreacting and sees himself as the second Leader of the princedom."

"A threat, especially an unconfirmed one, will drive them further apart," Tohmas added. Realization dawned on Carsh.

"We send Rydans to his border in the south?" Carsh guessed.

Tohmas' smile was proud. "And we offer Ranth words of wisdom as his prince panics."

Tamv pursed his lips but nodded at length. "I will send a team to harass Polthian."

They added the red and blue stone to the growing pile.

In silence, they looked at the remaining stones. Four were left; Tohmas picked up two at once.

"Nothor stands with Gaidol—they are brothers and cannot be divided—but we have little to fear from Nothor. When Gaidol falls, so does Nothor."

"They will fight," Tamv stated, and Tohmas nodded.

Carsh laughed. "Prince Dorakon will come after you personally, Tohmas."

"To his doom," Tohmas replied, and the second son of Tamv could only agree. His eyes fell onto the brown stone with grey. "But I think we should be striking at Trulin first."

"Trulin will fight?" the chief pressed.

"If I am careful how I present it, perhaps not. But if they do not immediately obey, we will have to go after them. Trulin cannot be allowed to gather strength."

"What advantages have we?"

"Lance," Carsh pointed out, but Tohmas shook his head with a frown that surprised Carsh.

"I don't know what he would do if we threatened Gaidol."

"You would count this man as a Follower then doubt his actions?" Tamv sneered. "Which is it?"

Tohmas fell silent. Carsh considered Lance a strong Follower, but he understood Tohmas' hesitation. Lance still spoke of Gaidol with great longing. If they attacked Gaidol, would Lance still follow?

At length, Tohmas said, "I may yet keep him if I am careful. But he will not tolerate being used as an advantage against Gaidol. We would do best to move quickly. So long as Trulin is already ours, Gaidol and Nothor stand alone. We can take them by force."

The two stones were added to the pile, and Carsh took out the white and brown stone of Trulin.

All eyes went to the final red and yellow stone.

Tohmas sighed. "The Princedom of Damoria is an enemy of Galanth. As soon as Prince Wevan learns of our purpose, he will attack. I cannot afford to lose Wayburn." The city itself was meaningless to Tohmas, but the symbol of his capital was vital. A Leader who could not defend his home could not be expected to defend anyone else. Wayburn was considered Tohmas' capital by the Esparans. He would be diminished if he lost it to Damoria.

"Rydans can defend it," Tamv said.

"The border, yes, but not the city itself. Esparans do not mix well with Rydans. For that, I will send back the Fyrd of Wayburn. With the other warriors joining us, we will not require the Fyrd here," Tohmas suggested.

Carsh thought Tohmas may have the statement backward; Rydans did not mix well with Esparan, not the other way around. He wondered if Tohmas had censored his words for Tamv's sake.

The chief gave one long nod of approval. "We will keep them out until you have finished with Gaidol."

The last stone dropped, and they paused to look at the pile. When Carsh turned back to his father, the chief's fangs were bared.

"Ambitious, my sons."

"As you wished?" Tohmas asked warily. Their father's approval was rare. His support had given both his sons prestigious ranks among the Rydans. His disapproval could easily revoke that honor.

"Your effectiveness is commendable. You have brought them to this point faster than I expected. I am pleased."

Since "pleased" was the highest commendation they would ever receive, the sons shared a victorious smile.

Tamv was the first to stand, but Tohmas and Carsh quickly followed.

"Go, enjoy the celebration," the chief commanded, and both sons took the kneeling position of waiting, heading the dismissal. "I will return to the Outlands after your battle is done, Tohmas. Burlotak will lead the Rydans. The Pack Runner will remain, as will Baont."

Carsh tilted his head in surprise, and Tohmas did the same. Tamv explained the decision in the next breath.

"I do not want to see Baont again."

Their salute, fist to shoulder, confirmed their obedience.

"Oh," the chief belatedly added, "and Schlavarai will remain."

Tohmas' lowered face brightened. Then the final dismissal came, and they were free to rise.

Their Followers were waiting outside, ready to fully announce their return to the First Clan.

Despite the activity in the Rydan camp below Kitable, there seemed to be little to watch. The Rydans danced around the fires, drank, and fought. A few stuck close to the house, but most came and went as chaotically as the busiest city's port. Women, their hair long enough to be used as cushions when they sat down, wove among the men. Children rushed between the legs of the crowds at full speed. Some women stayed with partners, but most seemed unattached, to be won by the most persistent courtship.

Kitable felt like he was watching the shorebird mating season on the lake.

At length, Tohmas and Carsh remerged and were swarmed by seemingly friendly Rydans. With this gathering, Tohmas joined the party.

Kitable expected Tohmas to look to Carsh for cues, but it rapidly became evident that the Prince of Galanth needed no guidance. Flawlessly, Tohmas danced, drank, and sang with the lot of them. Kitable had never seen his prince so at ease.

He did not understand. Even if they were allies, Rydans were dangerous. Had he been in the prince's place, Kitable would have been

terrified of making a mistake, but Tohmas joined the step-dancing without missing a beat then won a knife-throwing game. Once Carsh accepted the challenge next, the prince lost and, laughing all the while with wildwater in hand, wandered off.

He was promptly surrounded by women, who seem to have been waiting for such an opportunity. Although Kitable could not hear their words, it was clear what they were suggesting as they preened before him. Each woman wore a knife on her belt.

Without hesitation, Tohmas returned affections from a few different women until finally deciding on a tall, muscular woman who, despite the cold wind of the north, wore a buckskin dress that left her cleavage visible from across the lake. When they vanished into a low, branch-woven shelter, Kitable did not follow.

With Tohmas gone, Carsh left the area. Keeping one part of his mind on the tent where the prince was, Kitable let another part follow the stalking prime protector. Through the crowds, Carsh hunted, but the wizard could make no guess as to the prey until Carsh spotted it.

She was as tall and strong as the woman Tohmas had chosen and wore her hair pleated and folded up with a bone comb. She was speaking to three Rydan men and leaning against a fourth next to a fire, her clothing sparse enough to need the heat to keep the chill at bay. The prime protector's gaze fixed on her like a mountain cat sighting a deer. Although the woman did not, at first, appear to notice, the men with her spotted Carsh and immediately stepped away.

Her face twisted into a snarl, but Kitable did not hear what she shouted. Unlike the men, she did not retreat; she pulled her short knife in readiness. Carsh's one blade went away upon his final approach. When he grabbed the woman's wrist and twisted the blade from her grip, his hands were empty.

She shouted something further, but no one nearby moved to assist. Seeing Carsh's grin, Kitable's stomach knotted. Despite never having seen such a grin on Carsh's face before, he knew perfectly well what it meant.

Tucking the woman's blade into his belt, Carsh dragged her into a shelter kicking and punching.

Kitable released that portion of his mind, returning his full attention to the tent where Tohmas had vanished. At the least, he could ensure the prince was not intruded upon.

"Wait until morning. Rest here." Healing Mother Vera's words were soft, yet Sabian knew there was no give in them. He would not be allowed to leave if the healing mother did not permit it. There were soldiers on the door for that.

Sabian lay back onto the mat. A thick wool covering kept the cold of the wood from seeping in, and the many coal lamps warmed the waggon's interior. At the farthest wall, an altar to Pari—a large quartz stone engraved with aa zig-zag mountain sign—glittered in the low light. A white-robed man lay next to it with blood-soaked, bandaged wrists. Celebrant Calanor had been given a place of honor next to the altar, or perhaps the man was in need of the most blessings. His wounds were severe, his blood loss profound. Two protectors remained over him, obeying the prince's command to safeguard him.

There were worse places to sleep, Sabian decided. He had been given a place closer to the door, his wounds not as grievous. By morning, he would return to Carsh's side. He was warmer than he had been in mooncycles.

Before he could sleep, a familiar face leaned over Sabian. Protector Derry had left his vigil over Calanor to check on him.

"Your hand slip, kid?" the protector asked. "I never expected to see you visiting a waggon for a knife wound. I figured you were beyond making mistakes."

Sabian shrugged then winced when pain shot though his shoulder. His entire arm felt bruised. "This is what you get for sparring with someone who doesn't know how to use the flat."

"I've not seen you get hit by anyone you spar with, Sabian."

"I'm hoping people won't make a fuss about it."

Derry nodded wisely. "Well, you're better off than some." Sabian followed the man's gaze to Celebrant Calanor. The second protector watched over the unconscious man as a healing hand acolyte replaced

the bandages over Calanor's arms. The smell of burning flesh lingered in the waggon.

"Attacked by Rydans," Derry said. "Gods, they make me nervous. But our prince could convince the grass to tangle DoomDragon's feet, so I guess he can make the most of those brigands."

"What makes you think Celebrant Calanor was attacked by Rydans?" Sabian asked. His experience with Rydans had been limited to two individuals, but what he knew made him doubt Derry's assumptions.

The protector, now happy to have an audience, quickly replied, "Man's got no hands. They cut out his tongue too. That's too cruel to be—"

"Rydans would have killed him," Sabian countered. "They wouldn't go through the effort of maiming him. Someone was trying to silence him."

The protector looked pensive then shrugged. "The man should be dead. Apparently, this final cold snap froze his arms and stopped the bleeding. I suppose there's something appropriate about having a Celebrant of Totho saved by winter, but the whole thing makes my stomach turn." When Sabian gave no reply, the protector cocked an eyebrow and added, "I heard Calanor was responsible for the fires in the Temple waggons last fall. People say he ran off to join DoomDragon."

"Tohmas wouldn't defend him if he was traitor."

Derry nodded, his expression crunched in thought. "All I know now is that I have an unconscious, mute man under my care with specific orders to see him live. Problem is, the man doesn't seem to want to regain consciousness. Maybe I wouldn't either if I'd had both hands cut then frost-bitten black, but every time I look at him, I get the feeling he's already dead and nothing we do will change that."

Sabian could not argue. From what he knew of the fires, Calanor had already been betrayed by Celebrant Sedgan. His current state implied whoever had helped him survive the winter had betrayed, maimed, and abandoned him. What had the celebrant left to live for?

As the protector gave a final wish for Sabian's well-being, Sabian caught sight of movement. A sandy-haired boy was peering into the room through the door.

Timon, as the child had eventually introduced himself, had been surviving in Fixer City as an errand boy and visited Sabian whenever

his work allowed. He never mentioned the night Sabian saved him by confronting the masked arsonists who had burned the Temple waggons.

Seeing the boy's wide eyes brought the encounter back to Sabian with unsettling clarity.

"Derry," Sabian called, halting the protector's withdrawal. "That kid been coming in here?"

Following Sabian's stare, the protector caught sight of Timon as the boy ducked out of the waggon. "On and off. Keeps looking but doesn't come in. Seems harmless. We figured he was waiting for someone. Probably sticking his head in every Healing waggon's window."

Sabian shook his head. "I'll bet you a cycle's pay he's not moved more than a dozen paces from this waggon. If you want to help your celebrant, Protector, bring that boy to see him."

The protector lost his glare. "A friend of the celebrant?"

"It certainly wouldn't hurt," was all Sabian would promise.

After conferring with the other protector, Derry left the waggon and returned with the boy in his shadow.

Under the supervision of the protectors, Timon knelt beside the celebrant and, true to his faith, remained silent despite the tears that landed on his lap in the lamp light.

In the morning, before Sabian was allowed to leave, the celebrant woke.

It was hard to tell if the man was thrilled or heartbroken to see the child, but Sabian reasoned it was probably both.

The reunion as tender; the two treasured each other's company in the dawn. One arm touched the boy's shoulder in forgiveness, and the child lay beside his master, his head on the maimed man's chest. Together they lay, arms around the other, in perfect, sweet silence.

Sabian returned to his campfire, his shoulder aching with stitches and bandages. Still, the image of the celebrant, the acolyte snuggled against him, stuck with him. He had not seen love like that, the love for family, since his brother, Ciene, had died. He had known allies and squad members, even friends, but not family.

Seeing the overwhelming joy Timon had upon findings his master again brought the pain of Ciene's passing back to Sabian with potency.

For the first time, Sabian wept in grief, grateful that no one was around to see it.

From his viewpoint above, Kitable watched the Rydan's celebration. There was enough going on to distract Kitable from the uncomfortable knot in his gut. He was grateful when Tohmas finally remerged and Kitable could focus on the prince, guarding him in place of the prime protector.

As the fires burned low and the people slunk out of sight for a final time, the prince left the camp to visit the horses which had gathered in herds to the west and south of the camp. Answering Tohmas' whistle, a dappled grey mare joined him ono the trampled terrain, her winter coat wooly. Behind her, the herd dug at the snow, revealing patches of brush to snack on in the early morning's light.

Tohmas sat for long moments in the snow with one hand on the nose of the horse. When he offered the mare a handful of grain he had stolen from the sack behind the house, she ate readily.

After long enough for the cold to really settle in, Tohmas stood and made his way back to HillTop alone.

Kitable followed, watching as the prince snuck back into his own tent through the rip in the canvas. With Carsh gone, there was no danger of being detected. Kitable directed his Scry in, navigating around to the main entrance.

He arrived in time to see Tohmas pull off his shoes and kneel in front of his altar and the lamp there.

Kitable was debating interrupting when the prince's head abruptly whipped toward the bed. Kitable turned his Scry, fearing a threat, but he saw nothing. Knowing his Scrys lacked auditory, he attributed the prince's sudden alertness to a sound.

He began to reconsider when Tohmas slowly stood, walked over, and knelt beside the bed as if he was at the altar. Unable to see any reason for the change, Kitable moved in closer. The cot was empty, the blankets still laid out awaiting sleep.

When Tohmas spoke, Kitable was at a loss. The prince then paused and tilted his head, listening. After a few more words, the prince rose and sat on the sleeping furs as if beside someone.

There has to be someone there, Kitable decided. He reassessed the stacked blankets and decided one blanket might be imprinted as if sat upon.

The blankets beside Tohmas suddenly shifted and pulled back, and Kitable had his suspicion confirmed. Although Tohmas could see an intruder, Kitable could not.

Someone hidden from Scrys by magical shields would have triggered Kitable's spells. If he could not see the person, that meant *magic* could not see the person.

It had to be an untouchable.

Loni was the most obvious answer. Although she had been gone almost all winter, the woman was volatile.

But the more he considered it, the less sense it made. The prince was being courteous and unassuming. Loni worshiped Tohmas as the Champion of Inac. Would *she* not be kneeling to *him*? Why did Tohmas seem so cautious? *Why is he not behaving like a prince in the presence of a celebrant?*

When the answer struck him, Kitable dismissed it as too implausible. Then, when no other explanation sufficed, he considered it for a second time, trying to overcome his disbelief.

He did not believe in gods and never had. The idea of a god sitting among the stars above, dictating the course of time and space, had been introduced to Kitable too late; he had already known the workings of the stars, time, and life. There remained things unknown, but surely, in time, those things would be understood too.

Yet untouchables were always powerful celebrants. No one knew from whence their immunity to magic came except that it was not wizardry.

Could their resistance to magic be a gift from their god? And would the divinity not also be immune to magic?

More than one celebrant had called Tohmas the Champion of the Goddess Inac.

"Princes bow only to the gods," he'd heard said. Kitable had considered it to be the epitome of their arrogance, but under these circumstances, perhaps it had a more literal meaning. The prince was behaving like a man in the presence of his superior. In mortal terms, there was no one superior to a prince.

Kitable decided he did not want to know the answer. Tohmas was in no danger, even if the Goddess Inac was present.

Instead of meddling in the affairs of gods, Kitable let the Scry drop. It was the most prudent thing to do while he reanalyzed the evening and his entire view of religion.

Chapter 15

Carsh left Darcina early, wanting to be back with Tohmas by dawn. It took great effort to avoid waking her, but daylight was too close. She would forgive him for leaving. There would be time later.

Both camps—Rydan and Esparan—were quiet under a light snowfall as he crept back up the hill. A handful of the sentries were brave enough to wish him a good morning. He smiled or scowled at them depending on his whim.

Once at Tohmas' tent, Carsh surreptitiously checked on Sabian, pleased to find the injured boy at in his usual campfire. Had the wound been more serious, the Healing waggons would have kept him. Instead, he was bandaged but otherwise hale. *At least Sabian is right-handed.* The wound would slow him down a bit but not—

Something exploding interrupted Carsh's thought.

The Outlands only ever exploded when the volcanoes in the DragonTail Mountains were active, but there were no mountains here. Thinking it had to be magic, Carsh drew an extra blade. Puffs of smoke rose beyond the nearest row of tents. Protectors flooded in to surround the command tent. Soon Tohmas was present, having rushed out from his tent, sword in hand.

Nothing followed. The cold air passed through the tents, blowing up the snowbanks to dust them with flakes.

Carsh joined Tohmas, unsure. He searched for Master Kitable, expecting him. He did not initially find the master wizard.

CHAPTER 15

Is it not magic?

A new snap and hiss reached his ears. Fresh lines of fire, like burning wicks, snaked along the snowy ground between the tents. The four smokeless fires converged on a nearby storage waggon. There, the flames climbed the waggon and exploded.

Onlookers flung themselves down or behind cover. Carsh and Tohmas ducked but otherwise held their footing, ready. Magic finally arrived nearby; Master Kitable entered the area at a run. The wizard kept near the corner of the command tent as if wanting to remain unobserved. He needn't have bothered; all eyes were on the burning waggon.

Carsh still sensed no magic from the fires. Further confounding him, the waggon was intact. *What had exploded? What is our enemy up to?*

Behind a wall of flames, the door of the blazing waggon flew off its hinges, and a woman stepped out.

Carsh's heart skipped, and his chest tightened painfully for the second time in as many days. He had no fear of men, flyers, or death, but what he saw before him was none of those. Those were natural flames, not magical. The woman was not a flyer, but she stood among the fires without being burned. Her face was not even flushed.

Her beauty, as revealed by a long, golden dress that clung to her every curve, made him long for Darcina. Fiery red hair lay flat against her head and, unnaturally, did not move as she stepped down from the waggon's entrance. Her dress equally seemed immune to heat and flames, although it glistened like embers as she walked. Her skin flickered golden in some light and red in others, like the flames around her.

Tohmas acted first; he knelt. When his brother lowered himself into that submissive, waiting stance, Carsh dropped to his knees as well. As the first son of the chief, the only person Tohmas was expected to kneel to was Tamv. If he was kneeling, the woman outranked Tamv.

It could only be Inac, Goddess of Fire.

Even as he lowered his head, Carsh could see other people rushing forward. Every last one of the protectors, seeing Tohmas, knelt as well. Celebrant Sedgan emerged from behind the command tent and swiftly adopted the same position. His crowd of acolytes went with him.

For a long moment, no one moved. The only sound came from the roar of the fire that burned, yet did not consume, the waggon.

The woman's hoarse voice rose above the flames. "Come to me, my Champion!"

Carsh knew his brother well enough to read the apprehension on Tohmas' face. He was slow to bring himself to his feet. Carsh knew he was not to follow. In the presence of the Goddess of War and Lust, Carsh felt too weak to rise regardless.

As Tohmas walked over the new-fallen snow to the waggon, Carsh glanced up. He felt magic reach out to Tohmas briefly and tracked the source—Master Kitable. The spell, Carsh was certain, had been a defense, but he assumed it was useless.

Everything was useless. His blades, despite normally being a comfort, hung limp in his grip. He could not strike a goddess. Even if she wanted to kill Tohmas, Carsh was powerless to stop her. This was Inac, Goddess of Fire, War, and Lust. She could not be harmed by a mere mortal.

Inac had Tohmas kneel again at her feet once he reached the edge of the fires, and they conversed in words that were swallowed by the growl of the flames. His throat dry, Carsh watched from under half-lowered eyes. The camp was silent enough to let him hear his own heart pounding.

At length, the Goddess drew a sword from a scabbard. The air around Carsh tightened, and he struggled to breathe for a long moment.

The smooth blade reflected the fires brightly. It was Esparan in style, but the metal's sheen was silver not grey iron. Precious gems flickered over the quillon and the pommel, rough-cut and hardy, lending the sword a sense of purpose instead of ornamental ceremony. When she lifted it high, it was so light it moved like smoke.

Carsh lifted his head, as did the crowd, eyes fixated on the glittering sword.

"To the works of Fire," Inac announced for all to hear, "I give you SoulBurner. Only in the hands of the true ruler of Espar, as chosen by his people and accepted by the gods, will its full power be revealed. Into your keeping, my Champion, I bestow this gift."

The Goddess presented the green-coppered hilt to Tohmas. After a moment of further awed hesitation, the prince accepted it. The instant his hand closed around the grip, red light engulfed him. While most people ducked their heads again to shield their eyes, Carsh involuntarily

stood in alarm. But when the light dimmed, Tohmas stood with the blade in hand, unharmed and grinning. Carsh puffed out the breath he had been holding.

The woman had vanished in the moment of brilliant illumination.

Tohmas' sword was ablaze. Red light continued to lick off the surface of the silver blade well beyond reflections from the waggon's flames at his back. A crimson aura surrounded him as he knelt, turned the blade point down to the earth, and started to speak.

After only a few words, the crowd joined him, and Carsh lowered back into a kneeling position. His Esparan was good enough to allow him to speak Inac's prayer with the rest of them.

Kitable cast his daily hovering spells before sunrise as always but added several additional spells. He held plenty of shields in reserve, while powerful retaliation spells were keyed to a variety of circumstances.

Underway to the prince's tent, Kitable reviewed the spells and the sequences required to make them effective. The recitation kept him from overthinking the events from the night before. He had already reviewed the Scry, both in memory and through divinations. He still had no explanation for Tohmas' visitor the night before except that it could not be a god. Gods were things of faith and fantasy. Celebrants could preach all they wanted, but Kitable knew the gods were no more than mankind's attempts to justify their own existence and explain the world.

The lack of an alternative explanation nagged at him, but there were spells he did not understand too. Mysteries were interesting because they could be solved. Answers were not always obvious. This mystery would be solved after further investigation.

Kitable was part of the way to Tohmas' tent when something exploded. Four puffs of smoke rose disturbingly close to the prince's tent.

He sprinted the last distance but skidded to a stop when another explosion, this time centered on a waggon down from the prince's tent, went off. Although he activated Spell Sight, there were no magical auras to light up the dawn save for the wards of the prince's tent. A crowd

gathered, but no one attempted to put out the fires. There was no immediate danger, as the fires were not spreading. Everyone waited.

When a woman stepped out of the waggon, Kitable's hovering spells shook. He had learned to recognize the sensation; she was an untouchable.

The prince, caught in front of his tent, knelt. Everyone else followed. A goddess walked among them.

Kitable remained standing, his mind reeling. He *knew* a goddess could not be standing before them, but she certainly looked like one. She was stunningly beautiful, her brilliantly red hair lying unnaturally still down her back. She wore a strange golden dress and carried an ornate sword the likes of which Kitable had never seen. In every detail, she was the embodiment of the Goddess Inac.

Yet Kitable doubted.

The woman called for Tohmas, and the prince unflinchingly obeyed. Kitable warily tossed a shield onto the prince, feeling he had to try. The woman—goddess?—was untouchable. The spell would die the moment she touched him.

"You are not kneeling," a voice pointed out from beside him.

Shimmer Weaver had arrived at his side and was now breathlessly peering up at him. He was unexpectedly pleased to see her. Her faded skirt and blouse brought a flood of reality, giving him an anchor as his thoughts threatened to sweep him away. If another caster was present, he could not show doubt.

"Neither are you," he replied, thankful his voice sounded calm.

"I lost faith in celebrants and their gods a while back," Shimmer told him flatly. "What's your excuse?"

"I don't believe in gods," Kitable said, his eyes on the woman standing above Tohmas' kneeling form, a burning waggon behind her. The perfect skin of the goddess glistened like still water, casting sparkles around her and the prince.

"Odd to hear from someone staring at a goddess. But then, it's hard to believe in divinity when you can explain miracles." Without waiting for an invitation, she continued, "Those lines of fire that lit the waggon were probably grey dust. Dangerous stuff. You can get it in Lour, where they mine and mix it. Burns fast but not hot and gets consumed so there'll be no evidence. She must've soaked the waggon's

wood in something to get it to catch like that. I would've used liquid air. You can get it out of the south of Damoria. Gotta carry it in wax-sealed containers, but it burns slow. Since it'll ultimately light the wood itself on fire, she wouldn't have to worry about it going out."

Proving Shimmer right, the edge of the waggon's wooden frame was beginning to blacken.

"Then there's her ability to stand in the middle of the fire without burning," Shimmer continued. "She's not even flushed, which means she rubbed menthe on her skin before going in. That reflective surface is probably powered silver in ointment, although it could be ground glass. That's a bit more expensive and dangerous. She would have had to treat her hair and clothes with something—maybe watered famn sap—to keep it from catching fire, which would also explain why her hair and clothes are so stiff."

After a brief pause to catch her breath, Shimmer smiled sadly and finished, "And then there's her familiar face."

For the first time, Kitable concentrated on the woman's features. The flames made her skin reflect colorfully, but he could make out a familiar face.

It was Loni Firedancer.

"Why does she think no one will recognize her?"

"How many men look at her face? Besides, she's changed herself quite a bit. Her hair is clean and loose, not tangled. The paint around her eyes is gold, not black, and her lips are golden instead of Loni's deep crimson. She always wears striking paints on her face. When people look at her, that's all they see. It's a disguise. Take away those defining characteristics, and even the prince probably can't tell."

The prince's extended hand accepted the sword from the woman, and Kitable's shield spell broke.

"Demons. Spell broke," he grumbled. The loss of the shield did not surprise him. It probably had been Loni in the prince's tent the night before. She may not have been officially back in HillTop, but it was clear she had returned.

"She's untouchable," Shimmer reminded him.

"He didn't touch her." Even from a distance, Kitable had seen the prince carefully avoid so much as brushing a fingertip against the

woman. He assumed the attentiveness was respect, but it could have been fear.

Bright red light burst from the pair, briefly obscuring Tohmas and the woman. Kitable waited to hear Shimmer's explanation.

Once the light had dimmed and Tohmas knelt with his new sword, Loni was nowhere to be seen. Shimmer swallowed hard and said, "Then again, maybe the Goddess decided to take a guise like Loni's. Maybe some part of her has been in Loni all along. Who knows? Maybe she *was* Loni."

Kitable shot the girl a skeptical glare. "And why would I believe that?"

Her crestfallen expression made him regret his tone. The apothecary's daughter was paler than he had ever seen.

"Because even I do not know how to make a sword burn like that."

When Kitable looked back at Tohmas, Shimmer slunk away.

It looked like magical fire, but the red aura that undulated up and down the sword was something different. Although the woman had vanished in the flash of light, Kitable's spells trembled.

Tohmas rose and slid the blade into a green and silver sheath, the light winking out. Joining his awed protectors, the prince called Kitable over. The crowd moved in around the waggon, where Celebrant Sedgan began to preach. Kitable eyed it. Hopefully, when the wood caught in earnest, someone would prudently extinguish it.

Kitable approached Tohmas slowly, feeling for the shiver of magic with every step. It had vanished with the sheathing of the blade.

Tohmas cocked an eyebrow and asked, "Is there a problem, Master Kitable?"

I probably look like I've been turned upside down and shaken. Leaving a few paces between them, Kitable tentatively replied, "That sword..."

Tohmas grinned and reached for the hilt. "Amazing, is it not?"

"No, no, don't draw it!" Kitable shouted, scrambling back. "That light, that confounding fiery..."

"She said it would protect me from fire."

"Protect you? That's not even half of what that is! Not even a fraction! Not even..."

"Kit?" Tohmas pressed when Kitable became too flustered to finish his sentence.

He had to take a few deep breaths.

"The sword is untouchable. Only it can't be because an item cannot be untouchable. Still, it seems that light may very well have the same effect as my getting a kiss from your favorite celebrant. I don't want—"

"We should probably figure that out," the prince interrupted.

As much as Kitable did not want to see any more untouchable powers, he had to agree. "Here," he said, placing a small Tracker spell, like the one he often placed on Tohmas' belt, on the mud at Tohmas' feet. He backed away and invited Tohmas to draw the sword. As he had expected, the sword burned in quasi-magic fires, and the Tracker was dispelled.

"Put it away?" Kitable requested from a distance. Once the blade was sheathed, Kitable tossed Tohmas one of his trinkets.

While the prince held up the bauble and raised an eyebrow at him, Kitable attempted to cast a Tracker on Tohmas' belt. It failed.

Satisfied, he approached and extended his hand. Tohmas tossed him back the trinket. A feeling of magic came with the item.

Kitable censored his curses, trying to remain factual. In a quiet voice, not wanting others to overhead, he explained, "I cannot bind you even with the blade away. But you are not dispelling things per se; the trinket is unaffected. Once the light burns when the sword is drawn, it dispels everything."

"It is a miraculous gift from Inac herself," Tohmas said.

Kitable sighed. He thought of explaining the "miracles" as Shimmer had, but he had no answer for the sword itself. Its power was real. And contradicting the prince in front of a crowd would be ... a bad idea at best and disastrous at worst. He would take time to study the sword first then talk to the prince in private, he decided.

"We had better warn Master Clarin that your goddess is being generous," Kitable said instead.

"Can I get on with DoomDragon's defeat now?"

Kitable miserably nodded. "I take it this doesn't change your plans for the day."

"Not in the slightest. The day is blessed!" Tohmas called over his shoulder, leading the way into the tent.

Kitable dragged his feet after the prince. "Just warn me before you draw that thing!"

When there was a commotion, including unexpected pillars of smoke, Seria investigated with a discrete Scry.

She followed the smoke to a burning waggon and spotted Tohmas and his protectors, including the Rydan prime protector. Their attention was on a burning waggon.

A burning waggon was no reason for the Esparans to be kneeling. Seria did not understand.

It took the presence of a celebrant, who took his turn kneeling, to make her take a closer look at the waggon. When Tohmas moved and knelt again, Seria decided something was evading her Scry. She added Spell Sight, thinking to reveal concealing magics, but saw nothing new.

The prince reached out, and the Scry shook. Prince Tohmas vanished.

But the people were still watching, and the protectors did not seem concerned that their prince had disappeared. Their gazes continued to track movement. The prince must have shielded himself. Master Kitable was no doubt around somewhere. If her Scry had been detected, the wizard would protect his patron. He could even block her Spell Sight if he was being extra cautious. Surely, that was all it was.

Soon enough, the prince reappeared, and Seria reconsidered. She was still watching when Kitable approached him. The moment the prince reached for his sword—a new sword, Seria noted—Kitable stopped him. Her magic was still uneasy. Something had changed.

She moved in to closer to examine the new sword but saw nothing special. When Prime Protector Carsh tilted his head toward her, a hound scenting prey, Seria dropped the Scry. If the Rydan alerted Kitable, she would be in a fight she was not yet ready for. Dropping the Scry left no trail for Kitable to follow.

She spent a few moments reorienting herself. DoomDragon was waiting nearby.

"Well?"

She told him what she had seen, and not seen, but DoomDragon was not satisfied.

"Contact Clarin. I would hear more of this."

Within a candle, they had a full explanation.

CHAPTER 15

"A goddess stepped out of the waggon and handed Tohmas an enchanted sword called SoulBurner. As long as he carries it, he cannot be targeted by magic. When he draws it, it dispels magic within three paces. He will be testing it today. They are attacking."

Surprisingly, DoomDragon had nothing to say. The Northlander retreated to his tent alone.

Despite being tempted to Scry on him, Seria instead double-checked her spells, knowing that a duel with Kitable was fast approaching. She called for Master Terant.

The war would end.

Sabian awoke when the light of the morning had turned his tent into a humid, uncomfortable cave.

When he emerged into the cold air, he was surprised to find the area around the prince's tent crowded. He asked around and was pointed to the smoldering waggon nearby, which apparently had produced a goddess. Sabian was certain the man was leading him on until the guardians began to arrive at the tent. A pair of them went in talking about the enchanted sword Tohmas had received from Inac herself that morning. The celebrants were in a mad tizzy. No deity ever had been seen by so many. The Gathering of Inac was proudly preaching from every corner of HillTop.

Sabian had slept through a divine visitation.

His shoulder was sore but less so than he had expected. Leaving behind the pain pills the cutter had given him, he rushed through his morning routine and ate a hasty meal. Carsh had not chastised him, making him think there would be no morning spar today.

As Sabian was dousing his fire for the day, two unexpected visitors joined him. After seeing the condition of the Wind Celebrant the night before, Sabian was shocked to see him up. Calanor Blow wore his hood up and a scarf over his face, leaving only a slit for his grey eyes. He had reclaimed the robes of a celebrant from somewhere and wore them like armor, his arms tucked in the star-patterned sleeves.

Timon followed Calanor like an extension of the flowing robes. Dressed in white and grey, he bore the mark of the Wind God on his

NORTHLANDER

cheek prominently. Considering what had happened to the rest of the acolytes, Sabian was impressed that the boy dared publicly advertise his faith.

Sabian offered them food, but neither accepted. Just as Timon seemed about to speak, Protector Linco arrived at Sabian's shoulder. It was unusual to see the shortest protector without a smile on his face, but Linco had forced his expression into one of neutrality.

"They await you, Celebrant," he said blandly.

The celebrant lifted his head, peering at the command tent calmly. Although rumors were still circulating about the loyalties of the Celebrant of Totho, Sabian knew the suspicions should have been directed toward Celebrant Sedgan, not Calanor. Sabian had seen the masked arsonists in Inac's colors. Fleeing from HillTop had been a matter of survival for Celebrant Calanor.

"Prince Tohmas knows what happened at the Temple waggon fires," Sabian assured them. "You are protected here."

Calanor's slow nod answered.

"Very well," Timon whispered for him, standing and assisting the celebrant to his feet. The protector respectfully stepped back, bowing his head as they passed.

"You too, kid," Linco said, his typical grin returning. "Don't know how you got yourself injured, but you're going to have to suck it up for now. They need you. Come on."

"Me?" Sabian choked out. He straightened. "Carsh—"

"Prince Tohmas has requested you," Linco corrected. "Mind your manners when you're in there. Don't get too chatty or anything."

Linco chucked as he pushed Sabian forward gently, guiding him into the green lit interior of the tent. Sabian ensured he had a knife in hand as Carsh always did, but he chose his smallest one, not wanting to offend the protectors or the prince.

Within the tent, Master Kitable and Master Clarin sat opposite one another at the table with Prince Tohmas and Prince Barnon side by side, forming the third point of a triangle. Carsh paced behind the table, two blades playing over his hands. He did not acknowledge Sabian.

Calanor slowly lowered himself into the chair beside Kitable, Timon standing directly beside his celebrant. With the celebrant sitting, the child and he were now of equal height.

As Sabian arrived, unsure if he should sit, Master Kitable shifted back and drew his hands from the table in evident discomfort. Had the wizard been a man of the sword, Sabian would have thought he was going for a knife. Instead, the wizard sat his hands on his lap like a schoolboy trying not to fidget.

Clarin's discomfort was less subtle; the Prime Protector of Solta openly sneered at Celebrant Calanor then leaned over and warned Tohmas, "He fled to DoomDragon the night of the Temple waggon fires. He could be a spy."

Prince Barnon nodded pensively, but Tohmas snorted. "Do you sense magic on him?" Tohmas asked. Clarin shook his head, his frown deep. "Then how, lacking tongue and hands, do you expect him to be reporting anything, Master Clarin?"

Barnon joined in at once, following Tohmas' lead. "It is good to have the Wind god's support again."

Clarin sat back and sulked.

Raising his voice, Prince Tohmas said, "I welcome you home, Celebrant. Your safety is my paramount concern. I offer you whatever service you require and my oath to keep you safe."

Calanor nodded softly. Timon, acting as a voice for the celebrant, opened his mouth to reply.

Suddenly, Master Kitable kicked backward, throwing himself out of his chair. "Demons!" the wizard shouted as he scrambled away. "Not again!"

Carsh was on the table in the next instant, and Sabian snapped another blade out in readiness. His shoulder sharply throbbed, but his left arm still moved smoothly. Even Clarin shot to his feet, although he seemed to have no idea why. Tohmas was on his feet, his hand hovering over his sword's hilt, while Barnon clumsily drew his own weapon.

Everything paused. The only movement was Timon closing his mouth. There was no target, no enemy. Sabian did not know why Kitable had panicked.

Slowly, Calanor looked over at Kitable, prompting him to explain with a gaze.

Kitable rose to his feet with an indignant flare of his robes and stared back at Calanor. "Congratulations. You have found your faith, Celebrant. You are officially an untouchable!"

Clarin took a step back, but Sabian cocked his head, not under-standing the word. He kept both blades in hand, as did Carsh.

The acolyte looked at his celebrant and, either reading his eyes or speaking for himself, said, "He does not understand."

"Will you stop doing that!" Kitable cried. "It's bad enough that to touch you would end our spells! Stop making it flare out, please!"

Timon again looked at Calanor, but even Sabian couldn't read the celebrant's thoughts this time—he was baffled.

In time, even Kitable recognized their confusion. His voice calmed. "I do not know how, but you are sending out a wave of anti-magic that is coming dangerously close to..." He jumped another step back. "There it goes again!"

"He does not know what he is doing, Master Kitable," Timon said in a whisper. "It is not deliberate."

"I believe him," Prince Barnon interrupted.

"As do I," Tohmas added. "This is uncontrolled. He knows not what he does."

Although Kitable kept his suspicious frown, he reassessed the boy and the celebrant. "How do you know what he is thinking, Acolyte?"

The boy, seemingly surprised at the attention, shrugged. "I know what he wants to say."

"He is Sending to you," Kitable concluded. "He is manifesting magic-like powers, only they are untouchable. To me, it is a dispel." He looked pensive for a moment, then added, "This day is not starting well for us wizards."

Tohmas lowered himself back into his seat, and Barnon did the same, sheathing his weapon. Sabian mirrored Carsh; when the prime protector jumped off the table and took a position beside his prince, Sabian took the other side, near Prince Barnon, defensively. He would not show weakness to Carsh, no matter his injury.

The two worshippers met each other's stares. Master Kitable flinched again.

"He will try to control this power you describe," Timon promised.

Kitable's sour expression softened. "Sendings should travel in a straight line between the caster and the target. You seem to be Sending only as far as your acolyte, but in all directions. If you hit either me or Master Clarin with that, our spells will be affected. You need to, for

lack of a better word, aim. Concentrate your thoughts and send them directly to your acolyte. Do not just think out loud, and please, whatever you do, never 'speak' to me!"

"He will do as you ask," Timon said. "But you may wish to sit farther away."

"Fine. I am starting to think it will be a miracle if I get through the day without being dispelled," Kitable replied.

He got a sympathetic, though sad, smile from Clarin as they both stepped back to the table. Kitable took the chair as far from Calanor as was possible.

As the wizards retook their seats, Master Clarin said, "The day will certainly improve, for we will deal with our trio of wizards today. Ready for a duel, or three, Master Kitable?"

Calanor's eyes narrowed, and Sabian tensed. He did not know why, but something Clarin said had upset the celebrant.

Kitable shouted a curse and threw himself backward again, this time topping the chair and falling far from the table. Carsh and Sabian moved forward, shielding the princes, but it was too late. Prince Tohmas gasped. Confusion on his face, as if he had been hit in the gut and did not know why, he leaned over the table with both hands pressed against its surface.

Carsh's head swiveled from Tohmas to the rest of the table in frustration. Sabian could see no target either. If Tohmas was under attack, they needed to know the source. Training with Carsh had impressed upon Sabian the danger of wizards, but neither caster was moving. Master Kitable looked perplexed, Clarin banally concerned. And Tohmas had extended his protection to Calanor. Without the prince rescinding the order, Sabian could not harm the celebrant.

"*D'aems,*" Tohmas muttered at last, blinking as if to clear his eyes from sand.

"He is Sending to *you* now?" Kitable snapped, coming to his feet.

Tohmas did not seem to hear the question. Instead, he stared hard at the celebrant and demanded, "Are you absolutely certain?"

The importance of the answer was evident in the prince's voice. Timon checked twice with his celebrant before replying, "Without a doubt."

Releasing a sigh of resignation, Tohmas shook his head. Then he stood slowly, reaching for SoulBurner once more.

"Carsh, wisavi be goh. Flya be dearn'd."

Sabian translated the Rydan a heartbeat later: Wisavi Kitable was with them. The flyer—meaning Clarin—was a traitor.

Everyone moved.

Chapter 16

Any man who dearn'd— who betrayed and dishonored their chief— deserved death. While Tohmas had used Rydan to hide the declaration, to Carsh, it was clear—Clarin was a traitor. Worse, he was not a wizard; he was a flyer. He was using magic malevolently.

Carsh threw himself at the flyer. A magic shield kept him and his knives back, but the force of the attack still knocked Clarin backward off his chair, Carsh atop him. Carsh stabbed down with both hands. The blades were shunted aside by the barriers around the flyer.

He was aware of the Prince of Rabarch shouting something, but the words were irrelevant. The flyer had to die.

Clarin grunted out a word, and something invisible crunched into Carsh's gut, tossing him across the tent. As he fell, Sabian advanced. Carsh's Follower was attacking by the time Carsh found his feet and rushed the flyer again.

While Sabian ducked under Clarin's hand, the flyer activated a spell. Carsh felt the magic charging across the tent. Before it reached him, red light flooded around him, stopping the spell dead.

Seeing Tohmas holding his enchanted sword, Clarin cursed and quickly uttered another activation word. The flyer vanished.

"What, by the hells, is going on?" Kitable demanded in an exasperated voice. The dodging of untouchables, Carsh could tell, was wearing on their wizard. Kitable would not have understood the Rydan

so had taken no actions during the brief fray, at least none that Carsh had detected.

"Indeed! Explain this!" Prince Barnon added, drawing himself to his full height as if that would give his presence weight.

"Clarin has been working with DoomDragon," Tohmas said, sheathing SoulBurner so that Kitable could leave the corner he had withdrawn to. "Calanor recognized his voice. He heard it while in DoomDragon's company."

Kitable flatly cursed, making Carsh start. He had never heard the wisavi bother with swearing before.

"I'd better catch him before he goes back to them," Kitable said. With two more words, magic surged, and the wisavi vanished.

They paused, and Carsh took the moment to check his stomach for injury. Finding none, he shot a look at Tohmas. He wanted to hunt the flyer, but how was he to know where the monster had gone?

"We have to trust Kitable," Tohmas answered Carsh's unspoken question.

"I will not allow him to escape," Prince Barnon added. "Protector!"

The protector who popped into the tent lost his formal expression when Barnon said, "Have word sent to all the people of HillTop. Master Clarin of Solta is officially a traitor to Espar and should be killed on sight." To finalize the command, Barnon tossed the protector a token. Tohmas did the same, making the command doubly authenticated.

"Yes, my Prince," the protector stammered, surprise making his words skip. He rushed out.

Barnon was slow to compose himself, taking time to settle at the table and adjust his tabard. He had worn his red and black but now seemed to take exception to the black dragon's head on his chest and rubbed at it.

With both wizards gone, no one could tell them for sure, but Carsh suspected the boy was speaking for his master when the acolyte said, "Clarin will tell them everything."

Tohmas shrugged as he cautiously returned to his seat and spread his hands on the table. "Thankfully, he knows little."

"Little?" Barnon asked, his reddened face lifting. "But he was Sol's prime protector. He has been involved in your defenses extensively."

"He will not get far," Tohmas consoled.

"You trust Master Kitable to deal with him?"

"I do. And while Kitable keeps him busy, we need to get to business. Runnah!" A new protector—Protector Linco this time—popped his head in. "I need fifteen protectors in here for a mission. People like Derry or Geizer. Stealthy men."

Carsh chuckled, finally feeling confident enough to sheath a knife. He had always appreciated Prince Habal's tendency to select protectors with eclectic backgrounds. Tohmas had named two protectors known to be thieves in their previous lives.

In a matter of moments, fifteen of the self-selected sneakiest protectors stood in the room. Tohmas invited Sabian to leave his duties as Carsh's Follower and take a seat at the table. Opening a wax-wrapped package, Tohmas laid three blades on the table before Sabian.

"Thankfully, Clarin left before this much was revealed. Sabian, I need your skills."

Sabian shifted uncomfortably in his seat. Carsh frowned at him, and he stopped fidgeting.

"Your job," Tohmas told the protectors, "is to get Sabian within twenty paces of DoomDragon. Sabian, you need to score a blow against DoomDragon with one of these knives. All you have to do is draw blood. The poison will take him down. If you can, I'd like his body brought back to me, but if you can't, leave him. He's dead if we don't counter it." Tohmas took a deep breath in finality. "We can expect DoomDragon to be setting up his reserves on the east hill, so you can use the cliffs to block your approach and your escape."

"You know where DoomDragon will be?" Barnon asked. He studied the knives on the table from a distance as if expecting them to strike at him like snakes.

"He oversees the battles, which is why he was so keen to take the lake and keep the west hill. Now that the Rydans have the lake, he has only one place that works. That's where he'll be."

Carsh cleared his throat. "Pack Runna ken 'elp."

Tohmas cocked his head, pensive for a moment. Then he nodded. "We will have the Pack Runner join you. That's the man with the dogs you saw yesterday."

Carsh laughed at their aghast expressions. "'Ee be da best Rydan warrior," he said. The protectors stared at him, understanding coming

slowly to their faces. They knew Carsh was their better in one-on-one combat—he proved that at the morning spars—and he was Rydan. If Crawthran was the best, he was better than Carsh.

Tohmas explained further. "The Pack Runner is a knife dancer, a good man to have on your side. He and his dogs will be able to deal with DoomDragon's defenders."

"Meetin' ya ad da wahl," Carsh told them.

They looked at Tohmas for the translation.

"Gather at the east cliffs, behind the defenses. There is a tunnel under the snow, leading down to the lake. Once there, you can follow the shore east. It'll take you behind his viewpoint, so do not be seen. And don't wear tabards for this. Best if you're not recognized."

Carsh was impressed the protectors so readily accepted that. The Northlanders didn't abide by standards of war regarding identification, but the Esparan way of war would have required the tabards.

While Tohmas spoke, Sabian picked up a blade and turned it over in his hand. The directions done, all eyes went to Sabian.

"I am not an assassin," Sabian said, and Carsh balked. The boy had proven himself capable, especially for an Esparan. The prime protector had so much faith in his Esparan Follower that he was not worried about the boy's injured shoulder at all. That he might refuse had not occurred to Carsh.

"Are you implying a lack of skill or an objection of your conscience?" Tohmas asked as the boy slowly put down the blade.

"I may miss."

Carsh snorted.

"Demon shit. Your aim is impeccable, especially when you're stressed. I've not seen you miss a throw since Vait," Tohmas refuted.

"I missed in Vait," Sabian replied.

Tohmas glared at him. "You were a kid betting on a game. A lot has changed since then. You will make this throw."

Sabian had no choice. With a weak nod, he picked up the knives and their wraps.

"We'll start a scuffle to get you in. The guardians already know. Soon as I leave here, this begins. Go."

The protectors huddled together, swept Sabian into their midst, and left.

"I'll call my fighters. I hope Kitable is as good as you think he is," Barnon added.

Tohmas shrugged. "A smarter man than I by far. But we still have to hurry. We need to have things underway before our enemies realize their spy has been revealed."

Timon's soft voice reached out from beside Celebrant Calanor. "Good Prince, Celebrant Calanor requests permission to ride with you in the coming battle."

"I have a tendency of being in the thick of things, but so long as he is willing to brave that, he is welcome."

Carsh thought it wise; celebrants were favored by the gods. It would do well to have Totho's attention on their side for once. The Collector of Souls would no doubt approve of this winter battle.

Timon did not need to confer with his celebrant; he agreed immediately.

Then, with a grin Carsh loved seeing, Tohmas added, "You have given me an idea, Celebrant. *Runna*! Get me Celebrant Sedgan."

In the scuffle between Carsh and Clarin, Kitable had been too confused to attack. He had, however, thrown a Tracker onto Clarin's ankle.

The Tracker clung to the outside of Clarin's Molded Shield, following the wizard when he Relocated. Once Kitable heard Tohmas' explanations, Kitable located the Tracker and set an anchor on it. Another word activated his Relocation spell. Kitable was immediately at Clarin's location.

The low ceiling and cluttered bookcases of Clarin's vardo materialized around Kitable. Using the same spell Clarin had against Carsh, Kitable released an Ejecting Shield as he appeared, knocking the Soltan wizard into a wall. Kitable's next word, spoken before Clarin could roll over, locked a Seal spell over the vardo to stop any communication or Relocation spells. In the next moment, Kitable brought Spell Sight to bear.

Spell Sight identified a dozen defenses around Clarin, layered cleverly to require five or six dispels to get them all. Kitable sorted through

the auras, practiced at finding the pattern needed. The sooner this ended, the better.

In the flicker it took Kitable to contemplate his next spell, Clarin cried, "Kitable, stop! What have I done? Please!"

The terror in his voice made Kitable hesitate.

He had trusted Clarin more than he had trusted any other wizard in his life. They had defended BellRoost then HillTop together. Kitable felt he owed Clarin at least a chance to explain. What if someone was in error? Had the celebrant lied? *Will I kill based on Celebrant Calanor's word?*

"Tohmas identifies you as a traitor," Kitable said cautiously. He still sorted through the auras, seeking the path in.

Clarin, his mouth gaping wide, blanched. "I would never! Calanor was with DoomDragon! This is a trick to divide us; it must be. I am no traitor. It is the celebrant!"

His logic was dangerously plausible. Kitable knew the white horse bearing Calanor had escaped into the Northlander camp after the fires in the Temple waggons. The celebrant's return to HillTop to spread accusations was suspicious.

Clarin rose to his feet, and Kitable allowed it. His indecision held his spells at bay.

"You are the greatest threat to DoomDragon and his Northlanders. Dueling me will weaken you. If we fight, they will easily defeat you!"

Kitable was certain Prince Tohmas would not have accused Clarin lightly, but the Soltan wizard was making a reasonable argument. Guardian Carraway had identified Calanor as a guest, not a prisoner, of the Northlanders. *How can we trust a man suspected of arson and murder?*

If, as Clarin said, Calanor was lying, wasting magic on Clarin could be disastrous. Not only would he lose an ally, Kitable would be using up his hovering spells. Re-casting it all would drain his energy. He would be vulnerable to another duel, and he expected several today.

"That woman, Seria," Clarin continued, "no doubt seeks revenge for her capture. Black Agonies are not easily forgotten."

Right on too many accounts, Kitable thought.

Kitable triggered an Eight-layered Dispel, destroying the first two layers of Clarin's defenses.

CHAPTER 16

Only Shimmer and Seria had seen the Black Agony and Vox he had used to contain Seria. Shimmer would never have casually mentioned it to Clarin. If Clarin knew about the spell, he could only have learned about it from Seria.

Clarin retaliated, his lies over. Activating his own hovering spells, he sent two dispels and a Fire Burst against Kitable. The dispels were absorbed by concealed defenses, leaving his shields in place to deal with the Fire Burst. The attacking spell winked out without so much as a flicker of fire.

Kitable triggered three new attacks, but the glowing lines of color vanished as they hit shields Kitable had not seen despite Spell Sight. Kitable was surprised. He had not expected Clarin to be skilled enough to hide anything from him.

Clarin began full casting, giving Kitable time to destroy some of his foe's defenses with a combination of hovering and short full-cast dispels. Still, three visible layers remained by the time Clarin completed his casting.

Clarin's spell could not directly anchor on Kitable; his defenses prevented that. The spell instead appeared directly in front of him.

Kitable stepped back in shock. He had never seen anything like the wall that stretched across the width of the Seal spell in front of him. It shimmered, shook, flashed, and undulated in every color his Spell Sight could reveal. As near as he could tell, it channeled every element along every domain. It was protected against destructions, summoning, and alterations of every kind. Its purpose was obvious; the destructions would destroy a person.

No counter came to mind.

Words not spoken in casting during a duel were wasted opportunities, but Kitable was still uncommonly tempted to curse the glowing, flickering cornucopia of magic before him.

Had Clarin faked incompetence when he had been trapped by Kitable's Forced Confrontation spell? Or when he had so inefficiently cast the Relocation spell Kitable overheard? How could that man be the same who had created this abomination?

The spell advanced. Kitable stepped back and collided with the back of the vardo. With his own Seal stopping him from casting a Relocation spell and the door blocked by the immense wall, Kitable was trapped.

It took time to advance, giving Kitable time to further assess the auras. The Soltan wizard was still pouring energy in to expand it.

An open-ended spell needed continuous energy. If he could break Clarin's connection to the spell, it would stop.

It was, Kitable mused as he sat down with his back against the far wall, possibly the craziest thing he had ever attempted during a duel, but he saw no alternative. He sat down and activated a Scry. For location, he created it three paces ahead of him, on the far side of the wall.

He could not use spells that had to transverse the space between caster and target, but he could conjure or create through the Scry.

His detached vision showed him Clarin, bound to the spell and pouring magic into it through a visible thread. His defenses were still formidable. Kitable did not have time to break through more shields.

The threat was defended against destructive magic. He would have to be more creative.

Kitable invented the spell as he cast it, having never had the need for an open-ended eight-way alteration spell before. Once it was complete, he moved the Scry into Clarin's connection to the wall and, directing a powerful alteration, threw the channeled powers wide.

Clarin compensated, bending the lines of power to maintain his connection to the enlarging spell.

Free to adjust because his spell was also open-ended, Kitable shoved the powers up, twisting them. Clarin again turned the tether. Kitable switched angles and tried again. Clarin met his efforts.

Enervation seemed increasingly likely, but Kitable held on. His spell was smaller. He could hold it for longer than Clarin could.

If given enough time.

The spell continued to expand. When Kitable felt his foot ache, he knew he had run out of time. Desperate, he opened himself to the spiral of magic, drew as much magic as he could, and threw it all against the tendril. Gritting his teeth, Clarin reciprocated, pushing against Kitable's alteration with equal strength.

Kitable's foot stung sharply. He pushed harder, the flow of magic feeling like the rush of hot embers over his skin. The wall loomed closer, an avalanche threatening to suffocate him in magic.

In a blink, it lifted. The pain in his foot released, leaving an ache. Kitable dropped his Scry and drew back. Disoriented by the sudden

change of location, he stumbled and crashed into a bookcase. Books and trinkets scattered across the floor.

It was like coming up for air after diving for too long. All at once, the pressure of the magic around him was gone. The spell bearing down on him had vanished.

To his shock, so had Clarin.

Kitable verified the Seal; it was undisturbed. Spell Sight assured him that no powers were present on the far side of the vardo, but he dispelled illusions just in case. Nothing was revealed.

When he looked for his Tracker, Kitable had the impression he was trying to find a pebble at the bottom of a long, deep well. It took only a moment of searching for him to drop the Tracker in fear of falling in after it.

Clarin had pushed himself too far when using an open spell. Whether he was dead or just gone forever was irrelevant. It was over.

It took Kitable another three spells to exit the vardo without triggering a ward. He stepped out into the sunshine.

He glared at the chariot of Inac.

The day, despite his hopes, had gone from bad to worse. And by the shouts from HillTop, it was not over yet.

From the Match and Mixer's counter, Shimmer saw Caddic arrive at a sprint. The small boy ducked between two patrons, jumped onto the counter of the vardo, and whispered in Shimmer's ear, "He's casting." Proudly, he extended his hand.

Shimmer dropped a copper leg coin in his dirty, outstretched palm, and the waif skipped down. He left her wand on the counter before rushing back the way he had come, tattered coat trailing behind him.

He would then try to find the caster again, since they had learned that when there was magic at the vardo, it usually meant Clarin was on the move.

Passing off the patrons to her father, Shimmer took the wand into the back of Match and Mixer and analyzed it. Caddic's assignment had been Clarin's vardo. If the wand had activated, Clarin had been casting. Usually, that meant Relocation spell as Clarin never seemed to walk

anywhere these days. But the auras recorded by the wand were not the usual ones. In addition to *two* Relocations, there were defensive and offensive combinations.

"Gotta run, Papa," Shimmer called, leaping over the counter herself with her bag slung on one shoulder.

"Be careful, Shim!" Dust shouted after her.

Applying an alteration spell on herself, Shimmer gifted herself speed and headed for Master Clarin's vardo. Spell Sight was her next addition.

Before she could see the vardo itself, her vision was filled with auras. Most obviously, a Seal spell closed over the vardo. Untethered and permanent, even the wizard casting it would have to break through the spell to escape. It was not the kind of spell a wizard put up casually. Clarin was trying to keep something in.

She had been right; he was up to something.

Stopped in front of the vardo, Shimmer studied the colorful flashes of magic within the Seal. Every element and domain was present. A wall of magic was expanding, leaking between the cracks of the wood and shining brilliantly enough to leave her vision spotty. The amount of magic awed her. Never before had Shimmer seen a more powerful spell, not even when Master Kitable had used the enormous illusion to fend off the Northlanders. His magic was usually subtly potent, like a precise shot from an arrow, but this magic raged like a catapult. Shimmer trembled with the force.

An open alteration spell changed at a dizzying pace, matched by the flash and flicker of the wall spell within the vardo. The powers being channeled grew and grew until it felt impossible to contain even an ounce more.

Then, in an instant, it all vanished.

Shimmer released a breath she had unknowingly been holding. The air felt lighter. She blinked to clear the blinding spots from her vision.

For a long moment, nothing moved. The people around, oblivious to the tempest that had occurred in the vardo nearby, carried on.

Then, one by one, spells flashed, deactivating the Seal and unwarding the door. When the vardo door opened, Master Kitable stepped down.

The implications of his presence stunned Shimmer to silence. If *he* had been responsible, had that been a duel? Where was Master Clarin?

His glared up at the risen sun then checked his surroundings. His gaze found her. "Weaver," he growled.

Feeling his tension, Shimmer retreated two steps and lifted her hands out to her sides complacently. "I heard some magic was being tossed around."

"Heard? Demon shit. You were watching him. I take it you saw that?" As he descended from the steps of the vardo, he limped. Curiously, he was missing the front of one shoe. The tip of his exposed toes looked burned.

Shimmer nodded enthusiastically, knowing her eyes were wide in awe but unable to amend it. "I've never seen so much magic in one place before. That was amazing!"

"No," Kitable replied, "it was not. It was a flashy, sloppy spell countered by the proper application of conservative magic. Don't idolize power, girl. Idolize skill."

Shimmer scrambled out of the way, giving him a wide berth, but making to follow him. The master wizard's limp improved as he walked.

"Go home! This is not your fight!" he shouted without looking back.

She stopped, uncertain how far he would go to enforce the command.

"And stay out of my way," Master Kitable added before slipping out of sight among the tents of the camp.

Shimmer chuckled. "No way," she muttered as she set out on a circuitous route to Prince Tohmas' tent, certain the master wizard would soon be there.

Eventually, she thought. Might take him a while with that limp.

Prince Rairn stared at the Esparan army atop the hill, frowning deeply. The Esparans were moving. Seria had been right; they intended to attack now that the Rydans had seized the lake.

"He's got a lot of faith in his Rydan allies," Rairn commented, glancing to where DoomDragon stood below him. In an attempt to reclaim his authority, Rairn sat atop a warhorse adorned in leather and chain armor to match his. For the first time in mooncycles, he looked like a prince. "You said their numbers are still less than yours," Rairn said when DoomDragon gave no reply.

"We had allies arrive from the north," DoomDragon said, his voice a low growl. "If the Galanth leave their defenses, we hold the advantage. Tohmas must know as much."

The snow building the defenses up was almost entirely gone, except on the east hill facing DoomDragon's vantage point. The Esparan defenses were walls of soaking wet wood by now.

"Maybe he's counting on Kitable." Rairn shrugged. "If he wants to commit suicide, I'm happy to let him." Looking for support, Rairn glanced at the two wizards standing on the far side of DoomDragon.

Seria was the only one who noticed. She tilted her head, stopping short of shaking her head, but still disagreeing. "Kitable knows he is facing three wizards and their planning has been extensive. They are not underestimating us."

"But he *is* overestimating himself. He's placed trust in—"

At one time, no one would have dared interrupted a Prince of Espar, but DoomDragon tended to forget others were speaking. Rairn had become accustomed to it, as much as it irked him.

"Seria, tell your lover it is time. Your deception has served its purpose. Join him if you must but take Master Kitable out of this battle."

Seria's face lit up.

"I will go," Terant said, proving he had been listening. "I will take no chances. Tell Clarin."

Seria nodded, failing to hide her frown of disappointment.

She activated some magic Rairn could not see then squinted into the distance for a few moments. Her eyes going wide, she cursed. "I cannot find him!"

"For all the time you spend with him, how can you not define him?" Terant scolded.

"I *can* define him! I can't *find* him!"

"Have we a dead wizard?" Rairn asked the pair, but Master Terant shook his head.

"Not necessarily unless her definition of him includes breathing. Disintegrated or decapitated, perhaps."

"Tohmas does not normally draw attention to himself," DoomDragon commented absently.

"What are..." Rairn looked down. DoomDragon's eyes were on the ranks of assembled Esparan forces. A trio of riders had stepped out.

"Your eyes are better than mine," Rairn muttered, peering at the three horses in the distance. With some imagination, he could guess the lead horse to be a bay, but he would not have bet on it.

With a sweep of his hand, Master Terant created a spell in front of them. The distant shapes of the riders were magnified by a lens of stationary wind.

Rairn recognized the other two riders by their distinctive robes. A Celebrant of Inac, Celebrant Sedgan, rode on Tohmas' right hand. On his left rode a man dressed in white.

"But that is Tothonar!" Seria cried, glancing furtively at Master Terant.

Terant turned his cold stare on his apprentice. "You said he was dead."

"He was maimed and left in the snow!" she protested. "He could not have— "

If DoomDragon was shocked by the presence of the celebrant, he did not show it. Equally, however, the Northlander did not seem pleased. DoomDragon wore an expression of general annoyance, and Rairn could not decide if it was directed at him or not.

"The Winter Star protects his own. As the Wind willed, it is," DoomDragon said, but the answer did not appease Master Terant.

"Well, at least the celebrant has done us a favor this day. He is within reach of Tohmas. That demon-cursed sword will protect the prince, but he has not yet drawn it. Seria, target the celebrant," Terant directed.

Seria took a moment to pick a spell then activated it. Her face fell, and her jaw dropped. "I cannot. He must be shielded!"

With a quick word, Terant's eyes took on a shimmering, colorful shade. Soon the scintillating sight was glaring down at the girl next to him.

"There are no spells on either of the celebrants. Impossible child!" His next word was not Esparan, and Rairn guessed it to be a spell. The way the man pointed implied a more manual targeting, but still nothing changed on the field below. Tohmas, with his flanking celebrants, continued to walk forward.

Rairn considered giving the call to attack but decided to let Tohmas provide a larger target. The Prince of Galanth continued his calm approach, navigating the last of the southern hill defenses to stand between the armies.

"See!" Seria protested when the master's spell provided no satisfaction.

"The children," DoomDragon muttered to himself, "are bickering again. Shall we get on with—?"

The sentence stopped when light appeared around the trio of riders in the distance. Every set of eyes turned to examine the flare of red.

Rairn wanted to believe that the light was Master Kitable's doing, but he saw the truth on the faces of the wizards; the sword that Prince Tohmas had drawn was anything but magic.

The Galanth soldiers gave a cheer and filed out from behind the defenses, ready.

DoomDragon's words were calm. "Send a volley."

Answering DoomDragon's command, horns blared. A hail of slung stones lashed out at the enemy who had dared approach. Rairn had once doubted the effectiveness of stones compared to arrows, but after seeing the Hunters crack bones with their sling stones, he had gained respect for the weapon.

Along the west and east sides, the stones bashed against shields, producing a deafening clatter. But around Prince Tohmas, wind gusted down the hill, and the stones fell to the earth dozens of paces short. The red light added a flare that made Rairn growl.

"How the—"

"Another throw along the flanks," DoomDragon interrupted. "Move the central column to push the prince back. If they kill him, all the better." The commands were passed on hurriedly to runners.

"There!" Seria shouted.

Small bursts of light were knocking soldiers aside along the descent.

Kitable had positioned himself at the back of the advancing Esparan men. While Rairn identified him by his robes, he had to presume that Master Terant confirmed the identity with his colorful vision.

The way the Galanth caster's arm gestured made it look like he was waving at them. There may even have been a rude gesture in the mix.

"Master Terant, see to it," DoomDragon said.

"With me, Seria," Terant hissed. "We need to take this away from DoomDragon. We'll worry about Clarin's absence later."

The two headed toward the eastern fighting, and Rairn was left with only DoomDragon and a handful of Northlander Hunters.

CHAPTER 16

Tohmas and his celebrants held their position for only a heart-beat more then slowly retreated. The Northlander forces advanced on their position.

"I do not like this," DoomDragon rumbled.

Rairn took in a sweeping assessment of the battle then shrugged. "He's losing."

"Around the white rider, my warriors are unable to act. No one can touch Tothonar." DoomDragon pointed to the left. "Tohmas moves like he anticipated a retreat from the start." DoomDragon next looked east. "And where is the wizard now? The lights were but a fragment of his powers, and now they are gone. Was he baiting the casters?" In finality, he looked west and, at last, smiled. "The only place where things are as they seem is there. The Rydans, at least, are honest."

As Rairn opened his mouth to reply, his horse lurched and screamed. Pitched forward off the horse, Rairn caught a glimpse of a fur-covered man. DoomDragon pivoted, drawing his ax.

He glimpsed people approaching to the left, but the dead horse, its throat slashed, pinned him in the mud.

From the ground, he saw the Hunters move up to challenge a fur-covered stranger, but four hounds kept the guards at bay. The lithe Rydan, recognizable now that his fur coat parted, spun and attacked like a striking snake. The Hunters managed to push the attacker and his hounds away from DoomDragon but none landed a blow against the stranger.

With the war cries spurring him on, Rairn ripped his leg free. Pain from his ankle made his vision blank. When he finally blinked the lights from his eyes, a massive hound leaned over him, the snarling visage only a hand's breadth from Rairn's face.

Rairn threw himself sideways down the hill.

In the icy mud, he could not stop his descent. By the time he came to a halt at the bottom of the slope and looked back, the man in furs and his dogs were gone.

As was Darknim DoomDragon.

Hunters rushed the hill, the fighting distancing itself east over the water. Rairn rose to follow, but his ankle gave out under him.

The main battle was already slowing. Tohmas' fighters went into a full withdrawal. The last to retreat to their camp were the Rydans.

All went silent.

Chapter 17

"What, by the hells, was *that*?" Barnon asked when he arrived in Tohmas' tent.

Instead of arguing, Tohmas took the chair with the horn slung over it. The guardians had left. Tohmas' conversation with Rydan leader Burlotak had been exactly one word. Although Celebrant Sedgan had gone back to his Temple waggon, Calanor remained at the table. His presence meant Kitable had left after reporting that he had exchanged a few spells with two enemy casters before withdrawing. He was not in any condition to duel two wizards, not after defeating Clarin.

The battle, as Tohmas had expected, had been lost.

"Hundreds are dead or dying, Tohmas, for what?" Barnon exclaimed, tossing his hands in the air. "What did we accomplish with that row? Sol said you knew what you were doing! I trusted you! The Healing waggons are beyond capacity because of you and your stupid brigands, all too eager for a fight! What did you hope to accomplish? Why are there...?"

Barnon trailed off when Sabian was admitted into the tent. His clothing was soaking wet and spattered with someone else's blood.

Sabian lifted two daggers and asked Tohmas, "You want these back?"

Four protectors nudged past the boy and unloaded the unconscious man they carried.

"Consider them gifts. Be careful with them," Tohmas replied, unable to restrain his grin.

Finally, success.

The boy nodded as he numbly moved aside.

Protector Derry rolled the body over, revealing dragon scale as part of the armor. "Sabian's first knife got him under the arm as he went for the ax. Took another few flickers before he keeled over, but we got him. Only weapon's this." Derry placed the ornate dagger Tohmas had left as a *gef* on the table.

Barnon had been standing during his rant but now looked like he would fall over. His jaw dropped.

"Is that DoomDragon?" Barnon choked out.

It was for comments like this that Tohmas had sent Burlotak away. He did not want the Rydans seeing how pathetic the Esparans were when they did not understand.

"I would hope," Tohmas said. He retrieved the antidote Shimmer had delivered with the knives. He knelt beside DoomDragon and tipped the liquid down his throat.

"But we lost that battle!" Barnon exclaimed.

Tohmas took a long breath. Esparans needed to have their hands held. He had always known that much. Later, he would need Barnon.

"Yes, Barnon, I captured DoomDragon. I do not fight battles without intending to win. That's why I kept the snow built up on the east hill. Tunnels to the cliffs were concealed underneath."

DoomDragon's barrel chest heaved in a deep breath. His eyes, small like a bear's, blinked open.

Tohmas sat back on his heels. "The only person I need present is him." He indicated DoomDragon. "The rest of you can stay or go as you wish."

Sabian turned, but Carsh steered the boy into the chair beside Celebrant Calanor instead. He put a waterskin of wildwater in front of him then shooed the protectors out. The celebrant did not move. Mercifully, Barnon sat down. Evidently, there was something else the prince should have been doing, for he sent his prime protector out in his stead.

The prisoner took a few moments to fully grasp his situation, but once his eyes cleared, he smiled.

"Perhaps I was wrong about you after all," the big Northlander said in surprisingly smooth Esparan. His hands tied, he rose only to his knees, hands in his lap.

Still standing over the man, Tohmas reached for the ropes.

"What are you doing?" Barnon protested.

Tohmas chose the more Esparan reply once again. "Undoing his hands." The reply left Barnon sputtering, which was as close to silence Tohmas expected to get.

DoomDragon's expression was knowing. Tohmas felt as if his every gesture was being measured and, so far, had passed the man's tests.

"Master Clarin's dead in case you were wondering," Tohmas said, helping the Northlander to his feet.

"I had assumed. The others could not find him, and you are still alive." Confusing Tohmas, DoomDragon was still smiling, looking as pleased as a mason with a finished project.

"It's not often my enemies are pleased by my survival," Tohmas wryly commented.

DoomDragon froze, and his smile left from under his beard. His gaze was across the table, fixed on Calanor. Tohmas' words went unheard.

The celebrant's grey eyes glared out from under his hood, the feathers of his scarf dancing on unfelt winds. The silence between DoomDragon and the celebrant was heavy.

At length, the Northlander broke the stare and glared at Tohmas. "Is the celebrant a friend of yours?"

"Too great of an injustice has been done to Calanor for him to call me friend. In time, perhaps, I will earn that trust," Tohmas replied.

DoomDragon looked back at the celebrant. For several more moments, the two men stared at each other. At length, DoomDragon broke the silence. "The Winter Star protects his own. I am glad you are well, friend."

Calanor lowered his gaze. It almost looked like a bow.

"Friend" was not a word Tohmas had expected to hear used between DoomDragon and the celebrant.

This changed things.

DoomDragon's gaze swept over the rest of the occupants of the tent. He accepted Carsh with a swift nod but paused on Sabian. Tohmas

waited for the conclusion, surprised when the Northlander let out a short breath and moved on.

"No comment?" Tohmas asked, drawing DoomDragon's scrutiny to him before the Northlander could judge Barnon. "You are not offended that I used poison against you? Is that not cheating?"

To Tohmas' delight, DoomDragon cracked a wide grin. "Admitting that would be admitting I cheated when I sent assassins against you." He glanced back at Sabian. Sabian sat firmly, as good as any Rydan. "Wars should be made as short as possible, whatever the means. You chose your allies well. I admit, I am curious why the poison you used was not deadly." His grin was full of teeth when he added, "Mine was."

Tohmas matched the Northlander's grin and indicated the chair with the horn for DoomDragon's use. The Northlander lumbered over and sat down like a visiting relative.

Tohmas positioned himself nearer the exit in case DoomDragon attempted to flee. If the protectors got involved, DoomDragon was likely to end up dead.

If the conversation did not go well, that would be the outcome regardless. As far as Tohmas was concerned, this war ended tonight, one way or another.

"If I kill you, I may never get an answer to my question," Tohmas answered.

"But why would you expect me to answer your question?"

Satisfied he could get out of his seat faster than the older man, Tohmas sat across from his prisoner. He laid his hands on the table, trying to imagine it was another prince across from him. He corrected the thought in the next instant. DoomDragon deserved better than that.

"I had intended to take the answer from you by, as you put it, 'whatever the means,'" Tohmas said. "But now I offer you a chance to speak of your own free will. You see, my question is why do you do what you do? Who better to answer that?"

DoomDragon cocked his eyebrow, making it disappear under his mat of white hair. It was not refusal, so Tohmas pressed, "I came north thinking you wanted conquest, but that's not true, else you would have taken Solta years ago. You had the skill and the resources to do it, yet you didn't. I assume you have another goal." Tohmas spread his hands open in invitation. "I sent Lance to find that goal. I sought religious

inspiration, personal slight, or magic guidance. But he found your religion was the same as ours, and there was no holy inspiration. He learned you cared little about Prince Sol and had only just started to have an opinion on me, so we were not the reason. Worse, all your men—the Esparans and the Northlanders—thought that you *were* fighting for survival and territory. They did not know what your reasons were either."

"Anything else I should be discussing?" DoomDragon asked, his expression coy. He seemed to be enjoying the conversation as much as Tohmas was.

Tohmas sat back in his seat. "I concluded that the wizards who worked with you were your equals, not your masters or your servants. I suspected someone else was giving you commands, but now I have confirmed it."

The smile on DoomDragon's face settled firmly into place. All remaining tension vanished. Tohmas was struck by how comfortable he was with the Northlander despite having only known him at a distance over a season.

"Oh?" DoomDragon asked innocently.

Tohmas pointed at Calanor. "Why let him loose? I admit I know little of Northlander tradition, but the only reason I can think of to maim a man is to force his silence. But why spare him at all? Lance said you were his host. You called him friend just now."

For a brief moment, DoomDragon's eyes flicked back to Calanor.

"I think you didn't want to kill him, so you maimed him instead. But someone wanted you to kill him. You're following orders." He let the pause settle, then added, "This isn't your war. It would have been over by now if it was."

Tohmas met DoomDragon's stare and held it.

"So, you think we have a common enemy," DoomDragon said.

"If I am correct about why you do what you do and how much it must rankle you, then yes."

"This is ridiculous!" Barnon interrupted. "Just execute him!"

The words brought DoomDragon's attention to the Prince of Rabarch, but not in fear for his life. DoomDragon feared nothing, Tohmas was certain. He had seen it before, fear worn out of a man over a lifetime of fighting for survival.

CHAPTER 17

Under the dissecting stare of the Northlander, the Prince of Rabarch drew back.

"Ah, Prince Barnon," DoomDragon said, "your impatience is typical of your family, I understand. How is it your nephew dodged it? You, Prince Tohmas, appear to be more genuine than any Esparan prince I have ever known by a full measure."

Tohmas was flattered; a compliment from an enemy was worth twice that of one from an ally. And he felt the same. DoomDragon seemed more honest than any prince he had dealt with. His directness was refreshing, and Tohmas found himself liking DoomDragon, despite their disparate goals, all the more.

Ignoring Barnon's stammering half-replies, DoomDragon took a final deciding breath and said, "I have been in the service of Prince Marfaie of Tanble."

Carsh gave a laugh and promptly slid a waterskin of wildwater to the Northlander. Sabian was on his third or fourth swig, but there was plenty left.

"He is a Northlander, and he is lying!" Barnon exclaimed. "Marfaie has been dead for ten years! DoomDragon killed him! You cannot believe that this war has been anything except—"

"Why not?" Tohmas interrupted. "The evidence supports him. The tabards—Northlanders remove them from bodies, but why would they care or even know what they mean? And the cities in the north that Master Kitable saw? They were thriving! The Esparans in the north were not wiped out as you believed. Is it so hard to believe Prince Marfaie may be alive?"

The Prince of Rabarch paused, confusion on his features.

"I am tired of this harpoon in my side," DoomDragon declared. "It's time I looked harder on this side of the border for a solution." Before any of them could answer, he tilted the skin and asked, "Is this what you left in that waterskin by BellRoost?"

"It's Rydan wildwater, a drink," Tohmas explained.

The Northlander looked at the waterskin with a bemused smile under his whiskers. "I never got the courage up to drink it. It's still sitting in my tent." He took a large swig of wildwater then wiped the dribbling drink from his beard. "Not bad." With an appreciative nod

to Carsh, he stoppered it and slid the waterskin back. Without pause, Carsh took a drink of his own. Tohmas was next.

Once he had swallowed the burning liquid, he tilted his head and placed the waterskin where any of them could reach it for more.

"Your prince has you sitting out here doing what? Baiting us?"

DoomDragon leaned back in his seat, propped his feet on the table, and tucked his hands behind his head. "Bleeding out the sons of Zayban. Every year, he lets me advance only enough to keep Sol calling for help. Even now, he keeps Sol alive as a hostage to lure his brothers in. It worked," the man added, looking at Barnon.

"But it still makes no sense," Tohmas pressed, drumming his fingers on the table. "Why would Prince Marfaie care about the sons of Zayban? Tanble's too far north to even trade with them. There is no connection."

"You know perfectly well why, Tohmas." Barnon's soft reply, so unlike that of a son of Zayban, made Tohmas stop short. His head swiveled to him.

All formality was gone. This was not a prince, but a regretful uncle.

"I most certainly do not! What do you know, Barnon?"

With the attention of the tent on him, Barnon shrank into his seat. "Prince Marfaie is Prince Virrat's younger brother."

The name was not familiar. Chief Tamv's teachings had hardly touched the northern princedoms, and no one had ever said the name "Virrat" to Tohmas before.

"Who is Prince Virrat? And why would he have anything to do with this?"

"You must have been told! Every protector knows! The protectors who taught you—" Barnon objected.

Damn Esparans and their politics!

Tohmas' patience broke. Inac's fury boiled in his veins when he stood, grabbed Barnon out of his seat, and held him by his throat.

"I was *not* told. My protectors died when I was eight, Barnon, so the only thing they ever taught me was to respect sickness. Why is Prince Marfaie trying to kill the sons of Zayban?" he demanded a final time. On the next breath, there would be blood.

With his hand on the prince's collar, Tohmas felt when the Prince of Rabarch swallowed hard.

CHAPTER 17

"A moment in private, please, Tohmas. It is a family—"

Sensing the man yield, Tohmas dropped Barnon back in his seat. "DoomDragon has been trapped by this war as much as I have. You will tell us both."

DoomDragon contentedly smiled, enjoying the exchange.

Barnon looked like someone still had a hand to his throat when he said, "Before your Aunt Elinea married Prince Deiton, Zayban had been looking for a suitor for her. Prince Virrat of Tanble was one of the men who sought her hand."

For a moment, Barnon let his eyes meet DoomDragon's critical glare. His voice shook as he tried to regain his composure. "After a brief courtship, Virrat asked Zayban and was refused. Then we found out that Virrat intended to steal our sister away." The prince's eyes dropped to the table in embarrassment.

Tohmas could finally sympathize with the man. Virrat had been acting like a Rydan in taking Elinea. It was the brothers' duty to defend their sisters. If they had failed, Barnon had every reason to be ashamed.

"We intercepted them just outside town. He refused to release her. We fought. Virrat was killed."

"How did you know he was going to take her?" DoomDragon asked, his soft voice guiding Barnon.

"One of her ladies told us," Barnon confessed.

"She was not kidnapped," Tohmas realized aloud as DoomDragon nodded. "She wanted to leave with him."

"Claimed she was in love," Barnon admitted, shaking his head. "I was only thirteen at the time, and I didn't understand. Still don't, I suppose, but when we stopped them, she refused to leave him. Dragal struck first, but I do not know who struck last."

Tohmas paced, turning over the new information. Prince Marfaie had been thought dead near the beginning of the war with the Northlanders, the first casualty of note. There had been no official declaration of war. Sol had not known who he was fighting. Between princes, rules were observed, but with DoomDragon as his patsy, Marfaie did battle as he pleased.

Marfaie had to be brought out of hiding.

"So, we *do* have a common enemy," Tohmas said.

The Northlander sat forward. "My people want land and quiet. Marfaie's war is a feud that neither I, nor my people, have any part in."

"Nor I. I think we should end this, DoomDragon."

Carsh reached across the table and slid the wildwater back to the Northlander.

"Darknim," DoomDragon said, giving an acknowledging salute before taking another swig. "I am Darknim DoomDragon. I prefer to be known without title when among friends."

Tohmas' grin was wide enough for two men. "Then, Darknim, my friend, let me get that harpoon out of your side."

The Northlander laughed. "Tell me what you have in mind."

Visitor, Colt called to Kitable through his communication stone. *Important.*

Kitable heaved himself from his vardo's floor. Despite the late evening, sleep had evaded him. Meditation seemed the closest he would get to rest, if he could avoid further interruptions. He had so much to think about. Tohmas had relayed plans for the morning, including an alliance with the Northlander leader. Kitable was still trying to figure out what he thought about the idea.

He dismissed his complaints when he found Prime Guardian Vallant sharing a steaming cup of tea with Colt at the campfire.

"A word?" Vallant requested. He had the kind of voice that made questions come out as commands. If not for his respect for the man, Kitable would have resisted, but he had known the prime guardian longer than any other person alive, and that earned him instant acceptance.

Kitable sat on a log next to the glowing stone that worked as a campfire and accepted a cup of tea from his waggon driver. Although the stones looked like embers, Vallant had probably noticed there was no wood to this fire. Having a wizard for a patron meant Colt was never cold and never struggled to light a fire, even when fuel was limited.

"I'm supposed to tell you the name of the master wizard is Terant Palnon. Prince Tohmas thought you'd like to know." He left out the

source of the information, although Kitable assumed it had been DoomDragon.

The name was familiar. Master Terant was the author of various spells Kitable had been forced to copy as a child. To his knowledge, there had been nothing new from Master Terant in the last decade. Kitable had assumed the man dead.

Or perhaps Master Terant has simply stopped sharing his spells with others.

"Good to know," Kitable replied, running his memory over the spells attributed to Master Terant, seeking a trend. Perhaps it would help him prepare for the duels.

Long moments passed, but Vallant remained in his seat.

At length, Kitable cocked his head at the prime guardian. "Something further?"

"I heard a strange thing tonight."

"It's been a night for strange things," Kitable answered.

"Prince Tohmas doesn't know, but I was at the entrance of his tent." The prime guardian looked up slowly, his cup of tea held at his chin. It looked like a toy in his large grip. "I heard two of my friends died a good ten years before I thought they did."

Kitable cocked his head and waited.

Vallant took a sip of his tea then repositioned it in front of his beard pensively. He digested his words carefully, as if each was too precious to waste.

Probably still sees me as a scared thirteen year old. Not exactly the kind of person you reveal your soul to.

The prime guardian let out a long breath then said, "I sent my two best protectors with Tohmas when Prince Habal sent him into hiding. When Tohmas came back, he said their recent deaths had prompted him to return. But tonight, he said both died when he was eight."

Kitable leaned away. He had met Tohmas only once before Prince Habal had sent him away from the capital. Kitable had been on the verge of perfecting the hovering spell and had not paid attention to the visit from the prince's wife and son. Young Tohmas had shown no interest in magic. Their meeting had been tepid and uninteresting.

Now, he wished he had paid more attention.

"But if the protectors were dead, who raised him?" Kitable asked.

The glow of the heated stones reflected in Vallant's grey eyes as he stared down into the campfire. He sipped his tea once more. "You see my problem."

How much was a lie? Upbringing? Experience?

"He's never talked about it," Kitable admitted. Suddenly, it seemed strange that Tohmas had never discussed his life with his protector mentors. He had mentioned lapses in his lessons but never the circumstances of their demise. Kitable had never heard him mention either protectors' name. *Does he even remember them?*

Kitable uncomfortably adjusted his position. This was a dangerous topic. Colt was deaf, and the region surrounding his vardo was clear, but Kitable still checked the surroundings. If Prince Tohmas was hiding something, how far would he go to defend the secret?

What am I thinking? This is the son of Habal!

Kitable's loyalty to Galanth had been founded by Prince Habal's generosity nearly twenty years prior. His life of service to the family was repayment. It was all he knew.

"I need you to look into it," Vallant interrupted his thoughts.

"Now?" Kitable snapped loudly. He leaned in, sobering his voice. "We are about to end this war! I cannot go galivanting all over history and burning myself out before a battle. I'm likely to end up in a duel tomorrow with not one, but two wizards, including a master. I realize that probably doesn't mean much to you, but believe me, it's a big problem by itself! I should be preparing, not discussing conspiracies!"

Despite the tirade, Vallant stared at him. "Then don't galivant. Just get the answer. You're a smart kid. You'll figure it out."

Vallant tipped his tea into the dirt at his side, handed the cup to Colt, thanked the driver, and left the campfire.

Irritated, Kitable dumped his own cup and went back to his vardo.

Once he activated all the wards, Kitable leaned against the wall and pressed a hand to his forehead.

The idea would not be dismissed.

"How?" he asked aloud. "How did you survive alone?"

Tohmas could not have been alone at eight and survived to become an eloquent leader of armies. "No, you're never alone. You met Carsh when you were out there. He's why you know how to speak Rydan, and how to dance, and sing, and..."

CHAPTER 17

The tall blond woman he had seen the prince select the night before completed the thought.

"Habal, damn you, what happened? You hid him. Two protectors went with him, but neither returned. Fifteen years later, he showed up in Wayburn on a broken-down horse, and you welcomed him back like you had expected him! Did you ask him where he had been? Did you know? Habal, where did you send him?"

For the first time in his life, Kitable wanted the God Totho to be listening. He needed to talk to the ghost of his old patron, but only a god could reach the soul of the dead prince.

But Kitable was still flustered by the last deity who had walked among them and had no desire to entreat another.

His eyes went to his books. It was not possible for anyone, even a powerful wizard, to touch the soul, but what about a Reflection spell? The details would have to be exact to generate a true representation of the past, but he had done it before. Perhaps he could view Tohmas' return to Wayburn, or watch Habal send his son away. He could find the answer. He simply had to define it accurately.

He reached for the book but paused with it still on the shelf.

Now is not the time.

The imminent duels needed his full attention. He could not be unfocused by this mystery, as tempting as it was. The answer changed nothing about the plans for the morning. Kitable was still needed to defend the forces of Galanth against the Northlanders.

He lowered his hand and sat back down, breathing to bring back his calm. He could search for answers later. For now, he had to prepare for dealing with Master Terant and his apprentice.

He would discover Prince Tohmas' true history after the battle.

When Darknim arrived back among his people, he carried a blood-soaked stolen blade, which convinced the Esparans to not ask too many questions. He quickly assembled the people he required.

Terant had gone home to gather strength for attacking Master Kitable once more. Seria remained and, according to the Hunters, sulked.

Clarin was dead. In her typical way, Seria was more angry than sad. Her fury, for once, was directed at Terant and his patron instead of at Darknim.

Rairn yet lived, but his foot had been badly twisted. Darknim did not give the Prince of Barlaby time to wonder about his capture or escape; he gave the excuse that Tohmas had underestimated him and set about planning revenge with enough enthusiasm to keep them all too busy to think. Escaping from the enemy's camp earned him further notoriety.

In the dawn, Darknim visited the Earth Lodge. He had only to meet Elder Ela's stare to see the faint purple light of the Linking flare in a dozen directions.

His confidence had been failing for some time. Marfaie's war had always been emotional, but the closer the Prince of Tanble got to victory, the worse he became. Seeing Tothonar alive in Tohmas' camp had been the final blow. Ten years with Prince Marfaie had gotten Darknim and his people nothing. He had more respect for his enemy than his allies now.

"I will give you a moment to consider it," he said when he realized Elder Ela had seen his intentions for the morning and was now telling the Circle.

Elder Tril answered by yelping like a kicked dog and pitching forward onto the ice circle. His hands pressed onto the ice, hazy images formed.

An invisible force yanked Darknim forward. The Linking bored into his mind like a headache wanting to break his skull. In a flicker, the pain passed, and he could make out the images in the pool.

At first, Darknim saw himself bowing his head to Tohmas among kneeling Northlanders. Then the scene changed, and he saw the dragon ax swinging again. While the pennants of his enemies varied from white and blue to red and yellow, innumerable battles exploded in the ice pool. Shouts of pain and cries of victory mixed as horses charged down lines of spearmen and arrows darkened the sky.

But other scenes comforted him. Darknim saw himself sit at the great wooden table with Prince Tohmas and other men he did not know, sharing drinks and laughter. They clasped arms in friendship. He felt at home, welcomed and appreciated.

Finally, in a moment of blessed calm, Darknim saw a circle of people around a fire skinning elk and singing. His youngest son made spears while the boy's sister carved bone beads at his side. Darknim sat by the fire, his ax left in the hut.

The buzz of the Circle's thoughts vanished, leaving a profound silence. Physically, the force that had dragged him forward also dropped. He stumbled back several steps before finding his feet.

Elder Tril lay flat on his back with his eyes closed. The light of the Linking was gone.

In answer to his unasked question, Elder Ela explained, "He used his *Visaln* often in search of his Aspect, and so now it is stronger within him. He has not yet learned to control these new visions, but he will recover. Do not worry. A few moments are all he needs."

Sure enough, Tril stirred. The elder sat up, but his eyes remained distant and unfocused.

"His talents are in Divination. Was that the future we saw?" Darknim asked.

"Possible futures," Ela corrected, "but likely ones. The fighting will not end immediately, Darknim, but along this path, if you walk it well, we will eventually have peace."

"You approve of my choice, then?"

"Our faith is in DoomDragon, and our service is to you. This choice is yours."

"One requirement," Elder Tril interrupted, his voice firm as if addressing a field in battle and not a handful of friends around the ice pool. "The man we hunt must be met. Not to catch. Just words. We need words. We must speak to him."

The man they hunted would be Master Kitable. There was weight to the elder's use of the word "need" that made it impossible for Darknim to even consider refusing the request.

"I will make it happen."

With their reserved blessing settling his heart, he made his way to the door. He went the length of the tunneled entrance but stopped before stepping out into the dawn.

A *son* making spears, and his *sister* making beads?

"Elder Tril! I do not have a son or daughter!" Darknim shouted back into the cavern.

"Two boys carry your blood now," the elder said, his voice softening like a child falling asleep. "The girlchild comes with the new blossoms."

A soft thump followed. Darknim suspected Tril had collapsed once more.

He had no reply for the elder; he had lived too long and seen too many of his children die. In part, he was filled with disbelief, but at the same time, he was hopeful.

When he was done, he would go north and offer to take his sons and their mothers into his family. He hoped they would come forward.

By the time he reached the place from which he commanded his men, he had narrowed down the list of possible mothers of his daughter to four. She would be discovering her pregnancy soon.

Chapter 18

T ril woke from a restless slumber. It took him long moments to recognize his tent. Lingering wisps of visions played over his sore mind. They faded as the full light of dawn slipped through the tent flaps.

A drum sounded outside, and Tril's eyes snapped open. Ela's wrinkled face hovered over him, her smile broad.

A vision pounced on Tril, and he saw everything Darknim sought be yanked away. The plans for the morning went awry. Darknim DoomDragon, once the proud leader of all the north, was reduced to a puppet manipulated by a thread of magic. A beastly roar echoed through his ears. Fire streaked through a darkened sky.

"By the Winter Star ... he knows," Tril whispered.

Ela's face paled, but she asked no question, seeming to know more was coming.

Tril pushed himself up, and the tent spun around him. He staggered to his feet, new visions flashing across his mind. Relaxing family gatherings were replaced by war. Grasslands burned. DoomDragon stood, his head bowed, before a man in grey and black. A blade hovered before Darknim's impassive face. The sword flashed up. Relief flooded into DoomDragon as the sword neatly severed his head from his shoulders.

Ela grasped his arm, leading him, as she would a blind man, into the light of the morning.

"Spirits, no." Tril choked on the words. "I cannot let that happen!"

The visions shifted to the present. Darknim stood atop the rise overseeing the armies. When the horns sounded, the Northlanders would surrender. The Esparans would follow or be cut down by Tohmas' forces. All was ready.

It would not work.

Tril looked down on Darknim in his vision and, for the first time, spotted a thread of orange light attaching to the pendant around Darknim's neck. Years ago, Darknim had permitted the spell. It had become negligible and forgotten since.

The tiny touch of magic would be their downfall. Prince Marfaie still held power over him that Darknim did not recognize.

But spells could be broken.

Elder Ela gently shook his arm. It could have been with all her force, for she was frail, but it hardly moved him. "Tril? What do you see?"

Tril blinked aside the visions and realized he stood in the mud, surrounded by Northlanders. He saw fear in their eyes. He had been shouting. They knew he was an Elder in the Circle of the Raven. He had frightened them.

"Hope," Tril said, turning toward the rise. The dawn light reflected off the many drawn weapons of the camp around him. The visions, driven by his desperate hope, solidified. "Call the others!" he told her. "And then run!"

He took off at a sprint, his sight barely holding together.

They took position with the cleared forest at their back and the assembled Northlander and Esparan forces in the valley between the two hills. Spells and barricades now protected the vulnerable northeast approach. Rairn held a crutch to support his twisted ankle, but it hardly felt necessary as he stood, strong and proud, in anticipation.

"Revenge is sweet," he commented.

DoomDragon nodded slowly, his gaze distant. "I would be a fool to miss this opportunity," he said, but Rairn thought he lacked adequate enthusiasm.

"Master Terant would make this even—"

DoomDragon bristled, his voice taking on his more usual irritated tone. "I told you; Master Kitable is defeated. He has been trying to block the Circle, but they have worn him down. He is weak. Everything is in place. We go without the help of—"

"Change of plans, DoomDragon," a voice called, interrupting DoomDragon in a manner Rairn had never heard. The Northlander jumped, something else Rairn had never seen, and pivoted sharply to face the voice.

Master Terant stood calmly, his hands folded in his robes and a smirk on his usually dour face. Overwhelming his rather innocuous appearance, a dragon stood silently behind them where previously there had been only cleared woods.

While DoomDragon took a single controlled step back, matched by his nearby Hunters, Rairn's heart jumped into his throat, and he fought against a primal urge to flee. He was not alone; cries of shock and fear came over his shoulder from the army.

The beast was enormous, towering higher than an ancient fir tree. The pitchy scales reflected little of the dawn, as if absorbing the light for later use. The serpentine neck arched forward, keeping the head below the low clouds. Horns the size of oaks curled from the forehead in partial spiral over dark amber eyes. The beast stared ahead as if the army before it was insignificant and did not move, except for a rare, bored blink.

The clatter slowly settled, the general forces accepting that *this* dragon was on their side since their leaders were neither fleeing nor attacking.

Rairn swallowed tightly over the lump in his throat. Beside Terant, a thin man dressed in somber black and grey had also appeared. The emblazoned crest of the sword on the man's tunic marked him as a servant of Prince Marfaie. The man's amber eyes, identical to the dragon's, were as dispassionate as those of the beast.

A grin slid onto his face. It was impressive.

"An illusion? I dare say, Master Terant, yours is even better than Kitable's."

"This is no illusion," Master Terant said, gesturing to the mammoth dragon as he joined their vantage point. "Since we cannot wait, at least according to DoomDragon, this war will be finished today."

Watching Tohmas and his allies be immolated by a black dragon would be worth every suffering Rairn had endured since losing his princedom to the rabble of Northlanders so many years ago. Finally, he was certain he had chosen the right side.

Rairn looked at DoomDragon, expecting to see the Northlander full of similar enthusiasm, but the Northlander's expression was tightly controlled.

"Do you intend to stay? I did not expect to need you today," DoomDragon asked, his words stiff.

Master Terant let fall his hands. With a flick of a wrist, he summoned a short staff into his grip, its length flickering with runes. "I will remain to assist, just in case," the master wizard said. "That is not a problem, is it, little dragon? Prince Marfaie thought you were having doubts. I wonder why that would be."

DoomDragon frowned, his beard stretching with his disapproval. "I have given my patron no reason to doubt me."

Master Terant smugly shrugged. "Perhaps then, your thoughts betray you." He tapped his chest meaningfully.

DoomDragon's hand went to his sword-shaped pendant, the simple bog-iron ornament Rairn had seen around the Northlander's neck every day since their first meeting.

Realization dawned on his features.

The enormous man lowered his head in disappointment.

A laugh slipped into Terant's words. "A gift from our patron all those years ago. Did you never wonder how I always knew where you were? Did it never occur to you to remove it? I must have forgotten to mention the spells wrought into it. My sincerest apologies." The wizard turned to Rairn, his expression abruptly strict. "Prince Rairn, my patron extends you a warm welcome. He offers you a position of high authority in the forces of Tanble and power over the Northlanders. Your sole duty is to slay the Esparan princes who oppose you today. Your princedom will be raised to glory upon your success."

"You are giving me command?" Rairn balked, glancing at DoomDragon. *Certainly, the Northlander will object!* As much as Rairn wanted to consider himself DoomDragon's equal, he would not let that fantasy endanger his life. He could not believe that his luck had so suddenly changed.

Terant nodded. "Use it well. I will be pitting my magic against Kitable's. These Hunters..." He waved his staff, and DoomDragon's nearby Hunters stiffened. They grimaced and pulled against the invisible restraints but could not move. "...will stay here. They are the only ones who would oppose your command, having seen what transgressed. The others will simply see you as an extension of DoomDragon's will for now. As for the DoomDragon himself..."

Terant spoke no additional words, but something brought DoomDragon to his knees in the mud of the hill. His hands crossed in front of him as if bound, his head lowered in bow. The dragon wing ax towered over his shoulders, useless.

"There," Terant said. "Held nicely for you. We want him alive for now. As a man, he has outlived his usefulness, but as a symbol, he is priceless." Terant gave Rairn a final glare. "Prince Tohmas is expecting a surrender. Surprise him, won't you?"

"I don't have any fancy spells on me assuring loyalty," Rairn warned, eyeing the demeaning position DoomDragon had been forced into. *At least, I don't think I do. Wizards can't be trusted.*

Terant's tone was affable. "We share a purpose, and you are Esparan. We need no such assurances."

New strength entered Rairn, a confidence he had not known since the loss of his manor and city. He let drop the crutch, feeling he had no need of it. He was a Prince of Espar. Command was his. Now, he was guaranteed revenge against Tohmas.

His voice carried in the chill wind. "Spread the Northlanders out," Rairn commanded his horn blowers as he strode forward to see down the south-facing slope. He limped, but it was slight. "I want them interspersed among the Esparans so no one gets clever. Move the other Hunters to the west. Pit them against the Rydans when they charge. If they can take down reindeer, they can take down those horses."

Simple directions were echoed in the horns. More specific commands went out with the runners.

Master Terant joined Rairn in surveying the assembled forces as they reorganized. With a muttered word, the wizard's eyes were lit in glorious, shifting colors. The man who had arrived with him and the dragon, wearing bland black and grey and bearing the eyes of his beast, had no such adornments.

"Who is the man with you?" Rairn demanded, his eyes on the stranger.

Terant shrugged. "He is one of Prince Marfaie's foundlings. I think he's called Pattrik, but his name does not matter. He is bound to the dragon. Tell him where to send the dragon, and he will do it."

Rairn bared his teeth. He had thought the dragon suitable for intimidation, but if it could be used in more elaborate stratagems, the battle would be over before noon. "Send the dragon straight in." He thought for a moment about the people between the dragon and the Galanth camp, but they would either move out of the way or be crushed. "Tohmas will be leading. Let's see how well his flashy sword does against dragon fire, shall we?"

In the shadow of the black dragon, surrounded by magically incapacitated Hunters, Rairn felt his spirit lifted to the height of the clouds above him.

Finally, he would regain his rightful place.

With Prince Barnon, Carsh, and Kitable all vying for positions at his side, Tohmas felt crowded at his vantage point behind HillTop's barricades. The Galanth forces stood ready around the defenses as if in anticipation of an attack. That would change; they knew they were to attack soon. They needed only the signal which Tohmas awaited from Darknim.

Despite Tohmas telling the protectors to relax, every protector was mounted and fully armed. Carsh sat on Bashuran casually, but he had lost his coat and was wearing only his baldrics over his torso. Tohmas assumed he expected to be moving enough to stay warm. No one seemed to believe Darknim was sincere.

But Tohmas had found a kindred spirit in Darknim DoomDragon. Once the messy business of dealing with Prince Marfaie was done, Tohmas was looking forward to exchanging stories with the older man. There was much he could learn from the Northlander.

The sudden appearance of a black dragon in the woods behind their enemy stopped all such musings.

"A dragon?" Kitable asked, his voice quizzical but not panicked. "Remind me again. Did anyone mention a dragon in the planning for this? I don't remember there being a dragon."

"Is that real?" Barnon snapped loudly, his stare on Kitable.

Tohmas grabbed the prince's arm sharply. "Voice down," he warned. "Sound the up and ready," he commanded the horn blowers in a normal tone, "and make it sound jaunty!"

The horns gave the men something to think about for a moment.

Lowering his voice, Tohmas asked Kitable softly, "Is it real?"

Kitable grimaced and nodded.

Around Tohmas, the energy of the camp shifted. The fighters were breaking ranks, sidling back to be in a better position to run. Backed by the lake, there was nowhere to go, but that would not stop them once the first person bolted.

The Rydans on the west slope nearest the lake were unmoved. The horses arched their necks forward, tails swishing angrily, as if the dragon could be trampled if they tried hard enough.

Pleased Honest Justice had been readied, Tohmas mounted. Spotting High Guardsman Carraway an appropriate distance away, Tohmas shouted, "Carraway! Move the Fyrd of Arrow back to clear me a path. Me and the Rydans are taking out the dragon!"

He heard the soldiers whispering. *Good. I need this rumor.*

"We can't let the Rydans have all the fun!" Lance shouted back, bringing his warhorse a step forward from the ranks of his fyrd. Relief filtered through the ranks. It was, for now, powerful enough to hold the fear in check.

Grateful the right commander had been on hand, Tohmas laughed. "Then see if you all can keep up!" he goaded.

He looked down at his advisors, satisfied the forces would hold for now.

"As we predicted. You cannot trust Northlanders, Tohmas. He has proven it," Barnon said through clenched teeth.

"Not now, Barnon," Tohmas replied. "Kit? Remember in Polthian, when you were upset I didn't ask for your advice on the dragon on the road?"

"I remember," Kitable replied warily.

"So do you have a spell for moving dragons?"

"I'm sure I can think of something," Kitable said, but his tone lacked confidence. "Dragons tend to be resistant to magic. I believe that resistance gets more powerful as they get ... ah ... angry ... angrier."

Carsh barked laughter.

"So don't annoy it?" Tohmas asked, chuckling with the Rydan.

"How, by the hells, are you laughing at this, Tohmas?" Barnon demanded, his voice soft enough to not carry as the laughter had. "That beast alone could kill every—"

"I don't believe Darknim betrayed me, Barnon. I need to ask him what happened."

"You do realize we are coming with you, right?" Protector Sanba piped up, sidling his horse to block Honest Justice's path.

The protector had cleaned himself up but kept more of the beard than before, content in showing off the bristles of white and blond. He was still disproportioned and held his greatest muscles in his legs.

Still smirking, Tohmas insisted, "Follow only if you believe me. If you follow just to die, then go throw yourselves on your swords somewhere else. This will work. Darknim must not have known about the Black. The Northlanders are our allies. Am I clear?"

Sanba nodded stiffly, but his voice was tense as he asked, "How can you be so sure?"

"Because I heard no deception in Darknim's words."

"Then lead, and we will follow. I pray Inac is with us all." He delivered his final words with his eyes on Tohmas' sword.

Before Tohmas could kick Justice forward, Kitable and Carsh simultaneously flinched. Kitable snapped a word of command, and a rainbow of magic shot into the air above them, bursting to form a pearly sphere overhead. Fire exploded within the sphere, contained. While Tohmas froze, momentarily awed by the twisting sphere of magic fire, Kitable muttered another word and threw his hand out. Carsh winced. Tohmas assumed another spell had been triggered, but he saw nothing.

"Seems Seria's Master has entered the fray," Kitable grumbled, turning a critical eye to the distant slopes where the dragon stood. "That little bitch doesn't have the skill for those augmentations or for firing two spells at once."

"You're going to be busy then?" Tohmas asked, and the wizard nodded solemnly.

"Nothing I can't handle," he said. As the orb of fire above went out, Kitable cast a glare at the dragon and grimaced. "Blacks are naturally indiscriminate. If they summoned one to fight us, they must have enchanted it. If I can find the spell—"

Kitable paused, his eyes drawn sharply upward to the two figures descending from the clouds.

"Cocky bastards," Tohmas muttered. His fingers drifted to SoulBurner. "Archers..."

"He's shielded," Kitable said, positioning himself calmly between Tohmas and the enemy casters.

"Then give me a little space, Kit. SoulBurner and Carsh..."

"I'd rather you give *me* space," Kitable replied. Tohmas had heard this venomous tone in Kitable's voice only once before, when he had been discussing Seria after her capture. "I would rather not have to defend others during this. Protectors, get the prince to safety."

He's right, Tohmas had to admit. SoulBurner made cooperation between Kitable and himself impossible.

The dragon roared, and the enemy forces began their advance. Tohmas could not yet tell if there were Northlanders among them. Either way, he had no choice. The scales of a Black were reputably impenetrable, but he had been gifted a sword from the Goddess of Fire. If anything could cut those scales, it would be SoulBurner.

Yet a quiet corner of his mind quaked at the thought of facing a black dragon, god-blessed sword or no. If the fire ever reached him, there would not be enough remains to collect into an urn. Tohmas was, for a moment, terrified.

Rydan instincts kept the fear from showing. His voice had no tremor as he commanded, "Prince Barnon, cover the camp's defense. Prime Guardian Vallant, join Wayburn's Fyrd and follow the Rydans in. Our promise to Darknim remains. Harm no Northlander unless—"

"You cannot be serious!" Barnon interrupted.

"All you need to do is hold," Tohmas replied. "If I'm right, none of them will attack you, so you won't even be tempted."

He thoroughly enjoyed the expression of shock on Barnon's face as, followed by his protectors, Tohmas left the defenses and descended the west slope toward the Rydans. Lance's soldiers gave him the three strides of space he needed.

Burlotak met him on the front line and gave him a sharp-toothed grin as they positioned themselves at the front of the Rydan forces. Tohmas' Rydan Followers—each heavily armed and smiling broadly from the backs of their warhorses—subtly aligned themselves to follow in Tohmas' wake. The protectors created a formation at the front as if to guide the way.

"*Drago' huntin'*!" Carsh bellowed. A cheer answered, the enthusiastic whoop echoed by each Rydan warrior. With their weapons raised in salute and agreement, Tohmas' apprehension faded. His faked eagerness changed to genuine excitement.

The dragon's corpse would form a monument in honor of this day. He had no idea how, but he would kill the beast. Darknim and he would laugh about the day's feats around a campfire tonight.

Darknim had to be atop the east hill where they had cleared the forest. If Tohmas was lucky, the person controlling the dragon would be taking similar advantage of the view from the rise.

"We make a path to the vantage point, east hill," Tohmas called to his protectors as he tightened Honest Justice's reins. "If they think spears will stop a Rydan horse, they are mistaken!"

He switched to Rydan, turning on his saddle to call over his shoulder. "*Follo*!" His Followers stepped forward from the crowds and smartly slapped the salute to the Hand. "*Be makin' da pat*!" he shouted, gesturing toward the black dragon as it took its first steps through Northlander ranks. In only a few paces, it would be able to pick out Galanth fighters from behind the barricades thanks to its long neck. "*We be huntin' drago*!"

Turning his eye toward the vantage point, Tohmas drew SoulBurner, gave a battle cry, and kicked Honest Justice into a gallop.

The magic shot through the pendant and dug into Darknim's throat then his mind. The power burned every muscle, his vision overwhelmed by a haze of orange light. His body went limp like a puppet with cut strings. He dropped to his knees, distantly feeling the presence of the cold mud under him. Although he tried to move, nothing responded.

He cursed himself. Looking back, the ties of the pendant were obvious. It had weighed on him when his patron connected to him, heating when the magic was active. It had never occurred to him to remove it, which now seemed strange. The powers over his mind had been present intermittently for ten years, and neither he nor the Circle had seen it.

The black dragon took its first step into the fray, its motions taut. The dragon's handler gave Darknim a wicked grin before following it down, staying in the shadow of the beast where none would dare venture. Panicked cries rose from both armies.

As the dragon blasted a torrent of flame and death upon the enemy, Darknim felt a stab of guilt. He had given his word to Tohmas. Marfaie had forced him to betray it.

"Wait! Wait!"

Unable to turn his head, Darknim saw Elder Tril out of the corner of his eye. Panting from a long sprint, the elder waved his arms as he rushed to the top of the hill.

Although he could not move his body, Darknim found himself able to speak. "Tril is an honored Circle Member. You should heed him."

Rairn spun on Darknim, his face flushed. "You no longer command, barbarian! Do not tell me what to do!"

"Ignore the Circle to your peril," Darknim replied.

Rairn twisted back to the battle only to find himself face to face with the elder, who had moved up while his back was turned. Tril's grin was feral.

"Out of my way, old man!"

Tril did not move, nor did his snarling grin waver. His confidence seemed to worry Rairn enough to make the prince hesitate. Into the pause, Tril called, "Darknim, you called it a harpoon once. Did you see the barbed tip?"

Darknim tried to shake his head, but nothing moved. He saw the truth of the comparison. The barb had been real in the iron pendant around his throat. Now, the pendant was hot through the dragon scale he wore.

"No, I did not see it," Darknim answered.

The black dragon took another heavy step down the hill, its slow gait keeping pace with the human at its side.

Behind Tril, Ela and the five other elders arrived up the hill with hobbling gaits. Each elder wore the feathers or fur of their aspects, forming an unconventional crowd behind Tril and his wolf pelt.

"If it was a harpoon, then we would be without recourse. But it is only a spell," said Tril, his eyes mischievous. "Elder Vel, Seat of Destruction, we need your strength."

Elder Vel shuffled forward, her ruddy red fox skin singed. She was gaunt, her long nose emulating the animal she had taken as her Aspect.

As soon as Darknim met the piercing stare of the elder, the pressure on his chest vanished. His hands fell free, and the burn against his chest released. His mind jolted as if stunned by a blow but refocused with new clarity. He became aware of a void in his mind, where the influencing magic had been buried for more than a decade.

Darknim heaved himself out of the mud. He ripped the pendant from his neck and dropped it onto the hill, profoundly satisfied by the squishing noise it made when it landed in the muck.

Master Terant was nowhere to be seen. No one could replace the spell the elder had undone.

Prince Rairn pivoted to face him, his expression panicked. "Darknim—"

The dragon wing ax felt light as Darknim drew it from its place over his shoulders. The lifting of the spell freed his spirit as it freed his body. Now he could keep his promise to Tohmas. He would start by cutting down the prince who dared presume to control the Northlanders.

"Duck, Darknim!"

Darknim heeded Elder Tril's warning and dropped low instantly. The tip of the dragon's tail swept over him, coming from behind where he never would have seen it.

Prince Rairn, unable to move deftly without his crutch, caught a glancing blow from the tail. His ankle buckled. Darknim watched without remorse as the prince fell down the hill and out of sight. The tail soared over, the bone-white spikes of the tip hooking into a nearby stump and ripping it free. A flick of the tail threw the stump the length of the camp.

Darknim came to his feet cautiously. The Galanth soldiers were panicking, and scattered fires burned in HillTop, results of dragon breath. Someone was trying to keep the ranks in place within their camp, but it

was a tenuous hold. On the flank, the Rydans trampled a path into the confused Northlanders and their determined Esparan allies.

Turning in search of a horn—he had to signal the Northlanders—Darknim came face to face with Elder Tril. The elder's eyes flickered as if tracking multiple birds in flight, and his voice was distant. "Your ax is free," he said.

Darknim lifted the ax he had been gifted by the Circle upon receiving the title of DoomDragon. The artifact was older than the history of the Northlanders, but it had never been anything more than a well-crafted tool in his hand. He had sharpened it, bound the splintering wood of the handle, and oiled off the rust as it needed. It had been a good weapon, nothing more.

He was stunned to see the blade now. The flaking metal had a perfect black sheen. The emblazoned dragon along the shaft shimmered, casting a white glow that extended to the tip of each of the dragon-wing blades. It had no weight in his hand, but he had no doubt it was lethal. He dared not even test the edge.

Seeing the haft was now smooth ebony, Darknim peeled back the worn leather ties. For the first time, he saw a second figure on the shaft above the grip. The tiny person wrapped by the dragon's tail held an ax which was imbedded into the tail. He had always taken the rearing head of the dragon to be anger, but now he wondered if the snarling was pain.

"We named you for this," Tril said. "We did not know then, but now I can see it. You can slay the beast."

A roar thundered over them.

Horns first, Darknim thought. He had to signal the Northlanders to join Tohmas' forces.

"We will spread the word," Elder Ela interrupted, her wide eyes on him.

Darknim bowed his head to her. "I will slay the beast," Darknim promised.

Ela guided Tril to the other elders, and it took two of the elders to hold the youngest of them upright as links of purple light reached out to bind them.

"I will hold," Tril muttered to comfort the others, "but not for long."

Seeking in the chaos, Darknim spotted the foundling Terant had called Pattrik. The tiny man briskly walked beside the lumbering beast.

He expected to feel pity for the handler, understanding well the desperation of Marfaie's foundlings, but this man strutted, reveling in his power. Pattrik was not merely doing his duty, he was enjoying causing panic and pain.

Giving a final prayer to Totho for his people's survival, Darknim sprinted down the hill and leaped onto the trailing tail of the dragon.

The ax bit through the scales, straight to the bone. Hot blood spurted out. The next roar he heard was filled with pain. The amber eyes of the dragon turned to him as Darknim slid his ax free. He was pleased to find the clean blade easily came loose.

The white light tracing the patterns on the ax glowed brighter.

"Come on, beast! Let me give Marfaie a true reason to doubt me!"

The fanged jaw snapped down. Darknim DoomDragon brought his ax to meet it.

Chapter 19

Forty-five wizards.

As Kitable watched the two wizards descend toward him, the auras rising and changing around them, he added two more. *Forty-seven wizards.* Forty-seven wizards had tried to kill him over the course of his life. Forty-five wizards had died for the insult. Two more were about to follow.

Once, duels had terrified him, but the fear had faded with his extensive practice. When the hovering spell had been Kitable's secret, he had focused on landing an Eight-layered Dispel. It stripped away all defenses bound to the target and opened the path. After that, a simple, well-aimed destruction killed. Duels ended with the combination.

This was not that simple.

The balding man slowly drifting down had to be Master Terant Palnon. Dressed in black robes embroidered with grey, Master Terant boasted his patronage to Tanble as blatantly as Kitable did his loyalty to Galanth. His numerous trinkets shone in a multitude of colors under Kitable's enchanted vision, but the brightest of them was his staff. Complicated engravings imbued with magic covered into the shoulder-height staff, each flickering powerfully to Kitable's Spell Sight.

One more thing to analyze. Kitable had no doubt Terant was analyzing him as well, or perhaps he already had. In their last, albeit brief, altercation, Terant had cut through Kitable's defensive spells in sequence. Kitable had made efforts to better conceal his spells from

NORTHLANDER

scrys and divinations since, but this duel would reveal how successful he had, or had not, been. Neither of them would be landing quick Eight-layered Dispels in this contest.

Seria drifted down in a long black dress, her hair flowing far behind her as if independently affected by the forces that held her aloft. Despite her petite size, the auras around her glowed brighter than Terant's.

Focusing, Kitable assessed the auras. Seria had more spells; that was why her auras were brighter. Terant's were fewer but individually more complex, with elements and domains winding together tightly enough to appear as a single thread. The complications made identifying spells tricky. *And he's not limited to the spell books. These could be anything.*

By habit, Kitable identified their weakest elements or domains. Terant had only two shields against wind. Seria had erected a single protection against earth and had no defenses against light. *Foolish to underestimate light illusions,* Kitable thought. Deception could be deadly. That would be his way in.

Forty-seven and counting. Good thing I don't plan on playing fair.

No time wasted on words, Terant generated a multi-colored aura with the distinctive gusty pattern of destruction.

Kitable activated a simple spell—a light illusion that mirrored his surroundings. Without the means to see through it, Seria paused her casting. To her, Kitable had disappeared.

Terant was not fooled. He released his spell, and five elements rushed at Kitable. Determining there was no force magic in the spell, Kitable activated a Force Wall. He angled it to ricochet the spell toward Seria, who had to drop her flotation spell to dodge it.

As she fell, Kitable seized the opportunity to create an illusion of himself near Terant, complete with the many auras her Spell Sight would reveal to her. The presence of the many colors hid the trembling yellow aura that would reveal the image as an illusion.

Seria landed thanks to a quick spell and gathered herself. Finding Kitable's illusion, she attacked. In her eagerness, she failed to recognize Terant's proximity, and her Fire Blast crashed into one of Terant's shields. It dissipated, but the force still pushed the master wizard to the side and threw off the aim of his next spell. The glimmering blue and black spell crashed into the ground three paces from Kitable, a burst

CHAPTER 19

of stones and ice driving divots into the earth like a hailstorm where it landed.

Novel way of using water. That would have hurt, Kitable considered. He checked his defenses; water was weak. Creation and summoning of water was generally harmless, as being wet was not a problem. How had the man designed a spell that generated ice instead of water?

He did not have time to think about it. He needed to eliminate Seria and, at the same time, lay a trap for Terant.

Kitable used a three-way dispel to remove the first of Terant's two wind shields, trying to remove the wind defenses without being obvious. He tossed a second dispel at Seria, destroying three of her shields, including the earth defense.

Seria and Terant both activated spells. A dispel from Seria destroyed Kitable's illusion, and another water spell burst from Terant. The master wizard took a moment to add a force defense onto his, preventing Kitable from knocking it aside.

This time, Kitable bound the spell and used an alteration to turn it around. It barreled back at Terant.

To Kitable's surprise, Terant mimicked him, altering the targeting of the spell and sending it back at Kitable. Targeting a moving spell was tricky. Kitable had not expected Terant to be capable of doing it.

With his next breath, Kitable activated a short dispel, breaking Terant's binding to his spell, and then activated a second copy of the Turnabout spell. When the spell was altered, he angled it to the side, at Seria.

She attempted the same counter, but her targeting missed. The spell clattered against her Molded Shield, the impacts knocking her off her feet. The ice had been spikes this time.

Terant was casting something new. *Complex, but slow,* Kitable recognized. While the combinations were tricky to counter, they took Terant long to cast.

Kitable cast two spells in rapid succession. The first was quick; he activated an Eight-layered Dispel and manually targeted Terant. It was a rather poor use of the powerful spell, for it removed only two shields, but it took out the second wind defense.

For the next spell, Kitable had to full-cast it, which took time. He'd used the earth alteration spell a fair bit when digging tunnels for

ambushes in Barrow Hills, but this was the first time he used it aggressively. Seria was still prone. Only the Molded Shield defended her.

It was time enough for Terant to launch his spell—a monstrosity of seven colors lacking only the orange of thought magic. Overwhelmingly, the aura was alteration, although the cloud-like aura of creation was mixed within it.

Kitable relied on his shields as he finished his spell. Terant's storm cloud of powers raged around Kitable for a dozen heartbeats before petering out.

But Kitable finished his spell; like the hand of a buried giant, fingers of stone and dirt reached around Seria and her Molded Shield. Before she could counter, the earth pulled her down, destruction of the stone below her paired with creation above. Faster than a diving hawk, she was dragged deep into the earth, the tunnel she left behind closing over as fast as it was created.

For a moment, the two remaining casters paused. Terant's brow dropped low over his glittering eyes. He seemed to be debating retrieving his apprentice, but practicality won out. He faced Kitable once more. It would take her time to recover. Her Molded Shield meant she would not immediately suffocate. *Mores the pity,* Kitable considered. *Forty-six then.* If Seria did not step back up, he would have to worry about killing her another day. It was time to set the trap.

Into the pause, Kitable activated a wind spell, knowing the path was open. When he spoke to activation word, nothing happened.

He checked his spells, sorting through their bindings consciously. All were present. Terant's large attack had dispelled none of the remaining spells.

Alteration, creation, and ... binding? Did he alter my hovering spells?

Changing an activation word would render a hovering spell useless. It was beautiful in its simplicity.

The knot in Kitable's stomach tightened as he raced through options.

If that had been Terant's attack, it would be imperfect. Many of his spells with targeting code were defended against alteration to prevent subversion of the targeting portion. At least some of his hovering spells were still useful.

He turned and ran, the code for a large wind creation spell flying from his tongue, full cast at top speed. It would not be deadly—probably why Terant had left wind least defended—but it would buy him time.

Another attack, which Kitable had not seen, crashed into the space behind him. He thought he heard the master wizard curse.

Nothing was as simple as running. Even superb casters struggled to hit a moving target, particularly one that was moving in and out of their line of sight. Now, Terant had to keep up.

Turning briefly, Kitable released his wind creation spell, and a gust strong enough to topple a forest swept over Terant's flying position above him. Without defenses, the Tanble wizard flipped in the air and was carried a dozen paces to the north.

Kitable resumed his run, darting behind one of the shop vardos and out of sight. Without being able to anchor Kitable, Terant had to aim. The more things between them, the harder that became.

Continuing running, Kitable consciously dropped two of his hovering shields. He then picked a minor destruction to fire back at his enemy, hoping it looked like he was still to knock down shields.

When Kitable glanced over his shoulder, Terant, his robes and hair disheveled, was quickly closing the distance. Kitable fired his spell back at him, missing entirely in his haste.

A spell crashed into the vardo in front of him, setting it on fire. Kitable rushed behind the cover the vardo, protected from the heat by his shields. He heard a shout in a strong northern accent, and the entire vardo rose into the sky, denying Kitable a hiding place. Kitable fired a new destruction spell and disrupted another one of Terant's shields.

The mess of magic around the man was so bright Kitable started doubting his own assessment of it. *It's changed!*

Something landed at Kitable's feet, cracked, and started billowing black smoke. Kitable staggered back, chose a direction, and bolted. The smoke filled the area but did not seem to be dangerous. In fact, it hid him as he took refuge behind another vardo.

As he paused, the flash of nearby auras caught his attention. Recognizing alteration but lacking the time to fully analyze it, he tried to activate Burst spell.

How did Terant or his apprentice get ahead of me?

The Burst spell did not activate. It had been affected by Master Terant's earlier works. Apprehension tightened in Kitable's chest.

But to Kitable's immense relief, it was not Seria or Master Terant arriving at his side. Shimmer Weaver, dressed in her dancing clothes, had her hands out in surrender. In each open palm, she held a black nut. Her smile was sheepish.

"Just trying to help."

Kitable let out a breath, trying to slow his speeding heart. "I told you to stay away. If that wizard sees your magic, he'll kill you."

"I can handle myself," Shimmer replied tersely.

"Not against him, you can't." The smoke was clearing, swept away on the natural winds of the north. Kitable's defenses would obscure most, if not all, of the scrying spells Terant might be using, but it still would not take long for the master wizard to figure out where Kitable had gone. Or the wizard might start flipping vardos over and get lucky. Neither boded well for Kitable or Shimmer.

Kitable's eyes were drawn to the black objects in Shimmer's hands. "What are those? I saw no auras in the smoke."

Shimmer Weaver beamed. "They're alchemical, not magical."

She held out her hands, and Kitable took both acorns.

"I'll pay you for them later," Kitable said, and she beamed at his recognition.

Sensing she still did not appreciate the danger she was in, Kitable reached out gently and touched her forearm. He could not allow her to be so reckless.

"And Miss Weaver," he said, "*exanhol.*"

At first, her face flushed, and he could not tell if it was anger or fear. Then her expression fell. His Eight-layered Dispel, targeted perfectly through the contact on her arm, dispelled her down to the smallest of her trinkets.

"Stay out of this!" he said. Now satisfied Terant would follow only him, Kitable turned and rushed away.

"You bastard!" she shouted after him.

"Technically true," Kitable shouted over his shoulder. After only a few strides, he sensed the approach of a spell. He dodged it—his deflecting spells would not answer him—and continued his run, quickly pushing the young woman from his mind.

With a wedge of protectors leading, Tohmas took aim for the rise by the forest and ran Honest Justice at full charge. For all their experience against the Esparans, Northlanders had never faced Rydan steeds, let alone a charge led by a volley of well-aimed spears.

They folded away, opening the path.

Once beyond the front lines, the forces were unfocused, their attention divided by the Rydans and by the dragon behind them. Tohmas quickly found his targets were Esparan only. The Northlanders appeared to be withdrawing. *Some part of the agreement is being upheld,* he thought.

Leaving the Rydans to deal with the pressing masses, Tohmas used the enemy's confusion to make a road deep into the ranks. Enemies standing in his path met the deadly hooves of a trained warhorse. Those to the side met SoulBurner or Carsh's knives. His protectors came and went from his side, peeling off to deal with a threat then making their way back. By the time Tohmas reached the hill on the far side, the horses were soaked with blood, and he had a dozen protectors remaining with him.

Tohmas did not have to climb the hill by the woods to see there was no one there. Surrounding the vantage point, he was surprised to find few enemies in the frost and mud. A handful of Barlabian soldiers met the protectors. Soon enough, only Tohmas and his protectors remained in the area.

Tohmas checked on the dragon looming to his right. Something behind the dragon had attracted its attention, and its snake-like neck twisted back on itself to snap down beside its tail. The people around it continued to scatter, forgetting about human enemies in their desperation to get clear.

"My Prince!" a protector called. Protector Linco dragged an Esparan man forward and presented him to Tohmas.

Prince Rairn gathered himself, trying to wipe mud off but only smearing it over his white armor. He hobbled, favoring a swollen ankle.

"Unhand me!" Rairn snapped, reefing his arm from the protector's hold. With all the protectors moving in around them, the protector laughed and released him. But with his off hand, the protector cut the

prince's belt loop, freeing his sword. When the protector stepped away, he took the sword with him.

"As you ask," Protector Linco said complacently. He held his hands up as if in surrender, holding the prince's sword in clear view as he backed up.

Rairn blanched to match his armor. His head swiveled, taking in the surrounding protectors down to Carsh's toothy grin.

The coward reached his arms out wide, making no attempt at defending himself. "Princes do not kill princes," he reminded the protectors.

Tohmas grit his teeth, unsure if the Esparan tradition would hold him. Rydans had no such conventions. Anyone who became a threat could be killed. After Rairn's betrayal, Tohmas wanted the fool dead.

He felt the gazes of the protectors acutely. Tohmas was, in their eyes, a prince. He had to behave like one.

Mounted on Justice, Tohmas towered over Rairn, yet the Barlabian's smile was sardonic. He did not seem to see SoulBurner in Tohmas' grip.

"Prince Tohmas," Rairn greeted sourly.

"Rairn," Tohmas replied, dropping his enemy's title and making him flinch. *If I don't see you as a prince, will I be bound to the code between princes?*

Yes, but only for now, he decided.

"I insist you join me in HillTop. It's time we talk. Protectors, bind him."

Tohmas scowled down at the other prince as the protectors moved in. They did not seem to have rope with them, but some creative soul had found a belt from a dead man. It was, suitably, blood soaked but frozen.

"I am a Prince of—"

"And that is why, for the moment, you will live," Tohmas interrupted tersely. "Do not tempt me to change my mind." He addressed the protectors. "Take him into HillTop."

It was quickly settled; two protectors hoisted the prince onto the back of a horse and led him off.

Once Rairn was on his way, Tohmas searched the surrounding area. He needed to find DoomDragon, but identifying a single Northlander, even one as imposing as Darknim, among the forces was daunting. The area was clear, probably because of the dragon, but the distant armies

were still engaged in the slush and mud. Most of the Northlanders appeared to be withdrawing to the northern parts of their camps, leaving the Esparans to attack HillTop. They had breached the defenses in a dozen minor places. Prince Barnon was losing ground.

A horn sounded from beside the dragon, a call for Tohmas' attention. He could only guess who would be sounding it from so far behind the enemy lines, but it came with the identification of the Fyrd of Arrow.

Had they found DoomDragon?

If he could not find DoomDragon, he needed to find whoever was commanding the dragon. Either way, the logical place to look was at the dragon's side.

"Carsh!" Tohmas called, his brother immediately at his side. "Send half of the protectors back. Their horses will be useful against those attacking HillTop. The rest are coming dragon hunting with us."

Carsh guided Bashuran back to the protectors and snapped orders, selecting the protectors seemingly at random, but Tohmas noted the wounded were sent back.

Wounded or no, the protectors would give Barnon enough time to tighten his ranks and stop the invaders.

Carsh joined him once more as they pointed their steeds toward the dragon.

Darknim dove wide to avoid the dragon's snapping maw, improvising a roll when fire followed. The tendrils of heat chased him as he rolled through the snow, which quickly became scalding mud.

When the fire dissipated, Darknim regained his feet beneath the dragon.

Heat pulsed from the monstrous body, warming the scale armor on Darknim's shoulders and making his face flush. He looked up, seeking a tender underbelly to sink the ax into, but the body of the dragon was too far above. Only its limbs, each the size of the largest of the ancient trees in Barlaby, were within reach. Deciding a hamstring, if the beast had such a thing, would be a good thing to slice, Darknim chose a leg and sprinted toward it. Turning his run into a pounce, he sunk the ax

into the ankle of the beast with his full weight behind it. Heat pressed against him like tackling a bonfire.

The dragon screeched and lurched. The wounded leg jerked upward, taking Darknim with it. His ax sliced through the scales, dropping Darknim back to the wet ground. The ax landed beside him, edge buried into the mud.

Darknim lay for a moment, the cold of the ground soothing after the intense heat.

But the dragon wasn't going to defeat itself. He heaved himself out of the muck. Behind the leg, Darknim spotted the dragon's controller. A Galanth soldier approached the foundling from behind, stalking him for a kill, but the dragon's claw intervened, knocking the Galanth back with surprising speed.

The dragon's maw snapped up the unfortunate Esparan in a blink, cutting him in half with a chomp.

Something so large should not be able to move so quickly! Darknim cursed.

Strangely, the attack was apathetic. The beast killed but was no more aware of its actions than a tanner striking against a hide.

Darknim groped for the ax, seeing Pattrik gesture toward him next, an arrogant grin on his face.

End of the old, Darknim thought. This younger founding of Marfaie's seemed delighted to put down Darknim.

Following the pointing finger of its handler, the horned head of the dragon came around and breathed thick flames at Darknim. The impenetrable black scale around the legs would protect it from its own fire.

Darknim threw himself down, trailing the ax, and fell into a footprint the dragon had left in the mud. The flames licked over his head and hood but did not catch. Between the mud and blood, he thought himself relatively fire resistant, but he feared the heat which was known to turn even horses to ash. His face felt sun-burned already.

A pause lingered, and Darknim wondered if the dragon and its handler thought him immolated. Pulling himself clear of the footprint, he sought the handler, but the foundling was gone. Instead, Darknim found one of the dragon's feet nearby.

Seizing the opportunity, Darknim selected a toe and cleaved through the joint.

Blood gushed, and Darknim heard a double scream, one part dragon and one part human. Darknim rolled clear, using the cold earth to smother any spatter he might have collected before the hot blood scalded him.

The dragon brought its head around again, and Darknim found himself meeting its gaze. He hefted his ax, ready to take another chip from the enormous creature.

The dragon instead reared back, aiming its fire breath.

Before it could let loose the flames, its head pivoted away. Pattrik broke from the cover of the dragon's legs, fleeing a rider on a black warhorse. The rider was an Esparan man in a blue tabard, but that was all Darknim could tell before the dragon lashed out in defense of its handler.

Apparently, Darknim was not the only one willing to brave the dragon's proximity to get at the handler.

By some miracle, the dragon missed the Gaidolon and his horse, although the man was forced to abandon his attack on Marfaie's foundling. As the horse approached Darknim, the dragon reared again for fire, aiming to immolate them both in a wave of flames.

They both fled to a rocky outcropping. Darknim skidded through the slush first. Showing surprising agility, the Esparan sheathed his sword, leaned over hard and called a command to his horse. The horse slid through the mud, rounding the corner and lying down. Man and horse were protected in the lee of the outcropping when the fire soared over and around their cover. The hot air prickled at Darknim's lungs, and he lowered himself close to the cold ground to better breathe.

Ducked low, Darknim met the stare of the Gaidolon, who was doing the same. He suddenly recognized him.

"Lance Carraway, what are you doing?"

"Something very stupid," Lance replied. The man lifted his weapon a hand's breadth. "Should I be readying myself to face your ax, DoomDragon? My orders were to leave you be so long as you do not attack."

Darknim smiled through his mud-encrusted beard. The fire around them went out. "Tohmas is holding to his word, is he?"

The Gaidolon nodded stiffly. Commanding his horse to stay flat, he crept to look out. "We are to do battle only with those who oppose

us. And Tohmas is looking for you. Says this is a big misunderstanding." Lance unhitched a horn from his saddle, cleared the dirt from the mouth and blew a call.

"He is correct. I am not your enemy. The man with the dragon, on the other hand..."

Lance nodded. "I saw him. Thought it a bit odd, someone walking casually in that beast's shadow, so I figured he was important. But I can't get close!"

Darknim joined Lance in peeking out. The dragon was still only two dozen paces away, but it was again looking elsewhere. Pattrik yelled directions from its far side.

Lance whistled lightly, and the horse rolled to its feet, its black coat mud-colored. He was quickly mounted again and let out a long breath. "Right, no problem. Just kill a dragon. Or something..."

Repeating the horn call, Lance left the cover of the rocks and charged under the dragon once more, aiming for the foundling.

Spitting mud to clear his own mouth, Darknim pulled himself up to the top of the outcropping. With Lance distracting the dragon, Darknim use his vantage point to launch another attack. He took the dragon in the elbow, and the limb buckled. Nearby, Pattrik screamed and clutched at his right arm in mirror. Pattrik's voice cracking, his instructions increasingly terse.

The sway of the dragon as it withdrew its foot drove the incoming fire wide of Lance as he charged. To Darknim's dismay, the handler dodged Lance's swing.

Darknim slid down the smooth scales of the leg, cutting a gouge from the elbow to the already-damaged wrist. His armor smoldered in the heat, his furs singed in some places and burned to ashes in others. The dragon scales on his shoulder survived, protecting him from the impossible heat, but his gloves were nothing but rags by the time he landed.

"Won't be putting weight back on that one!" Darknim shouted. "Come on!"

The dragon screeched. It moved awkwardly now, two of its four legs wounded. It did not lash out as Darknim expected, but he assumed it was obeying Pattrik. The dragon stepped away. With one stride, DoomDragon was before the beast in perfect line of fire.

Pattrik was there, standing at the dragon's side, but favoring one leg and holding his right arm delicately. The man's confidence was gone, replaced by consolidated rage. Darknim was the cause of this pain, and now he would die.

From the side, a group of Esparan riders charged in.

Darknim let out a laugh as he recognized the lead rider. Only Tohmas would be mad enough to be charging the dragon through the soft terrain.

"The handler!" Darknim shouted through his laugh, pointing at Pattrik. "Take out the handler!"

At first, Darknim was unsure he had been heard, but then Tohmas redirected his horse. The handful of protectors with him followed.

The foundling's expression sharply switched to panic. The dragon abandoned the fire breath at Darknim and lunged to intercept, crushing two protectors and knocking a third prone.

But Tohmas' horse leaped clear of the snapping jaw and charged in. With a swift cut, he cleaved Pattrik's chest in half with his glowing sword.

The stoic march of the dragon broke, and the black dragon screeched, making the warhorses skitter. Its wings flared out and tossed stones like hail across the field.

Darknim paused, waiting to see what the beast would do now that it was free. He started to make his way to the Esparans, certain he needed to at least explain himself.

A trio of riders—the prime protector and two lower-ranked protectors—flanked Tohmas when Darknim joined them, keeping one wary eye on the dragon that thrashed aimlessly. The horses flattened their ears, and their nostrils flared, but none bolted as their riders leaned in to comfort them with soft voices.

Prime Protector Carsh's enormous black stallion stared down the dragon as if wishing it was a little smaller, so he could trample it.

"Well, at least it's not taking sides anymore," Tohmas said as Darknim arrived. "That ought to keep it away from HillTop. Good to see you. We still on?" With his empty right hand, the prince extended his fist to Darknim.

Darknim eyed the gesture, not sure if he could believe the good will of the Galanth man. The hells themselves seemed to have risen from the earth to take over the battlefield. The sprawling chaos around them

was a far cry from the organized exchange they had agreed upon. Many lives had been lost because of this betrayal, and Darknim was shocked Tohmas did not blame him for it.

But Elder Tril's words lingered with Darknim. He wanted the life the elder had seen in the visions. He would fight for it even if it meant taking down a dragon. He trusted this man more than he had ever trusted Prince Marfaie.

He knocked his fist against the prince's as the dragon lashed out, sending fire across the camp ahead of it. It stepped forward, advancing on the HillTop while striking with teeth and tail all around. Northlanders and Esparans were tossed equally in its wake.

"Apparently, it's mad," Tohmas commented dryly.

Darknim matched the prince's calm, hefting his ax. "Course, it's a Black. I suppose the only way this slaughter ends is with it dead."

Giving a helpless shrug, Tohmas smiled. "You are the DoomDragon, aren't you? This is what you are meant for! Carsh, I'll draw the head down. See if you can hit an eye. The wings seem to be soft between the ribbing, but I'm going to have to get its attention. I'm not sure SoulBurner will bite through scale but—"

"My ax will," Darknim said. "I need to get close to something vital."

They both looked up where the dragon blew fire into an arch, sweeping its head from left to right. Its eyes were blood red now, deep enough to seem black in the overcast light. "How about the head? I think they need their head," Tohmas suggested.

"Done," Carsh said, shocking Darknim. He had forgotten the sound of the man's voice.

Darknim's spirits lifted. He felt like he was a boy once more, running down caribou with friends.

With the eyes of a hunter, Tohmas assess the dragon for a moment more. The beast was moving away as if forgetting about them. Darknim took that to mean the dragon had no desire to avenge its handler.

"Protectors," Tohmas said, pulling a token from a pouch, "take a message to Prince Barnon. He needs to move everyone to the lake shore. This thing is too close."

The two remaining protectors paused, exchanging glances. The man on the white horse edged forward, accepted a token, but asked, "You trying to get rid of us?"

"I am. You'll be of no use right now. Between SoulBurner and his ax, we're the only ones who have a chance. You stay with me and you're collateral damage."

The pair of protectors lingered a moment more then nodded. Although the men were hesitant to leave, the horses were quick to agree about the choice of direction and left at a barely controlled gallop.

"The fire..." Darknim cautioned when he realized they were leaving all forms of cover and were about to attract the beast's attention.

"Inac will protect us," Tohmas declared, lifting his sword. "Keep close!"

Chapter 20

Barreling through Fixer City, aiming toward the lake cliffs, Kitable used the cover of the waggons and the smoke screen acorns to delay Master Terant. Still, a dozen spells had been resisted or blocked by his various defenses by the time he broke into the Temple waggons circle at the heart of Fixer City.

Seeking to delay his foe a few moments at least, Kitable cast a Wind Barrier behind himself. The wall of blustering gusts shot up from the ground. He added an Extension—full-casted as his hovering one did not answer its activation word—making the sheet of wind a hundred paces wide and high.

Knowing he had only a few moments before a dispel broke through, Kitable quickly located Celebrant Calanor standing at the top of the stairs to Totho's waggon. His acolyte was at his side as always.

"Don't say anything!" Kitable cried, stopping opposite the fire. Once he was certain the untouchable was not going to speak to him directly, Kitable tentatively circled the fire and approached the stairs, feeling all the while for any hint of flaring powers that might dispel him. "There is an enemy wizard on my tail. You can turn the tides on him better than anything I can conjure up."

Calanor's approving gaze was fixed on the Wind Barrier Kitable had created. The celebrant nodded slowly.

Of course, the Celebrant of Wind would appreciate such a spell, Kitable mused.

"He will close on me quickly," Kitable explained. "I've opened a gap in my spells. Once he is within a dozen paces, talk to him. If you can dispel—"

"Will you not be struck as well?" the acolyte asked. Since he had felt no untouchable powers, the boy spoke only for himself.

"Absolutely. But I'll be ready for it. With your help, Acolyte, this ends here," he explained quickly then handed Timon a pouch.

As Kitable moved away, Terant came through the Wind Barrier. Instead of fighting the wind, Master Terant drifted through an alteration-made opening, sparking energy as he gathered power. Around the Temple waggons, the people who had remained despite Kitable's arrival now fled. Soon only the celebrant, his acolyte, and Kitable remained in the waggon circle.

Kitable squared himself up and selected his most powerful attack. It was one of the few he had left that he could count on to answer him, having been protected from Terant's manipulations.

Kitable's had been inspired by Terant's spell at the fires and improved upon it. The Uncover spell was layered to eat through defenses, one after another, in every conceivable order. It would brutality strip defenses like concentrated salt acid on flesh. It was a spell he was proud of.

Terant said a single activation word, and the Uncover spell was summoned away before even touching the first of the Tanble caster's spells.

Foreboding trickled into Kitable. If he could so easily counter such a spell, Master Terant was the most powerful wizard Kitable had ever fought. It hadn't occurred to him that he might die in this confrontation. That risk was fast becoming realized.

Terant paused, his dark robes flapping around him as he hovered a dozen paces in the air. Kitable waited an extra moment. He had removed his closer two binding defenses and had no shields that would block a physical advance. If Terant moved close enough, he could stand between Kitable and his defenses. An opportunity to bind the enemy directly was impossible to ignore.

But Terant did not advance. Instead, the master wizard sneered and shook his head. His face wrinkled in a deep scowl. "You're too clever to leave an opening like that."

Midway through the sentence, Kitable fired another spell. The minor destructions destroyed two shields, but it was like chipping at a mountain with a chisel.

Seeing he could not lure the master wizard closer, Kitable called, "How loud can you shout, Celebrant?"

Calanor stepped down slowly and, with a sweep of his enormous white sleeve, tucked Timon behind him. His grey eyes fixed on the floating wizard across the fire from him, and his chest rose in a deep breath. With the exhale, Calanor threw his handless arms up, his tethered feathers flying around him.

The wind answered. Stronger than any "speech," a gust of wind swooped through the area, spinning around the central fire pit and lifting the ribbons of Totho's Temple waggon. Kitable's hovering spells were caught by the gale and ripped from their bindings as the untouchable magic coated him like oil. Active defenses and items were yanked away or dispelled. In a blink, he was, in magical terms, naked.

Terant's expression delighted Kitable as he tried to counter Calanor's "spell" and failed. The Fly spell suspending the enemy wizard disappeared, dropping Terant sharply. He shouted a command word, but the item or hovering spell Terant sought to activate did not answer. The man landed heavily in the mud and slush.

Kitable wondered how long it would take Terant to figure out what had happened.

"Timon!" Kitable shouted.

The acolyte leaned out from behind his celebrant and tossed Kitable his pouch. Opening it, Kitable selected a dart, which instantly morphed into a dozen. Following his line of sight, the darts flew through the settling campfire and struck Master Terant as he scrambled to his feet. Tiny holes burned through the robes and into flesh. None were lucky enough to kill.

Two wasted words followed as Terant seemed to try to activate his staff first then another item. By the time he discovered the extent of the dispel Calanor had achieved, Kitable had selected a stone from the pouch and taken aim. The Force Cage sealed around the caster, ready to contain any further spells.

CHAPTER 20

Kitable activated a Reduction spell on the Force Cage and finally relaxed. *Gotcha.* Dispelled, trapped, about to be crushed, this was the end of Master Terant.

As much as he wanted to turn away, Kitable knew he had to watch. The roof of the Force Cage touched Terant's head and realization crossed the master wizard's face. A quick glance around was all he needed to make his decision; Terant reached deep into his robes and, disappointing Kitable, activated a concealed item that had survived the untouchable powers.

Kitable rattled off a Spell Sight, so he saw the purple cloud-like spell stretch out across the battlefield and vanish over the horizon. He could not cast fast enough to stop it. In a blink, Terant was gone.

Silence settled over the campfire circle. The Force Cage, now visible as green bars to Kitable, shrank down to nothing and vanished as well.

The pause lingered. The sounds of distant battle finally caught up with Kitable, carrying with it the roar of a dragon. Cold air now cut through Kitable's robes, his protective spells gone. He was covered in sweat, still panting from his run, and his hovering spells were gone.

Calm reason cut through the silence. The untouchable magic spared items hidden in the folds of Terant's cloak. Good to know.

A new greasy feeling reached him, making him instinctually flinch. It was pointless. He was already as dispelled as he could be.

When the stone in his hand went dead and Spell Sight fell from him, Kitable corrected himself. *Now* he was as dispelled as he could be. Celebrant Calanor was "talking" to Timon again, and the acolyte was close enough to put Kitable in the wave of powers.

"He escaped?" Timon asked for his celebrant.

"We seem to have scared him home," Kitable agreed. He turned his attention to the battlefield on the far side of the hill and to the black dragon tearing through the forces. It seemed to be limping. "I'd best clean this up. If we make the place unfriendly enough, he'll probably think twice about returning. Thank you for the help, Celebrant. You'll be pleased to know that trick will not work twice, so I will not be bothering you again."

He heard the acolyte's reply as he left the clearing. "Totho is always pleased to help you, wizard."

Once out of sight of the Temple waggons, Kitable took a moment to lean back and take a deep breath. His heart was still racing, his legs were throbbing from his sprint, his skin felt greasy from the contact with untouchable magic, and the cold within him from the lack of spells was deepening.

But the battle raged on. There was a black dragon to deal with.

He pushed off the wall and trotted on. His head was clear at least. He'd not managed to enervate himself this time. Maybe he would get through the day without exhaustion for once.

He cast as he ran back to the barricades and had to admit his optimism had been unfounded. By the time he reached the front lines, now wearing a dozen protective spells and another dozen hovering attacks, he felt enervation sinking in.

And none of the spells were nearly as impressive as the ones he had worn earlier that day. He did not have the time, or energy, to cast those again.

Letting out a weary sigh, Kitable looked at the dragon that was eating and stomping both armies equally. Although he stood on the rise of the HillTop, he still had to look up to see the head of the monster.

Kitable started casting as he made his way down the hill.

Frustratingly, he would have to get closer.

Allied once more with Darknim, Tohmas led the way in. If it had been a milder natured blue or green dragon, or even the more benevolent silver or gold dragons, he could have hoped to trade with it or bribe it into leaving, but the hot-tempered magma dragons were unforgiving and ruthless.

Darknim's ax being able to cut through black dragon scale was fortunate, but they still had to get the man close.

Tohmas gazed up at the beast far above them and saw the head raising away.

"We didn't scare it off, did we?" he quipped.

"No, it does that before blowing fire," Darknim calmly replied.

Tohmas tightened his grip on SoulBurner, and he felt the fiery aura intensify. "I guess we find out if the Goddess was honest about her

protection," he said. He glanced at Carsh, comforted by his brother's calm stance. "Stay close," he warned, lifting the sword above him so the aura surrounded all three of them. The fire came down like a waterfall, cascading immolating heat. Tohmas watched it fall, and for a moment, his heart stuck in his throat. No one, he was certain, had seen this sight before and lived.

But where the fires reached the red aura of SoulBurner, they parted like a river around a boulder. The heat leaking through softened the earth underfoot.

"The Goddess delivers!" Darknim shouted. The old warrior jumped up and down in place like a child with a new pony. "Blessed are we! And damned be the beast!"

The fire subsided, leaving a field of mud and stone where once snow had been. The dragon's head withdrew slightly, and Tohmas thought he saw a flicker of surprise in its expression. For a moment, the irises went white.

White with fear, Tohmas thought, raising the sword that much higher. He gave Honest Justice a kick. The sweaty warhorse obeyed, but Tohmas sensed reluctance. Bashuran never wavered, carrying Carsh unerringly toward the dragon. Darknim split to a side, ducking between the feet in search of a target while Carsh and Tohmas kept its attention.

The next breath of flames was weaker, more a wishful swat. SoulBurner's aura protected both charging horses. The dragon's jaw snapped down. Honest Justice veered right, and Bashuran went left. Moving faster than Tohmas had ever seen, Bashuran spun in place, reversing his charge to avoid the teeth of the dragon. When the dragon's head snapped passed, Carsh threw a knife. It hit the left eye perfectly.

The dragon merely squinted. Tohmas had been hoping a knife to the eye would cause the beast a bit more distress.

In his distraction, Tohmas did not see the dragon's front leg sweeping toward him. Honest Justice was no fool; he swerved. As the horse righted, Tohmas felt his steed's muscles shift into panic. His control of the warhorse slipped.

Knowing he had to decide between dropping his sword to reclaim both reins or simply let the horse run without him, Tohmas chose the latter and leaped from Justice's back.

His landing was not as elegant as he would have liked, but it ended with him still holding SoulBurner and lying in the shadow of a huge, uprooted stump. Sitting up put his back to the stump and his face to the dragon.

The dragon stomped down at Carsh, and Bashuran again demonstrated the agility of Rydan steeds by stopping instantly. The enormous foot crashed down in front of him. Carsh threw another knife, this one longer. He hit the same eye, and this time, the dragon pulled away sharply and screamed.

Tohmas shoved himself to his feet and sprinted back into the fight. Before he could reach them, Bashuran was forced to dodge another stomp. The horse paused. The dragon dove in. Although Bashuran kicked at the snout, the dragon's teeth snagged into Carsh's back, plucking him up like he was a rag toy. It had been a near thing, but Carsh dangled from the dragon's tooth by his baldrics.

Tohmas' feet found extra speed. He reached the dragon's injured foot. Taking SoulBurner in a double-handed grip, he stabbed the blade into the open wound and deep into the finger. He had to withdraw immediately as the hot blood spurted and threatened to scald him.

The dragon screamed and released Carsh.

From a place two paces back, Tohmas watched helplessly as his brother fell from a height of several stories. The dragon was still screeching in pain, but Tohmas could only think about the deadly plummet.

Carsh could not survive that fall.

I'll kill every black dragon in the world, he swore. After I tear this one to pieces.

A flash of light interrupted Carsh's fall. Gently supported by a magical force Tohmas could not see, the Rydan lowered to the ground.

Tohmas' chest was still tight. Carsh had not struggled. Even when returned to the ground, he did not immediately come to his feet. Carsh was not moving.

The dragon turned its red-hot stare onto Tohmas now, and Tohmas met it squarely. Not bothering with sending fire into SoulBurner's aura, the dragon lunged in with teeth and horns. Tohmas stepped forward, ducked under the strike, and stabbed up hard into the chin as it passed over him. The scales resisted most of SoulBurner's bite, but spurting

blood sizzled into the mud as Tohmas pulled clear. Spatters caught his clothes, leaving holes in his leather armor and blisters on his arms.

Numb to the pain, Tohmas slipped out from under the head and came up beside the face. The dragon's eye blanched for a second time. Tohmas stabbed SoulBurner, brought overhand, into the white eye next to the knives Carsh had already thrown. Unlike the short blades, the sword delved deep into the globe and nipped into the bone of the orbit.

The cry from the dragon deafened Tohmas and made him stagger back. The earth shuddered as if anticipating a blow.

SoulBurner stuck in the bone. When the head wrenched away, SoulBurner was pulled from Tohmas' grasp.

His stomach sank. Inac's protection was gone. Although Tohmas pulled his knife and retreated toward the tree stump, he was an easy target.

The dragon thrashed its head in the air above as if trying to toss the blade off, but all too soon, Tohmas found the red-eyed stare of the good eye on him. Tohmas pulled back farther, thinking of taking cover behind the stump but not wanting to put his back to the dragon. He was in the shadow of the roots when the snout lowered and blew smoke at him. With a snarl to show its teeth as long as spears, the dragon lunged.

A burst of magic light appeared, and the dragon missed its strike. Seeing spots himself, Tohmas dove for cover. A shadow passed over him, a person leaping from the top of the toppled stump.

Blinking to clear his vision, Tohmas saw Darknim clear the stump, land on the dragon's snout, and sprint up the horned head without breaking stride. The dragon lurched, but the Northlander held his footing for long enough to crest the head and reach the base of the skull, where he hooked his boot on a scale and cleaved his ax down between the dorsal spines of the beast.

The ax did not stop there. Strike after strike, Darknim DoomDragon sliced through scale, muscle, bone, and spine. The dragon thrashed, trying to throw off the attacker, but Darknim, impossibly, could not be dislodged.

The shrieking abruptly stopped. The neck buckled, and the head pitched forward. With a thump that could be felt for leagues, the head thundered into the slush, pulling the body with it and sending a hail

of mud and rock across the field. The eyes were glazed by the time the spray of dirt settled.

Speckled with mud, his arms scalded, and his shoulder now reminding him of his previous injury, Tohmas made his way out from the stump. In the cold air of the north, the black scales and oozing muscles steamed. Patches of blood melted the remaining snow, revealing ripped grasses and thick mud.

He had to jump, but he managed to reach SoulBurner's pommel and was pulling it loose when Darknim landed in the mud beside him. How the older man had kept his feet during the fall of the body, Tohmas had no idea.

The Northlander cleaned his face with a gloved hand. With the mud went the spattered blood and gore that was still steaming.

Darknim said something. Tohmas rubbed at his ears but still only heard ringing.

"What?" he shouted back at Darknim. The Northlander laughed, the man bending double in hysterics.

The ringing slowly clearing, Tohmas searched the emerging crowd for Carsh. Not seeing him, he whistled, not caring that the people nearest him winced at the volume. If Carsh had fallen, all of Espar would know his anger.

"He's over here!" Kitable's voice made it through, drawing his attention farther up the slope, to the edge of the HillTop defenses. He had not even realized they had come so close to the camp in the fight, but there was Kitable, standing atop one of the short walls. "I caught him in time. He's dazed. Give him a—"

Carsh rose slowly off the wall where he had been sitting, his goatee brown instead of blond. As he stood, his staggering step made Tohmas' heart wince. Outwardly, he held firm. There were Rydans starting to reach them. Showing weakness could not be permitted.

Once he had centered himself, Carsh shook himself like a dog, spraying dirt in all directions. Then, with a deep breath, Carsh made his way to Tohmas' side.

In respect of Carsh's strength, Tohmas did not meet his brother halfway. As he waited for Carsh to join him, he glanced over at Darknim, who had begun to gather his senses from his hysterics.

"What did you say earlier?"

Darknim first wiped his face again, the tears from laughing having run the mud down to his beard once more. "I asked, 'how was that?'"

"I told you they needed their heads," Tohmas replied, reaching up and getting a grip on SoulBurner once more. With a final yank, SoulBurner came loose, and the bright red light surrounded them. A flick shook the boiling blood and ooze from the blade. He wiped it clean, sheathed it, then turned to find Darknim sitting on a root, happily soaking his feet in the slush.

"Burned the bottom off my boots!" DoomDragon lifted a foot to show his callused feet protruding. Blisters were already rising.

"If that's the worst that happens today, I'll be happy," Tohmas said. The ringing in his ears was lessening, but he suspected it would last several days.

Carsh returned to his side. When his brother turned to face the gathering crowd, Tohmas spotted two bloody gouges stretching from Carsh's shoulders to his pelvis. Stitching would be required, but the bite wound was not deep enough to kill so long as it was tended soon. His had bruising around his ribs, making Tohmas believe Carsh had not been dazed at all. Some ribs had been broken, and he had been badly winded. Even his tattoo of a snarling mountain cat on his chest was black with bruises.

But he was alive.

"Dragon be breakin' ma baldric," Carsh said with a frown.

Tohmas let a conserved smile out. *He's well enough to be joking.*

"I'll make you one myself!" Darknim declared, his laughter renewed. "I like this man!"

With the laughter, which was slowly percolating through the on-looking crowd, the tension of the battlefield released. Weapons were sheathed. Both armies were free to see to their wounded. Kitable finally decided SoulBurner was not coming back out and joined them.

Tohmas eyed the wizard, who shrugged.

"Neither are dead, but both are on the run. Seria—"

With a sputter, a mud-coated body sat up beyond the walls. Compared to the burly protectors or Hunters, the body was a child. When she cleared her face, Tohmas realized it was female and familiar.

"Oh, look," Kitable said, his voice darkening with every syllable. "She finally got out."

The next word was something magic, and Tohmas saw the small woman jump as if she had been poked. He imagined he could see her flush under the muck.

"Wait, please," Darknim interrupted, pushing past Kitable. He helped Seria to her feet. "If you cast, woman, I will cut you down myself. Plans have changed."

The wizard nodded mutely, pulling her long hair to one side and wringing out the dirty water. Her eyes locked onto Kitable's. Kitable stared her down with cool anger.

"If it was not for Terant and Prince Marfaie, Clarin would still be alive," Darknim said.

Seria swallowed hard. She broke the stare with Kitable to check her surroundings. All at once, she recognized she was without allies.

"Sit down," Darknim said, pointing to the stump next to the dragon's head. "Join us in our alliance, or I will knock you over myself."

She sank onto a root.

Darknim's gaze searched the area. "Rairn?"

Tohmas nodded toward HillTop. "Tied up by now. What say we convene by a fire? I'm getting a chill, and you need new boots."

"Very true. Lead on, Prince Tohmas. This war is over."

The horn call for final cessation sounded behind them as they made their way into HillTop, leaving Kitable to stare down at the petite caster.

"Play nice, Kit," Tohmas called.

Kitable's shrug was non-committal, but Tohmas left it. He trusted Kitable would act in Galanth's best interest.

Behind them, the Rydans began a hesitant harvest of the dragon body, digging into the wounds caused by DoomDragon's ax to get at the muscle. Where the smooth black scales were intact, no blade could pierce.

A dozen defenses, along with a handful of attacks, jumped to mind. Kitable's spells, freshly cast and ready, were poised. He had dispelled her. Seria was at his mercy.

It was easier to see her as an enemy. How does the Northlander's request fit into things?

She stood slowly, her eyes on him for a reaction. He was reminded of their meeting in the Weaver's tent. She had been cleaner then.

"If we are working together," she said softly, "perhaps I can have a moment of your time, alone?"

He was tempted to cast another Vox as an answer but held himself in check.

"Do you have any idea how often Clarin made that request of me?" Kitable replied, looking down at the filthy caster. "I turned him down every time. Turned out he was trying to get me alone so he could kill me."

His paranoia could no longer be called paranoia now that it had been justified. Clarin had proved again that Kitable could not trust other wizards.

But he did not have to trust Seria to get information from her, and he was in the better position. "But since you are dispelled, and since my patron has requested we make efforts toward cooperation, I will give you one moment. Use it carefully because it will not come again."

"Did you kill Clarin?" she asked bluntly, all polite pretenses gone from her voice.

"Your lover," Kitable understood. "Was it Inac or Ocea, I wonder?"

Since it was evident he would not answer her question without hearing the reply to his own, Seria eventually straightened and lifted her chin confidently to say, "Inac, mostly. He was an entertaining distraction." Her pride was at odds with her grimy exterior.

"You sent him to Prince Sol."

Seria shrugged. "Yes. We arranged for him to befriend Sol, and then we killed the previous prime protector so Clarin would get the position. Did you kill him?"

Kitable let out a sigh. "You'll no doubt hear the story soon enough. The truth is Celebrant Calanor identified him, Tohmas and Carsh challenged him, and I dueled him. During the fight, we both used open-ended spells. He drew too deep. So yes, I killed him. I pushed him. He fell."

Seria fell silent, making Kitable doubt her earlier assertions about the relationship being lust, not love. "It seems I am without allies now," she said after her pause.

"And so you shall remain. I am not as trusting as my prince is."

When she slunk forward slightly, Kitable dropped his crossed arms to have his hands ready.

"I have been an apprentice to Master Terant for more than six years, but he has taught me all he can. It is because of him that Clarin died. I do not wish to be next. I follow power. I would follow you."

By the time she finished speaking, she was only a hand's breadth away. Kitable held his ground. She had no hovering spells with which to threaten him.

"When you told Tohmas that, he laughed at you. I am tempted to do the same."

"If you would teach me..." she suggested, but her sentence fell off when her lifted hand hit his Molded Shield.

"I want nothing to do with you, Seria. Your moment has passed. If you are ever within fifty paces of me again, I will put that Vox back on you."

A muddy handprint remained on his Molded Shield when she let her hand drop. Heeding Tohmas' request, Kitable left her alive as he walked away.

He soon caught up with Tohmas and Darknim. Prince Barnon met them at the defenses, his expression a mix of joy and confusion. He seemed as likely to hit Darknim as hug him.

"So what now?" Prince Barnon was asking as he too joined the unlikely friends in their stroll into camp in search of warmth. "Can DoomDragon tell them to give Sol back?"

"You will have to fetch your brother," Darknim answered. Kitable activated a Lie Light. It remained white as the Northlander added, "I will help you."

A crowd gathered behind the two leaders, a mixture of Northlanders and Esparans. They milled about, looking nervous and giving each other large berths as they vied for positions nearest the leaders.

DoomDragon pivoted when he reached the top of the hill, the viewpoint from which so many battles had been overseen. Casting a sweeping gaze over the crowd, he began speaking in Northlander. It sounded roughly like Rydan, but Kitable found it incomprehensible.

He was apparently not the only one having that problem.

"Kit?" Tohmas asked. "Translation?"

Kitable quickly cast a Translation spell while holding his Lie Light still at the ready. Although he worried about having Rydans suspect magic in play, none of the southern barbarians, besides Carsh, were in the area to hear.

He had missed some of the preamble but caught the rest of the Northlander's speech.

"...believed our future had to be with the Esparan princes, and I still believe this. Now, however, it is *our* future to make. We will have our homes, our glory, and our territory. But we will take them by marching *with* allies, instead of marching *for* an enemy. If you believe the DoomDragon was named, then march with me. I will take our freedom from the liar Marfaie. We will take our place as rulers of the north."

Kitable expected DoomDragon to be surprised when the Esparans also cheered his conclusion, thinking the Northlander would have no way to know that he had translated the words for the onlookers. Yet Darknim DoomDragon only nodded to Kitable upon the cheer, acknowledging the spell.

Kitable had watched the Lie Light surreptitiously throughout Darknim's speech and was impressed that no lies were spoken. He almost dismissed the spell as Tohmas began to speak, but curiosity had him hold it for a moment longer.

The Translation spell continued to do its job, translating the Esparan into Northlander for those who needed it.

"We came here as three different peoples," Tohmas said. "Esparan, Northlander, and Rydan. Three is a bad number. It is one short of the four elements, the four seasons, the four gods. It is the number not quite complete. Do not think of us as three people now, but as one people, one purpose. That purpose is justice, and we will seek it at the gates of Arcott, where Prince Marfaie must be brought before the justice of Inac!"

The Lie Light swirled blue at Tohmas' last sentence.

Kitable felt cold and uncertain as the two leaders headed into HillTop in comradery.

If they were not going to march against Marfaie for justice, then why?

Epilogue

As festivities took over the camps, Kitable retreated to his vardo. He set the defenses against magical intrusion despite knowing the Circle of the Raven, DoomDragon's team of casters, now defended HillTop as well. Master Terant had retreated north. Without DoomDragon to provide the warriors, Terant had no fodder. Esparans loyal to Prince Marfaie were on the run. For now, there was quiet. Celebrations were permitted, at least for everyone else.

Kitable needed rest, but that was nothing new. Thankfully, there was no enervation. Although his hand shook as he closed the latch, he had the strength to make tea and eat before sleeping.

As he finished a wrap of bread, Kitable's eyes fell onto a book sitting a finger's breadth out from the rest on one of his bookcases. He had dislodged it after speaking to Vallant, and now the prime guardian's request returned to him.

I need you to look into it, he'd said.

Kitable walked across the room and pulled the book of spells off his shelf. The pages cracked when he laid it on the table. He flipped through, knowing the spell he wanted was toward the end.

Uncertainty slowed the action, and when he reached the Reflection spell, he paused.

Fifteen years of Prince Tohmas' life was still shrouded in mystery. And the swirl of blue in the Lie Light after the battle added to the problem. Tohmas had promised justice, yet he had lied.

But Kitable liked his patron. Tohmas respected his knowledge and had trusted him when others wanted little to do with him. Kitable would have obeyed Tohmas to fulfill his oath to Habal, but he now considered Tohmas a friend.

Placing his hand on the book, Kitable drew a long breath.

Do I want to know the truth?

He knew how at-home Tohmas was among the Rydans. Normal Esparan etiquette was often forced, and large gaps were present in his knowledge of Esparan culture, yet Rydan traditions came easily to him. Kitable could blame some on the lack of family growing up, but there was more to it. He'd known that for a while.

Resigned, Kitable pulled his hand off the book and cast the spell. He needed to pose a question to guide the spell. Magic existed across multiple times and worlds. If Kitable made an error in assumption or detail, he could bring forward scenes from another time entirely, making the spell useless. He had to be specific.

Since the answer seemed likely to lie among the Rydans, Kitable fixed on the easiest target: Carsh.

Kitable had thought Tohmas' protective exile from Galanth had been close enough to the Outlands for him to make friends across the border. Yet his relationship with Carsh was far more than that. Besides, that theory did not explain the knives Carsh used like an extension of his arm or how Tohmas could so easily behave like a Rydan.

Tohmas was never alone. Now, Kitable was ready to find out why.

Painstakingly, Kitable defined Tohmas and Carsh. Ready, he asked his question. "Why are they friends?"

The scope of the question, he realized quickly, had been too broad. Although he braced himself, the magic flooded into his mind, the kaleidoscope of colors tangling to form images. Unlike a Reflection on a single moment, a thousand things defined a friendship, and Kitable was witness to them all.

The first scene was of two thin boys throwing rocks at crows in a field of tall grass. The Esparan boy's features were sickly and thin, but his skin was already darkened by the sun. Both boys cheered when the Rydan's throw knocked a bird senseless. They carried it home as a prize.

From there, time flew.

Spearing fish on the river then fixing the spears that had chipped on riverbed stones. Picking leeches off each other by a campfire. Quail roasted for dinner and the eggs eaten as a delicacy. Patching a torn sleeve and trying to scuff the new hide to make it blend in with the old. Bandaging a deep gouge on Carsh's arm where he'd slipped with his bone knife. He needed Tohmas to tie the knot on the moss-packed bandage.

Kitable grasped at the images, trying to hold on to details as they raced by.

Carsh's chest tattoo took form over a dozen scenes, Tohmas standing by, denied the tradition. Although his Rydan friend hid his pain, Tohmas knowingly brought Carsh several meals as he healed.

Fights joined the flashes of life among the Rydans. From fisticuffs and wrestling matches as children to bare-blade duels as teenagers, in every exchange, the two boys were smiling.

More Rydans entered the scenes, a wary eye on Tohmas at all times although Tohmas dressed and moved as a Rydan.

As a young teenager, Carsh stood by a fire and took a cut across his arm. Kitable recognized the Rydan who delivered the blow, the howling wolf-like man who had killed the goat in HillTop. At Carsh's side, Tohmas received a similar slice across his hand. Both boys stood firm, blood oozing from their wounds, as the fur-covered attacker slipped away into the forest. Once he was gone, they bandaged each other's wounds.

Soon the fighting was real, and the teens were standing back-to-back among enemies, all the while grinning like they were play fighting with deadly blows. Kitable saw Tohmas answer a whistle, storming into a crowd of enemies and suffering a dozen injuries. He arrived at Carsh's side in time to kill the enemies and carry his wounded friend out. A nearly identical scene followed, the roles reversed; Tohmas took a spear to his thigh and fell, but a whistle brought Carsh and his blades to the rescue.

These scenes of violence were broken by campfire drinks and good-natured ribbing. There were wild rides on horses tall enough to make even Tohmas stand on tiptoe to reach and climbs on snowy cliffs far above solid ground. A hundred cuts turned into a hundred scars, and all the while, Tohmas and Carsh were side by side.

When Kitable regained consciousness, he lay flat on the floor, staring up at his ceiling. Each vision was the barest flash buried in the blink of his eye. He continued to sort through them, trying to glean the last detail as they faded. He had been given his answer.

None of the visions had contained another Esparan. Kitable had not seen protectors. From the first vision of the boys throwing stones, there had been no Esparan influence in Tohmas' life.

Tohmas and Carsh had not just been friends; they had stood side by side in a hundred death-defying encounters and laughed about the outcomes together.

Kitable sat up and rubbed his head. There was blood on his hand; he had hit his head. He pressed his hand against the wound until he found a shirt to hold against it, his thoughts tangled.

While the official story claimed Tohmas had been tutored by his two assigned protectors in isolation, Kitable was now confident Tohmas had spent his fifteen years with the Rydans in the south. The Prince of Galanth was Rydan in every way except blood.

Kitable closed his eyes, leaning back on his bed.

He had to tell Vallant. But what would the old warrior say?

Why had Tohmas lied about the protectors and their deaths? Why hide his Rydan beginnings? Tohmas' departure from Galanth had come at a time of peace with the Outlands. Although the relationship had often been tenuous, the Rydans were considered opportunistic brigands, not enemies. There had been a Rydan boy raised in Galanth too, Kitable recalled.

Kitable opened his eyes, the cluttered rafters of the vardo coming into view. The light was dimming. Sunset cast the vardo into an orange haze.

The son of the Rydan chief, a young man by the name of Bragn, had been in Galanth on and off during Tohmas' absence.

"An exchange?" Kitable's voice cracked.

Sitting up, he activated an enchanted lamp, the stars and moon pattern on it casting projections onto the walls. Once he could see, he found his tea. It was cold.

Bragn had vanished after Tohmas' arrival, that much Kitable knew. The young man had visited often with Habal over the same fifteen years, always accompanied by two older Rydans.

Like Tohmas' two protectors.

If he remembered correctly, Prince Habal had been in the room with Bragn, the two Rydan advisors, and Tohmas when he had collapsed then died shortly thereafter. It had been a mere three days after Tohmas' return.

The event now struck Kitable. If Tohmas had been raised among Rydans, had Habal not been in a room with effectively *four* Rydans and no defenders? Had Habal known of Tohmas' history? Vallant certainly had not; he had been shocked by the early loss of the protectors. If Habal had thought Tohmas raised by Esparan protectors...

The book still lay on the table, open to the Reflection spell.

Kitable drank his cold tea, staring at the flickering star-shaped lights on the page. His head wound slowed its bleeding, but there was still fresh blood on the shirt when he checked it.

More things I do not want to know. Yet he had to find out. What had happened the day Prince Habal had collapsed? His heart sank as he wondered.

Had Tohmas been involved?

Putting down his tea, Kitable kept the shirt pressed against his head as he cast again. He defined Tohmas carefully, using every aspect he could think of from Tohmas' bright blue eyes to the scar on the bottom of his foot. He called up his memories of Habal, defined the old prince as well, then finished by setting up the circumstances: a closed room; five occupants; the prince collapsing. In closing, he asked his question.

"What happened to my patron?"

The event was short compared to the cascade earlier. As if standing in the corner of the room, Kitable watched the death of Prince Habal unfold.

Tohmas sat at his father's side, perched on the edge of a plush seat while Habal sat back comfortably. The Rydan Bragn, his vest opened to show a striking hawk tattoo, sat across from them with his two escorts at his back. A fire blazed behind the trio, making them sweat. The escorts wore no armor and carried no weapons, unlike Bragn who was armed with several short knives. Tohmas wore an ornate knife, one Kitable had seen often until it had been gifted to Darknim. He looked uncomfortable on the seat and was closely watching the Rydans behind Bragn.

They were discussing relations with the Outlands, Tohmas telling tales of battles fought and how the three clans were now one under a single chief.

Tohmas was mid-sentence when Bragn launched off his chair and dug his knife into Prince Habal's gut. Habal did not even have time to flinch. Bragn's hand fell over the prince's mouth, blocking his cry.

The prince toppled forward as the Rydan withdrew his blade.

Tohmas came to his feet, his knife in hand, but he hesitated. As he reached for his fallen father, Bragn pulled him away by his shoulder. Although Kitable did not understand the Rydan words, they were harsh and accusatory.

Reefing his shoulder from Bragn's grip, Tohmas growled and replied in Rydan. Tohmas stepped deliberately between Bragn and Habal, his knife up in threat. His message was clear; he was defending the fallen prince and chastising the chief's son for attacking.

Bragn snarled and attacked, but he was outmatched. With practiced ease—Kitable had seen the maneuver in the other Reflection several times—Tohmas caught Bragn's wrist, twisted the arm, and without hesitation, stabbed the Rydan's knife into his back.

The blade must have reached the heart. The Rydan was dead before he hit the floor.

Nearby, Habal gurgled, unable to draw enough breath to call for aid, still bleeding. Tohmas knelt and applied pressure to Habal's belly, his lips pressed in concentration.

At last, the other Rydans came forward, having remained motionless throughout the exchange. One knelt beside Tohmas and the other across from him, both speaking calming words. Agitated, Tohmas spoke harshly at first, his words still guttural Rydan too fast for Kitable to understand. But as the Rydans laid their hands on Habal, Tohmas' ire faded. Their words got through to him. He allowed one to pull him back gently while the other tended to Habal.

To Kitable's shock, the Rydan *cast*.

An illusion fell over the dying Prince of Galanth. The wound and the blood vanished. Only then did Tohmas call for help, his hands washed clean with the aid of the Rydan escort. The summoned healers could not see the injury bleeding their prince out. Bragn's body had vanished as well, another spell cast by the two strange Rydans.

Habal died within a few candles, his wound hidden and untreated. Tohmas watched on, his face stone.

The Reflection ended. Kitable was once more in his vardo facing the lantern. He was chilled despite the warming spells on his home. The bread he had eaten swirled like sour ale in his stomach.

He had seen so much yet now had more questions. Had Tohmas known of the deception? Condoned it? Ordered it? How were there casters among the Rydans that went uncontested when the Rydans professed to hate casters of all kinds? Had Habal's death been deliberate?

Only one person had the answers: Tohmas.

Kitable owed Habal everything. If Tohmas had been complicit in his death, their friendship and their alliance was over.

He would have his answers.

THE END.

SNEAK PEEK OF ESPARAN

Esparan

With every breath, Rakhund felt the absence of the dragon's soul like a gaping wound in his chest. He knew the sensation would eventually fade to a dull knot and join the one that lingered from his first fallen dragon, but for now, the lack of the soul gnawed at him like a disease.

After nearly two centuries, the great black dragon Rakhund had enslaved was dead. The memory of the sensation still made Rakhund's rage rise. Without his dragon, he was weak. He needed his prestige back immediately.

By the time Rakhund's patron heard about the loss, Rakhund intended to have remedied the problem. He would never dare be seen without the soul of a dragon bound to his, even if the humans did not recognize it.

Rakhund left his home in the volcano's caldera and traveled alone into the wilderness of the north. Unconcerned by the last of the winter's winds and snow, he hunted with his eyes on the skies. His black robes hid his features but did little against the chill. For that, Rakhund had his spells and his natural scales. He crossed great distances through the rocky terrain, requiring little by way of rest and nothing by way of sleep.

At length, he felt the presence of dragons. He followed them back to their lair.

For days, he watched the pair. His dragons had been Blacks before, the strongest of the Magma dragons. Dominating Blacks had put

Rakhund into positions of authority among his kind once. But the demonic creators of the great dragons had enchanted them to die once their masters were gone, and too few of the escaped dragons had bred before the spells sapped them of life. Finding a Black once had been fortunate. Now, it seemed likely to be impossible. Besides, there were no others of his kind to impress.

Taking two dragons, even if they were Reds, would suffice. It would take twice as many spells, but the resistance of each individual dragon would be easier to manage. Reds were less vicious and less clever compared to their volatile, larger cousins. Rakhund's last Black had been a veteran of the demon wars, sturdy and experienced in resisting a demon's hold. Two younger, naïve Reds would be easy.

Setting a seat in the moss of the stony fields, Rakhund cast spells for days, pulling in the powers of his core and building it together. He used the magic to craft a composite stone, built pebble by pebble from the hills of the dragons' own home, their sacred place. Once he had two such creations, each the size of his fist, he imbued them with magic, fashioning a spiral of confusion. Confused, they would never defy him.

At midday, when the beasts were sleeping, Rakhund crept into the cavern home of the red dragons. Hidden by magic, he placed the first stone onto the steaming wrist of the bull dragon and let it fuse to the scales. The spells flickered to life.

As he placed the second stone onto the female, the bull awoke, his nostrils flaring. His roar was instant and fierce. Rakhund thought he understood it;

"Demon, I smell you."

But it was too late. The stones worked their powers over the mind of the beast, and the dragon's search was uncoordinated. While Rakhund sat, hidden in illusions but in the open, both dragons searched for him. Too confounded to hone in on the source of the smell, they had not found him by the time his next spells, which had to be set by touch, were ready.

When Rakhund bound himself to their souls, both dragons went still. He felt their fury, for they recognized what had been done and despised him for it, and he was comforted. He had lived his life with that hatred seething within him. He had felt incomplete without it.

Rakhund forced the larger bull dragon to carry him as a rider back to the hills outside of Arcott. The innate heat of the dragon, hot enough to scald exposed flesh, was nothing against his scales.

With the souls of the dragons now held, Rakhund reported to his patron. Dragons were again ready to be commanded.

An army marched against Prince Marfaie now and needed to be destroyed. That was fortunate, for Rakhund wanted to kill something.

Glossary

Barlaby: Far north princedom of Espar. Overrun by Northlander
    CURRENT PRINCE: Prince Lorian Rairn.
    COLORS: White and White.
    CREST: None

Calendar: Universal calendar pre-dates the Demon Wars. Roughly based on the moon's phases:
    YEAR: Eight mooncycles of forty days, and one mooncycle (the ninth) of a variable length, thirty-five or thirty-six days.
    MOONCYCLE: forty days.
    HALFCYCLE: twenty days.
    QUARTERCYCLE: ten days.

Celebrant: Esparan priest, traditionally assigned to a single deity of the four. Overseeing a group of Acolytes.

Clandac: Central Esparan princedom.
    CURRENT PRINCE: Prince Dragal Galanth. Eldest son of Zayban.
    COLORS: Blue with Gold.
    CREST: Scythe

Companion (Black rank rope): Esparan Companions are not soldiers by profession. They become soldiers when they are required, but have other occupations.

Currency (Esparan)

> LEG: Wedge-shaped copper coin with a hole in it for threading on a string.
>
> TABLE: Eight legs strung together.
>
> SLIVER: Wedge-shaped silver coin with a hole in it for threading on a string.
>
> SLICE: Eight slivers strung together.
>
> SPOKE: Wedge-shaped gold coin with a hole in it for threading on a string.
>
> WHEEL: Eight spokes strung together.

Damoria: South west princedom of Espar, corner of DragonTail mountains and Outlands. Enemy of Galanth.

> CURRENT PRINCE: Prince Wevan Damoria.
>
> COLORS: Red with Yellow.
>
> CREST: Dragon

Espar: The overall region north of DragonTail mountains.

Esparan (race): People of Espar. Pale skinned and featured peoples. Religion of four elemental gods.

Forsinth: Princedom of Espar, known for pottery and claywork. Close ally to sons of Zayban

> CURRENT PRINCE: Prince Deiton Darvin-Galanth. (Widower of Elinea Galanth)
>
> COLORS: Brown with Silver.
>
> CREST: wine pitcher

Galanth: Southern Esparan princedom on borders with Outlands.

> CURRENT PRINCE: Prince Tohmas Galanth. (Son to Habal Galanth)
>
> COLORS: Green with Silver.
>
> CREST: Tree

Gaidol: Princedom of Espar with prolific trading routes. Borders contentiously with Trulin. Close ally to Nothor.
    CURRENT PRINCE: Prince Dorakon Lodaton
    COLORS: White with blue.
    CREST: Shark

Guardians (Red rank rope): Each Esparan city had a single Guardian named by the Prince. A Guardian may or may not have a Prime status, depending on the size of the city.

Inac: Esparan fire god. Female. Also known as the Bitch Goddess, Dame Justice, Lady of Lust, Warrior Queen.

Knock: An Esparan gesture of agreement. Originally from a time of blood-bonds, where the two people would press their fists together and cut across the two hands to bind their words and spirits. More recently, no cut is used, just the knock of fists.

Lour: Western princedom of Espar along the Crescent and DragonTail mountains. Deep iron mines. Finest metalsmiths in Espar
    CURRENT PRINCE: Prince Loritat Naygan.
    COLORS: Gold with Grey.
    CREST: Anvil

Meloch: Far north princedom of Espar, currently overrun by Northlanders
    CURRENT PRINCE: Prince Garit Carnilan. Deceased.
    COLORS: Black with Red.
    CREST: Raven

Northlander (race): Race of the far north; a hardy people organized into clans but united by a Circle of the Raven, which comprises of magic-users. When the circle is complete (7 members), they name a DoomDragon (all clan leader).

Nothor: Eastern coastal Esparan Princedom. Known for shipping and mechanical innovation. Close ally to Gaidol.

    CURRENT PRINCE: Prince Neillen Lodaton.

    COLORS: Green with Gold

    CREST: Ship

Ocea: Esparan water god. Female. Also known as the Maiden, The Benevolent Mother, the Weeping Goddess.

Polthian: Esparan Princedom on southern border, close to Outlands.

    CURRENT PRINCE: Prince Emacen Polthian.

    COLORS: Blue with red.

    CREST: Eagle

Pari: Esparan earth god. Male. Also known as the Mountain King, The Beast Lord, The Traveler, Healing Presence.

Prime (single strand of silver in a rank rope): A distinguishing rank above the main associated one in Esparan ranking. For example, a Prime Protector would be one step above a protector and command them.

Protectors (Green rank rope): Bodyguards of a Prince of Espar. Commanded by a prime protector.

Rabarch: Esparan Princedom.

    CURRENT PRINCE: Prince Barnon Galanth (youngest son of Zayban Galanth)

    COLORS: white with red

    CREST: Dragon head

Rydan (race): Tribal people of the south Outlands, consisting of three clans (First, Second, Third), each ruled by a Chief. Primarily raiders and nomads, with a strong emphasis on horsemanship. Rydan horses are powerful warhorses, bound to a given master for life.

Solta: Central princedom of Espar, currently under siege by Northlanders.

> CURRENT PRINCE: Prince Sol Galanth (Second youngest son of Zayban)
> COLORS: Red with back
> CREST: Shield

Tanble: Northern Princedom of Espar, currently overrun by Northlanders.

> CURRENT PRINCE: Prince Vornan Marfaie (believed deceased)
> COLORS: Black with grey.
> CREST: Sword

Totho: Esparan wind god. Male. Also known as the Tempest, The Gust, North Star.

Trulin: North East Espar Princedom. Breeders of powerful warhorses.

> CURRENT PRINCE: Prince Kelland Trulin.
> COLORS: White and Brown.
> CREST: Horse

Wardens (Blue rank rope): Under the Guardians, these are permanent Esparan soldiers who guard the city and maintain the peace. The number of Wardens answering to a Guardian depends on the size of the city. If a call comes from the Prince, the Wardens become responsible for a company of ~20 companions.

Wisavi: A wise-man and advisor to a Rydan Chief.

Author Bio

At a young age, Deborah's rampant imagination kept her up, lending great detail to all the terrible things lurking in the night. In desperation, her mother suggested she invent her own stories to distract her brain. She has been doing that since, channeling her ideas into sword and sorcery-style fantasy novels and shorts.

In her other life, Deborah is a veterinarian. She lives in Sooke, BC, Canada with her husband of 13+ years, their two sons, and three demanding felines.

WWW.DLAMBERTAUTHOR.COM

INSTAGRAM: @dlambertauthor
TWITTER/X: @dlambertauthor
FACEBOOK.COM/DLAMBERT42

Book Club Questions

1. Do the characters seem realistic to you? Do they remind you of anyone you know?

2. Did any sections surprise or upset you? Why?

3. Lance and DoomDragon's dinner shines light on their respective characters. What does each character get out of the exchange?

4. Did you laugh anywhere in the story? Where?

5. More than one character has a change of heart and swaps sides. Are any surprises to you? Would you have done the same?

6. Do you agree with Tohmas' refusal to pay ransom for Sol? Why or why not?

7. Moving beyond their long history of animosity, Carsh defends Kitable against the Pack Runner, even calls him "Family." What makes someone family? Does Carsh's definition meet current views?

8. Do you believe that Tohmas and DoomDragon's respective efforts to assassinate each other are dishonourable? Is it at odds with our current views of how wars should be fought, or would it be acceptable today to assassinate an opposing leader?

9. Was SoulBurner truly gifted by the Goddess Inac, or are you skeptical like Kitable? What evidence do you have for true divine power in the series?

10. In the epilogue, Kitable learns what happened to Tohmas' father. How do you feel about the discovery? How do you think it will impact Kitable's position? How does it change your view of Tohmas?

**Discover more at
4HorsemenPublications.com**

10% off using HORSEMEN10